AMERICAN NOMADS

N.L. MCLAUGHLIN

This is a work of fiction.

Printed by:
Twisted Sky, LLC
ISBN: 978-1-7367059-1-9

Proofreading provided by the Hyper-Speller at
https://www.wordrefiner.com

Cover art provided by Meagan McLaughlin
MeaganEMcLaughlin@gmail.com

Contents

To Robert,
My best friend who always believes in me…even when I don't.

"There was nowhere to go but everywhere, so just keep on rolling under the stars."

— Jack Kerouac, On the Road

"There's a race of men that don't fit in,

A race that can't sit still;

So they break the hearts of kith and kin, And they roam the world at will.

They range the field and rove the flood,

And they climb the mountain's crest; Their's is the curse of the gypsy blood,

And they don't know how to rest."

—Robert W. Service

Chapter One

"That is some next level Bullshit. Do you not remember what happened in Montana?"

Craig shrugged. "I held my own."

"Uh, huh," scoffed Cyrus. "Who fell into the river?"

"That's not the point."

"It is, very much the point," stated Cyrus, "Quit dodging the question. Who fell in the river?"

"The rock was slick. And the current was wicked fast..."

"Did Finn fall into the river? How about Teague?"

"Come on," Craig protested, "Finn grew up with Preppers. Comparing me to him is like putting a Nascar driver up against a Soccer mom."

"You realize you just made my point," said Cyrus.

Craig did not reply.

"Look," said Cyrus. "You and I can hold our own most of the time, but when it comes to wilderness survival, we're out of our element." He paused. "You wouldn't survive more than a couple of days in the wild. Without help, neither would I."

"I don't know," replied Craig, "I mean, come on, we're not talking rocket science."

They stood alone on the dark country road—not a single home or business as far as the eye could see. Cyrus couldn't recall the last time he saw a vehicle of any kind. It was hard to believe Austin was a few miles away.

The sun had set hours ago, yet the temperature had changed little. Humidity hung heavy in the air, creating a thin layer of moisture that clung to his skin and dampened his clothes.

He lifted the dreads off the back of his neck and mopped away the sweat with an old bandana. "You think what you wanna think, but I'm just gonna say if the zombie apocalypse ever happens, the first thing we're doing is gettin' on over to wherever the hell those Texas boys are. The rest of the world would go to shit. But those boys..." He shook his head. "They'll be kickin' back like it's just another day."

"Actually," interjected Craig, "Teague's from Louisiana. He's Cajun."

"Texan, Cajun—it don't matter," said Cyrus. "Their crew has some serious survival skills. And we do not."

Craig shook his head. "Come on, hear me out. All I'm saying is it can't be that hard. I've played enough video games."

"You did not just say that out loud!" Cyrus spun around to face Craig. "Are you serious?"

"You know what I mean."

Cyrus laughed. "There's so much stupid in that statement, I don't even know where to start."

He sighed and shook his head. "Why the hell do we always end up talking about this trash when we're in the middle of nowhere? Seriously. Why does this never come up when we're in the middle of a city—in broad daylight, surrounded by lots of people? Let's just find the trailhead. I'm all done with stupid talk for the night. We can finish this conversation when we're on the beach in Tampa."

A warm, gentle breeze rustled the leaves of the trees. A cacophony of frogs and crickets surrounded them in the dark. It never ceased to amaze him how loud nature could be. To his right, he spied a narrow path cutting through the tall grass. *Bingo!* He thought.

Stepping off the roadway, they followed the trail as it led into a vast meadow. The tall grass; thick and gnarled as it was, slowed their pace. Cyrus couldn't help but wonder how many chiggers were hiding in the weeds, waiting for their chance to hop on and feast. As far as he was concerned, of all the creepy crawlies out there, chiggers were the worst. Just thinking about the tiny creatures was enough to conjure up phantom itchiness and tingling skin.

They cleared the meadow and hiked up a small hill, stopping in front of an old, abandoned farmhouse.

A remnant from an era long passed, the house was an impressive sight with its large windows, generous front porch, and steep gables. Even in its current decrepit state, it was remarkable.

The faint sound of music and laughter seeped through the cracks around the boarded-up windows.

A small creature scurried from the shadows, disappearing into a cluster of shrubs nearby. Overhead, perched on a branch high in a tree, a barn owl hooted. It glared down at them, blinked once, then spread its massive wings and took off into the night.

Cyrus stepped cautiously onto the porch. The boards creaked and moaned under the weight of his heavy boots. Above the weather-worn front door, the words 'Hotel Austin' were scrawled with faded, black spray paint. On the door itself, 'Wanderers welcome. All others fuck off!' was carved deep into the wood as a warning.

With a loud, sustained creek, he pushed the door open. "I see the owners haven't gotten around to fixin' things up yet," he said, over his shoulder as he stepped across the threshold.

Broken glass crunched under his feet. All manner of debris littered the floor—used cigarette butts, empty candy wrappers, and old food wrappers. Open holes in the walls, exposed the lathe and gave a view into the room adjacent. Graffiti covered every accessible surface. The air reeked of booze, stale cigarettes, and mold.

Across the room, what remained of the fireplace stood against a backdrop of grimy, old wallpaper, broken fixtures and what could either be graffiti or blood. In places like these, it could be either one.

A young woman sauntered out of the kitchen. Smiling—beer bottle in hand, she swayed her hips to the music playing behind her as she strolled toward the newcomers.

"Welcome travelers," she said. She stopped in front of Cyrus and stared boldly into his eyes.

A flush of warmth spread throughout his body.

Her hair was an unruly mass of brown dreadlocks that hung along her jawline. Across the bridge of her nose, a small cluster of freckles gave her a childlike appearance.

"Got a name?" She asked, smirking as she played with a gold ring on her bottom lip.

"Um, yeah. Cyrus. This here is Craig."

The young woman shifted her gaze to Craig then back to Cyrus. She flashed a coy smile. "I'm Mollie."

Cyrus shuffled his feet.

Mollie stared—her dark brown eyes gazing into his soul.

Unable to think of any words to say to this fascinating creature, he stood still and smiled awkwardly. Behind him, Craig snickered.

A slim, blond man wandered out of the kitchen. Several years older than Mollie, he had the look of a drifter with his short hair and scruffy beard. Cyrus recognized him right away.

"Mollie, what the hell? You walked away with my lighter," he slurred.

Never taking her eyes off of Cyrus, Mollie replied, "Mags, this is Cyrus and Craig,"

Mags chuckled and reached out his hand. "I know these two. How the hell are ya doing? Last time I saw you was in New Orleans." He paused and rubbed his chin. "That was a wild time."

Cyrus never thought he would be glad to have someone interrupt a conversation between himself and a beautiful woman. But here he was. He smiled. "Yeah, yeah, something like that. How many others are here tonight?"

"I wanna say seven, plus our group. So, about eleven," Mags replied. He turned to Mollie. "Am I missing anyone?"

Mollie shrugged.

Mags shifted his attention back to Cyrus. "One group's in the first bedroom at the top of the stairs. The other one's down here in the parlor."

"Anyone we know?"

"Nah," replied Mags. "At least I don't know any of 'em. They're two different groups as far as I can tell. The ones in the parlor are all greenies. They're young and stupid." He scoffed. "I had to yell at 'em a little while ago—idiots were setting off firecrackers! Inside!" He rolled his eyes. "We're literally sitting in a giant pile of kindling. How dumb can you be? You should have seen the looks they gave me! Like they've never been told no in their entire lives." He scowled. "I don't remember us being that dumb or entitled when we started out. Do you?"

"Man, I'm sure we were pretty stupid. Maybe even more so." Cyrus smirked and shot a sideways glance at Craig. "In fact, some of us still haven't grown up."

Mags chuckled. "Yeah, yeah, yeah, I hear ya. Hey, we're hanging in the kitchen. Wanna join?"

Cyrus had to admit, spending a few hours getting to know Mollie was tantalizing. But exhaustion had already set in. "Nah, man," he replied. "We got an early hop tomorrow."

"We've been walking for hours," added Craig. "I for one, just want to crash."

Mollie sighed. She slowly scanned Cyrus from head to toe. "Whatever. Y'all are missin' out, though." She turned and meandered back to the kitchen.

"Well, suit yourselves," replied Mags. "I'd probably try to sleep up in the attic tonight. The middle bedroom's ours. I can't guarantee we're gonna be quiet." He winked.

Turning to stroll back to the kitchen, Mags called over his shoulder, "Oh, and be careful on the stairs, some treads in the middle are about to go. If you crash through, you could seriously hurt yourself. Broken bones suck."

Thankful for the warning, Cyrus headed toward the stairs with Craig. At the threshold of the parlor, he paused and peered at the occupants inside. Mags didn't exaggerate—they were young. Far too clean for seasoned riders, their clothes lacked the usual wear and tear. The teens glared at him. After nodding a quick hello, he left them alone.

He pulled out his flashlight and climbed up the stairs, taking particular care to test each tread before applying his full weight. At the center of the staircase, he discovered the weak boards, exactly where Mags said they would be. He set his foot down—the step groaned and buckled. Not wishing to crash through, he shifted his body and hopped over the weak steps, landing safely at the top.

Passing the first room, he peered in to find three people sitting on the grimy floor. Deep in conversation, they passed a liquor bottle between them. Seeing him standing there, they halted and nodded in greeting. One of the men held the bottle in the air, offering to share. Cyrus decided he liked this group better than the one downstairs. After politely declining the invitation, he and Craig continued down the corridor.

To their left was the bathroom—or rather, what remained of it. A sliver of wood was all that was left of the door. The old toilet, blackened with mold and filth stood alongside the grimy, claw-foot tub. Shards of broken mirror lay scattered around the fractured sink.

In the next room, soiled clothing, empty bottles and discarded cigarette butts littered the floor. The room reeked of the musky scent of sex, cheap whiskey, and stale smoke.

At the end of the hall, he paused at the entry to another bedroom. This one was larger than the others. An old, stained mattress lay in the far corner against the wall. Across the room, two large windows overlooked the rolling hills below. A rat squeaked and scampered across the floor, disappearing into a dark corner.

Cyrus glanced back at Craig, who wrinkled his nose and shook his head.

He didn't want to stay in that room either.

They turned and climbed the second flight of stairs to the attic.

At the top was a vast open room—an enormous wooden cavern. Exposed rafters soared overhead like the belly of an old seafaring ship. The peculiar scent of mothballs permeated the air.

Startled by the intruders, two birds launched into the air, escaping through a hole in the roof.

"Skylight's bigger than I remember," joked Cyrus.

Craig smirked and studied the hole. "Ah, nothing like an unobstructed view of the stars." He slapped Cyrus on the shoulder. "Also, bonus, if it rains, we could shower right here."

Cyrus shook his head. "Let me just say, if it rains and you strip down while I'm in the room, I will beat your naked ass."

Craig grinned. Mimicking Mollie's tone and gestures, he responded, "Whatever. You'll be missin' out though."

They cleared a space near the wall and laid out their sleeping bags.

Muted voices floated up through the floorboards along with the familiar scent of weed.

Craig pulled his beanie off of his head. "At least the neighbors aren't too loud tonight," he said as he folded the hat with the Bruin's B facing up and set it on the floor.

Within minutes they were both fast asleep.

Cyrus awoke to shouts coming from downstairs. He lay there, eyes closed, listening. A faint hint of smoke permeated the air.

Rubbing his eyes, he sat up. "Yo, Craig, you awake?" No response. He reached over—Craig's sleeping bag was empty.

Something was wrong. He picked up his flashlight and clicked it on. Smoke whirled around in the beam. He scanned the area. No sign of Craig. The smoke grew thicker. His eyes stung. He sat there, trying to clear the fog of slumber from his mind and make sense of what was taking place. Down below, he could hear pounding feet running on wooden floors. Someone yelled.

Craig bolted into the room. "Dude, we gotta get out now! The place is burning!" He grabbed hold of Cyrus's arm and yanked.

"Wait! Our gear!" Cyrus pulled back.

"Let it go." Craig shouted—fear in his voice, "We don't have time. The whole downstairs is in flames!"

They rushed down to the second floor and halted. People were yelling and running everywhere. An ominous red glow emanated from the stairs. Through the heavy smoke, they saw the silhouettes of two people disappear into the crimson haze. Suddenly, the crashing noise of splintering wood echoed throughout the house, followed by ear-splitting screams. Acrid, black smoke filled the air, making it impossible to see or breathe. Cyrus struggled to inhale.

Craig grabbed him by the arm. "Come on!" He shouted, as he dragged Cyrus along. Heavy smoke whirled around them. His eyes watered and his lungs burned as each breath drew in more of the noxious smoke. Feeling their way along the wall, they pushed through the doorway of the nearest bedroom and found a window. Using his elbow, Craig broke the glass. Fresh air! Cyrus leaned out and inhaled deeply, filling his lungs. His chest spasmed. He coughed uncontrollably.

Below them stood a narrow overhang—this was their way out. Craig stepped backward and signaled for him to go first.

Cyrus climbed out of the window and stepped down onto the metal roof. Slanted and smooth, the surface made it difficult for him to maintain his footing. Slipping and sliding, he shimmied his way to the edge and jumped down to the ground where he watched as Craig jumped and landed beside him. Safe from the fire, he lay there on the ground, hacking and wheezing as he expelled the smoke from his lungs.

Inside the house, a woman screamed.

Cyrus jumped to his feet and sprinted around the building, trying to find a way in. Angry red flames consumed the front porch. Smoke billowed out of every crack and crevice. As he rounded the corner to the back porch, the kitchen door burst open. A young man tumbled out onto the ground, shrieking as he frantically batted at his clothes.

Without hesitation, Cyrus ran to him and snuffed out the flames.

"Your friends still in there?" He asked as he stood up.

The kid nodded. It was one of the teens from the parlor.

Reaching out to help him to his feet, Cyrus declared, "We need to get them out of there."

The teen didn't take his hand. A look of panic swept over his face.

Shaking his head, he scurried backward on all fours. Without saying a word, the boy jumped to his feet and took off into the woods.

"Goddam coward!" yelled Cyrus. He turned to Craig. "Looks like it's up to us."

Craig remained still and silent.

"Come on," pleaded Cyrus. "You know we can't leave those people in there. They'll die. We have to help whoever we can."

Craig nodded solemnly.

It was obvious Craig didn't want to go back inside the burning building. In all honesty, neither did Cyrus. He wanted to run off into the woods and get as far away as possible. But he knew there was no way he could live with himself if he didn't at least try to save some of the others.

He stepped onto the small back porch and looked inside. Heavy smoke billowed in the air. Orange flames licked around the doorframe leading into the living room. A profound sense of dread crept over him —he pushed it back.

More screams erupted, followed by the sound of pounding feet as the people upstairs ran around in terror.

Cyrus covered his face with his arm and charged into the house.

In the living room, heavy smoke made breathing difficult and hindered his vision. Were it not for the flames burning so bright, he wouldn't have been able to see anything. Crouching low, he made his way to the bottom of the stairs.

At the entrance to the parlor, he paused and peered inside. Red hot flames consumed the entire room, ravaging all in its wake. He stepped sideways, bumping his foot against something soft and heavy. Looking down, he found a body buried under burning rubble.

He kicked off the flaming debris, grabbed hold of the body and pulled. Craig placed a hand on his shoulder. Cyrus stopped. The boy was dead, there was no helping him. Sad at the senseless loss, he surrendered the body to the flames and stood up, turning his focus on the stairs. Orange, red, and blue flames climbed up the walls, illuminating the area with an eerie glow. Able to see the entire staircase for the first time, he realized why no one had tried to use them.

Halfway up, trapped in a gaping hole, were two bodies twisted around one another, engulfed in blue flames. Burned beyond recognition, their mouths frozen in perpetual screams.

The old house shuddered and buckled. A blanket of flames undulated along the ceiling like an angry sea of fire.

He glanced over at Craig—they locked eyes. Craig made the sign of the cross and kissed his Saint Christopher medal.

The house moaned. The eerie sound of splintering wood crept through the walls. A thunderous crash rang out as what remained of the dilapidated old house collapsed in a fiery heap.

Chapter Two

Four weeks later; outside of Tulsa, Oklahoma

PERCHED ATOP AN EVERGREEN TREE, FINN STUDIED THE LAY OF THE land. Carried on a cool breeze, the fresh scent of pine wafted through the air. The rolling landscape spread out before him like a diorama. Lush green grass carpeted the ground, sprinkled here and there with clusters of trees and shrubs. A pair of train tracks meandered along the hillside, disappearing around a bend.

Overhead, a flight of swallows darted about catching bugs in midair like tiny, daytime bats. Finn envied their ability to soar high in the sky. To be able to cruise the warm air currents—wild, alone, and free. He couldn't imagine a more perfect life.

In the prairie below, a group of deer grazed; one large buck and four does. He watched as they nibbled their way into the woods and out of view.

Several yards away, stood the remains of an old, yellow farmhouse. Surrounded by fallow fields, tall grass had overtaken what remained of the building. Weedy vines crisscrossed their tendrils around the outer walls, shrouding the building in a blanket of green. Beyond that, stood the remnants of a small barn. The wooden structure had collapsed long ago, leaving behind the rusty, metal roof to rest on the ground as if it were the top of an underground bunker.

A sudden blast of warm air exploded from the south. Whirling and churning, the gust caused the tree to sway. Clinging to the branch, he waited for the movement to subside. The air calmed. The steady, cool breeze returned. Finn turned his gaze toward the warm wind—off in the distance, the leading edge of thick, gray clouds gathered. A storm was brewing.

Returning to the clearing to join his friends, he found Zac and Cash were still busy playing a game of poker.

Zac studied the cards in his hand. A cluster of dark, auburn curls poked out from under his black hood. He nodded as Finn approached.

Seated opposite him was Cash, wearing a predatory smirk while flipping a coin around his fingers. He waited patiently for Zac to make a move.

It was quite difficult to beat Cash at card games. He was always one step ahead. Over time, the others came to realize it was a losing proposition, so they avoided getting into challenges with him. Zac, however, could never accept defeat. He would win at some point—or he would die trying.

Zac grimaced and peered up at Cash. "You better not have any cards up that sleeve of yours."

Cash flashed an innocent smile. "Me? Nah. No need to cheat, I've already got you beat."

Zac groaned and stared back down at his hand.

A few feet away, River was busy cutting Teague's hair. Her slim frame hovered over him as her long blonde dreads fell askew across her face. "Quit movin'!" She scolded.

"Aye-ye-yi! Woman," shouted Teague, "I ain't movin'—you're yankin' my head around!"

Finn smiled and sat cross-legged beside him.

"Hold on," River said, as she pulled her hair up into a ponytail. "All right, that'll make it easier."

She lopped off a few sections of Teague's blond hair, then paused and wagged the scissors at Finn. "Don't disappear. You're next."

"I don't need a haircut," he protested.

River shoved her fingers into the mop of wavy, dark, brown hair on top of his head. She tousled the unruly mess, then pushed it aside, exposing a blue eye. "It's grown past your eyes." She flipped the hair to the other side of his forehead, exposing an amber-brown eye. "We only ever see one eye at a time anymore."

Finn twitched his nose. "Maybe that's how I want it."

"Well, letting your hair cover your eyes like that will mess up your eyesight. I'm cutting it, so get used to the idea, mister, and don't wander off." She glared, daring him to argue.

Finn rolled his eyes and gestured toward Cash. "Doesn't look like you got a hold of him, yet. I can wait till he's done."

River shook her head. "He's not getting his cut."

"It's longer than mine!"

Cash laughed and ran his fingers through his hair. "She likes my luscious, brown locks long." He flashed a crooked smirk at River.

River scoffed and set her focus back to Teague ending the entire discussion.

"See anything interesting out there?" Asked Teague.

Finn gestured toward the tree line. "There's an old, run down farmhouse on the other side of those trees." He pointed. "Oh, and a storm's brewin' to the south."

"Comin' our way?"

"Stop moving," hissed River.

Finn shrugged. "Not sure. It looks like it might, but it could just veer off and leave us alone. Too soon to tell."

Teague nodded.

"Dammit! What are you, five?" Demanded River. "I just about nicked your ear that time." She turned to Finn. "Stop distracting him or he's gonna end up losing an ear."

"I'm not with him because of his ears. Losin' one ain't a deal-breaker." He winked at Teague.

"Uh huh. Of course, you would twist my words into something else. Thank you for dragging that right into the gutter," scolded River.

"Gutter? What is this gutter of which you speak?" Asked Finn, feigning ignorance.

"You know what you meant," replied River holding her ground.

Finn flashed an impish grin. "I don't know what you're talkin' about. I was referring to his mind. I'm with him for his brilliant mind and kind heart."

"I took it as his mind too," added Zac.

"Yep," chimed Cash. "I, too, took his comment as being purely wholesome in meaning. It appears as though you were the only one to take his comment in a dirty way."

"Nice," she nodded, "Go ahead. Twist it around," said River, as she glared at the group.

Finn shrugged. "Well, if the dirty mind fits..."

River pointed the scissors at him. "Don't piss me off, I'm holding a sharp object and I'm not afraid to use it."

"Wouldn't be the first time someone came at me with a sharp object," he laughed.

"This is true," agreed Teague.

"Why do I even try?" River shook her head and sighed.

"Truth be told," said Teague, "We wonder the same thing sometimes."

River responded by pointing the scissors at him. "Stay still!"

Holding back laughter, Teague and Finn shared a conspiratorial grin as River went back to work on his hair.

A gust of warm air blasted through the meadow, picking up several of the playing cards, carrying them off into the field.

"Well, damn," Zac sighed, as he tossed his cards on the ground. "There goes another deck."

The air warmed—the wind blew. To the south, an ominous, dark cloud moved in their direction.

"That does not look good," said Teague. He stood up and put his shirt on. "Looks like the storm is gonna hit us. Finn, think we could ride this out in that farmhouse you saw?"

"I think so."

Gusts of wind whipped back and forth. The sky turned dark, olive green. The air became damp and heavy with humidity.

Finn picked up his pack. "We should go now."

Dark clouds swallowed up the sun. Lightning lit up the sky, followed by a low rumbling sound that reverberated all around. Large droplets of rain plummeted to the ground.

"Follow me!" Finn yelled, as he ran toward the woods.

At the tree line, he pointed out across the meadow. "That way, on the other side of those trees."

The sky exploded with light. A tendril of lightning reached down and touched the ground, followed by a loud crack. Electricity filled the air. The hair on Finn's arms stood on end.

The wind howled through the trees. Hail mixed with rain as it poured down sideways.

Teague picked up a hailstone the size of a quarter. "Maudit! This is gonna hurt!" He exclaimed, "We better do this quick."

Finn waited as his friends readied themselves. A quick nod from Teague, let him know it was time. He turned his focus to the open field, took a deep breath and ran. Small balls of ice pelted down on him, stinging as they struck his face. His wet clothes grew heavier with each stride.

Halfway through the field, tornado warning sirens went off. A flurry of movement erupted as the herd of deer burst into the clearing, trying to outrun the storm. Finn and the buck nearly collided. Unfazed, the deer sprinted past and disappeared.

Lightning flashed. Thunder rumbled. He ran full speed, through the trees, emerging on the other side where the old farmhouse stood. A quick glance back assured him that his friends were holding their own. He pointed to the house, the others nodded and sprinted for shelter.

Inside the building, panting, they dropped their packs and pushed back their hoods. Finn reached out to Teague and wiped away a small spot of blood on his left cheek.

"Looks like one got me pretty good," Teague laughed.

"Everyone else okay?" Asked Finn.

Winded and soaked to the bone, they were all fine.

Broken glass, animal feces and building debris lay all over the floor. In the kitchen, holes in the walls, exposed old, paper-wrapped electrical wire and rusted iron, plumbing pipes. The whole building smelled of dirt and animal urine.

Outside, the wind raged, causing the old house to creak and sway. Hail pounded against the metal roof. Bang, bang, bang—like firecrackers. The siren continued to wail. Finn questioned whether the building could hold. Based on the looks on everyone's faces, they were wondering the same thing.

The siren stopped. Four loud beeps sounded over the speaker followed by a calm voice stating, "Take cover immediately."

Frantically, Finn and the others searched the house for a secure place to hide.

From the kitchen, Teague shouted as he pointed out the back door. Buried beneath a mound of grass, an old, concrete storm shelter sat hidden along the side of the house. They ran toward the structure.

Finn grabbed hold of the rusty metal handle and pulled with all his strength. It moaned and bent—then snapped off in his hand. Still holding the useless piece of metal, he turned to his friends hoping someone had an idea.

Cash ran back inside the house and returned with a metal pipe. "Here!" He handed it over to Finn.

After placing the end of the pipe over what remained of the handle, Finn pulled. The latch did not give.

Zac stepped up beside him. "Gimme."

Grasping the pipe with both hands, Zac pulled. The muscles in his neck and arms strained. Blood vessels and tendons became more defined as he exerted every ounce of power he could rally. The rusty metal screeched in protest, then finally, the latch gave way. With another great yank, Zac hoisted open the door. Both he and Finn peered inside the hole.

A foot of dirty water covered the shelter floor. The fetid stench of the stagnant liquid violated Finn's senses. He recoiled and covered his nose. This was going to suck.

He stepped back and looked around at his friends as the storm raged. There was no other choice, they had to go in.

The speaker sounded its eerie warning one more time.

A funnel formed in the clouds. Transfixed, he watched in awe as the finger stretched down to touch the ground, ripping trees out by their roots. Flinging them through the air like toothpicks. Churning and swirling, the dark cloud moved slowly, picking up everything in its path.

A blast of air nearly knocked Finn off of his feet. It was time to get inside. Hand over his nose, he joined the others in the shelter and slammed the door closed with a loud bang.

Chapter Three

STANDING IN THE DANK SHELTER, LISTENING TO THE STORM RAGE outside—Finn waited. Drenched from head to toe, the icy water chilled him to his bones.

Hail and rain crashed down on the metal door—pop, pop, pop—like a cascade of marbles falling from the sky. Outside, it sounded as though a freight train was passing by. Finn's ears popped from the pressure.

In need of a distraction, he turned on his flashlight and searched the shelves behind the stairs. Two old MREs and a couple jars of preserves covered in mold. He shook one, then placed it back down. Examining further, he discovered three mason jars covered in cobwebs hidden on the bottom shelf. Smirking, he lifted one, wiped it off, and held his flashlight against the glass, showing off the clear liquid inside.

"Well, at least this day isn't a total loss," Teague quipped.

Finn popped the seal and opened the jar. He smelled the contents and flinched. "Smells like paint thinner."

Teague took a sniff, then cringed. "Mais oui! That means it's good."

Finn raised the glass to his friends. "To Zac, our corn-fed country boy, and his ridiculous strength." He took a large drink. The clear liquid warmed the inside of his mouth, burning as it went down his throat and into his belly.

"How is it?" asked Teague.

"Tastes like it smells," Finn gasped, as he passed the jar. "It burns."

Teague raised the glass to his friends. "Bonne santé!" Then he took a swig and passed it to Cash.

"You gonna take a pull?" Zac asked, impatiently.

Cash nodded. "I will, I will. Let's just wait a minute to see if they die."

"They're good. Give it here." Zac said, as he snatched it from Cash. He raised the jar in the air. "To found whiskey, the best kind there is."

Two hours passed—the storm dissipated. Finn wasn't sure when the siren stopped screaming, but he was thankful it did. The alcohol helped to stave off the chills. Buzzed and feeling antsy, he was ready to get out. He climbed the ladder and peeped outside. The rain continued to fall at a steady pace—no wind and no hail.

He crawled out of the shelter and ambled up to the back porch, picking up a rusty metal tub along the way. "I can't believe this old place is still standin'." He said as he tossed the tub onto the wood floor.

Soaked to the bone, he took off his wet pants and shirt and draped them over what remained of the railing. River disappeared into the house. She returned a moment later wearing a gray and black flannel shirt. In her arms, she carried her wet clothes and three blankets. She tossed one blanket at Teague, another at Zac, then hung her clothes on the railing and wrapped the other blanket around her shoulders as she sat down.

Finn walked inside in search of anything dry to burn. He returned with a pile of scrunched up newspaper and small bits of wood. Placing them in a heap in the center of the metal tub, he looked around at the others, "Anyone got a lighter or anything?" he asked.

Teague handed him a flint stone.

Once again, the moonshine proved useful. After taking a swig, he doused the paper with the pungent-smelling liquid. With his Bowie knife, he struck the stone, causing bright, yellow sparks to fly. After a few strikes, a wisp of smoke rose from the pile of paper. He leaned close and blew on the fledgling flames, coaxing them to life. In no time at all, a warm fire illuminated everyone's faces with an orange glow that waved and flickered like a belly dancer.

Finn leaned back against Teague, who wrapped the blanket around them both. At last, a moment of calm. He listened to the rain falling on the metal roof as he basked in the fire's warmth. He closed his eyes and relaxed.

In the house, a phone chimed.

"It ain't mine—my battery's been dead for at least a week," said Zac.

"Mine died the other day," replied Teague.

Finn shook his head.

River shrugged.

"I suppose it's mine then." Cash walked inside. A moment later, he emerged, staring at the tiny screen in his hand. "Um, guys, something's up."

Apprehension buzzed through Finn's body as he waited for more information.

"Gunner wants us to get onto the server," continued Cash. He lifted his phone in the air. "I don't have a good connection."

Finn stood up. "Hand it here."

He climbed on the railing and reached above the roof. The signal was still not strong enough. He typed a message to let Gunner know about the issue.

The phone chimed with a response, "All right, I can fill you in via text."

Finn climbed down and sat beside Teague again. Anxiety washed over him while he waited. No one said a word.

A moment later the phone chimed again.

Finn read the message aloud. "There was a fire at the Austin Hotel a few weeks ago. The whole building burned to the ground. Several riders died inside."

He halted reading. "Christ!" He stared at the screen in disbelief.

Realizing the others were staring at him, waiting, Finn glanced up, "Cyrus and Craig were in the house."

Looks of shock swept over the faces of his friends as the reality of what Finn was telling them took hold.

Like a movie playing in slow motion, images of Cyrus and Craig flooded his mind. Cyrus with his big, muscular frame. His warm, friendly smile. Craig with his signature, cocky grin.

"Are they okay?" River asked, her voice quaking.

He shook his head. "According to Gunner, they didn't make it out." He blinked a tear from his eye and turned his focus back to the phone in his hand. "Is this real?" he typed.

"Yes," replied Gunner.

Finn typed, "How do you know it was them?"

He stared at the tiny screen, biting his nails as he waited. Teague put his hand over Finn's and pulled it away from his face. Ordinarily, this would irritate him, but this time, he was too numb to care.

The phone chimed with Gunner's response, "They sent me a text a few weeks ago saying they were stopping overnight at the Austin squat. They wanted to know if anyone else was nearby. I heard nothing from them after that."

As Gunner typed more, Finn conveyed the latest bit of information.

The phone chimed, and Finn read aloud, "Porter got wind of a major fire at an old, abandoned farmhouse outside of Austin. He did some digging and confirmed it was the rider squat. Yesterday, he posted on the server to see if any of us were in that area around that time. That was when I told him that Cyrus and Craig were there. He did some more digging and found out that two of the unidentified bodies they found in the debris, fit their descriptions. The bodies were burned too badly for proper identification, so they sent them off to a local mortuary for immediate cremation."

Finn shook his head. His heart pounded in his chest. He wanted to yell or punch something.

He typed another question. "Are you sure it's not a mix-up?"

Gunner responded, "Have you heard from either of them lately? It's like they dropped off the face of the earth. I haven't heard a word from them since that night. It's them. When you get a chance, Porter posted the official reports with all the details on the server. You can read it all there."

Finn wiped his eyes, then typed. "What happened to their bodies?"

Gunner responded, "The fire burned so hot, there wasn't much left. The county sent the remains they could identify along to their relatives. They stored the unidentified ashes at a county mortuary on the outskirts of the city."

Finn waited as Gunner typed more.

"The others already know. We chatted about it over the server. You guys have been out of touch for a while. We need someone to go there, collect the remains, and then bring them down to Stoney's where we can hold a proper memorial."

Finn relayed the info to his friends, then responded, "Count us in. Who's gonna get the ashes?"

The phone chimed. "That's what we're trying to figure out," replied Gunner. "We're all in transit, trying to make our way to Texas. Where are you?"

Teague leaned close. "What's he sayin'?"

"Someone needs to go get the ashes." Finn's heart raced in his chest. He sighed, then said, "We're the closest group, which means it's on us."

"You up for that?"

Finn shrugged. "We don't have any choice."

Cash spoke up, "You know, we don't have to do it if you don't want to. Some of the others could do it. Or, Zac and I can go get the ashes, then meet back up with you guys somewhere else."

Finn shook his head. "We can do it. As a group." He said struggling to hide his anxiety.

"You sure?" asked River.

"I said, we can do it!" He snapped.

Finn typed a message on the phone. "We're outside of Tulsa. We'll get their ashes and meet up with y'all in Terlingua."

The phone lit up with a response from Gunner. "I realize this is difficult for you. I wouldn't ask if it wasn't necessary. Nate and I are already heading down if you run into any trouble, give us a shout, and we'll come running."

"OK," typed Finn before putting the phone down.

Teague leaned over his shoulder. "You sure you're gonna be okay?"

Finn nodded, but he wasn't sure. A sense of cold dread washed over him. *Why did it have to be Austin?* He spent years running from that place—he vowed he would never go back. *Never say never.*

Finn stared into the flames—his mind blank.

First thing in the morning, they were catching a ride south.

Pitch black. Eyes open wide—searching. Darkness. The sound of muffled voices echoed around him. Something heavy held him down—suffocating. Panic bubbled up inside. He lay there paralyzed. A scream trapped in his throat.

Finn woke with a start, breathing heavy, hair damp with sweat, unsure of his surroundings. Slowly. he realized he was in the shabby room of the decrepit farmhouse. The room was dark; it was the middle of the night.

He stared up at the ceiling and wiped his eyes.

Isolation and stark, cold fear washed over him. He reached out to touch Teague, then withdrew his hand.

Afraid to close his eyes, he crept out of the room and sat outside on the old porch. The cool night air was a welcome change.

Leaning forward—elbows resting on his knees, he covered his face with his hands and wept.

Chapter Four

A LONE RAY OF SUNLIGHT CAST ITS BEAM INTO THE DARK ROOM, landing on Cash's face. He turned to the side—it made no difference. If he didn't know better, he would think someone was shining that light to prank him. He knew this was a foolish thought. His friends weren't messing with him—the sun was.

After another futile attempt to avoid the irritating ray, Cash surrendered to the morning and sat up. A sharp, piercing stab shot through his skull, causing him to wince in pain. His head was heavy, as though it was filled with sand. Feeling nauseous, he leaned back against the wall and studied the tiny particles of dust dancing in the sunbeam.

A few feet away, Zac slept—blissfully free of the annoying beam. Cash wanted to kick him, to wake him up. After a short, internal debate, he decided that would be a dick move. He opted instead to get up, find some water and wait for his hangover to subside.

Staggering out onto the front porch, he found Finn.

"How the hell are you the first one awake?" Cash asked, as he sat down on the step. "You drank more of that poison than I did." He rubbed his head and groaned. "It feels like tiny gnomes are trying to push my eyeballs out of my eye sockets."

Finn flashed an empty smile—the kind of smile that never makes it up to the eyes.

"Don't take this the wrong way," said Cash, "but you look like shit."

Finn didn't respond.

Something was off. He studied Finn closely. Puffy, red, bloodshot eyes, skin a little more pale than usual—all typical signs of a person who was deeply sad.

Aren't we all right now? He thought.

Sadness washed over him. Cyrus and Craig were dead, and they were going to get their ashes. On top of it all, as if the universe couldn't help but show off its twisted sense of humor, they needed to go to Austin to do it. Of all places. Why did it have to be there? Finn's personal center of hell. The Fates were assholes.

He sat in silence, glancing over at Finn, wondering what his thoughts were.

The sound of heavy footsteps pounding on the creaky floor grew louder as the person came near.

"Good morning, ladies." Bellowed Zac, as he shoved Cash into Finn. Pain shot up through his head, bringing with it more nausea. Without pausing, Zac stepped off the porch, walked over to the edge of the house—still in plain sight—and relieved himself.

River wandered outside. She stretched and yawned. Tilting her head to the side, she swept her hair away, exposing the delicate curve of her neck.

If Cash were to dream up his perfect woman, it would be River. From the moment they first met, he was smitten. Everything about her was perfection. Her face—her big green eyes—the tiny dimple that appeared just to the side of her mouth when she smiled. Physical features aside, she was strong, brilliant and independent. She was also fiercely loyal to her friends.

Family was sacred to River. She would do nothing to hurt them. Boyfriends were a different story—they were disposable. He had seen enough of them come and go to know he didn't want to be among their numbers.

Teague wandered out onto the porch and handed River her shoes. "You shouldn't walk around here barefoot. Lots of broken glass everywhere."

Good old Teague—always the parent.

He crouched down in front of Finn and sized him up. "Comment ça va?" He asked.

"I'm ready to get started," replied Finn.

Teague nodded and handed Finn a bottle of water. "Drink up," he said. "Flush some of that alcohol out of your system. You look like shit." He stepped off the porch and disappeared around the side of the house.

Finn wasn't the only one who was ready to hit the road. On this particular morning, no one was in the mood for lounging around. Within the hour, they were packed and ready to head out.

As they walked away from the house, the destruction left behind by the tornado was on full display.

Giant shards of metal and various sized chunks of wood were strewn about as if someone had tossed them aside like garbage. Around the side of the house, a swath of upturned earth ran in a straight line from the meadow, halting beside the remains of the old barn. The cyclone had torn out a twenty-foot section of trees—roots and all, casting them aside like a pile of Lincoln Logs.

Sprinkled throughout the wreckage were the tiny, broken bodies of at least a dozen sparrows. Hopping over the lifeless creatures, Cash couldn't help but think how lucky they were that none of their bodies were laying amid all this mess.

The meadow was unharmed. This was normal for tornados—one home could survive without a scratch while its neighbor would be demolished. The level of damage depended on where the funnel touched down. Pure luck of the draw.

They walked across the field and into the trees, emerging along the side out just in time to hear the train whistle blow. Staying out of sight, they hunkered down in the brush and waited.

Cash watched as the engines passed. They were waiting for the right car near the end of the train. Hopping on close to the engines increased the chances of them being seen, especially during the daylight hours.

At last, the end of the train came into view.

Bursting from the trees, he ran alongside the tracks, keeping pace with a boxcar. Reaching the door first, he grabbed hold of the frame and pulled himself up. Finn was next. After tossing their packs inside, they helped the others on board.

They were on their way. Oklahoma City was a couple hours away, so there was time to relax and enjoy the scenery.

Sitting in the open door, Cash pulled his phone from his pocket. He scrolled through his photos, pausing on one of Craig. Blue eyes, dark hair, Bruins beanie. Flashing his middle finger.

He smiled, remembering the first time they met.

Before running into Finn and Teague, Cash rode the rails alone. It wasn't because he didn't like other riders. He enjoyed the times he traveled with others. It was just that more often than not; he preferred solitude. Being alone gave him time to think.

It was late October, and he made the mistake of staying in the Denver area for too long. Winter was setting in. It was time to head west.

He thought the Fates were on his side when he caught a ride in a boxcar. However, that ride didn't last long. When the train pulled into Grand Junction, Bulls were everywhere—searching inside and between the cars. Cash needed to get out or risk being arrested. Listening through the walls, he waited until they were busy with another car, then jumped out and hid among some brush at the far end of the yard.

Several hours passed. The sun had set. Because of the cold, no guards or engineers were out. After slinking down several alleys, he came upon a train that was heading west. Thankful to be leaving the cold behind, Cash hopped on between the rear engine and a gondola filled with gravel. The metal of the ladder chilled his fingers as he climbed up and slid over the ledge onto the bed of rocks.

It was a lumpy, uncomfortable ride. At least he didn't have to worry about falling off—might freeze to death, though. He wrapped himself in as many clothing items as possible and hunkered down.

It wasn't too bad until the snow began to fall. Tiny, delicate The flakes grew in size. The snow accumulated.

Shivering, he rummaged through his pack to find anything he could use to protect against the weather. Having always preferred warmer climates, Cash didn't have much cold weather gear.

Mental note—get some fucking gloves and a goddamn hat. He thought as he pulled every article of clothing out of his pack.

A swirl of icy wind whipped around him, lifting several items and hurling them into the wind. Scrambling, he dove forward, leaning against the lip of the car, he caught them in midair. "Ha! Got it!" He yelled. Holding up a middle finger to the sky, he shouted, "Fuck you!"

Something moved in the corner of his eye. He looked into the window of the rear engine and found two men staring back at him. One was a large man with dark skin and a head full of dreads—the other was tall, skinny, and pale. He was wearing a smirk the size of the Grand Canyon. Cash didn't know who they were, but he knew, without a doubt—they were not engineers.

As he stared at them, dumbfounded, the skinny guy handed money to the other one. *Some sort of bet? Who the fuck are these guys?* He wondered.

The large guy held up a clipboard with the words "Wanna come inside?" scrawled on it.

Wanna come inside—no, I think I'd rather stay up here and freeze my ass off.

Cash nodded.

The skinny guy grabbed the clipboard and wrote something. He held it up. "You know the drill. Gas, Grass or Ass."

Before Cash could respond, the big guy snatched the clipboard, read the note and shook his head. He shoved his buddy, who then scrawled something else on the clipboard, then held it up again. The words gas and ass had lines drawn through them, the word grass was still visible—this time with a question mark and a smiley face.

Cash laughed. He pulled a baggie from his shirt pocket and held it in the air. His two new friends nodded with enthusiasm, then quickly helped him climb over to the engine.

The warmth of the cabin was a welcome change from the frigid cold outside.

"I'm Cyrus and this is Craig."

"Cash," he replied. "How long have you two been riding in here?" He cupped his hands together and blew on them.

"We hopped on back in Grand Junction," replied Cyrus.

Cash nodded. "Same place I did. I didn't see you."

Craig chuckled, "Well, we watched you scurry up that ladder and hunker down in the bed of rocks. It's wicked cold outside, you had to be freezing your ass off out there."

"I was," agreed Cash. He lit a joint and handed it to Cyrus. His fingers tingled painfully as they adjusted to the warmth of the cabin.

Cyrus exhaled. "We had a little bet as to how long you were gonna make it out there. He bet you'd only make it an hour or two. I bet longer."

The money exchange made sense now. Cash decided he liked these two.

They traveled in the rear engine all the way to Salt Lake City. From there, they made their way west and finally south to Venice Beach, where they spent the next three months camping along the beach.

Zac clapped a hand on his shoulder, "Earth to Cash. Get ready."

They were coming into the train yard outside of Oklahoma City. The others were already standing around the door. Cash got to his feet and readied himself.

Zac flashed a cheesy grin, "See ya on the ground, jackass." Then he jumped.

Cash watched as Finn went next, followed by River. It was his turn now—he nodded to Teague and jumped. Landing on the gravel, he rolled with the momentum and came to a full stop on his feet. He brushed himself off and looked around.

Being in a large city was a rare occurrence for their group. They spent most of their time away from all the hustle and noise. For Cash, this was like being home. He enjoyed the commotion. The others, however, were a different story. Having so many people around made them uneasy. They didn't mind spending time in urban areas when they had to, but they preferred being as far away from mainstream society as possible.

Hungry and eager to find out all the details about the fire, they found a small diner and settled into a corner booth. While filling their bellies, they charged their phones and took advantage of the free Wi-Fi to access the server and learn everything they could about what happened.

Chapter Five

AFTER SUNSET, THEY HIKED TO THE TRAIN YARD AT THE EDGE OF THE city. Crouching low among the brush, an uneasy feeling crept over Teague. The last twenty-four hours had been a whirlwind.

First, the tornado which, on its own, would not have been a big deal. Over the years, they had seen their fair share of natural disasters. When you live outdoors, you learn how to endure whatever nature throws your way.

Finding out about Cyrus and Craig—now, that was awful. Thinking about them made him sad. It was hard to believe he would never hear Cyrus' deep laugh or Craig's sarcastic comments again. The world was going to be a different place without them in it.

On top of it all, making everything that much worse, was the fact that they were now heading to Austin. He was sure going back there was bringing back a whole torrent of emotions and memories for Finn. Memories Finn took great pain to forget.

Teague studied him in the dark. Aside from the obvious exhaustion due to lack of sleep, nothing seemed odd or out of character so far.

Something his "Paw paw said years ago came to mind. *"You can't run away from your past. It's a part of you—how you became who you are. Embrasse le. It ain't goin' nowhere. Until you do, neither are you."*

Remembering the old man brought a smile to Teague's face. The long summer days at the old house on the river—just the two of them. Fishing off the back porch in the middle of the bayou, his bare feet dangling inches above the murky water. The rickety sound of the old screen door when it slammed shut. Thwack! The deafening noise of millions of frogs calling out for mates in the twilight hours.

At the cabin, there were no rules. Out there, Teague wasn't a boy— he was a man. They slept in till the sun made it too hot to be indoors and stayed outside until the mosquitoes chased them back inside for safety. On that porch, Teague had his first taste of moonshine and tobacco. Or course, Paw-paw swore him to strict secrecy. Maw-maw was never to know. Sweet and loving most of the time, Eugenie Leveaux was a force to be reckoned with when she got angry. It was best not to trigger her ire.

He spent hours listening to the old man's stories of adventure and struggle, peppered with various bits of wisdom. In the eyes of young Teague, his Paw-paw was the most amazing man in the world. He wanted nothing more than to grow up and be just like August Leveaux.

The train whistle called out, startling him from his reverie. Anxiety washed over him. This train was hauling oil tankers—some of the most dangerous cars to ride.

They did their best to avoid these. Clinging to the narrow, open frames, feet dangling in the open as the railroad ties pass below in plain sight, didn't lend itself to comfort or safety. Riding suicide is what they called it—a fitting name. One wrong move and a rider could fall between the cars, onto the tracks. It would make for a gruesome end.

He pulled a bottle of water out of his backpack and took a long drink before handing it off to Finn. "I ain't gonna lie, I sure wish this train was haulin' grainers. Tankers suck."

Finn glanced back at him. "Can't be too choosy when you're gettin' a free ride. Besides, a little danger now and then spices things up." He winked.

"Yeah, but your version of spicing things up usually ends up where I'm pullin' your ass out of some mess," replied Teague, "There's a lot of yelling, confusion and chaos. And, oh yeah… blood. There's usually a fair amount of blood."

Finn flashed an impish grin. "What's life without a little pandemonium? Besides, just think how much I've single-handedly helped you hone your stitchin' skills."

Teague nudged him. "Couillion."

The whistle blew. Ten cars passed—fifteen. A seemingly endless parade of filthy oil tanks slithered by like a black snake in the night. Eighteen—it was time.

Bursting out of the bushes, Teague ran up alongside the moving train.

Cash and River climbed on board first. They split up—Cash on one car—River on the other. They moved aside to make room for the others.

Teague was next. He grabbed hold of the rail and hoisted himself up while Zac climbed aboard the opposite car. So far, so good. He reached out to help Finn.

The train jerked forward and gained speed. They clasped hands. Suddenly, the metal wheels kicked up a large rock. Careening through the air like a bullet, it bounced off the side of the tank and struck Finn on the side of his head. The force of the impact caused him to swing hard to the side. Barely conscious, he lost his grip.

"Finn!" Teague yelled. Muscles straining, he held tight. The jerking motion, coupled with the weight of Finn's body, conspired to pull them both onto the tracks.

Zac was on his feet immediately. He stretched across the coupling between the two cars while Cash held him steady. Below, the tracks whizzed by.

River wrapped her arms around Teague's waist and held tight.

Teague tried to pull back, but the train lurched, forcing Finn's body to pitch to the side, pulling his arm along with it. He howled in agony as his shoulder ripped from its socket. His arm grew numb.

He held on—he was not letting go.

Zac grabbed hold of Finn's belt and heaved with all his might. After much effort, they managed to pull Finn between the cars. He was safe.

Leaving Finn in the care of River, Teague took a moment to survey the damage done to his shoulder. He lifted his arm. Pain shot through him like a hot knife. He took a deep breath and attempted to rotate it back into place. Intense pain exploded through his arm and shoulder. He wasn't going to be able to reset it without some assistance.

"I'm gonna need your help," he said to Zac.

Zac nodded.

"I'll lie on the frame. You're gonna grab hold of my arm and put your foot against my rib, right around here." He pointed to the area below his arm.

"When I say go, pull my arm toward you, steady and firm. Don't yank it. Just pull steady and firm. I'll let you know when it's back in. Got it?"

Zac nodded once again.

Teague was grateful that Zac was the sort of man he was—he did what was necessary with no special treatment or coaxing. In moments like these, Teague always tried to put the other person at ease. This time, however, he was in too much pain to care.

Holding on to the rail, he laid down and reached out to Zac, who grabbed hold of his forearm.

After adjusting his grip on the railing, Teague took in a deep breath and nodded.

Zac's foot pressed hard against his side as he pulled. Slow. Steady. Pain erupted in Teague's shoulder as the tendons stretched. Unable to hold back, he howled in agony.

He lashed out. "Just pull the goddamn thing! Hard!"

Pain exploded. He screamed. This was excruciating. Teague was sure the tendons in his arm would snap. Nausea washed over him as his shoulder popped back into place with a dull thud.

Zac let go.

Teague lay there, waiting for the queasiness to subside, staring up at the night sky—thankful that the pain was decreasing. His shoulder throbbed, and his entire arm tingled as though it were being jabbed by thousands of tiny needles. He sat up, leaned against the back of the tank and sighed.

It was time to set his focus back on Finn. He pulled him close, having Finn rest his head across his lap. He was barely conscious. Due to the darkness, Teague was unable to see the full extent of the injury.

Crimson blood gushed from the wound. Teague pulled a wrinkled and soiled bandana from his backpack. He pressed it against Finn's head.

Warm blood seeped through the cloth, oozing between his fingers. He continued to apply pressure, hoping the bleeding would stop, or at least slow down.

Finn's body tensed and spasmed. He was having a seizure. Teague knew this was coming. Years ago, when Finn was thirteen, he suffered a horrible attack. It was pure luck that he survived. Since then, any serious head injury would trigger multiple seizures. These instances didn't happen often—only a few times in the past four years.

Teague stroked Finn's hair and whispered, "Shhh, shhh, shhh. It's okay."

He didn't know if Finn even knew he was there during these episodes. Regardless, it was the only thing he could think of doing until it passed. If nothing else, this small act helped Teague stay calm.

Finn's body relaxed.

The first episode was always the worst. Teague continued to apply pressure to the wound. He wanted to sleep. His shoulder throbbed. He was done with this ride.

Less than twenty minutes later, another seizure hit. Once again, he held Finn close, whispering. This one would not last as long.

Finn's body calmed. Teague rested his head against the tank and relaxed to the sway of the train.

During the night, Finn had two more episodes. Each one shorter than the last, yet still terrifying considering their circumstances.

. . .

As dawn broke, the landscape changed, a city came into view.

It was a long night for everyone. Teague needed to get onto solid ground where he could patch up Finn and give his own shoulder some much needed care. Neither of them were in any shape to travel. His body ached with a dull pain that spread deep into his bones.

Finn sat up and pulled the blood-soaked bandana away from his head. A trickle of blood streamed down his cheek. Holding the soaked cloth out in front of him, he squeezed. Crimson liquid seeped between his fingers and splattered on the gravel.

Teague handed him another bandana. After folding it, he tied it around his head.

The whistle blew.

They were rolling through the center of town. It was time to jump.

Finn went first.

Teague watched as he landed on the ground, rolled once and came to an abrupt stop, shaking his head. Even in his current state, Finn could land on his feet. All of this came naturally to him. He made it look so easy. It was one of the many things Teague admired about him.

River nudged him. It was his turn. He tossed his pack onto the ground, then jumped and landed effortlessly. He stepped aside and watched as the others landed in a relatively perfect line along the tracks. They brushed themselves off and collected their gear.

To their right stood a concrete wall, covered in graffiti. To their left was an area covered in overgrown brush. They turned and disappeared behind the cover of the shrubs and trees. Hidden from view, they threw their packs down and dropped to the ground, exhausted.

Teague kept a watchful eye on Finn. His body trembled when he moved—his eyes glassy and unfocused. He was pale—more so than usual.

Finn sighed and laid back against his pack.

Teague leaned over and wiped away the crusted blood from his hair and face. He watched as Finn's eyes rolled up into the back of his head. His body tensed. His back arched.

Weary to the bone, Teague moved closer and whispered once again as Finn's body spasmed.

"Shh, shh, shh, it's okay."

Chapter Six

DISTANT, MUFFLED SOUNDS SURROUNDED HIM. EYES CLOSED, TINY sparks of light flashed around the edges in the darkness. Everything was far away—detached. Finn focused on the voices. He knew they belonged to his friends, but he couldn't make out what they were saying.

The ground pressed hard against his back. His right hand rested in the grass—the cool blades soft against his fingers. The smell of damp earth. He strained to open his eyes—his eyelids were lead blankets, refusing to cooperate. His head hurt like hell.

Slowly, he realized he was coming out of another seizure. Oh, how he despised these things. The pathetic weakness. The lack of control over his own body.

At last, able to open his eyes, he reached up to touch his head.

Teague caught his hand and gently forced it back down along his side. Smiling, he leaned over and looked him in the eyes. "Ah, I see you decided to join us again."

Teague's face came into focus. The silver ring in his left eyebrow. His pale blue eyes.

"Another one?" It was a rhetorical question.

Teague nodded.

"How long was this one?"

"Not long," replied Teague. "How're you feeling?"

"Weak, foggy, pathetic. How long was I out of it?"

"A couple minutes. This one hit as soon as you put your head down. Thank God it waited till you were lying down because we're all too tired to carry you." Teague grinned. "We've been waiting for you." He slid the bandana aside to peek at the wound.

Finn flinched at the painful tug as the cloth pulled loose from the sticky, coagulated blood.

"That needs some stitches," said Teague.

Finn nodded.

"Can you sit up? You can take a few hits from that joint." Teague motioned toward Cash, who sat across from them watching the exchange. He exhaled a cloud of smoke. "Hopefully, it'll numb some of the pain."

Finn sat up—his body trembled. He tried to run his fingers through his hair, but there was so much dried, crusted blood, they got stuck part way through. Disgusted, he wiped his hand off on his thigh.

With shaking hands, Finn took a large hit from the joint. The trembling stopped. Instant calm washed over him.

Beside him, Teague rummaged around in his pack. He pulled out a shirt, sniffed it and recoiled. "Well, it ain't clean, but it's gonna have to do." He laid it flat on the ground and pulled out his sewing kit along with a small bottle of hand sanitizer. After placing them on the shirt, he turned to the others. "Anyone got any dental floss? Not mint. Oh, and bandages, gauze—this is a big one."

As the others gathered what items they had, Finn pulled out the flask filled with the leftover moonshine from the storm shelter. He took a swig, then placed it down on the T-shirt with the rest of the items.

Teague looked at him and asked, "You ready?"

"About as ready as I can be," replied Finn, forcing a wry smile.

"Tête de cabri," said Teague, as he tapped his head, "I suppose that's a good thing in this case."

Finn sighed and gave a quick nod.

"Okay, let's do this." Teague rubbed hand sanitizer on his hands. "Put your head back, we got to clean it first."

Finn scooted back and leaned sideways, tilting his head.

Using the bottle of water, Teague flushed out the wound. He moved the hair aside and poked around, taking care to remove all the bits of debris. Finn swore he could feel each hair follicle as it moved. The world spun, creating an odd sensation of detachment. A stinging splash of cool liquid brought him back to earth.

"Jesus!" exclaimed Finn, flinching and trying hard not to pull away. His eyes watered.

"I know, I know, moonshine stings a little," Teague said calmly, "Hang in there."

Finn relaxed.

Teague used the lighter to sterilize the needle. As he watched, Finn couldn't help but chuckle over the care he was taking. Why bother? There was enough dirt encrusted deep inside the crevices and lines of Teague's fingers to contaminate the needle all over again.

He took another swallow of the moonshine, then settled back. Turning his head to the side, he closed his eyes and waited for the inevitable.

Finn did his best to ignore the pain, but he could feel every torturous stitch. First came the sharp stab as the needle forced its way through both sides of the wound, then came the weird, skin-crawling sensation as the thread moved through his flesh. Eyes watering, he went between bouts of sharp pain and pure revulsion.

"Relax. If you struggle, it's only gonna hurt more," Teague whispered.

A faint smile crept across Finn's face as the words echoed in his mind. His thoughts trailed back four years ago, to the night they first met.

Chapter Seven

Four years ago. Austin, TX

COLD, FRIGHTENED AND ALONE, FINN RAN THROUGH THE DARK CITY streets. Heart pounding in his chest, each breath was hot fire in his lungs. Leg muscles screaming out from exhaustion, he halted at the end of the Lamar Bridge.

Gasping for air, he leaned against a concrete post and peered down to the water below. He scanned the riverbank, searching for a place to hide. To rest. Under the bridge, he spied a hidden area tucked away between the deck and the first arch. Perfect.

He glanced backward. The street was empty. Not a single person in sight. Without a sound, he hopped the rail and scrambled down the uneven steps.

Pausing one more time, he listened for any sign that he was being followed. All he could hear was the river coursing by and the pounding of his own heartbeat. He was alone. Relieved, he scurried up along the concrete arch, worked his way around the columns and finally sat still.

Having run four miles from the east end of the city to the river downtown, exhaustion swept over him. His hair was a sweaty, tangled mess on his head. The cool night air on his damp skin chilled him to the bone. Limbs weak and throat dry, breathing was pure misery. Shivering, he pulled his legs to his chest, wrapped his arms around, and rested his forehead on his knees. Pain, fear, and anger washed over him. He broke down and sobbed.

Curled up under the bridge, Finn lost track of his surroundings. He stopped crying and stared down at his feet, listening to the sound of the river coursing below. He was numb. His mind blank, he rocked back and forth.

A soft, shuffling sound emanated from his right. Someone or something was moving around. An uneasy feeling crept over him. His body tensed as he strained to listen.

An unfamiliar voice interrupted the silence, "Uh, y'alright?"

It was close—too close.

Startled, Finn scurried back up the arch. He glanced over to see a skinny, scruffy-haired, blond teen kneeling beside him. His clothes tattered and dirty, it was obvious he was another street kid. *Where the hell did he come from?* Finn wondered. He looked around in panic.

"Whoa, whoa, whoa calm down!" the teen said, as he raised his hands, palms out toward Finn. "I ain't gonna hurt you, mon ami. I saw you sitting here, and you looked like you needed some help." He placed his hands down on his thighs and stared.

His mind blank, Finn did not respond. Panic swelled inside him. His heart raced.

The teen cleared his throat and spoke again.

"Mais oui. So, I see you're not gonna say much." He smiled. "That's fine—your call. Let's start easy. I'm Teague." He offered his hand to Finn, who glared at him, unmoving. After a long, uncomfortable pause, the teen finally let his hand drop back to his thigh.

"Okay." He ran his fingers through his hair. "Uh, you want some water or food?" He gestured to his pack.

Finn flinched—Teague flinched.

Teague sighed and rubbed his chin. He smiled and became more animated.

"What? Do I smell bad?" He lifted his arm and sniffed. "Ech! Yeah, that's vile." He wrinkled his nose. "Well, that explains why you won't talk. Okay, so yeah, that's rank, but in my defense, showers are scarce. And honestly, I'm not bathing in the river right now." He shook his head. "It's cold, cold. If it was warmer, that would be a different story...."

Why is he talking to me about showers? What the hell is that accent? Thought Finn.

Riveted to the spot, Finn's mind told him to run, but he could not move.

Teague continued to rattle on, "The nights have been chilly lately, wouldn't ya say?" He leaned closer.

Finn scrambled to his feet. Stepping backward, he slipped and almost fell into the river. Teague jumped up and grabbed hold of his arm.

Bad move.

Finn wrenched his arm away and swung a hard right jab that landed on the side of Teague's jaw. With a howl, he cupped his hands over his mouth.

"Fils-putain!" Teague cursed through his fingers. Lowering his hands, he sneered and spat blood into the river below. Nostrils flaring, he tilted his head to the side, balled his fist and punched Finn in the nose.

Pain shot up through his head as he slammed back against the column. Nose bleeding, he regained his footing and swung again.

This time Teague blocked him. He punched Finn in the stomach, knocking the air out of him. Before he could regain his wits, Teague got him into a headlock. Finn struggled to free himself, but Teague held on.

Shaking his head, Teague hissed through his teeth, "Nah, nah, nah, couillion. I ain't lettin' go till you calm down, jackass!"

Finn struggled to free himself, but Teague had the advantage of both size and strength. Realizing he would not get out of this by fighting, he calmed and waited.

Teague spoke again. "Trés bien! I see you finally understand the situation here. Calm the hell down. If you struggle, it's only gonna hurt more."

That last sentence triggered a renewed sense of panic in Finn. He whimpered and thrashed about.

Teague tightened his grip. "Okay, okay, so that was probably the creepiest thing I have ever said to anyone, and I do mean ever. Sorry. I did NOT mean that how it sounded."

Unable to get free, Finn relaxed again—he listened.

Teague loosened his grip. "All right, I'm gonna let go. Do NOT swing at me again, or I promise you, I will kick your ass and toss you into the river. Clear?"

Finn nodded his head.

As promised, Teague let go.

Breathing heavily, Finn stepped back and adjusted his clothes.

"Now, let's try this one more time, shall we? My name is Teague." Once again, he offered his hand.

Finn stared at the extended hand. Apprehensively, he accepted. "Finn."

"Hoo Lawd! We have a name!" Teague flashed a cocky smirk. "Okay, Finn, what brings you here to my bridge, and why the fuck did you hit me?"

Teague spoke with the thick drawl of a country boy. Some of the words he used were French—at least they sounded that way. Such a strange combination.

"What?" Finn's voice cracked. He stared at Teague. *Is he serious?*

Teague's language confused him. He seemed okay, but then so did the other street kid Finn trusted a week ago. He didn't want another repeat of that whole nightmare.

"You heard me, couillion," Teague responded. Tapping his forehead with his fingers to the cadence of each word, he said, "Est tu fou? Someone comes up to offer you help, and you respond with this feral bullshit where you haul off and punch 'em in the face! Not cool man, not cool." He shook his head.

Finn's mind whirled. He couldn't believe he was being scolded for defending himself. *What the hell does he want?*

Undaunted, Teague continued to talk. "Are you even gonna say anything, or are you just gonna stand there slack-jawed starin' at me?"

"What the hell is wrong with you?" Finn snapped, "What do you want from me?" His throat ached with each word.

Teague took a slight step back. His face relaxed. He blinked, then spoke in a friendlier tone. "Okay, look. I realize we got off on the wrong foot. Let's backtrack. I was trying to sleep over there, minding my business." He gestured toward his pack on the other side of the arch. "I saw you come inside and heard you crying. You're a freaking mess. I thought, pauvre bête, this kid could probably use some help."

"I wasn't crying," replied Finn.

Teague nodded his head and smirked. His eyes sparkled with amusement. "Uh, huh—sure," he said, "Regardless, I've got a little food in my pack... water too. I'm only guessing, but it looks like you haven't eaten in a while."

Finn nodded.

After gesturing for Finn to stay put, he took a step backward and walked along the barrel to his pack. A moment later, he returned with a bag of almonds, half a sandwich, a bottle of water and a gray hoodie. He tossed the hoodie at Finn and sat down on the concrete.

Watching Teague's every move, Finn put on the hoodie and sat down. The sight of the food and water reminded him how hungry he was, he couldn't remember the last time he ate. Weak and exhausted, he rubbed his head. His mouth watered.

Teague popped a bunch of almonds into his mouth, showing they were okay to eat. He then handed the bag over.

Finn was feeling better about this strange teen. After getting a good look at him, he didn't seem all that terrifying. He supposed he was a year older than himself. Maybe fifteen. He had an expressive way of speaking. Finn got the sense that if you paid close attention to Teague, his face would reveal his thoughts. So he watched.

Teague broke the silence. "It's a little chilly to be without a jacket."

"Yeah, it is. Thanks for the hoodie."

"De rien," replied Teague.

"Is that French?"

Teague grinned. "Sorry, it's habit. Where I grew up, it's just the way folks talk."

"Where's that?"

"Southern Louisiana. Cajun country. What about you? You from around here?"

Finn nodded.

"Got a home to go back to?"

Finn shook his head.

Teague nodded. "You're gonna need a pack and a jacket then. We can find those later."

"I got my own gear," replied Finn, a little more confident, "Just some basic things, including a coat."

The look of surprise that swept across Teague's face made Finn smile.

Teague grinned. "And where is this?"

"At the State Park at the south end of town. I was camping out there. About a week ago, I came to town to get a few supplies, and well, things happened." He let his head hang low and paused. "If you want, you can come with me, and I can share some of my food with you. To pay you back."

Teague smiled, nodding his head. "Well, mon ami, that sounds like a plan." He hesitated, then said, "Can I ask you a question?"

Finn nodded.

"Are you wearin' contacts?"

Finn looked down, suddenly self-conscious. "No."

Teague seemed to sense Finn's discomfort—at least, he didn't bring up his eyes again. They spent the next couple hours under the bridge, discussing everything from the weather to the ins and outs of sleeping under an overpass. It surprised Finn to find out that Teague knew quite a lot about hunting and surviving in the wild.

When the morning sun rose, they left the cover of the bridge and walked their way across the city. From that day on, they were inseparable.

Back in the clearing, Teague finally tied off the last stitch. He rinsed the wound one more time, then applied the clean gauze, holding it into place with a fresh bandana tied around Finn's head. "I think you'll survive now," he declared, as he handed the remaining supplies back to their original owners.

Finn sat up. His head ached a little, but overall, he was feeling much better. He rubbed his head then looked around at his friends, "So, where the hell are we?"

Chapter Eight

Zac doused a bandana with water and cleaned his face. "Denton. It's a college town in north Texas." He pulled up his pant leg, exposing a deep scrape along his shin. It surprised him that it wasn't deeper—it sure felt a lot worse when he scraped it across the coupling last night.

Last night. What a shit show. He barely placed his feet on the frame when the rock hit Finn in the head. From there, it was pure instinct. Zac didn't even stop to consider the logistics of leaping across the coupling the way he did. His only concern at the time was making sure that Finn did not die. It was a good thing Cash had his back.

Finn was always getting into something. And Zac was always there to help drag him out. He didn't mind—he would do anything for his friends. Family was everything. Finn was just the stupid brother who hadn't figured out he wasn't invincible yet. Besides, if Zac wasn't able to help, it would have all fallen on Teague's shoulders. He couldn't do that to him.

He glanced over at Teague, who was busy changing his blood-soaked shirt. A large, purple bruise covered his shoulder. *That's gotta hurt.* Thought Zac. When Teague asked him to help pull his shoulder back into place, Zac worried he would mess it up somehow. That he would pull too hard and make the injury worse. Teague didn't have any concerns. He seemed to be sure that Zac could handle it. That was the story of his life. Everyone around him believing he was capable and steady when deep inside he was just as scared as the rest of them.

Zac wiped away the crusted blood and dirt from the scrape on his leg. Once finished, he poured a little moonshine over it to kill any germs. He was good to go now—ready for whatever the day offered.

Finn rummaged through his backpack. "So, we're not even in Dallas?"

"Nope," replied Zac.

"That sucks. When's the next ride out?" Having found a semi-clean shirt, Finn pulled it over his head.

Teague interjected, "Not until tomorrow at the earliest. Neither of us is up for another hop today. I need a good night's sleep." He pointed at Finn. "You do too."

"Teague's right," River stated. She was wiping her face and arms with a damp cloth. "We already agreed we were not leaving for a day or two. Took a vote. You have no choice. We're gonna stay here, and you're gonna rest." She pulled out a strip of fabric and used it to tie back her long dreads.

Cash was busy brushing his teeth. He pulled the toothbrush out of his mouth and spat toothpaste on the ground. "We already told the others. They're okay with the delay since none of them are even close right now."

Finn nodded. "Seems like y'all have it figured out. What's next?"

"We're gonna head into town. The square is that way." Zac pointed. "We'll find something to eat, then figure out where we're gonna spend the night."

"Have we been through here before?"

Teague shook his head. "We haven't. Cash and River have though."

"Only once, a long time ago," replied River, "It was nighttime and only for a few hours so I don't remember much."

Cash closed up his pack. "I've been here a couple times. The square is cool. Lots of musicians and artists around. We should have no problem shoring up our cash reserves while here."

Finn put on his sunglasses. "Okay then, let's check out this town."

After stashing their packs among the shrubs, they left the cover of the brush and walked out onto the street.

A small neighborhood of neat, single-story houses on their left—a large, warehouse-style complex with a group of tall grain silos to their right. In the distance, high above the other buildings, the clock tower of the old courthouse stood tall. Turning right, they headed in that direction.

Standing at the corner, waiting for the light to change, River slapped Zac on the arm. Across the street stood a small shop with the word, Scrap, hand painted on the concrete block wall.

"Yeah, I see it," he said.

"Can we stop? I wanna stop," she asked aloud.

"We'll see."

She giggled, hooked her arm around Zac's, and waited for the light to change.

It was unusual for River to get excited over a shop. When she did, it was noteworthy. Looking over at the store—the signs in the windows —Zac could see why. The shop looked like a treasure trove of miscellaneous items. He wondered if he could find an old lamp cord in there —their wires made the best snares.

Stepping onto the curb, Cash came up from behind and grabbed River around the waist, pulling her away from Zac and the shop entrance. He lifted her over his shoulder and carried her down the sidewalk.

"No, no, no, no!" shouted River. Her long legs kicked in the air.

"Damn it, Cash! Put me down! Seriously! Zac! Teague! Somebody! Anybody?" She nodded her head toward the others who were walking behind them laughing, then flipped them off with both her hands.

As they rounded the corner, Cash put her down. River straightened her clothes, then struck at him playfully. He drew back to avoid her blows.

"We'll stop later," Teague said, walking past her with Finn, "That way you ain't carrying trash around with you all day. Or at least, we're not."

Zac stopped next to her. "Let's go, woman," he said, shaking his head as he nudged her. "Stop messing around."

River slapped his arm. "A lot of help you were."

Zac chuckled. "Cash seemed to have it all under control."

She slapped him again.

They walked past a building with rusted, old décor outside. Once a turn-of-the-century house, it was now a draft house. As River pulled out her phone to take a picture, Zac jumped into the rusty tub on the front lawn and pretended to bathe.

"Finn, Teague, come on, let's get a photo," she said, positioning herself in front of a large, green, lettered stand.

"What the hell does this say?" asked Finn.

"Lil' d," replied Cash, "Looks like you're supposed to stand between the big L and little l. Like you're the 'i' in Little d."

"Little d?"

"You seriously don't know Denton's nickname is Little d?"

Finn shook his head.

"Dallas is Big D. Denton is Little d." Cash shrugged. "I guess they had to come up with something to be different. How did you grow up in Texas and not know that?"

"He's not from North Texas," replied Zac, "this area is a whole other place compared to the rest of the state."

"Aren't you from North Texas, though?" asked Cash.

"Nah, man," Zac shook his head, "East Texas. That's another, completely-different place."

"This state's too damn big," said Cash, shaking his head.

Thinking about his home town brought back a flood of memories for Zac. Giant trees—open pasture and rolling hills. The smell of fresh-cut fields. The way the cows called out when it was time for their cubes. He wondered if the old family home looked the same. Had the rickety, old barn fallen down, or was it still hanging in there?

He remembered his dad with his big laugh and his big heart. There was no greater compliment for young Zac than to hear people say how much he was like his father.

"He sounds like my dream old man." Craig's voice, with its distinct Boston accent, cut through his memories.

"When I was a kid, I'd imagine my dad walking through the front door." Craig took a hit from the joint they were sharing. "He'd have this amazing reason for leaving." He chuckled. "You know, like he was a spy or some shit."

Zac leaned back on his hands. His feet dangled over the calm water of the lake as they sat on the pier. The night sky was dark and full of stars.

"That never happened though." Craig took another hit and handed it to Zac. "My dad was a spineless piece of trash who left his pregnant girlfriend. He never came back. He probably doesn't even know he had a son. Wherever he is, I hope he's miserable."

Craig lay down on the uneven boards of the pier and stared up at the sky. "I'll be honest man, I think I'd rather have no dad at all than an amazing one like yours, that died suddenly. It's way less painful."

Way less painful. Thought Zac, as he swirled his feet in the cool water. He supposed Craig had a point. Having nothing was probably better than having something great and losing it.

"Come on Zac," River called out, "Stop your daydreaming, let's go."

He shook his head to clear his mind. Enough thinking about the past. The present was all that mattered. Leaving the little bar behind, he caught up with River and Cash.

Chapter Nine

Parked cars lined the street—not a person in sight. This was a perfect opportunity. Coming up alongside a black SUV, Finn grabbed the handle and tugged. It opened easily. He slipped inside.

Outside, Teague stood watch while the others paused farther down the road.

The car reeked of cheap air freshener and stale smoke. Finn rifled around, searching for anything of value. In the console, he found a ten-dollar bill, a disposable lighter and some CDs. He pocketed the money and the lighter. As he reached over to open the glove box, he glanced out the window. Aside from his friends, the street remained empty.

The glove box contained a car manual and charger cables for a ridiculous number of devices. *Why so many of these stupid cords? How many devices do you need?* He wondered.

After one more pass to be sure he missed nothing, he climbed out of the car and closed the door.

As they strolled down the street, he tried the doors of two other vehicles—both locked.

The next car they came upon was a red sedan. He glanced around, making sure there was no one around, then he hopped inside.

A cheap, plastic dream catcher and Mardi Gras beads hung from the rearview mirror. He pulled them down and tossed them aside. Next, he opened the console. Jackpot. A twenty-dollar bill, just waiting for someone to take it. He never understood why people left cash in their vehicles like this. Oh well, all the better for him. He stuffed the money in his pocket.

Digging around a little deeper, he found a pill bottle. He emptied the contents into his palm—two pink allergy pills, orange painkillers, and some unidentified white pills. He popped two of the orange pills into his mouth and pocketed the rest, then tossed what remained over his shoulder into the back seat.

Back in the console, he found a gift card for a coffee shop. Flipping open the ashtray, he found a small disposable lighter on top of a pile of coins. He dumped the contents on the passenger seat and sifted through, gathering all the quarters, dimes and nickels—leaving the pennies.

He pulled down the passenger visor. Nothing. As he flipped down the driver's side, a photograph floated onto his lap.

A young couple smiled up at him as they held their newborn baby in a hospital room. Beaming. Mom's hair in a messy, high bun on top of her head, baby swaddled in a light-blue blanket, face frozen in a tiny yawn. The wholesome image was topped off with the dad hovering protectively over them both. He stared at the picture, then crumpled the photo into a ball and tossed it over his shoulder, onto the back seat.

In the corner of his eye, he could see Teague shaking his head. Finn flashed a sheepish grin and shrugged.

Teague wasted too much energy on the feelings of others. In Finn's eyes, if these folks didn't want someone like him to come along and take their shit—they should lock their doors.

After one final look around, he climbed out and closed the door.

They circled around the old stone courthouse. Small shops lined the street—a pizza shop, pawn shop, 24-hour diner. An old movie theater that had seen better days, two bars, and an old-time candy shop. Finn was excited to see that one.

The clock tower chimed, echoing around the empty square. It was now nine o'clock. They climbed up the giant stone steps of the courthouse and sat down under the shade of the covered landing. A cool breeze rustled the leaves of the trees. Across the street, a woman with long, black hair—shaved on both sides—was busy placing a placard outside of the tattoo shop. Behind her, the light in the shop window flashed OPEN.

Finn pulled the gift card from his pocket and leaned over to River, wiggling the card in the air.

"Oh, my God, yes!" she said, smiling and jumping to her feet.

He stood up and turned to Teague. "You comin'?"

"Nah, you go on; I'm just gonna sit here for a while," replied Teague, as he leaned back on the stone steps. "Get me an orange juice, though."

"I'm with him," said Cash, "But I want a coffee." He leaned back alongside Teague.

"Well, I'm coming," said Zac, as he got to his feet.

Entering the shop, the smell of fresh coffee was overpowering. Trendy music played through the speakers. A gauntlet of empty tables stood against the brick wall on one side. On the other stood the service counter. Finn sauntered up and met the gaze of the clerk who was busy wiping off the machines.

"What can I get for you guys?" asked the young man. He had messy hair, tattoos and ear gauges. The name tag pinned to his chest read Jackson.

Finn smiled, handed over the gift card, and asked Jackson to check the balance. After confirming the amount, River and Zac immediately stepped forward to discuss their options. This allowed Finn some time to look around.

To his left, stood a long table covered in baskets, filled with various fresh baked items. Cookies, brownies, muffins and bagels. The enticing aroma of cinnamon and chocolate wafted through the air. His mouth watered.

He peered up at the counter one more time, River and Zac had Jackson's full attention. They appeared to have forgotten all about him. Craftily, he reached down and grabbed several treats, stuffing them into the pockets of his camo pants. This was the exact reason why he preferred them to plain jeans. He looked up one more time—Jackson was busy.

Feeling confident that he wasn't seen, Finn walked to the refrigerator against the wall and pulled out a bottle of orange juice and a bottle of cold water. He stood there, feeling the cool air wash over him, wondering whether he could fit either bottle into his pockets. They were already too full—anything more would not fit. He closed the door and returned to the counter.

"Will that be all?" asked Jackson.

"Yeah," replied Finn.

Jackson smirked. "You, um, sure you don't want a few more baked items? Another brownie, maybe? Or perhaps a few more cookies?" He raised an eyebrow and stared at Finn.

The candidness of that statement stunned him like an electric shock down his spine. Heart racing, he made eye contact with Jackson—not sure what would happen next. To his surprise, the young man quickly winked and flashed a coy smile.

"It's all good man," said Jackson, "I just wanted to let you know I saw you. You're good. Had I not just finished restocking that table, I wouldn't have known you lifted anything. Didn't even see you move… and I was watchin' for it." He smiled.

Finn stared, unblinking. Unmoving.

"Seriously," said Jackson, "Relax. You've got some skills."

Unsure how to react, Finn remained silent.

"So, do you want anything else?"

Finn slowly shook his head, "Nah, we're good." Behind him, River and Zac were silent.

"I'll get your drinks," said Jackson, as he turned and began moving things around the machines.

Finn kept a watchful eye while the barista went about his task of making the drinks. His gut told him that Jackson was okay, his head was telling him not to trust this stranger.

Pacing nervously, like a caged raccoon, it felt as though the whole encounter was taking forever. He wanted to leave the shop.

Jackson finished the drinks and handed them over. Smiling, he held out a small, brown bag and filled it with cookies. Next, he reached into his tip jar, pulled out all the bills and stuffed them into the bag, then handed it off to Finn.

Not sure what to say, he cautiously took the bag. Whenever people were nice for no reason, it caught him off guard. In his travels, he had met plenty of these genuinely nice people. Especially in these small towns. He should be used to it by now—but he wasn't. His instinctive distrust of outsiders ran too deep.

"A couple blocks down Locust, there's a food cubby," said Jackson, "It's right in front of a daycare—you can't miss it. Anyway, there's usually canned goods and packets of dried soup in there for folks to take as needed. There's also a free library cubby on Elm."

Apparently, Jackson was no stranger to drifters. Feeling a little more at ease with him, Finn nodded. "I'll keep those in mind." He reached out and shook Jackson's hand. "Thanks, man,"

"No worries, man," replied Jackson, "Take care."

And just like that, the exchange was over.

Back on the sidewalk, River leaned close. "That was super sweet of him, and he's kinda cute."

"Yeah, he didn't have to do that with his tip money," said Zac.

"I know, right?" said River, "Oh, my God, Finn, you were like a rock standing there. You looked so calm after being called out for stealing. You were freaking inside, weren't you?" She laughed.

Finn said nothing. He didn't listen to the rest of their conversation as they walked back over to the others. Lost in his head, he was busy recounting the whole event—trying to see if he missed some sort of trap that Jackson laid for him to fall into.

River and Zac described the encounter in the shop while Finn pulled the items from his pockets and passed them around.

"Playing it cool, huh?" whispered Teague.

Finn sat down and sighed with a "pshhh," under his breath, as he handed over the small bag.

Teague peeked inside, pulled out the money, and held it up. "Do I even want to know?"

Finn shook his head. "He's just a cool guy. At least that's how I read him. I think."

Teague nodded, as he put the cash away.

Three hours later, the clock tower rang out twelve times. Cash jumped to his feet and hit Finn on the shoulder. "Let's go check out the rest of this Podunk town."

Finn stood up and straightened his clothes. "Who's comin'?"

River wrapped her arm around Zac's shoulder. "I think we're gonna see if we can't get some locals to donate to our cash reserves."

Zac nodded, "Sounds like a solid plan."

She walked over to the trash can and pulled out a small cardboard box. Flattening it out, she said, "This'll do nicely."

"What's it gonna be today?" asked Zac.

River shrugged. "We'll play it by ear. Let's set up across from the tattoo shop."

Zac brushed himself off. "Wish us luck."

"Good luck," was the collective, monotone response.

Finn turned to Teague. "You comin' with us?"

"Nah, not this time," replied Teague, "I'll be here when y'all get back. Hey, Cash, try not to let him get his ass beat. I'm not up for anything strenuous today." He winked at Finn.

"I'll do my best," chuckled Cash.

Finn shook his head and rolled his eyes, as he and Cash walked away.

Chapter Ten

NESTLED AWAY IN THE CORNER BOOTH AT THE DINER ON THE SQUARE, Beth and her friends were having lunch. Same diner. Same booth—same food. Never a change. Table littered with empty plates. The smell of ketchup and mustard permeated the surrounding air. Her friends were busy chatting about something—she didn't hear much of it. Twisting a lock of dark, brown hair around her finger, Beth stared out the window.

Across the street, a girl with messy, blonde dreads and her red-haired, male companion were panhandling. The girl, holding a card-board sign in her hands, would engage passersby. More often than not, the person would drop money into a cup the young man was holding.

Laughter erupted around Beth. She wished her friends would be a little more quiet. If only they would just stare at their phones, like they always do, and be quiet.

"Looks like that weird girl from middle school liked your post." Liz glanced up at Kara. "Why are you even friends with her?"

Kara shrugged. "I've known her for years. She's not that bad."

Liz snickered, "Well, you should get rid of her. She's weird and having her on your friend list makes you look weird too."

"Looks like Kai posted," interrupted Eli.

"Oh, my God! Did he?" squealed Kara. Peering down at the little screen, she scrolled down to read the comment on her most recent selfie.

Eli shook his head and teased, "Look at you being all giddy."

Sitting beside Beth, Liz was busy using her phone as a mirror to apply her lip gloss. "I think Kara has a crush," she teased. She nudged Beth with her elbow. "Wouldn't you say so?"

"Huh?" replied Beth. She glanced around the table at her friends. Through the entire conversation, none of them had looked at one another. They were all focused on their phones. Beth wondered if she stuck her tongue out at them—would they notice?

"God! Where are you today?" asked Liz, as she stared at her reflection. "Hello. Earth to Beth." She sighed and shook her head.

Beth stared back at her. Was she joking? Was she annoyed? Beth could never tell. Liz was a very hard person to read.

Of their group, Liz was by far the most popular. She was beautiful with her warm, brown skin, hazel eyes and long, wavy hair. She wore the best clothes and was always at the forefront of the hottest, recent trend.

Kara was best described as Liz's shadow. Slight of frame, with dark, blonde hair and blue eyes, she copied everything Liz would do. Beth could hardly blame her. There was a time when she too tried to copy Liz—then she realized it was impossible. She would never be as cool, confident, or beautiful as Liz.

Eli was Beth's longest friend. They had known each other since kindergarten. He was the reason Liz and Kara allowed her to join the group. People used to tease that one day, they would get married. They agreed that they hated when people joked that way—they were best friends. That was all. Besides, as far as Beth could tell, Eli had a huge crush on Liz.

Beth shrugged. "I don't know. Maybe, I guess."

Liz chuckled and shook her head. "Sometimes I wonder about you Beth."

Beth turned on her phone and looked up Kara's post. She scrolled through the comments. Some people she knew—others she didn't. All posting emojis or GIFs. Occasionally, an adult commented. She scrolled past those. She stopped at a comment by Kai, a popular kid from their school. A simple, single-word post, "cute" was all he wrote.

She rolled her eyes, opened her own page and scrolled to her latest post. A selfie she took earlier that day while waiting outside her house for Eli. Not one comment. The only "likes" were by her mom and aunt. Suddenly, a heart emoji followed by a smiley face appeared in the comments. It was from Eli. She peered up to see him grinning at her.

"Oh great! More drifters. Just what this town needs," scoffed Kara.

Beth glanced over to see Kara staring out the window. Her comment had piqued the interest of the others who were now peering out across the street.

"The guy looks kinda hot." Laughed Liz.

"I didn't know you were into hobos." Kara teased.

"Well, if they're hot…" Liz Giggled. "Beth seems enthralled. She's been gawking at them forever."

Beth's face grew hot. She scraped her mind for something witty to say in response. Nothing.

"So, which one do you like Beth? The girl or the guy?" Kara asked with a taunting smirk.

Beth wanted to reach over and hit her, or at least spill a drink onto her lap. She did neither. She fiddled with her phone, then glanced out the window again.

"Ok, Beth," said Eli, "what's the deal? Looks like they're just another couple of drifters who rode the train into town. Nothing new. You've seen these types before. What gives?"

Beth shrugged, painfully aware they were all staring at her. "I don't know. They seem different. Don't they? Like they're really happy." She looked around at her friends.

Eli glanced out the window. "I suppose, if being homeless, riding trains, sleeping in the dirt and god only knows what else could be considered being happy."

Liz sighed. "I will say it again, that guy is pretty hot."

"Meh," added Kara, "I'm not really into gingers."

Beth turned her gaze back to the duo outside, hoping this would end the conversation. It did not. Ignoring her friends, she stared at the couple across the street and tried to imagine where they were from. What sort of adventures they've had. She wondered what it was like to be so free.

Liz interrupted her thoughts when she shoved her. "You in?"

Confused, Beth looked around at her friends. "In what?"

Liz sighed. "We're all going to my house to hang out. Are you coming?"

Beth didn't want to spend the rest of the afternoon listening to Kara prattle on about herself. She wanted to meet the young strangers. She glanced over at Eli, who shrugged slightly. "I think I'm gonna wander around the square for a while, then head home. Y'all go have fun."

"Suit yourself," replied Liz. She climbed out of the booth and paid the check at the counter.

Walking out of the heavy, wooden doors, the sunlight was warm against Beth's skin. She hadn't realized how cold it was in the diner until she walked outside. After saying goodbye to her friends, she watched as they rounded the corner and disappeared.

Alone, she turned around and sauntered across the street toward the strangers.

"Greetings!" said the girl with the dreads, as Beth approached. "Care to contribute to our cause?"

She was smiling, not the kind of smile you would feel uneasy about. This was a genuine, welcoming smile. Up close, Beth could see how beautiful this strange girl was. Tall, with the frame of a dancer. Her deeply tanned skin made her green eyes stand out like gemstones. A tiny, green stone sparkled above her top lip.

Beth couldn't help but feel a little jealous.

"It all depends," said Beth, attempting to sound casual, "What exactly is this cause?"

The blonde traveler smiled. "We have some family things we need to take care of in Austin. We could use some cash to help us out."

A car rounded the corner and blasted its horn. Hanging out the passenger window, Kara shouted, "Bye Beth! See you tomorrow! Try not to get abducted!"

Beth cringed. *Oh god! Why did she just do that?* She thought. She could hear the laughter from the car as it drove around the courthouse and finally disappeared.

"Hi Beth, I'm River," the blonde girl said with a smile.

Still feeling the sting of embarrassment, "I-I'm sorry about my friends. She didn't mean that."

River was unfazed. "No worries." She shrugged. "Beth. I like that name." She gestured to the young man sitting on the ground nearby. "This is my brother, Zac."

Zac stood up and moved closer. He said nothing as he looked on with his serious, dark, brown eyes. A tiny Texas star tattooed on his right temple. His skin was as bronze as River's, no doubt due to all the time spent outdoors. Tall, broad-shouldered and muscular, Beth imagined he could be quite intimidating when he wanted to be. She smiled and said hello. An easy, friendly smile crossed his face in reply.

"So, you gonna contribute?" asked River, one more time, as she wiggled the cup in front of her.

"Oh, right," said Beth, as she dug around in her pockets. She dropped a five-dollar bill into the container. Noting the band printed on River's T-shirt, she blurted, "Oh! I love that band!"

River handed the cup to Zac. "Ever see them live?"

Beth shook her head. "Nah, last time they came through the area, we couldn't get tickets."

"We worked a festival in upstate New York last summer," replied River, "We got to see them play from the backstage area. It was cool."

"Wow! How exciting." The sudden rush of envy came roiling up inside Beth. The way River casually tossed that bit of information out there as if it were a typical thing to experience. Beth wished she could brag about doing those sorts of things. "Do you do stuff like that often?"

River shrugged. "Sometimes. We have a few friends who do it a lot. From time to time we join them. It changes things up—makes life more interesting."

"Wow," sighed Beth, "I bet you have lots of cool stories to tell."

River grinned, glanced at Zac, then turned back to Beth. "Tell you what Beth, I'll share some of those stories with you if you walk on over to that pizza place with me and buy us a pizza." She winked.

River's candidness shocked her. "Um, what?"

River chuckled. "It's simple. You buy us lunch and we tell you about our travels. It's a tradition."

"Tradition?"

Still smiling, River replied, "Tradition. Throughout history, whenever travelers came into a village, the locals would feed them and give them a place to rest. In exchange, the travelers would share stories of the places they visited and the things they did along the way."

Zac snickered.

"So, what do ya say?" River asked, "Wanna buy us lunch?"

Beth looked at Zac, then back at River. "Um, sure. I can."

"Yes!" shouted River, she handed the sign to Zac, then put her arm around Beth's shoulder, "Let's go then, shall we? I'm starving."

They turned to walk away. Zac did not come along, instead he turned and headed toward the courthouse.

"Where is he going?" asked Beth.

"He's gonna go hang with our friend until we get back with the pizza," replied River.

Beth wondered who that friend might be. She didn't see anyone else nearby. She decided to wait and find out; she had so many questions for River about their travels.

Inside the pizza place, waiting for their food, River told Beth about the time she and her friends worked the festival, allowing them to hang around backstage with the bands. It all sounded so fun—so exciting—so opposite of anything she had ever experienced. She wanted to hear more.

"How long are you guys gonna be in town?"

"Well, that all depends," replied River, "two of my brothers had a mishap so we might need to stick around for a day or two. Know of any good places to spend the night?"

"I do," replied Beth with a little too much enthusiasm.

"Well, don't hold back, where is it?"

"At the south end of town," replied Beth, "there's a forested area along the river near an old wooden bridge."

River nodded slowly. "Sounds interesting."

"Locals call it the Goat Man's Bridge."

River leaned closer. "The who?"

"Its actual name is Old Alton Bridge," continued Beth, "Everyone around here refers to it as the Goat Man's bridge. It's pretty secluded. You could camp there. No one would notice."

The man behind the counter called out Beth's name. The pizza was ready.

As they stepped out onto the sidewalk, River hooked her arm around Beth's. "You're gonna have to tell me about this Goat Man. Come on and meet the guys."

Chapter Eleven

W<small>ALKING AWAY FROM THE COURTHOUSE,</small> C<small>ASH LAUGHED TO HIMSELF</small> over Teague's admonition. As if he, or anyone else, could ever keep Finn out of trouble. Finn was a unique person. He didn't like most people. Most people didn't like him either. To say he was abrasive would be an understatement. Finn had a knack for reading people. He could pinpoint what made them uncomfortable, then zero in on that and push until the other person snapped. Most of the time, Cash found that amusing. Sometimes it made him nervous. Finn never seemed to consider that one day, he could find himself face to face with the wrong person. Teague would say that Finn lacked the ability to properly gauge threat levels. That was his way of saying that Finn was fearless—in a stupid way.

Entering the candy shop, swing music played in the background— oddly fitting, as Cash immediately felt as though he had wandered into another era. The sweet smell of chocolate wafted through the air. Walking past a group of coolers, the sheer number of different flavored sodas overwhelmed him. Collectible, candy tins filled the bins in the center of the isles.

This place was heaven.

Finn stood at the other end of the shop by a wall of containers filled with a rainbow of colorful candy. He glanced over at Cash and flashed a wry grin. A clerk stood nearby—watching.

The lack of any other patrons this early in the day meant they had the undivided attention of the shop clerks. They would have to stick to what they could afford.

Back on the sidewalk, Cash teased Finn with the bag of candy as he popped a piece into his mouth. Finn responded by pressing him against the display window of a record shop and stealing the bag away. The people inside glared angrily at him. He smiled, then quickly walked away.

They rounded the corner and came upon a restaurant with outdoor seating. The aroma of French fries and burgers assaulted his senses. He was getting hungry. In the corner, four, college-age girls sat at a table.

They waved at him.

Flashing his charismatic, crooked smile, he waved back.

The girls giggled.

Hoping that Finn would be up for taking a break while he got to know the girls better, he tapped him on the arm.

Finn sneered and stalked away.

Cash sighed. What was he thinking? Maybe next time. He waved goodbye to the girls and caught up with Finn.

Down the street, a silver motorcycle rounded the corner. Shiny chrome sparkled in the afternoon sun. Radio blasting an old, rock song while the low growl of the motor echoed off the buildings, it rolled up in front of a dive bar and came to a stop. The driver cut the engine. The street was silent. Standing by, Cash and Finn watched as the couple dismounted and removed their helmets. The woman fiddled with her purse, then placed it back into the saddlebag and closed the lid.

Bingo.

Pretending not to care, they waited for the couple to walk into the bar. As soon as the door closed, Cash leaned over and peered into the darkened windows. The couple took their seats at the bar.

While Finn stood watch, Cash strolled over to the motorcycle.

After a quick scan of the street, he tested the saddle bag. It was locked—this was not a surprise. It was also not a deterrent. Locks like these were nothing for him. They were almost an insult to his abilities. He pulled out his multi tool and used it to work the lock open. Smirking, he flipped open the compartment and pulled out the bag. A cloud of flowery perfume reminiscent of spring time lilac flowers exploded into the air as he opened the snap. He sneezed.

Over by the window, Finn signaled for him to hurry.

Moving quickly, Cash located the wallet. It was light brown, one of those large styles that older women carry around. The kind that match their designer handbags. He popped it open and rifled through the contents. Credit cards, ID, photos and a checkbook. A small stack of bills was tucked neatly in the side pocket. All twenties. Nice. Not a bad haul. He stuffed those in his pocket. Holding the wallet up, he let the accordion-style photo holder unfold. Smiling faces of children peered up at him. These had to be her grandchildren. A joint popped out and landed on top of the bag. *Ah! Grandma, you are a sneaky woman.* He thought. He picked it up and sniffed. He could barely smell the weed over the heavy scent of lilac. He sneezed again. Wondering what else she may have stashed in there, he groped around the bag one more time.

From his post by the window, Finn whistled.

Cash glanced up to see him mouth the words, "Time to go."

He set his focus on the contents of the bag one more time. Nothing. Looks like Grandma only had the one joint. He tossed the wallet back into the bag and slammed the case closed. As he walked away, Finn materialized beside him as if he had been there all along.

They spent the next hour exploring. Unable to find anything else of interest, they finally decided it was time to rejoin the others.

Waiting at the corner for the light to change, a cursory glance at the courthouse steps told him there was another person with his friends. From where he stood, he couldn't make out much, but he could see it was a girl with long, brown hair.

He struck Finn on the arm. "Looks like Teague and the others made a friend."

Finn squinted his eyes and made a guttural sound. It was either a groan or a growl—either one would have been possible.

As they approached, Cash tried to make out what details he could of the newcomer. She looked like a typical, suburban, high-school kid. Long, brown hair, bronze skin and a round face that made her look very young.

Busily talking with River, the girl laughed and stepped backward, accidentally stepping on Cash. Startled, she jumped forward and spun around, nearly falling.

He caught her by the arm. "Woah," he said, as he looked her over. She was short. Probably around seventeen with big, doe-like, brown eyes. A shiny, blue stone sparkled on the right side of her nose.

The young girl stood silent. Her face a pale shade of red.

"You okay?" He asked, releasing her arm.

She smiled and ran her fingers through her hair. "Um, yeah. I'm sorry."

"You should be a little more careful," Finn said with an icy tone.

"I-I'm sorry," she replied, staring at him with wide eyes.

"Just in time," said River, "Beth, say hello to Cash and Finn."

"Hello Cash," said the girl, as she reached out her hand. He took hold of it gently and leaned forward. Reaching his other hand behind her ear, he pretended to pull out a piece of candy. He held it out for her.

She smiled and accepted the offer.

"That was pretty good. Do you know any other tricks?"

Cash winked. "I sure do."

"Careful with this one Beth," warned River, "He's tricky."

Beth turned her attention to Finn, who was standing silent, watching the whole exchange. "Hello Finn," she said smiling.

Finn stared.

At least he wasn't growling.

Cash pulled out the bag of candy and offered it to Beth. "Want some?"

She reached into the bag and pulled out a piece. "River was telling us about some of your travels."

Finn snatched the bag away from Cash. He glared at River.

Beth continued nervously, "Riders come through here all the time. I've spoken with a few of them before."

Finn scowled at Beth. "Anyone ever tell you not to talk to strangers?"

Tension hung heavy in the air.

In an effort to lighten things up, Cash quipped, "Ah, good, ole Finn making friends and influencing people." He lunged for the bag—Finn pulled it away, causing a small scuffle to erupt.

Beth laughed.

"Well, I was telling the others, I know a place where you could camp," she blurted.

Cash made another dive for the bag, and Finn kept it away.

"Really?" asked Cash, attempting to reach beyond Finn. "Where would that be?"

"At the south end of town," replied Beth, "There's a wooded area along the river near an old bridge. It's called the Old Alton Bridge or, as everyone around here calls it, the Goat Man's bridge."

"Wait, the what?" Cash asked, as he suddenly stopped messing around.

"She said the Goat Man's Bridge," replied Finn, smirking.

Beth smiled. "Yeah, the Goat Man. It's an old legend here in town." She shrugged. "It's one of those stories parents tell their kids to scare them from being too adventurous. Aside from local teens and the odd college kid, no one hardly ever goes there, so you can camp there for days and be fine."

Finn looked past Beth and nodded at Teague while wiggling the bag of candy in the air. Teague shook his head in response, so he tossed it over to River. He turned to Beth. "Well, I ain't gonna lie, I am intrigued." He brushed past her and sat down alongside Teague, leaving her to stand, awkwardly shifting her feet and running her fingers through her hair.

It was obvious to Cash that Beth was feeling uneasy. Who

wouldn't? Finn was an expert at making people uncomfortable. He reveled in it. She was either going to work through it or go away like so many others have done before. Cash sighed and sat down on the steps.

The aroma of pizza overwhelmed his senses. The smell of the melted cheese, grease and tomato sauce made his mouth water.

Finn peeked inside the box. "Any mushrooms?"

"Yes. There's a couple slices. Just for you," replied River.

He smiled at her and pulled out a slice. Teague handed him a small bottle of hot sauce. The two of them put it on everything. They liked their food to hurt. After drowning the pizza in sauce, he shoved more than half into his mouth at once, smearing grease and red tomato sauce around his mouth in the process. Chomping heavily, he swallowed loudly. Without even a pause, he shoved the rest of the slice into his mouth, causing even more red, tomato mess to ooze out of the corners.

Cash watched with a mix of disgust and humor. Finn ate food like it was about to disappear. It was a sight to see. Watching him eat like that, one could almost see what it must have looked like when cavemen devoured a mammoth.

Finn swallowed and reached back into the box for another slice.

Unable to take it any longer, Cash slammed a paper napkin against Finn's chest. "Dude," he said, shaking his head, "you got a little something…" He pointed to the corner of his mouth.

Finn twitched his nose and wiped his face, then glanced over at Teague, who grinned and nodded in approval.

After finishing the second slice, he wiped his face, then said, "Okay, Beth, you have our undivided attention. Tell us about your bridge."

Chapter Twelve

RIVER WATCHED THE APPALLING SPECTACLE THAT WAS FINN DEVOURING food. From time to time, she peered at Beth, surveying her facial expressions and body movements, trying to glean what she thought of it all. These boys were a lot to take in at first. She recalled when she first stumbled upon them—how unusual they were. That was quite a while ago.

She had been hopping trains for roughly a year and a half. Mostly, keeping to herself, she would occasionally tag along with a small group, but that never lasted long. River found that she didn't like the drama that took place whenever groups gathered. It took too much energy—too much effort to keep up with it all. Life was simpler alone.

After spending the winter along the soft, sandy shores of Tampa, she decided it was time to hit the road. The sameness of it all bored her. She needed to move. One night, she hopped a train heading west.

Exactly where she was heading didn't matter. Winter was over so any area of the US would be fine.

Enjoying the solitude, she rode for days, hopping from one train, only to catch another within hours. It was grueling. When she landed in Roswell, New Mexico she decided it was time for a hot shower and some rest. She rented herself a cheap motel room. For the next two days, she languished in bed until noon, ate too much junk food, watched television and relaxed in a nice, hot bath.

In the evenings, she prowled the city streets. Drifting from bar to bar, she collected money from tip jars, swiped billfolds from unsuspecting men, and snagged more than one wallet from the purse of an intoxicated woman. It was all too easy.

River was great at avoiding unwanted scrutiny, or so she assumed. On the third night, she captured the attention of a group of four men. They followed her from one bar to another. Each time she was confident she lost them, only to discover they were not far behind. She walked faster—they kept up. She wanted to run, but she feared if she did, they would overtake her. There was no way she could outrun them all. Searching the dark street, she needed to shake them.

Focusing all her attention on the men behind her, she rounded a corner and ran headlong into a dark-haired man.

"Hey there," he said, flashing a crooked smile.

Behind him, sitting on the curb, were three more men—all roughly the same age. The worn clothes, unkempt hair, and bronze skin—she knew right away they were Nomads. She glanced back—her followers had stopped. They were hanging around just far enough to appear innocent yet close enough to keep an eye on her. It would be best if she led them to believe these were friends, so she turned on all her charms and whipped up a conversation.

In his hand, the dark-haired stranger held a metal flask.

River stared directly into his eyes. "Care to share?" she asked, deliberately standing inches from him. This made him uneasy. It also gave her stalkers the impression they were friends.

A deep, red blush spread across his face. "Um, yeah. H-here," he sputtered. He handed over the flask, then wiped his palms off on his legs.

The cool metal had a slick film of perspiration on it. Continuing to stare, she cleaned off the opening, then took a swig. She smiled. "What's your name?"

His mouth moved as though he were formulating words, but none came out.

Behind him, his friends howled.

Another dark-haired man sauntered up. His hair a mass of unkempt waves that made him look as though he had just awakened from a nap. A pair of red-rimmed sunglasses covered his eyes. River found that odd. *It's night time. How could he see anything?* She wondered.

He wrapped his arm around his silent friend's shoulder. "Cat's got your tongue?" he asked.

A blond man with blue eyes appeared on the other side of the quiet one. He smirked and leaned close. "Someone put a gris-gris on him."

The mute one could only shake his head.

"Maybe he swallowed the wrong way," said the one with the glasses.

"It's possible," responded the blond. He poked the silent one's cheek. "He look a little rose to you?"

"More like bright red," Mr. Sunglasses chuckled. "Actually, he kinda looks like a deer caught in the headlights of a truck."

They laughed. River almost felt bad for him.

"Cash!" he shouted. "My name is Cash." He shoved the other two away. "You guys are assholes."

The blond one blew him a kiss. The one with sunglasses simply snickered.

"Hello Cash, I'm River," she replied. "What're your two friends' names?"

The blond leaned forward. "Teague." He pointed to Mr. Sunglasses. "This is Finn."

Finn didn't move. The smile on his face had vanished. He stared. This made River uneasy.

The last friend sauntered up. He stood beside Finn. "I'm Zac," he stated. With hardly a pause, he continued, "Those four guys down the street, they ain't friends of yours. Are they?"

His tone was so matter-of-fact, it threw River off guard. She didn't quite know how to respond.

She shook her head. "No, no, they aren't."

Zac nodded. "You know they're following you?"

"Yeah, I know," she replied a little uneasy about how exposed she felt at that moment.

For the first time, the others took note of her stalkers.

Zac peered down the street. "They say anything to you? Harass you?"

"No."

Finn stepped forward and called out, "Hey, yo! Assholes! You got a problem?"

One man hollered a response, but River couldn't make out what he said.

"Maybe you should just move along before I have to kick your asses!" shouted Finn.

Someone yelled back, "Come on down here and let's see who gets their ass beat."

"Aight!" replied Finn, and he stomped straight for them.

"I'll go," Zac said to Teague. He brushed past River.

Teague and Cash glanced at one another. Then they too followed Finn.

The encounter didn't last long. A little shoving and a lot of cursing later, the four men stormed off, middle fingers in the air. She was glad for that, she didn't want anyone to fight for her.

"Thank you," said River. "I didn't really know what to do about them."

"That why you came up to us?" asked Cash.

She didn't want to admit the truth. It made her feel weak and manipulative. She nodded.

"Well," he said. "It's a good thing you did. I'm glad we could help." He flashed a crooked grin. "Want to hang with us? Just to be sure they don't return."

River found his smile charming. He had a mischievous air about him. Not malevolent—lighthearted. She agreed to stick around for a while.

They spent hours wandering around the city. To her surprise, she enjoyed their company. She laughed so much her belly hurt. They had a familiarity about them. She didn't want the time to end, so she encouraged them to stay at her motel. Over the next few days, they teased, laughed and wormed their way into her heart.

Four days after they met, they all hopped a train heading west.

Finn had finally had his fill of pizza, so he asked Beth about the bridge.

Beth cleared her throat and fidgeted. "The actual name is the Old Alton Bridge. Its nickname is the Goat Man's Bridge—there's a local legend about a ghost that haunts the area."

"Wait, a what?" asked Cash, pausing between bites.

"She said a ghost. The Goat Man," River replied, trying to help Beth feel more at ease. "Pay attention."

"For real?" he asked.

Beth nodded. "Like I said, it's hidden. They built a new bridge years ago for cars to drive on, but they left the old wooden one in place. It's a historical marker now, a walking trail." She flipped her hair to the other side. "The woods are thick down along the river bank. No one ever goes there. You'd have it all to yourselves." She flipped her hair one more time.

Teague leaned back against the step. "I don't know. What're your thoughts?" he asked Finn.

Before he could respond, River chimed in. "You already know there's no way we're gonna leave this place without checking it out." She winked at Beth, who seemed to loosen up a little. At least the hair flipping and fidgeting slowed down.

"Are there any houses near?" asked Teague.

"Nah, not really. People say they get the creeps when they're there at night, so they stay away. The kids around here are boring. No sense of adventure," she said, attempting to sound cool. River cringed. She knew the guys caught that. *Please don't harass her.*

Finn and Teague flashed a smirk to one another.

"Mais non!" said Teague. "How tragic to have no sense of adventure." His words dripped with condescension.

Beth's shoulders hunched. She flipped her hair again.

River felt awful for her. "Don't pay any mind to them Beth, they're just being assholes." She shot a warning glare at Teague. "Where is this place again?"

Beth shifted her body to face River. "The south end of town near a high school. It's a long walk from here, but it's doable."

As annoying as the guys were, River knew they weren't being malicious. She hoped Beth could see that. Done with their shenanigans, she hopped to her feet and placed her arm around Beth's shoulder in a show of solidarity.

They stopped laughing.

"Sometimes y'all have no manners," she scolded. "It's okay, Beth, I think the bridge sounds like a great place to spend the night. Doesn't it, Cash?"

Cash swallowed his pizza and nodded with a thumb's up.

"How about you Zac?"

He liked to hang back and watch how unfamiliar people interacted with the group. Though more open to newcomers than Finn or Teague, he wasn't prone to jumping right in with anyone he didn't already know.

He shot a knowing look at River and smiled. "I'm in."

"So, what do ya think?" River asked Teague. The best course of action was to convince him first, and he would get Finn to come along. Finn always did what Teague wanted him to do, even if he didn't like it.

"I think we should at least check it out, right Finn?"

Finn didn't reply. He was glaring at Beth.

Ignoring him, Teague continued, "We'll need to get our gear before we head over there." He stood up. "Well, Beth, looks like you're our tour guide. Let's go check this place out."

River hooked her arm around Beth's. "Okay, you heard the man. Let's go." The two girls led the group away from the square.

Walking down the street, each of them took turns checking the doors of the parked cars. At first, River thought nothing of it until she noticed Beth's demeanor change. This was all just a regular part of their lives, but Beth was more than a little nervous. River wondered what she could say to make her feel a little better.

Cash sprinted past them to be in the lead. He tried the door of a parked SUV and found it unlocked. Looking up, he smiled at everyone and hopped in.

A few yards away, River and Beth stopped and waited under a tree. Beside the car, Teague stood sentry, while Finn and Zac joined the girls.

Beth ran her fingers through her hair. She glanced around nervously.

River stood close. "We check all the parked cars, vending machines, or newspaper stands for cash or other valuables. You get money any way you can—finding it's a better way than others."

Beth flashed a pathetic smile. This only made River feel worse. It was so obvious that Beth was trying hard to fit in.

"What are some of the other ways?" Beth asked. "I mean, you said, taking money or finding money is better than… what?"

To River's surprise, Finn replied. "Well, you can beg for it or you can always get it the old-fashioned way by earning it."

"What kind of jobs?" Beth asked him.

"Huh?" He was biting his nails, as he watched Cash and Teague.

"You said you can earn money. What are some of the ways you can do that?"

River watched this exchange with a great deal of interest. That Finn was even talking to Beth was a good sign.

He stopped staring down the street and shrugged. "Sometimes odd jobs." He pulled his sunglasses down to look into Beth's eyes. "And occasionally it's doing things that aren't necessarily legal."

"Your eyes!" Beth exclaimed, causing Finn to push his glasses back up.

His face turned deep red.

So close. Thought River. It almost looked like he was warming up to Beth. Now he might close off completely.

Beth quickly apologized. "I'm sorry. Are your eyes two different colors? Did I see that right?" she asked.

Finn turned away. "Yeah, they are."

"Lots of people love Finn's eyes," said River. "It makes him uncomfortable. The rest of us think it's cool." She nudged him, hoping he would lighten up.

"Well, I think they're cool too," said Beth in her gentle voice. "You shouldn't hide them."

"Awesome. I'll keep that in mind," Finn replied with a derisive tone. He twitched his nose and turned his focus back to Teague and Cash.

Just like that, the conversation ended. They stood in agonizing silence for several minutes as they waited.

Time crawled. Cash was taking forever. River wondered what was taking so long. When he finally emerged from the SUV and rejoined the group, she was more than a little relieved. His witty conversation helped brighten the mood. River was grateful for that. It was a much-needed change. After a brief stop to collect their gear, they proceeded along their way.

They trekked for miles, past small stores, apartment buildings, churches and auto shops.

Passing a neighborhood park, they decided to take a break. They found a shady spot near a small pond. Ducks swam, geese lounged on the shoreline, a cool breeze rustled the leaves of the trees. River sat with her feet dangling in the cool water, face uplifted toward the warm sun, eyes closed.

"You know, we could stay here tonight," said Cash. "That brush over there looks dense. I bet no one would see us."

"I wanna see the Goat Man," replied Teague, smiling.

"Somehow, I knew one of you were gonna say that," Cash responded. "But I thought it was gonna be this one." He pointed at Finn.

Beth leaned closer to River. "I never asked what brought y'all here to town."

"Well," replied River. "We were heading south toward Austin, and we ran into some trouble."

"What's in Austin? Some friends of yours?"

"You sure ask a lot of questions," interrupted Finn.

River scowled at him, then replied to Beth. "You could say that. Truth is, we have some business to take care of down there before we head further west."

Beth nodded and said nothing more.

Damn it, Finn. Stop being an ass. Thought River. Even Teague seemed to warm up to Beth. Sometimes she wished that Finn wasn't so antisocial.

After an hour enjoying the stillness of the pond, it was time to move on.

By late afternoon, they passed a high school that sat across the street from a small chapel.

They turned down a rural road and walked about a quarter mile when Beth stopped, spun around, and gestured with her arms.

"This is it!" she shouted.

River took in the area. Beth did not exaggerate it was private. To their left, a gravel parking area lay hidden among large trees. Beyond that, a path receded into the woods.

"You're shitting me, right?" said Cash, piercing through the silence. "I mean, seriously? I get that it's out of the way, I'll give you that much, but... that forest."

He swatted away invisible bugs. "I'm already getting itchy from all the mosquitoes. I can feel malaria coming on. Come on, guys—it's not too late to go back and camp over by that park."

Before he could complete his sentence, Finn had already bolted down the path. River chuckled. She took hold of Beth's hand and followed.

Still standing in the middle of the road, Cash called out, "I've seen horror movies that start out exactly like this." He slowly followed. "Just so ya know, it didn't end well for most of the characters."

A few yards down the path they came to the old wooden bridge.

"So, this is the Goat Man's bridge, huh?" asked River.

Beth nodded proudly.

"Doesn't look very eerie to me." Cash said, as he nudged Zac.

"It's still daylight," said River.

Below the bridge, murky water flowed, framed by sand bars. Thick woods enveloped the entire area creating the mirage they were far away from civilization.

Finn pointed out along the river. "I bet we can find a place to camp just past that bend over there." Without waiting for a reply, he hopped over the rail and ran into the woods.

They followed the river bank until they came to a private clearing. Water on one side—thick woodland on the other.

"So, what do y'all think?" asked Finn.

River looked around. The sand beneath her feet was soft and fine. She listened to the birds singing in the trees. "I like it—it's kind of wild and ignored." She hesitated, then added, "Like us."

Cash chimed in. "I'm with her. I guess I kinda like it too."

With Beth's help, River chose a patch of flat land alongside an embankment. After tramping around to create a flat area, she pulled her tent out of its sack and directed Beth on what to do. It was funny to watch her struggle. River supposed Beth had done little camping in her life—at least not tent camping.

The tent was almost finished, all that remained was to bang the stakes into the ground. River peered up at Beth, "So, do you live nearby?"

Beth shook her head. "My house is across town. On the north end."

"Isn't that a long way? How are you gonna get back there tonight?"

"I guess I hadn't thought that part out just yet." Beth shrugged.

River didn't want her to leave. "I know! You can spend the night with us! You can share my tent with me."

Beth lit up. "Really? That would be so cool!"

Laughing, she spun Beth around and walked back over by the fire where Zac had just finished laying out his sleeping bag. "Beth's gonna spend the night with us," she announced.

"Well, my sleeping bag isn't made for two," quipped Zac. "But we could make it work." He winked at Beth.

River shoved him. "She's gonna stay with me, jerk."

Cash sat down beside the fire. "You sure, Beth? My hammock has plenty of room." He began shuffling a deck of playing cards.

River scoffed. "Stop being a creep."

Based on the shade of red that had washed over Beth's face, she was feeling a little uncomfortable. "Don't listen to them Beth, they're just messing around," assured River.

Moments later, Finn and Teague joined them. The crackle of the fire mixed with the mellow, flowing sound of the water made for a calm setting. River loved the smell of a campfire. To her, that was the smell of home.

Zac pulled out his flask of moonshine, took a swig, then passed it around.

Chapter Thirteen

WATCHING HOW THE GROUP INTERACTED WITH ONE ANOTHER, BETH could see their bond was much deeper than mere friends. They were a family.

Based on their accents, she tried to glean where everyone came from. River was definitely from the south. She had that familiar twang in her speech. Zac, with his tiny, Texas star, was obvious before he uttered a single word. Finn had spoken little, so she didn't have enough to go on. Cash sounded as though he were from somewhere out west. And Teague, well, she couldn't figure out his accent at all. He used what sounded like French words from time to time, although they didn't sound like the fancy French she had learned in school. His was more slang. When he said ask, it sounded like 'axe.' Words like this or that came out sounding like 'dis' or 'dat.' At one point, she thought he said 'mais oui' but it sounded like 'may weh.' She never heard anyone speak that way.

"All right, Beth, time to fill us in," said Cash, "what's the story of this Goat Man?"

Beth cleared her throat. "Well, the story goes that sometime back in the 1930s, there lived a black man named Oscar Washburn. He and his family had a goat farm north of the bridge. Oscar was well respected in the area as an honest, hardworking businessman. Most of the people in town really liked him."

The flask made its way to her—she sniffed the contents and flinched. The pungent smell of pure alcohol made her nostrils burn. Not wanting to be the odd one out, she held her breath, closed her eyes and took a sip. It was awful. She cringed and swallowed the liquid. With a shudder, she handed the flask over to River. Saliva pooled up in her mouth. She swallowed again, hoping the horrible flavor would go away soon.

Regaining her composure, she continued, "A few people in town were Klansmen. I don't need to tell you that they didn't like that Oscar was such a successful businessman." She looked around the circle to be sure they were all paying attention. "Anyway, the story goes that one day he posted a sign on the side of the bridge saying, 'This way to the Goat Man,' or something like that."

"This angered these Klansmen. So, one night in August, in the darkness with their headlights off, they rode over the bridge to his farm and dragged him away from his house. They lynched him right up there off the side of the old bridge."

She pointed to the bridge.

Everyone's gaze drifted over to the bridge, then shifted back to focus on her.

Beth continued, "At some point, after not hearing any sound, they felt as though something was wrong. They looked over the side. That's when they realized that he wasn't there. In fact, there was no sign of him anywhere. In a panic, they all went back to his farm and murdered his whole family in cold blood. No one ever saw Oscar Washburn again. No one knows if he died on that bridge and his body floated away or what." She paused for emphasis.

"The legend goes that if you drive across the bridge with your headlights off, the Goat Man will meet you on the other side with his red eyes glowing in the dark."

Silence.

Cash burst out laughing. "What a load of pure bullshit. I mean, come on. Red eyes glowing."

Laughter.

"No, no, no, it's all true!" shouted Beth.

They stopped to hear her out.

"I have a friend whose neighbor spent the night here one time. He said he heard the hoofbeats of the Goat Man crossing the bridge."

More laughter.

Zac put his arm around her shoulder and gave a light squeeze. "Beth, you're adorable," he said, as he pulled away.

River leaned against her and gave her a little hug. "I adore you, little girl. You are way too cute."

Offended, Beth struggled to mask her feelings. Her friends teased her all the time—she was used to that. It hardly bothered her anymore. However, being laughed at by this group made her feel awkward —defensive.

From across the fire, Teague said, "Well, I was hoping for something a little more supernatural. I mean, that was okay. I suppose…" He let his voice trail off as he smirked with Finn.

"Don't listen to him, Beth. I liked your story," said River, "Teague's just a snob when it comes to ghost stories. He can't help it— it's because of where he grew up."

Eager to change the subject and happy to learn where he was from, Beth turned to Teague. "Oh yeah? Where's that?" The petulant tone of her voice made her cringe. She didn't mean to sound that way.

Teague seemed not to notice. "Southern Louisiana," he answered.

So that's what that accent was! She thought. She was happy that he was talking to her instead of laughing at her. For the first time since she met him, she didn't get the vibe that he was mocking her. "Oh! I bet there are lots of cool ghost stories where you're from!" she blurted, "We went to New Orleans once on vacation, but I was young. I don't remember too much, just this old cemetery with all the crypts above ground."

"Where the hell is the flask?" demanded Cash.

"Hold up, I got it right here," replied Zac. He took a big gulp, then handed the bottle back to Beth, who held her breath and took another sip—it wasn't so bad the second time.

River took the flask from her. "So, Beth, tell us about yourself. What's an adorable thing like you doing in a town like this?"

Beth didn't know what to say. There was no way to make her life sound interesting. They were all looking at her—waiting.

"Well, there isn't much to say," she sighed, "I was born here. Lived in the same town, in the same house all my life. Same schools, same friends, same bedroom. Kinda boring, huh?" She glanced over at River, then Zac. She didn't want to look at the others, she could only imagine how dull that sounded to them.

River smiled. "Actually, it sounds lovely. I didn't see much of your friends. What's your family like?"

River's encouragement gave her the courage to go into greater detail. "My friends are okay. Eli and I have been friends for as long as I can remember. He was in the back seat of the car you saw drive past." Recalling the scene at the square with her friends in the car made her cringe.

"My mom and dad are pretty normal, I guess." She shrugged. "Dad works for a cabinet making company and my mom is a nurse. I have a brother. He's older than I am. I don't see him much anymore, he's a jerk. He wasn't always that way, it just sort of happened out of the blue. One day we laughed about games and how normal our parents were, the next—he was a total dick who yelled and punched things. He moved out about a year ago."

The flask was in front of her again. This time she didn't hesitate. She took a large drink and continued. "Aside from Texas, that one trip to New Orleans and some areas in Oklahoma, we never traveled much. I really want to travel. Someday, I hope to see all the places I've read about and seen pictures of."

She stopped talking and looked around at everyone. They were all a couple years older than her. She guessed they had all been out on their own for at least a few years. They used the word tribe to describe themselves, and after spending time with them, she agreed—they were a very, close-knit tribe. Beth envied their friendship. Sure, she liked her friends, but she would never really consider any of them to be as close as these people were. She wondered what it would be like to be one of them.

"So, enough about my boring, little, suburban life," she said, "How old were y'all when you left home?"

"Seventeen," replied Cash.

"Yup, me too. Seventeen," said Zac.

"Thirteen," muttered River.

Over on the other side of the fire, oblivious to the others, Finn and Teague were wrestling. When she first met them, Teague was stand-offish—snarky. As for Finn, well, he was a jerk. Seeing them interact with one another in this intimate setting was like seeing two different people. She watched as Teague brushed Finn's hair out of his eyes and smiled, causing Finn to respond with one of the most beautiful smiles she had ever seen. Such a sweet gesture. It was like she was watching two different people. She couldn't look away.

They stopped when they realized everyone was staring at them. "What?" said Teague, as he shifted his body to sit up.

Beth grinned and replied, "How old were you when you ran away?"

"Ah, fourteen," he answered, "though, to be fair, I didn't run away. I walked. Out the front door in broad daylight."

Beth turned her gaze to Finn and waited for his response. He was biting his nails, staring into the fire. Teague reached up and pulled his hand away from his face. Another one of those sweet things couples do.

Finn whispered, "Fourteen." Then glanced away.

He sounded sad. Beth wanted to know why, but figured it would be better to let it go. Things were going well with him right now. She didn't want to ruin that.

She turned to River. "Looks like you were the youngest. How did that happen?"

River sat up, adjusted her seat, and cleared her throat. Her face became serious as she began her story.

Chapter Fourteen

"WE LIVED IN MEMPHIS IN A CRAPPY, TINY HOUSE IN A CRAPPY AREA of town," River said, as she stared into the fire. Remembering that little house and the time she spent there, was bittersweet and painful. "My mom left when I was a baby. I never knew her. Growing up, it was me, my dad, and my older sister, Dawn. She was three years older than me."

She pulled out a photo of Dawn, posing confidently with her long, red hair and big, green eyes. Dawn was gorgeous. River remembered how she looked up to her big sister—she was her hero. A dark wave of sadness washed over her. She could hardly believe so much time had passed since she heard Dawn's voice. Fighting back tears, she handed the photo to Beth.

"Dawn was so smart. She was tall and gorgeous and so, so strong. For as long as I could remember, I wanted to be just like her."

Beth stared in silence at the picture. This gave River a much-needed pause. It gave her the chance to calm her emotions. Beth handed the picture back. She put it away in her back pocket.

Cash handed her the flask. Thankful, she took a large swig, then wiped her mouth with the back of her hand. She passed it over to Beth before continuing.

"Things weren't great. Most months we had a hard time paying rent, and there was hardly any food in the house. Lots of booze though —my dad loved to drink." Like a remnant from a bad dream, her father's face appeared in her mind with his deep-set wrinkles and permanent, five o'clock shadow. It was well known around the neighborhood that Jacob Greene was an angry, violent drunk.

"I can't tell you how often he would pass out on the floor of his bedroom, unable to make it to the bed. He got violent, too."

"Dawn usually took the brunt of it all. When he got worked up, she would send me to our bedroom and tell me to put on the headphones and listen to music. I would stay there until she came back and told me it was okay. Once or twice I tried to listen at the door. There was always a lot of shouting and cursing."

She took a deep breath. Her hands trembled. Cash reached over and placed his hand over hers. The trembling stopped.

"One day after school, Dawn told me to pack a bag because we were leaving. I didn't ask why—I knew. And I was happy to be getting out. We hid the bags under our beds. As soon as he passed out, we took our things and snuck out of the house. We ran to Mason's house—he was one of Dawn's friends. He tried to convince her to either stick around or at least let him come with us. When she refused, he cried. I think they were dating or something." River shrugged.

"Anyway, we snuck away to the bus station and got on the bus for Nashville. Dawn figured, it being a big city, odds were no one would find us there."

Dawn's face came swimming back. How she held River close and promised her everything would be okay. River knew she had nothing to fear. Her big sister would always be there to keep her safe. She forced back the sorrow that smoldered below the surface, threatening to erupt.

"We stayed in Nashville for a few weeks, then moved on to Birmingham, next to Jackson, Mississippi. We would stay in a city for anywhere between two weeks and two months. It all depended on what Dawn thought we needed to do. When she said it was time to leave, we would leave."

"I don't know if anyone ever came looking for us. I do know, no one ever found us."

River paused and glanced over at Beth. She could see her own sadness reflected back at her.

"Wow. Where is your sister Dawn now?" asked Beth.

"She's dead," answered River flatly, as she picked up a thin branch and poked at the fire. Red embers fell out onto the sand. She pushed them back into the flames, catching fire to the end of the branch. She snuffed it out by burying the tip into the sand.

"God, I'm so sorry," stammered Beth, a slight hint of panic in her tone. "I didn't know."

River didn't want Beth to feel bad about any of this, she knew Beth wasn't deliberately trying to upset her. "How would you?" she asked, "There's no way you could have known."

"We had been traveling for about two-and-a-half years from one city to another when we ended up in New Orleans," continued River, "We stayed there for almost three months. Dawn seemed to have given up. Most of the time she was angry—the rest of the time she was sad. She started doing drugs—lots of drugs. Pills, powder, you name it. She even shot up. She was falling apart. I worried about her. I went down to the free clinic and got some overdose medicine just in case..."

River hated remembering this part about her sister. How broken, sad and desperate she was. She cleared her throat.

"One night, in a doped-out state, she broke down and told me the truth about our father and the things he used to do to her when he thought I was asleep. She told me the reason that we left when we did was that she was afraid he would do that to me too."

The fire crackled and popped as tiny embers hopped out and fell to the ground. Once again, River poked them back into the fire. It was a welcome distraction.

No one said a word.

She was thankful for the silence. *God, this is so hard.* She thought.

River sighed. "She told me what she had been doing to earn money to keep us fed and to pay for our shitty motel rooms. All the strange men. She said she couldn't do it anymore. She broke down."

"I told her she didn't have to do that anymore, that we would be okay. I was older and could help a lot more. I cleaned her up and held her until she cried herself to sleep. For the first time ever, she actually felt smaller than me. Weak."

The flask made its way back to her. She swallowed a huge gulp, stared at the fire, then took a second and passed it along.

"Later on, during the night, I woke up. She wasn't there beside me, so I checked the bathroom to see if she was okay." River breathed deeply. Tears welled up in her eyes. Her bottom lip trembled. "During the night, she had filled the tub and climbed in. She slit her wrists and quietly let herself bleed out. When I found her, she was already dead—been that way for a while."

"She left a note on the sink. It only had four words on it."

"I'm sorry baby sister."

"That was it." River sniffled, sighed, and wiped her face. Cash put his arm around her—she leaned against him. *Why does this story never get easier to tell?* She wondered. Would she ever be able to look at the image of Dawn and not want to scream?

She sat up and wiped her eyes. "I ran out and called 911. The coroner came, and I hid across the street while they were there doing their thing. They took her body away. I never saw her again after that. I don't know what they did with her—if she's buried somewhere or not..."

Did her ashes get stored in some county facility like Cyrus and Craig?

Tears streamed down Beth's face. She was such a sweet kid. There was something about her that River really liked. She smiled as she leaned forward and wiped Beth's cheek.

"Girl, stop that," River said with a lighter tone and a forced smile.

"There was this old squat in New Orleans. Everyone knew that the people who stayed there were train hoppers. I wanted to get away, so, I hooked up with a small group of 'em. They were sketchy, but they were willing to bring me along." She smiled. "I traveled with them to

Houston, then on up to Fort Worth. After that, I rode for about a year and a half. Mostly by myself, sometimes with a few other riders I met along the way. I travelled all over the southeast and southwest. Met a lot of interesting people."

The memory of that house came flooding back to her. The acrid smell of stale smoke, B.O. and alcohol. She remembered the first person to talk to her was a straggly rider named Mags. With his round, purple-tinted sunglasses and laid-back style, he made her feel welcome. He took her under his wing and showed her the ropes. Thinking of him made her smile. She wondered where he was right now. Probably somewhere near a beach. That was his favorite place to be. Wherever he was, she knew there was plenty of beer, good music and other riders.

She realized the others were staring at her. Gesturing to the rest of the group, she said, "I met up with these jokers in Roswell. Somewhere along the way, they became my family, and now I can't get rid of them."

Beth wiped her face. She sniffled then asked River, "Can I give you a hug?"

"Sure," replied River. Beth already had her arms wrapped around her neck before she finished the word. River's heart melted. She wondered what it would be like if Beth came along with them. She wondered if the others would even consider the idea.

Chapter Fifteen

POP, CRACKLE, POP. ZAC BROKE A TWIG AND TOSSED THE PIECES INTO the fire. A somber mood hung in the air as they sat in silence, listening to the crackle and hiss as the flames devoured the wood. River's story was hard to hear. It surprised him that she shared it. He knew how painful it was for her.

As he stoked the fire, he noticed Beth staring at him. A questioning look on her face.

He smiled.

"Well?" she asked.

Zac glanced around at the group, then back at Beth. "Well, what?"

She pointed to her temple. "I'm gonna guess, based on that tiny star, that you're from Texas."

He nodded.

"Where?"

"East."

"So, evasive," said Beth, "Are you gonna make me ask?"

"Ask what?"

Beth sighed and shifted in her seat. "Come on." She flashed a sweet smile. "What's your story?"

He shook his head. "I don't have one."

"Come on," pleaded Beth.

He sighed. "Well, like I said, I grew up in East Texas—on a farm. Not a big one, but enough for some cows, chickens, a couple dogs and some barn cats. Before you ask, 'cause everyone does, yes, I drove a tractor and yes, I worked in the field with my dad."

"How many people in your family?"

"Four. My mom, dad, little brother Cole and me. My Meemaw lived with us too. So, I guess that makes five." He pulled out a photo of him with his little brother standing together on their front porch. He remembered that day. It was his thirteenth birthday. Cole was four years old. Those were the best times. Before the accident. He smiled as he looked down at the little guy with his mass of red, curly hair and big, toothless smile. *I hope wherever you are, you're still smiling like that.* He thought.

He handed the photo to Beth. "We weren't rich. Money was always tight. I don't remember ever feeling like we were missing out, though. My folks did the best they could with what they had. My dad was great — he had these huge, calloused hands." Zac looked down at his own hands. "He busted his ass every day and helped people who needed it whenever he could. He used to tell me that it was the responsibility of those of us who were strong to help the ones who were not."

A pang of sorrow struck as Zac thought about his father. His infectious laughter and ready smile. Mason Wade was a giant man with a heart to match. He remembered a time when he believed everything his dad told him about good people, bad people, and responsibilities. It was all so pie-in-the-sky. Life on his own had taught Zac that the real world didn't work that way.

"What about your mom?"

He sighed and let his thoughts wander to his mother. "Her name was Melody. We got our hair from her." He smiled. "Most of the time, she wore it up in a ponytail. When she took it down, though, it was beautiful. She held her own on the farm—she was not afraid of getting dirty."

"She sounds amazing."

Zac nodded. An image of his mom rushed forward in his mind. The afternoon sun cast a warm glow on her red hair as it blew in the warm breeze. She smiled at him as he climbed off the school bus. This was their ritual. Every day after school, his mom would meet him at the edge of the driveway. As they picked their way back to the house, Zac would tell his mom all about his day. She would listen with great interest, always ready to laugh at the funny bits.

Oh, what he wouldn't give for one more stroll down that driveway together.

Beth handed the photo back. "So, tell me more."

He stared at the picture one more time, then tucked it away inside his wallet.

"My Meemaw was exactly what you would imagine. Supercool, old Texas lady with a real hard edge. She smoked, drank and cussed a lot." He laughed. "She was an expert shot, too. I once saw her take out a coyote in the middle of the field—in the dark. It was going after our newest calf. My parents were out, and she was watching us. We could hear the pack howling. They were signaling to one another, moving closer. Meemaw wasn't about to let one of her babies get hurt. She grabbed the rifle and went out back, cussing and yelling. Took that coyote out with a single shot. The rest of the pack ran off."

"Wow," said Beth, "She sounds amazing."

Zac nodded, a joint made its way to him. *Why does it smell like lilac?* He took a hit, then passed it on.

Beth took a hit and coughed. She was not a seasoned smoker. When she could breathe again, she asked, "So, did you get to feed the cows and stuff? I went with my school once to a farm where we got to bottle feed the baby cows. They were so cute."

"I got to be there when they were born. There wasn't much bottle feedin' to do, their mamas took care of that."

"Do you ever go back to visit?"

Zac stared at Beth. Where to begin? He shook his head. "There's nothing to go back and visit." Someone handed the flask to him. He took a swig, then continued.

"Just before my fourteenth birthday, my parents got into an accident with another driver on the interstate. It was dark and foggy. The other driver didn't know where he was going. A deer jumped out into the road, he swerved to miss it. The two cars collided. No one walked away from that crash—not even the deer."

Peering into the fire, he remembered that night, watching from his bedroom window as the Sheriff's car crept down the driveway. Blue lights flashing, it seemed to move in slow motion. Unable to hear what was being said, he snuck out of his room and listened at the top of the stairs. In the living room, his Meemaw cried uncontrollably while the Sheriff did his best to console her. Zac wasn't sure what was going on, but he knew deep inside, that his life would never be the same.

"I remember the shock." He glanced at Beth. "It's kinda surreal. When you're a kid, you don't think that your parents will ever die. That only happens to other people. To old people."

He paused and wiped his face.

"After that, Meemaw did her best to take care of us. I did my best to fill my dad's shoes, but I just couldn't keep up. The fields went fallow. We did what we could—it just wasn't enough.

No fields meant no hay. So, we had to sell off the cows. Next, the equipment. Like I said, money was always tight. With my dad gone, it just got tighter and tighter. I did what I could as far as helping out and earning cash. Meemaw got a job in town."

"Is your Meemaw still alive?"

Zac shook his head.

"I was almost sixteen—in high school. One day, toward the end of the school year, our Principal came into my class and called me out. I figured it was because of the fight I had gotten into the day before. It wasn't. She walked me down to the counselor's office and closed the door. The sherriff was there."

He took another hit from the lilac scented joint, handed it to Beth and waited for her to stop coughing. "My Meemaw collapsed at work and died. Right there, on the floor of the grocery store in the middle of stocking some shelves."

"Just like that." He snapped his fingers. "Things went to shit."

"Cole stopped talking. I mean, not a single word came out of his mouth. They sent us to live in a group home. It sucked, but at least we were together. Cole was terrified. He wouldn't even sleep alone. Every night, he'd crawl into my bed, take up all the covers, and snore like hell. I didn't mind. He needed me—needed to know someone was still around."

Tears began to well up in his eyes. Most of the time, he tried not to think about Cole. The feelings were too raw.

Zac took a sip from the flask. He licked his lips and continued, "We moved from one family home to another for a little over a year and a half. One day, our caseworker came to the house and sat me down to tell me that a family wanted to adopt Cole. Since I was seventeen, they didn't want me. I was too old."

"Families don't want teenagers. Too much baggage, I suppose." He shrugged.

"To her credit, she put a good spin on the whole deal, trying not to let it sound as shitty as it really was."

"Wait," interrupted Beth, indignation in her voice, "I thought Family Services was supposed to keep families together! Why wouldn't they let you take Cole to live with you?"

Zac flashed a rueful smile. "Apparently, I've got anger issues," he said, using air quotes for emphasis. "A couple weeks earlier, I got into a fight at school. There was this scrawny, feminine kid. Everyone thought he was gay and left him to fend for himself. One day I saw him getting roughed up pretty bad by two, older kids around the back of the gym. The other guys were double his size."

"I couldn't let him get beat like that." Zac shook his head. "I stepped in and, well, I don't remember every detail, but I do remember how great it felt to beat the shit out of both of those assholes. They were pretty messed up."

"It took the Principal, the shop teacher and the coach to break us apart. They sat us down and tried to make sense of it all. That was when the little scrawny kid turned on me. The little bastard told the adults that I started the whole thing."

He shook his head. "I should have let him get his spineless ass beat to a pulp. Just walk away and mind my own business. Who knows, maybe they would've considered letting Cole live with me. Instead, I got labeled a problematic, violent teen with anger management issues. That sealed my fate. Cole's too."

Zac looked at Beth again. "I'll be honest, hearing that caseworker talk that day, man, it felt like a hot poker in my gut. I knew what she was getting at. I brought it all on myself."

"She went on about me being just a few months away from aging out of the system and how that meant I would have to move out and away from Cole—how this was the best thing for him. Prattling on about how he needed a proper family with a mom and dad."

"I never wanted to punch a woman in the face so hard in my entire life. But I didn't. I couldn't really talk, but I think I muttered some sort of agreement—this made her feel better, and she went on about more crap."

"I can't recall anything else she said. Must've blocked it all out."

"The next day, they picked up Cole to take him to his new family. Nobody said a thing about it being permanent. They didn't want him to get upset over the fact I wasn't going with him. I played along and pretended I would see him later. He hugged me, and he left. That was the last time I saw him."

He sat up and cleared his throat. "I left that night. Packed my things and walked out the door." Pointing at Finn, he said, "I ran into this crazy bastard not long after." He chuckled. "The rest is history."

"Ever wonder where Cole is now?" asked Beth.

"From time to time," he replied, "I hope the family that adopted him was every bit as amazing as the caseworker said they were. That he's living in a big house, celebrating birthdays and all the holidays."

Zac stared down at his feet. *I hope that when he thinks of me, he doesn't think I abandoned him.*

He ran his fingers through his hair and sighed. "Maybe someday I'll look him up. I don't know." He shrugged and stared into the fire.

They sat in silence. Pop, crackle, pop. In the darkness, frogs croaked, and crickets chirped.

"Wow," interrupted Cash. "You guys are just downers tonight. We need to lighten things up around here."

Zac agreed. He was done feeling sad—he was done thinking about this. "Well, speak up Cash, tell her your story."

Beth jumped at the bait. "Yeah Cash, what's your story?"

He shook his head. "Not much to tell."

"Well, how did you meet everyone?" asked Beth.

This brought about a round of laughter from the group.

"Wait, what's so funny?" she demanded.

The laughter grew louder.

"Okay," she said, glancing around, "now you have to tell me."

"All right, all right," said Cash, "I'll fill you in. But first, I gotta go take care of some business." He walked over to the edge of the trees and disappeared into the darkness.

Chapter Sixteen

WITH EACH STEP, THE EARTHY SCENT OF DECOMPOSING LEAVES DRIFTED into the air. He really liked that smell. As much as he enjoyed the action of the city, Cash also reveled in the quiet and peace that came with being in the woods. The unique sensation of being the only people in the world. He could understand why the others loved it so.

Laughter broke out. Standing in the dark, he heard the unmistakable sound of Teague's voice, followed by a retort from Finn. Another burst of laughter. No doubt they were teasing someone. Those two loved to pick. And they were great at it. They had a unique way with one another. A silent form of communication. A bond that Cash had never observed between two people before. That's how Finn and Teague have always been—how he hoped they always would be. He thought back to the first time he ever set eyes on them. In an empty rest stop in the middle of nowhere.

After recently parting ways with a trio of Nomads, he found himself in Las Cruces, where he met a girl named Camille. She had long, dark, brown hair, big, brown eyes, and a gorgeous smile.

The night before they met, she had stolen money from two of the meanest-looking guys he had ever seen. Cash knew this because he ran into them as they searched for her. Camille never said a word about it. The only thing she told him was that she was on her way to Austin to see her cousin. He knew she thought she had played him. What she didn't know was that he didn't care what angle she was working. He just wanted to sleep with her. He introduced her to the art of train hopping and the two set out for Texas.

They landed in a small town, west of San Antonio. Still having a good distance to go before arriving at their destination, they snagged a ride from a man named Todd. Tall and thin, with long, greasy, blond hair, he was perhaps one of the most sketchy-looking people Cash had ever met. And that was saying a lot.

Todd babbled incoherently all the time. When he spoke, his words came out slurred. The surrounding air filled with the stench of stale tobacco and weed. He had a tendency to forget what he was saying mid-sentence. More than once, he used his knees to steer as he lit a cigarette.

They careened down tree-lined country roads. Potholes dotted the asphalt, water had washed out entire sections in the low areas, cutting the road down to a single lane.

After traveling for over two hours, Cash couldn't stand it anymore. At the first sight of a gas station, he told Todd to pull over and let them out.

There they stood, on a bleak strip of road in the middle of nowhere Texas. Todd peeled out, kicking up a heavy cloud of dust and debris as he drove away.

The little shop was closed, so Cash, needing to take a leak, wandered around the rear of the building. When he returned, he found Camille sitting on the curb beside the air pump, his pack, suspiciously by her side. He wondered whether she had taken anything. That was how deep their relationship was. He didn't trust her.

On the road, a sheriff's car rolled by. He stopped, turned on his lights, pulled a U-turn and rolled into the driveway.

Cash couldn't help but note the irony of it all. They drove for hours along that shit hole road and saw nothing. Not one damn thing. They finally get away from the toothless hippy, and then a cop shows up. *Of course, he would.*

The deputy climbed out of his car and approached. "Howdy," he said. He stood six feet away, legs spread apart, left hand resting on his belt while his right hand rested over his handgun. The strap on the holster already open.

"You folks got some ID on y'all?" he asked.

Just what he needed, thought Cash. He sighed, pulled his wallet from the side pocket of his pack and handed the card over.

The deputy scrutinized the ID, looking down at the card, then back at Cash. He smirked. Cash was very familiar with that grin. It was the same one everyone flashed when they found out his full birth name. He steeled himself for the incoming joke. Everyone had a joke.

"Your momma a fan of country music by any chance?" he asked, struggling to hold back a laugh.

Cash did not reply, it wasn't really a question.

The deputy's face became serious once again. "Washington state. That's a long way away. How'd y'all end up here?"

"We got a ride a few towns back," replied Cash. "Driver just dropped us off here a few minutes ago."

Still holding on to Cash's ID, the deputy asked, "Where y'all heading?"

Cash responded once again, "Austin." He glanced over at Camille, who had been dead silent the whole time. She did not look well.

As though noticing her for the first time, the deputy turned and said, "You too, young lady, I'm gonna need to see some ID."

Camille shot a terrified glance at Cash. Trembling, she jumped to her feet and bolted.

"God dammit!" cursed the deputy. "Stay there," he ordered, then ran after her.

Time crept. Cash had no idea why she ran. He tried not to think of a reason; the possibilities were too many—all of them ended in him being arrested. *Should I run the other way?* He wondered. The thought was quickly swept aside when he recalled the deputy still had his ID. More nervous than he had been in a while, he waited.

It didn't take long for them to return. Camille's face red and blotchy, hands cuffed behind her back, tears streaming down her face. Dried leaves in her hair.

The deputy placed her inside the vehicle, then walked back over to Cash.

"You gonna give me a problem?" he asked. His hand, once again, rested on the handle of his sidearm.

Pissing off a Texas cop was not high on his list of things to do. Cash shook his head. "No, sir."

"That's a wise decision," stated the deputy. "Now, stay put while I run these IDs." He spun around and went back to his vehicle.

The next couple minutes ticked by like hours. Cash knew he didn't have any real reason to be worried, but, like a school kid in the Principal's office, he worried anyway. He scraped his mind, trying to see if he could find any reason at all that the officer would have cause to search him. He remembered a small baggie containing weed was in his left shirt pocket, just waiting for the deputy to come along and find it.

God, please do not let him check my pockets.

The officer climbed out of his vehicle. He opened the door to the back seat, leaned forward and stated, "Camille Lin, you are under arrest..."

When he finished reading her rights, he paused and asked, "Do you understand these rights?"

From where he sat, Cash could not hear her reply.

The deputy closed the door and strode back over to Cash.

Please don't check my pocket. Please don't check my pocket... Cash begged repeatedly in his head as though warding off an evil spirit—or praying.

"All right Johnny, you're free to go," said the deputy, as he handed Cash's ID back to him.

Cash was confused. He couldn't think. "Um, what?" The deputy's words finally made sense. "Oh, okay. Thanks," he replied.

"I suggest you not be here when I come back around in a couple hours," the officer warned. Without another word, he got back into his vehicle, and drove off.

Cash stood there, silent. A cloud of dust and debris encircled him. When the dust settled, there was no sign of the cop or Camille. Just him, standing there in the middle of nowhere. Alone. He picked up his pack and walked.

As luck would have it—for Cash, there was always luck to be found—a truck rolled up. The driver, a friendly, white-haired man in denim overalls, offered him a ride to the nearest rest stop.

It was early evening when he was dropped off. The building was large, clean and brand new. It even housed a modern storm shelter. Outside stood a tall water tower, play structure and several vending machines.

Unfortunately, there were no trucks anywhere. He sat down on the plastic slide and looked around. Until that moment, he hadn't realized how exhausted he was. Hungry, too. He pulled out his wallet—it was empty. All his money was gone. *Well, Damn.* Camille had ripped him off. He couldn't really be angry about it, considering that some of that money came from her wallet the night before. Rifling around in his pack, he found the remains of a chocolate chip cookie. He shoved it in his mouth and scanned the area.

The only vehicle in sight was a run-down, tan sedan. It's occupant, a creepy man with pockmarked skin and greasy hair, sat transfixed, staring at something on the other side of the building.

Cash followed his gaze.

Two teenagers sat under an old oak tree. One dark-haired, the other blond. In their own private world, they laughed, wrestled and talked. Oblivious to everything.

Cash looked around the facility again. No other cars. The rest stop was in the heart of nowhere. No large city nearby. No small city either. *Where the hell did they come from?*

Cash glanced back at the creepy man. Still watching—like a predator stalking prey. A chill ran up his spine. Inner conflict roiled. Should he warn the two teens? Should he do something? But if he could do anything, what would that be? Did he really want a confrontation after the whole run-in with the sheriff? Would it even be worth it?

What if he was reading it all wrong? What if the creepy guy was really a friend of theirs? *That's probably what it is. No need to be concerned, Cash. It's none of your business anyway, so let it be.*

He settled back on the slide, closed his eyes and listened to the sound of the birds singing.

A burst of laughter and the sound of footsteps on the concrete walkway.

Cash opened his eyes. The dark-haired teen was heading his way. Bright smile on his face, he strolled past Cash as though he wasn't there. His steps light and happy as he disappeared into the men's room.

A car door creaked open. Cash watched as the creepy guy did his best to close the door as quietly as possible. Fixated on the restroom, he glanced over at the other teen.

Once again, Cash followed his gaze. The blond one was busy reading a small paperback. He never even looked up as the creepy guy snuck into the men's room.

Cash strained his ears, listening for... he didn't really know what for. Something. Anything. His heart pounded. The longer the silence, the more intense his heartbeat. Nervousness coursed throughout his body, creating energy that demanded to be discharged. Leg twitching, he ran his fingers through his hair.

Shit. Shit. Shit.

He peered over at the blond teen—nothing. Head still buried in his book.

Look up, dumbass.

His body was intent on making him move. Against his better judgement, Cash crept over to the men's room and placed his ear against the metal door.

BANG! Something heavy yet soft hit the door from the inside, causing a vibration that bumped the door against his head. He pulled away. Muffled voices and scuffling ensued.

His worst fears were being realized.

You are not seriously gonna do this, are you? He stepped back. *Just walk away.*

Another crash, this one sounded like glass breaking or something more substantial.

Christ! That kid is being destroyed. Knowing this, could he really walk away and let the kid die or who knows what else?

A holler—then silence.

That was it. He was going in. He braced himself, then leaned forward with his shoulder and charged through the door ready for a fight.

Standing before him, breathing heavily, blood streaming from his nose, stood the dark-haired teen. He glared at Cash. His face contorted with rage. Behind him, the metal stall wall was bent and twisted in on itself. Overhead, the cold fluorescent light buzzed and flickered. The creepy man lay at his feet, unconscious, on the cool tile floor. A pool of crimson blood spread out from the wound on his head.

Behind Cash, the metal door swung closed with an eerie creak.

The teen stared with a cold, challenging eye. No fear. No guilt. Not a hint of remorse. Just a glare, questioning Cash if he were going to be a problem too.

He bent over the unconscious man's body and pulled the wallet from his back pocket. Ignoring Cash, he set his focus on the contents.

"Well, Dennis, you suck," the teen's voice bounced off the tile walls. It was deep. Much deeper than one would expect from one so young. He flipped the billfold to the floor. Smirking, he folded the money and stuffed it in the pocket of his camouflage pants.

Ah, a sense of humor Cash could work with.

"You know," said Cash. "You should go through all the pockets." He grinned mischievously as he approached the troll on the floor.

The kid flashed an evil grin, then stepped back, allowing Cash to rifle through the rest of creepy man's pockets.

A pocket knife, a vial of what appeared to be coke and car keys.

"I'm Finn," said the teen, as he reached out his hand.

"Cash." He looked over Finn, noting the blood and unfastened leather belt. "You okay?"

Finn nodded and buckled his belt. He studied his reflection in the mirror, turned on the water and used a paper towel to clean away the blood from his face.

As they left the restroom, Cash trotted over to the cleaning closet. He pulled out the yellow caution sign and placed it in front of the door.

Under the tree, the blond teen finally took notice. A questioning look of concern spread across his face. He got to his feet.

"Time to go," Finn said calmly.

Cash tossed the keys into the overgrown grass.

Without another word, the trio walked off into the brush, leaving the rest stop behind.

Cash buckled his belt, made his way back to the fire and reclaimed his seat alongside River. Zac handed him the flask—he took a drink and passed it along. Finn and Teague were messing around again, off in their own little world. He wondered what it would be like to have such a close partner in life. He watched River as she laughed with Beth. The orange light from the fire cast a warm glow on her features, highlighting that little dimple. A wayward dread fell across her face. She brushed it aside.

He pulled out a baggie of weed and rolled a joint.

"So, Cash," said Beth. "What's your story?"

He took a hit, exhaled and placed his hand against his chest. Shaking his head, he replied, "My story? Nah, I don't have a story. Seriously. I grew up in Spokane. Before I met these guys, I used to think my life sucked, my family sucked. I was absolutely convinced that I had the shittiest existence ever. I realize now that my parents were just poor, working-class. They didn't have a whole lot of options or opportunities. In hindsight, it wasn't really all that bad."

"How did you start hopping trains?" Beth took a hit.

He ran his fingers through his hair, "Well, like I said, I believed that life would be better anywhere that wasn't home. One day, after yet another argument with my old man, I met up with some Nomads who were heading to Seattle, so I hitched along. I was hooked."

Thinking of home brought no strong feelings. It was almost depressing how little thought he put into his life before. To him, it was as though that was just a placeholder period. A temporary scene. One where he waited until he was big enough, smart enough, strong enough to get out on his own.

"Have you spoken to your dad since?" asked Beth.

Cash nodded. "Yeah. I didn't for about a year, then... I don't know." He shrugged. "Whatever negative feelings I had toward him were just gone."

He thought about how he felt the day he left. The anger and frustration. With each hop, the rush of new places and new experiences changed his state of mind—his state of being. The negative emotions evaporated, leaving behind no trace—like morning dew in warm sunlight. Over time, he saw the world much more clearly. He understood his parents a little more.

"I called him one Sunday morning. I knew the old man was gonna be home—he loved to sleep in and lounge around that day," he said. "Anyway, he picked up and to my surprise, he wasn't an ass. Instead, he talked to me like a man—not like a stupid kid. It was the best conversation we ever had. We talked for hours, until my phone battery died."

"Have you been home to see them since?"

"Yeah, several times," replied Cash. "For a day or two. Even brought these guys a couple times."

River smiled. "His mom made some great meals for us."

"I cannot tell you how much I enjoyed watching his old man kick his ass in poker," laughed Zac.

Cash had to laugh at that one. His dad was probably the only person he knew who could always beat him at cards. No real surprise there—he was the person who taught him how to play.

Finn stood up and reached his hand out for Teague. Pulling him to his feet, he said, "On that note, we're goin' to bed now. Good night, y'all." They walked over to their tent.

"Try to keep the noise down so we can sleep," Finn said, as he held the tent flap open and gestured for Teague.

As Finn crawled inside the tent, Cash called out, "Keep the noise down? Us? You seem to forget who makes all the noise around here at night."

Laughter.

Finn let the tent flap fall, then he reached his hand out and flipped them all off.

More laughter.

Everyone else remained by the fire until the moonshine ran out. As the flames waned, River and Beth made their way to the tent where they settled in for the night.

Cash staggered over to his hammock. Within minutes, he was fast asleep.

Chapter Seventeen

EYES CLOSED, TEAGUE LISTENED TO THE SOUND OF THE WATER flowing along the sandy shoreline. In the trees, birds chirped and whistled. Red and orange light filtered through his eyelids. He inhaled. The smell of dank, sweaty clothes assaulted his senses. He wrinkled his nose and rubbed his eyes.

Without looking over, Teague already knew Finn was not in the tent. More than likely, he was outside fiddling with the fire. It was normal for Finn to wake early—he was a light sleeper. However, ever since they received the news about Cyrus and Craig, Finn was not sleeping at all. The first night, Teague figured it was because of the upsetting news. Then came the injury. Finn sort of slept then—if you could consider being knocked unconscious sleeping. He had hoped that last night, Finn could finally rest. He didn't.

Teague stretched, then pulled his pants on and crawled out of the tent.

The morning sun was bright—too bright. Holding up a hand to shield his eyes, he scanned the area. Crouched in front of the fire Finn was barefoot, wearing only his jeans. His hair an unruly mess on his head. Busily fanning the fledgling flames to coax them to life.

Sitting beside him, chatting away, was Beth.

Teague smirked. *Finn must love that.*

Taking care to avoid the dirt, he stepped into one boot. The next one was not so easy. While hopping around on one foot, he struggled to get the boot on. All the while, Beth giggled at his antics. After nearly falling over more than once, both boots were finally on. He buttoned his pants and joined them by the fire.

"Morning," said Beth. Her voice a happy contrast to what he was used to hearing in the morning. The thought that she resembled a young child struck Teague—just waking up, happy to see everyone around them.

He nodded. "Morning." He sat down next to Finn, then leaned close and gave him a peck on the cheek.

"Did you sleep?" He asked.

Finn's face twitched. "Yeah." He picked up a pot filled with water and placed it on top of a small circle of rocks at the edge of the fire.

Teague wasn't buying the reply. Finn was great at conning people who didn't know him. That didn't work with Teague. With all the little, uncontrollable ticks and twitches, Finn's face betrayed his true feelings and thoughts every time. When his face twitched, he was covering something up—lying.

When he twitched his nose, he was processing things—sorting through his thoughts.

A tick in his left eyebrow meant he was surprised—in a good way.

When he flared his nostrils or clenched his jaw, he was getting angry. And when the left corner of his mouth twitched—ever so slightly—fists were about to fly.

Teague turned his attention to Beth. "How about you? Get some sleep?"

"I did," she replied, "And you?"

She was either naturally energetic first thing in the morning or trying desperately to overcome a sense of awkwardness. He couldn't figure out which one.

"I did," he replied, smiling, "We had a hell of a night the other night. After all that excitement, I needed to sleep. It was great."

He watched as Finn stoked the fire, then got up and walked to the tent. Crawling halfway inside, he rummaged around noisily.

"That's a cool tattoo," blurted Beth. She pointed to the compass above his heart. "I see Finn has the same one between his shoulders. I like it."

"Thanks."

Uncomfortable silence.

Finn returned with three envelopes of instant oatmeal, two bowls and some utensils. He reached into the flames to move the pot, then quickly jerked his hand back. He must have scorched his fingers. The water was ready, so he added the oats.

Beth interrupted the awkward silence, "What happened the other night?" She paused. "If you don't mind me asking, that is."

"Say again?" asked Teague.

Beth gave a sideways shrug. "You said you had a bad night the other night. What happened?"

Teague glanced at Finn, who was staring down at the pot. No doubt trying to avoid conversation.

As they waited for breakfast, Teague told Beth all about the accident on the train the night before and how, had that not happened, they would not have ended up in Denton, but continued to Austin.

Finn divided up the oatmeal into the two bowls and handed one to Teague. He handed the other one to Beth, then ate directly from the pot.

Beth turned and asked Finn. "Did it hurt when he was stitching you up?"

Finn shook his head and swallowed. "Nah, not too much. You get used to it if it happens enough."

"Happens enough?" she asked, "Do accidents like that happen often?"

"Not really," he replied.

Teague scoffed.

"All right, maybe it happens more often than some of us would like," Finn said, as he rolled his eyes.

"That's better," snickered Teague.

"That's a nasty bruise you got there Teague, does it hurt?" asked

Beth.

"It does," he responded, as he moved his arm in a circular motion. This created a dull ache deep inside. His hand was weak. He clenched his hands. "But I'll survive." He winked at her.

She seemed to be more comfortable with them. Her face became thoughtful. "Can I ask you a question?"

"Sure."

"What was it like for you, growing up?"

Memories washed over his mind. The sweet fragrance of honeysuckle drifting through the air. Spanish Moss hanging heavy from the trees. Humid, oppressive heat. Playing in the bayou all day, sleeping on the screen porch at night. The heady scent of Angel's Trumpets. Leelahs. Mosquitos and the painful sting of cow killers.

"It was swampy." He grinned. "In a lot of ways, it was a good time for a while, then it all changed and went to shit."

"What was your family like?"

"My maw-maw and paw-paw raised me for the first eleven years of my life." Their smiling faces flashed in his mind. "My maw-maw was a big, southern lady. If you spoke out of turn, she had no issues slapping you back into place. The rest of the time, she was overfeeding you and always ready with the hugs."

"Paw-paw was a war vet. Korean War, I think. He had a mean streak when he drank brown whiskey, which wasn't all that often. He's the one who taught me how to fish and hunt."

Across the fire, Zac stirred. Curled up in his sleeping bag, he opened his eyes.

"Mornin'," said Teague.

Zac responded with a sleepy nod of his head in acknowledgment. He unzipped his bag and sat up. After rubbing his head, he pulled out a bottle of water.

"What about your mom and dad?" asked Beth.

Teague scoffed. "Ah, that putain. Her name is Grace. She didn't come around much. She was busy living her best life in the city." He shrugged. "I imagine having a kid would be a damper on your party lifestyle. She was too busy sleepin' around to care about her kin."

"As for a father, I don't have one. Or at least I don't know who he is. I'm pretty certain it wasn't an immaculate conception, not with old Grace." He shook his head and smirked. "Once when I was twelve, I asked her if she could tell me anything about him. She said she dated several men during that time, and couldn't be sure who he was. On my birth certificate, in the box where the father's name should be, it only says Unknown."

Grace always brought up dark feelings. When he was little, and she came to visit, he would do his best to impress her. More than anything, he wanted her to like him—to stay with him or take him with her. That never happened. As the years passed, his desire for her love and acceptance slowly gave way to deep disgust.

"I-I'm sorry," stammered Beth, "I didn't want to bring up any bad feelings."

Teague felt bad. He didn't care much for making others uncomfortable or upset. There were plenty of other opportunities for people to be upset—he didn't enjoy causing it.

He shook his head. "Don't apologize, I kinda lose my composure sometimes when she comes up. It ain't you. It's her."

He smiled. "My maw-maw and paw-paw made up for her. For every way that she was selfish and horrible, they were the exact opposite. It's hard to believe that two people like them raised a kid like her."

"What happened to them?" asked Beth.

Teague sighed. "Same thing that happens to all of us—they died. First the old man. A few months later, she followed."

Finn leaned against him and gave him a gentle shove. After shoving him back, Teague continued. "It was for the best. After the old man died, Maw-maw was a mess. She just gave up on everything. Even stopped leaving the house. She would send me to the shops for food and things. It was like her turn couldn't come soon enough. I guess that's what happens when you lose your soul mate. A part of you gets lost with them."

"That was when Grace moved back in with her small army of dirt bags."

Cash shuffled up and sat down, yawning. "You people are loud.

What the hell is all the talking?" he said, somewhat sleepily.

"I'm sorry," said Beth, "We didn't mean to wake you up or anything."

"Ah, don't apologize to him," said Teague.

"Yeah, he needed to wake up his lazy ass anyway," Zac chimed in.

Cash punched him in the arm, then grabbed his water.

Beth turned back to Teague. "So, was that when you left?"

Teague shook his head. "Not right away. Grace took over the house. I got to see up front and personal the way she lived her life. All the drugs, boozin' and losers. When I was little, the old man, and I built a treehouse out of old pallets in one of the giant trees out back. I moved into that full time. I was just waitin' for the right time to leave."

Teague thought about his days in the treehouse. The loud parties every night. Sneaking down into the kitchen to steal food. Not because anyone would refuse him, but because he did not want to interact with any of the people in the house. His treehouse was the only place he could call his own.

"Anyway," Teague continued, "Sometime around my fourteenth birthday, I packed up and walked out. Didn't say goodbye. Just walked until I got tired, then curled up and slept. Woke up the next day and did it all over again. It probably took 'em a week before they even realized I wasn't around. You know?"

Teague looked around. All the grave faces. He needed to change the mood.

"It ain't all bad. Had I never left, I would've never met this scrawny, little, scared kid."

Finn shook his head. "I wasn't that scrawny."

Laughter.

"Dude," chided Cash, "you were pretty, damn scrawny when I met you. And that was a good couple years after you two met."

Teague nodded.

Cash chuckled. "Yeah, I can only imagine how spindly you were."

"Twigs for arms with giant feet and hands—like a puppy," chortled Teague, "And a head full of out-of-control hair." He tousled Finn's hair.

Finn pulled away.

River's tent flap burst open. She put her shoes on and walked over to the fire, carrying a tin cup filled with water. After placing it on the rocks at the edge of the fire, she sat back to wait.

"The princess has graced us with her presence," teased Cash.

River punched him in the arm. "Shut up, peasant."

Looking around at everyone, she asked, "So, what is everyone up to this morning?"

"We were just chatting," replied Teague, as he winked at Beth.

"Ah, cool," replied River, her water ready, she prepared her tea.

"Beth, is there someone who's gonna be worried or angry about you being out all night?" asked Teague.

Beth shook her head. "Not really. My mom and dad work a lot. They usually leave me to do my own thing. Sometimes we'll go three or four days without seeing one another."

"So, what you're saying is that odds are, no one is at your house this morning. Right?" asked River.

Beth slowly replied, "Yes."

Without skipping a beat, River asked, "Can we use your shower?"

"Oh, my God! A hot shower!" exclaimed Cash.

"What is this hot shower of which you speak?" asked Zac.

"Mais oui! A hot shower would be great!" said Teague.

"Sure!" Beth answered. "When was the last time you guys had a shower? It sounds like it's been a while."

"We had cold showers a week ago. Hot showers are scarce," answered Teague, as the others nodded in agreement.

"Hey, can we do some laundry too?" asked River, "I know, we're asking for everything, but it would be nice to put on clean clothes after a nice, hot shower." She smiled.

"Yeah, sure, no one will care."

"So, where's your house at?" asked Teague.

"The north end of town—it's gonna be quite a walk from here. We might just want to catch the bus.

Teague nodded. "Trés Bien!" he said aloud. "Alright y'all, time to pack up! We're headin' over to Beth's house."

Chapter Eighteen

RIDING THE BUS TO THE NORTH END OF TOWN, RIVER SAT NEXT TO Beth while Cash, seated across the aisle, practiced card tricks.

One row in front of him sat Zac, who was busy sketching in a small sketchbook. His expression was one of deep concentration as his pencil moved with purpose on the page. She wondered what he was creating. At the back end of the bus, Finn lay with his head resting on Teague's lap. Finn's focus set on the book he was reading, while Teague stared out the window, unconsciously twirling a lock of Finn's hair.

The hum and sway of the bus was soothing. Quietly enjoying the sound and movement, River allowed herself to fantasize about what it would be like to have Beth join their group. To have a sister again. It wasn't that far-fetched, Beth got along well with everyone so far— well, almost everyone. She peered over at Finn. He wasn't overtly hateful toward Beth, but he was being awfully dismissive. He could be so abrasive, sometimes. She sighed.

It was mid-morning when the bus finally dropped them off at the edge of a neighborhood full of neat, single-story, brick homes. As far as the eye could see, small, brick houses sat one after another along the tree-lined street.

Beth was fidgeting again, so River wrapped her arm around her shoulder. "How far from here?"

"Fourth one on the left."

"Well, then," said River encouragingly, "lead the way."

They sauntered along to the steady purr of air conditioning units. All built around the same time, each home was almost identical. The sole distinction from one to the other was the color of brick. Gray, tan or red. Stopping in front of one, Beth spun around. "Here we are, home sweet home."

The little house stood silent. Red brick exterior with white trim. Garage off to the side, set back from the street. In the front yard stood a giant oak tree. A tired, old swing hung off the lowest branch.

River went up to the tree. The swing ropes were old and frayed. The wooden seat rotted. She nudged the swing once, then twice. She imagined Beth as a small child giggling while swinging higher and higher—so high, she could touch the fluffiest of clouds overhead. A smile spread across her face.

Back on the doorstep, Beth opened the door and gestured for everyone to come in.

Upon entering the home, Cash tossed his pack on the floor and announced, "Mom, Dad, I'm home!" He then flopped down on the sofa and put his feet up on the table.

River placed her backpack down and took in the cozy surroundings. "This is nice Beth."

"The kitchen is this way," said Beth, as she closed the door and strode across the room.

River followed.

In the kitchen, Beth showed her where everything was. She was nervous, which made her rattle on. River found this adorable. Beth was going on about drinking glass type and style when Cash walked in and interrupted her mid-sentence.

"Where's the shower?" he asked, leaning against the doorjamb.

"Oh, follow me!" replied Beth, "It's the second door on the right." She called over her shoulder. In the hallway, she opened a closet door. "Towels are in here."

Cash pulled out a clean, folded towel. He held it against his face and took a deep breath.

"Ah, it's so soft." He inhaled one more time. "And it doesn't smell like ass."

Zac appeared in the hall. Without saying a word, he reached into the closet and pulled out a towel, then strode to the bathroom. Cash grabbed him by the shoulder and shoved him backward into the wall. Zac responded by grabbing Cash and pinning him against the opposite wall.

Beth chuckled as she, and River did their best to stay out of the fray.

"Are you two gonna get in there?" demanded River. "Or am I gonna have to kick someone's ass for taking up precious time?" She glared at both boys.

They let each other go, straightened their clothes, and once again, headed to the bathroom. Bumping into one another in the doorway sparked another wrestling round.

Beth giggled. "Are they always like this?"

River nodded. "Most of the time." She wrapped her arm around Beth's. "Let's let them figure this out on their own. Is there another bathroom? With another shower?"

Beth smiled. "Sure, follow me."

She escorted River down the hall to the master bedroom. Without pause, River strolled across the room, toward the shower. "Awesome!" She said, as she kicked off her shoes and removed her T-shirt.

Somewhere behind her, she heard the door to the bedroom open, then close. Beth must have left her alone.

The tile floor was cool against her feet. River stared at her reflection in the large mirror that spanned the wall above the sinks. She played with her hair, then inspected the things on the counter. A bottle of contact lens solution, toothbrushes, and toothpaste. On the shelving unit behind her, bars of soap, lotion, face cream, and talcum powder, all organized neatly. Picking up a small jar of face cream, she sniffed the contents—the scent reminded her of something, but the memory was too far away. She closed the lid and put the jar back where she found it.

She turned on the shower, then wandered into the bedroom as she waited for the water to warm. In the far corner of the room, near a large window, stood a small vanity table—makeup strewn across the top. River never understood people's obsession with makeup. She opened a bottle of foundation and sniffed. It smelled of chemicals. Wrinkling her nose, she closed the bottle. In the small mirror, she studied her reflection—all her freckles and imperfections.

Grinning, she spun around and continued exploring the room.

A wooden jewelry box sat centered on a large dresser. Instinctively, she glanced over at the door, then raised the lid. Gold and silver rings lay atop a tray of red velvet. Some had gemstones, some did not. Small dividers held various styles of gold and silver earrings. She lifted the tray. An ornate, slender box caught her eye. Inside was an elegant bracelet made up of three rows of rubies and diamonds in a staggered sequence. River lifted the bracelet and put it on her wrist. The gems sparkled like tiny stars as she moved her hand. So beautiful. *I bet this is worth a fair amount of money.* She thought.

Staring at her wrist, River debated taking the piece of jewelry. She knew the guys would do it with no hesitation. Guilt washed over her. *I can't do this to Beth.* She removed the bracelet and placed it back in the box. After closing the lid, she turned her attention back to the shower.

She held her hand under the running water—it was hot. Perfect. She stripped off her remaining clothes and climbed in.

Warm water cascaded over her from head to toe. She stood there, face lifted up, eyes closed, feeling the water stream down as it warmed her body.

Looking down, dirty water swirled around her feet and down the drain. *Yeah, that's gross.* She laughed to herself, then grabbed hold of the nearest bar of soap and held up to her nose. Lavender flooded her senses—she loved lavender. Immediately, she went about washing herself, basking in the water's warmth, as the fragrance wrapped around her in the steamy air of the shower.

Chapter Nineteen

BETH BLUSHED AND QUICKLY TURNED HER HEAD AWAY, NOT BEFORE noticing that River had the same compass tattoo as Finn and Teague. It was on her right shoulder. As she left the room, she wondered whether Cash and Zac had one. *Is it a group thing?* She pondered as she closed the door.

Back in the hallway, Cash and Zac were still scuffling over who would shower first. Snickering, she skirted past and entered the living room.

Finn stood by the fireplace. Seeing her, he held up a framed photo. "This your family?"

Beth took the picture from his hand. The smiling faces of the Sepulveda family in all their happy, middle-class glory, stared up at her. Alicia, her mom, was an older version of Beth. There was no better description. Same height, hair color and round face. Frank, Beth's father, stood towering over them. He was a rugged, handsome man, tall and fit with a head full of dark, brown hair. And sitting beside Beth was her older brother Tomas.

She nodded.

"Y'all look happy."

"Yeah, everyone is always happy and smiling in photos. You never see pictures of the bad times. We were younger back then." She placed the frame back on the mantle.

Finn shook his head. "Not all families have happy pictures—sometimes there ain't enough happy times to photograph."

He picked up a photo of her brother Tomas. "How much older than you is he?"

"About four years," she said. She looked at the image. Tomas was handsome with his dark, brown hair and big, brown eyes. She wanted to change the subject. "Do you have any brothers or sisters?"

He shook his head. "No."

Beth nodded. He was so guarded. She had never met anyone who was so sealed off before.

"So, where's he now?" asked Finn. "Your brother."

Beth shrugged. "I haven't seen him much in the past several months. Tomas moved out almost a year ago. There was a big blowup, and he left in a huff."

There was a time when she and Tomas were very close. She looked up to him in that special way that little sisters look up to their older brothers. To her, he was a hero—she knew, no matter what, her big brother would always be there. After his twentieth birthday, that all changed. She wasn't sure what made it happen, she just knew that it was around that time that he became a different person. He was violent and angry most of the time. He made it impossible to be around.

Finn said nothing. He stood still, staring at her in that creepy way of his—like he was studying a lab animal.

Teague walked past, stopping at the end of the hall. "Those two couillions are gonna be at it forever, or at least till one of 'em gets tired and gives up." He turned to Beth. "We might as well do laundry while we wait. Where's the washer at?"

"It's over here," answered Beth. Happy to be free of Finn's watchful eye, she crossed the kitchen and opened a door. "Everything you need is in here."

"Let's get to it!" said Teague, as he walked back to the living room. A few moments later, he returned, arms full of dirty clothes. The pungent odor of sweat was so strong, Beth could smell it from several feet away.

"Thanks for lettin' us use your house like this, Beth," he said, as he shoved dirty clothes into the washer.

"It's no bother at all. I'm glad I could help," she replied. Then, in a moment of honesty, she added, "Actually, it's been great hanging out with y'all. I know this is weird, but I feel comfortable around you. Like friends I've known a long time." She let her voice trail off as she realized both of them were staring at her.

Oh, god, I'm rattling on again. She thought.

Beth smiled at Teague then glanced at Finn. The expression on his face was strange, almost menacing. *Was that a sneer?* It was only there for a moment—perhaps she imagined it. *Stop reading so much into things.*

Finn took his shirt off and handed it to Teague, who had just done the same. He tossed them both into the washer.

"Uh, what are you doing?" asked Beth.

"Laundry," replied Teague. He winked and bent down to pull off one boot, then the other. He peeled off his dirty socks and tossed them in.

As though she wasn't there, Finn emptied the contents of his pockets. He placed them on top of the dryer along with his belt and Bowie knife, then removed his pants and added them to the washer.

"Can't wash it if you're wearin' it," said Teague, who had removed his pants and added them to the mix. He turned on the machine and closed the lid.

If Beth thought she was uncomfortable before, the two of them standing there in their boxer shorts made it even worse. *Thank god, they left those on.* She felt the blood rush to her face. They walked past her and into the kitchen where Finn hopped up on the counter. Teague went over to the refrigerator and pulled out some eggs, bacon, butter and a bottle of hot sauce.

Oh, my God. They're seriously going to cook in my kitchen in their underwear! Okay be calm—this is no big deal. She told herself, trying to ignore their lack of clothes. She pulled up a stool by the island and sat down.

Cash entered the kitchen. "Ah, eggs! And bacon!" he said excitedly.

"Zac won, huh?" taunted Finn.

"Ha ha, yeah, whatever. I let him go first," replied Cash. He looked around and grinned. "I see we started the laundry?"

"Wait, this is normal?" asked Beth.

Cash snickered, "Yeah, you should see the faces of all the people in the washaterias when they do this. Sometimes the old ladies will stare, with a huge smile on their faces, and other times, they'll walk out angry and disgusted. These two will sit there in their shorts for hours —oblivious."

"Y'all don't get embarrassed or self-conscious that strangers are staring at you? In your underwear?"

Finn and Teague looked at one another, shrugged, and shook their heads.

Cash put his hand on Beth's shoulder. "Look, Beth, one thing you need to know about these two—they're feral. Well, that one is for sure," he pointed at Finn, "you know what that is, right?"

Without waiting for a response, Cash explained, "A feral animal is one that used to live with people, but then something happened and it was abandoned—left it to survive on its own. Because they once lived among people, they have no fear of 'em. They may look and act harmless, but the truth is they're worse than wild—far more dangerous."

He pointed at Teague. "This one still has some social potential, but deep inside, he's every bit as twisted as that one. They honestly could give two shits about what other people think of them—this is one of the many reasons we love 'em."

Finished cooking, Teague divided up the food. Beth watched in horror as both he and Finn covered their eggs and bacon with hot sauce. Her dad was the only person who could tolerate that stuff. It was way too hot for her. It didn't seem to affect them at all.

River entered the room, a towel wrapped around her head. "Do I smell bacon?"

As she stole a piece from Cash's plate, she looked at Finn and Teague then at Beth. "I see they got to the laundry first." She smiled at Beth and gave her a little hug, as she said, "You'll get used to us."

Beth gestured to Finn and Teague. "One of you can use my parents' bathroom if…"

Before she could even finish her sentence, both of them had taken off down the hall to the master bedroom.

"Aw, man, y'all had bacon?" said Zac, as he entered the kitchen.

River handed him a plate. "I saved you some."

Cash bolted to the bathroom.

"Don't let them freak you out," River said to Beth. "When I first met them, I didn't know what to think. These boys are weird sometimes." She nodded toward Zac who was busy eating.

"But I honestly couldn't imagine being with any other group of people or even being alone again. They grow on you." She winked. "Like a fungus."

Beth could see what River meant. They were quite endearing. Weird, but in a good way.

They finished up their food and cleaned up the dishes.

Waiting for the others, River turned to Beth. "So, where is your bedroom? I'm thinking it's full of stuffed teddy bears with a ruffled bed skirt and matching curtains," she teased.

Beth was dreading this part. "If you promise not to make fun of me, I'll show you."

"Cross my heart and hope to die," replied River.

The hallway was empty and quiet. Beth let the door to her room swing open, gesturing for River to enter. "Here it is in all its little-girl glory."

Please don't think it looks stupid and childish.

River sauntered around the room. Past the shelves overflowing with stuffed animals and collectibles. She smiled as she ran her hands over the curtains—they matched the bedding. In the corner, over by the window, sat Beth's writing desk. She looked over the items attached to a pin board that hung on the wall.

"These are your friends from yesterday." She pulled the photo down.

"Uh, yeah," said Beth. She pointed at each person. "That's Liz, Eli, and Kara."

"Are y'all close?"

Before Beth could reply, a flurry of activity erupted in the hallway as Finn and Teague bumbled into the room. Hair wet, and carrying towels, they stopped and looked around.

"Ah, it's Beth's room," said Finn. Teague pulled a teddy bear off of one shelf and tossed it over to him. Finn caught the bear and hopped onto Beth's bed. He leaned up against the pillows with one arm behind his head, holding the teddy bear in the other.

Aside from Eli, Beth had never had a boy in her bedroom before, let alone one in his underwear. She was trying to ignore how uncomfortable she felt, but it didn't help that he was lounging around on her bed. *How red is my face?*

River scolded, "All right, all right, time to get out of here. It's Beth's room. Don't embarrass her—this is her private domain." She shoved Teague toward the door, then reached out her arm for Finn. She pulled him up onto his feet and shoved him in the hallway.

Back in the kitchen, Teague went back to the laundry. Cash, finally out of the shower, came into the kitchen rubbing his wet hair with a towel.

Finally, they were all in one place. Time to ask her question. "Okay, so I have to ask," said Beth, "the compass tattoos. I noticed that Finn, Teague and River all have the same one, just in different places."

River was smiling at her.

"Do you have it too, Cash?"

He nodded and showed his left forearm.

"How about you, Zac?"

He nodded.

"What's it mean? It seems like there is some sort of meaning behind it." She paused as she waited for a reply.

"A compass is the symbol of a traveler," explained Zac. "Sailors used to believe that getting a compass tattoo would protect you through rough waters and ensure that you'd always find your way home."

He lifted his right shirt sleeve to show Beth the tattoo on his upper arm. "Seemed kind of fitting for us—since traveling is all we do. That's why I designed this one."

Beth touched Zac's arm and ran her finger along the tattoo's outline. His words struck a chord deep inside—one she didn't even know existed until that moment. She wondered what it would be like to run away with them and never look back.

"You, ah, finished feeling up his arm?" asked Cash interrupting the moment.

River scoffed and hit him.

Beth blushed and let her hand drop away.

Chapter Twenty

Tick, tick, tick... shhh. Finn leaned against the back of the folding chair. The backyard was awash in warm, afternoon sunlight. He tilted his head up to the sky and closed his eyes. Tick, tick, tick... shhh. Several houses away, a lawnmower droned. The smell of fresh-cut grass drifted in the air.

He was tired. The kind of deep, bone-weary tired you get when you haven't slept in days. It was taking a toll on his body. A weird sense of detachment, almost like a cloudy force field between him and the others, was creeping in.

Eager to get back on the road, Finn was not happy with all the delays. Yes, the shower was great, and the clean clothes—a bonus. But enough of this. They needed to get going. They had a job to do and all of this lounging around was getting in the way. He wanted this whole business behind him.

To make things worse, River was becoming more enthralled with Beth by the moment. It was written all over her face. He did not want another person tagging along—let alone one as clueless as Beth. He had to get everyone back on the same page.

Finn sat up and looked around at his friends. "Anybody check when the next train heading south is comin' through?"

"I hadn't bothered checking with Porter yet," replied Teague.

"Don't ya think we should? We've been here long enough."

Teague cocked an eyebrow. "It's only been one night. I think it's a little soon to say we're off schedule." *That was condescending as fuck.* He thought. Frustration welled up inside him. Looking around at the others, they were all paying attention, yet no one spoke up.

Trying to conceal his irritation, Finn replied, "One night can be too many. Do we even know how long they'll store the remains at the mortuary? For all we know, they could have already gotten rid of them."

Teague sighed—as if he were talking to a child. "Then I suppose we're already too late then, aren't we?"

Finn pinched his eyes closed and rubbed his head. This was going nowhere. There was a low buzzing sound in his head.

"Look, Finn," said Teague. His tone was less condescending, more intimate this time. "I realize you want to get this over with. We all do. But we had a bad start. It's been one thing after another. Maybe a little break is in order, so we can relax and become whole again. I doubt the county has done anything with the remains yet. One more day ain't gonna hurt anything."

"One more day?" Shouted Finn. "What the hell do you mean, one more day?"

This time River chimed in, "He means we should stick around for one more night, then head out fresh tomorrow. Don't take this the wrong way, but it looks like you—more than any of us could use a little downtime."

Christ! There it is. They already decided. He thought. Without even consulting him, they decided that they would push this whole night-mare out even longer. *Of course they did.* This was just another trip for them. No big deal. *They probably don't even care if they get the ashes or not.* The buzzing gave way to a high-pitched whine.

"So that's it, then." He glared at Teague. "Y'all have decided we're staying another night. Any other decisions I should know about?"

Teague shook his head. "Don't go there. No one is plotting against you. The fact that your mind went there only proves you're not thinking right. C'est bête."

Did he just call me stupid? Finn was ready to go off. He opened his mouth…

River placed her hand on his arm. "Look, baby, we all need a little more rest to recover. First the storm, then Cyrus and Craig, followed by you damn near getting yourself killed. We're all a little run down. Some of us more than others." She flashed a sweet smile at him. "One more night. We can relax today, then get a good night's sleep and head out tomorrow. We need this—you need this too."

His thoughts whirled. Was he overreacting? Was he exhausted and not thinking right? Was he being stupid? No. He was trying to stay on task. *Was she hinting that I'm the reason they want to lounge around for another day? Bullshit! This isn't about me, this is all about her wanting to play with her new pet, Beth. And what the hell is Teague up to?*

Finn rubbed his head and looked down at his feet. His body tingled with weakness. His head hurt.

Teague placed his hand on his shoulder. "Maybe one more day to rest would be a good thing."

Finn caved. "You win. Y'all are probably right. We can head out tomorrow."

Finn could feel the tension dissipate—his body relaxed. The whining in his head stopped. He leaned back against the chair, closed his eyes and listened to the sprinkler again. Tick, tick, tick… shhh.

"On another note," said River, "Beth is nice."

Finn didn't open his eyes—he knew she was looking at him.

"Yeah, I like her," replied Cash.

Of course, he's gonna kiss her ass.

River chuckled. "Well, for once I can say thank you, Finn. If you hadn't gotten hurt, we wouldn't have ended up here, and we wouldn't have met Beth."

Finn opened his eyes and leaned forward. "Wow," he replied, "Next time I get my skull nearly broken, I'll be sure to remember it ain't all bad. At least River will be able to make a new friend now."

144 · N.L. MCLAUGHLIN

Cash chuckled. "The way you are, that will probably be in a day or two."

This caused the others to laugh and tease him.

He shook his head. "All y'all are assholes sometimes."

The back door swung open. Fresh from her own shower, Beth came outside to join them. Seeing everyone laughing, she asked, "What did I miss?"

Cash pointed at Finn. "Just poking fun at Finn—same old, same old."

Here we go. Thought Finn. For a fleeting moment, he considered getting up and walking away. He looked at Beth. "I have no idea what he is talking about."

"Yeah, uh huh?" said Cash, smirking. "Man, I love you like a brother, so believe me when I say you either got a death wish or your judgement is garbage. Maybe, you're just plain insane. What is it you say, Teague? C'est Fou?"

Laughter.

Finn shook his head. "Wow. That's savage."

"Nah, man, I'm gonna agree with Cash on this one," said Teague. "You've come up with some asinine ideas."

Finn turned to Beth. "Don't believe 'em. They're all talking shit."

"Dude, come on," said Cash. "Some of the most terrifying moments of my life—NO, scratch that, ALL of the most terrifying moments of my life—followed you saying the words; I got an idea."

"I'm gonna go with Cash on this one, man," added Zac. "When you say, *you got an idea*, it always ends up with something crazy happening."

Finn wracked his brain to find a memory to prove they were wrong. He couldn't find one.

"Hey," said Finn, "My ideas always work out—maybe not in the exact way originally intended, I'll give you that—but they do work out. Right?" He looked over at Teague for back-up.

Teague smiled and wagged his head slowly from side to side. "I ain't so sure you could say things work out. Most times, it's more like things go wrong, like horribly wrong, and then we're all just doin' what we need to in order to get through it alive or in one piece.

Finn bowed his head in mock defeat. Teague wrapped his arm around his shoulder and kissed him on the side of his head. Finn relaxed and leaned against him.

Laughing along with the others, Beth asked, "All the times you could have gotten hurt or died. Don't y'all ever want to stop?"

"Stop?" asked River.

The laughter died down—everyone listened.

Beth shrugged. "I don't know, stop traveling. Settle down, maybe? Have a home? Okay, it all sounds stupid coming out of my mouth right now."

"A home?" asked Finn, his tone mocking. He leaned forward in his chair. "What do you think makes up a home? Are you talking about a building filled with a bunch of shit you don't need?"

Beth blinked, she looked like a deer caught in the headlights of a car. She shrugged. "A home is a lot more than just the things you put in it."

"Yeah?" asked Finn. "Like what?"

"Family. Being with the people you love. Safety. Security," replied Beth.

"My family travels with me." He nodded at Teague. "Safety and security, from what exactly? What are you so scared of?"

"I don't know," admitted Beth. "The world can be a pretty harsh place."

"Home can be just as harsh," he snapped.

Beth nodded.

Finn scoffed. "Safety is a bullshit, fairy tale. It's a carrot they dangle in front of you, to keep you in line."

Beth stared.

He realized she was uneasy with the way the conversation had gone. *Too bad. She brought it up.* The pain in his head returned.

"You know, we're all gonna die one day, right?" He said, "Nothing you can do is gonna change that." Finn looked around at the others. "I think we're all pretty much of the mindset that we'd rather live life on our terms, even if that means that sometimes we're not safe."

"Do you ever worry about getting into trouble for living how you do?" she asked.

"In trouble with who?" He demanded. "No one's paying attention. Here's a little hard truth for you, Beth—the rules only apply to the fools who choose to follow them. The rest of us do what we want. And nobody does a goddamn thing about it."

Irritation bubbled up inside him again. He looked down at his feet. The buzzing in his head was back.

"Y'all are brave," whispered Beth.

"Brave?" asked Teague.

"Yeah, I mean you packed up and left without being afraid of anything," replied Beth.

"I wouldn't say we weren't afraid of anything," responded Teague. "I mean, yeah, we left behind everything we knew, but, trust me, it wasn't 'cause any of us were fearless. Some of us had nothin' to stick around for."

Beth nodded.

Zac interrupted, "I didn't have to leave. I could have stayed where I was and waited till I aged out of the system. Though, I probably would have been homeless after that, anyway." He shrugged.

Cash chimed in, "I'm pretty sure if I stayed in Spokane, I would be well on my way to dying of liver failure or drug overdose—there was nothing there for me anymore."

River sighed. "I, for one, am glad Dawn decided for me. I love this family. I wouldn't trade it for the world."

Those last words had such a sad tone to them. River hardly ever spoke of her sister. When she did, there was always an undertone of deep sorrow. Of a loss so profound, she could never be whole again. Her sister left behind an empty void—a void she might look to fill with Beth.

Finn glared at Beth. He gave Teague a quick nudge, then stood up and said, "I'm bored. Let's get out of here and do something."

Chapter Twenty-One

THE WARM AFTERNOON SUN MADE FOR A VERY PLEASANT STROLL BACK
to the square. River walked alone with Beth as the others lagged. Her
affection for Beth had taken her by surprise. Not having much in
common with most other females, she never gave much thought to
their companionship. Spending this time with Beth, however, brought a
yearning to the surface.

How great would it be to have a sister again? She couldn't help but
wonder.

They took their time, wandering along the sidewalk. Beth pointing
out various little shops she found interesting while the guys took turns
poking around all the parked cars. There would be a whistle, then
River and Beth would move to the side and wait; talking and laughing
the entire time. One more whistle, to signal all was clear, and they were
on their way once again.

Each time they stopped, River took care to study Beth's reactions.
At first, she was uncomfortable, eyes darting around, shuffling her feet
while flipping her hair. But after a while, she seemed to settle into it.

It was mid-afternoon when they arrived at the old courthouse. After
circling the building, they settled on a shady spot in the grass, under an
old oak tree.

"So, what are we gonna do now?" asked Beth.

River shrugged. "Any thoughts?" She looked around at the others, hoping for some input.

Finn lay in the grass and closed his eyes. Teague lay down alongside him.

Zac pulled his hood up over his head and leaned against the tree.

River turned to Cash. "Wanna go wander around?"

He smiled and stood up, holding one hand out for Beth, the other for River. A moment later, the trio set off to explore.

A pub-style restaurant stood at the corner with several, small tables for outdoor seating. Cash grabbed River by the arm, stopping her in her tracks, and nodded toward a couple seated at one table. They were paying their bill. He didn't have to explain; she knew what he was getting at.

The couple placed money into the small, black folder, then finished their drinks and walked away.

River turned to Beth. "You stay here and wait. Okay?"

Beth nodded, she looked confused and more than a little apprehensive. River smiled reassuringly.

Cash sauntered over to the table as River moved closer to the front door.

It swung open and the unsuspecting waiter came outside. Pretending to stumble, she grabbed him by the arm, and spun around, so his back was facing Cash. He reached out and held her arm. Good. She had his full attention. Peering over his shoulder, she watched Cash move in on the table.

She flashed her most innocent of looks. "Oh geez," she said. "I'm sorry."

"You all right?" asked the waiter.

"Yeah, yeah, I'm fine," replied River, as she smiled at him and looked him in the eyes. "I'm sorry. I wasn't paying attention." She continued to talk, all the while maintaining eye contact.

At the table, Cash had finished what he was doing and walked up to River and the waiter.

"You being clumsy again?" he asked. "This girl is always running into people. Sorry, man." He smiled at the waiter.

The waiter nodded.

"Well, thanks again," said River. She winked and walked away.

When they were out of earshot, she wrapped her arm around Cash's. "How much did you get?"

"Fifty."

She stopped walking. "Let me guess, you didn't leave any money to pay the bill, did you?"

Cash smirked and shook his head.

"Such a dick." She shook her head and scolded, "You know that that poor guy will have to pay for that ticket out of his own pocket. You should have only taken the tip and left the rest to pay for the food."

"Eh, he'll survive," he replied.

River sighed. "You're spending too much time with Finn. He's rubbing off on you."

Beth was silent through all of this as she kept pace, staring down at the ground.

"You okay?" asked River.

Beth looked up and stammered, "I-I'm fine."

She didn't look okay. In fact, she looked nervous—uncomfortable.

River needed to find a distraction—something to pull Beth out of the obvious funk she was in. A few yards ahead, she saw her answer. A small ice cream shop, all decorated like an old-style soda fountain. Perfect! She grabbed Beth's hand and tugged her inside.

The smell of ice cream and sugar wafted through the air. Swing music played in the background. Beth perked up. This was what River was hoping for. Minutes after placing their orders, Beth's mood turned around. She was back to being her usual bubbly self.

As they left the shop, a voice called out from up the street. "Beth! Beth! Wait up."

It was the girl who had shouted out the window of the car the other day. River recognized her as Kara, Beth's friend from the photograph in her room. She was walking with the other two, Eli and Liz.

"Where were you today?" demanded Liz. "I tried to call, but you didn't pick up."

"Yeah, we thought you were sick, but I see that's not the case," said Eli, as he looked over River and Cash.

"Sorry, I was busy," replied Beth. We were hanging out."

There was an elusive tone to her voice. She wasn't acting like a person talking with dear friends—it was more like she was interacting with people she wanted to be free of.

"I'm Eli," said the boy, "This is Liz and Kara."

River introduced herself and Cash, then watched the interaction between Beth and her friends. There was a relaxed familiarity about them, but it appeared as though Beth was being a little distant. She wondered if this wasn't wishful thinking on her part.

Beth's friends wanted her to go with them. This would be a good time for River to get with the guys alone and try to make her case for a new addition to the group. After several minutes of prodding and convincing, she persuaded Beth to go. After making sure Beth knew they would be waiting for her under the tree, they exchanged a quick hug, then parted ways.

When River and Cash returned to the tree, they found the others hadn't moved at all. River plopped herself down beside Zac. Cash sat down near Finn—who was still lying on the ground with his eyes closed.

On the steps of the courthouse, a band prepared to play. Feedback whistled through the air as the lead singer tapped his mic. The drummer tapped his drumsticks together while counting out loud, "One, two, three...." Music blared out across the open square.

Scanning the area, Cash said, "Well, this is quaint."

"At least the music isn't bad." She laughed. It was so loud. The drum and bass vibrated through the ground.

Finn sat up.

River was dying to share her thoughts with the others. She didn't know how long they had before Beth returned and she wanted to have this discussion without her around.

"What do y'all think of Beth?" she blurted.

"She's nice," replied Cash.

Zac nodded.

"She's young," said Finn. Turning his face toward the band, River watched a sneer sweep across his face, then disappear.

"We were all young like her before," she countered.

Finn shook his head. "Not that kind of young. None of us were ever that kind of young."

His dismissive tone annoyed her. He wasn't even giving Beth a chance. "You say that like she's stupid. She's pretty smart."

"I think you're only seein' things you wanna see," he retorted.

"How so?" she demanded. Frustration was giving way to anger.

Teague interjected, "River, what exactly are you getting at?"

Before she could answer, Finn replied, "She's thinkin' of having Beth come with us."

River shrugged and nodded as she searched their faces for any sign they were open to the idea. She could tell by Zac's expression, he was mulling it over. She knew Cash would agree with her. The only one she had to convince was Teague.

"Why not?" she asked. "She's smart, she's funny, she likes us. Come on, it'll be fun to have her around. Come on, Zac—you agree... you know you do."

Zac grinned. "She is cute."

"You can't go on what he says—he's thinkin' with the wrong head!" shouted Finn.

Zac agreed and laughed. "This is true."

River hit him. "Be serious," she scolded.

"Hold up, hold up," said Cash. "If River is serious, we should at least consider it."

Thank goodness for Cash. She thought.

Finn's voice cut through the air like a car slamming on its brakes. "And now you're just kissin' her ass."

"Hold on," said Teague. "Cash is right, we should consider it." He gestured toward River. "Do you really wanna ask her to come with us?"

River nodded. "I do." *Come on, Teague, please agree with me.*

"What makes you think she would even be interested?" he asked.

This was her chance to plead her case.

"Come on, she's been with us non-stop since we met. I feel a connection with her, and it's obvious she feels one too." She gestured toward Finn. "Even with him being a dick to her, she sticks around."

Finn scoffed. "She's green."

I'm gonna hit him. River leaned forward. "We were all green at one time."

"Greenies get you killed," replied Finn. "Just ask Cyrus and Craig about that… oh, wait! We can't 'cause they're dead!"

"That's not fair! she shouted. "We don't know who started the fire."

"Actually, we do," seethed Finn. "You read the reports. You know, some of the kids in that fire were too young to be seasoned riders. They were green. You also know that no seasoned rider would ever leave a lit candle next to whiskey bottles in a building that run down."

River took a deep breath and opened her mouth, ready to shout.

Teague put his hand up. "All right, we already know Finn's opinion and River's." He looked at Zac and Cash. "What do you two think?"

"Honestly?" asked Zac. "I'm up for it. Finn's right, she is green. But I don't see why she couldn't learn." He shrugged. "It could work."

Thank you, Zac. Thought River.

"I think she's fine," said Cash. "Like Zac said, I think she could learn quick enough."

Yes! That's two. She sighed in relief.

"I guess that leaves you," Finn said to Teague, his voice dripping with venom, "What're your thoughts?"

Teague sighed and rubbed his chin. "I think if River wants to try it, we should consider it. I also think we should consider what Finn is saying. He might have a point."

River and Finn scoffed. They glared at one another.

"We also don't have a clue," continued Teague, "what Beth would think about it all. I mean, we don't even know if she would want to come along." He turned to face Finn. "You should give her a chance. I'm asking you to do that—for me."

Yes! He's on my side! Suck it, Finn! River struggled to contain her joy.

Finn seethed.

"All right, let's take a vote," said Teague. "All those in favor of asking Beth to come along with us, say aye."

"Aye!" shouted River.

"Aye," added Cash.

"Aye," said Zac.

"Aye," said Teague. He poked Finn. "Come on."

Finn shook his head. "Whatever." He pointed menacingly at River. "But if your pet gets in the way, does something stupid, or just fucks things up… you're cleanin' up the mess."

"Woo-hoo!" she shouted. *Now to wait for Beth to return.*

Finn stood up and brushed himself off. "I'm walkin' around," he said. Without another word, he stalked away, vanishing into the crowd.

Chapter Twenty-Two

"ONE, TWO, THREE...." MUSIC BLASTED FROM THE SPEAKERS, startling Finn awake. *Jesus Christ.* He thought. The ground beneath his body reverberated with the base. It rattled his brain. He sat up.

Everywhere he looked, the square teemed with people. Families and couples were milling around. The music was loud. Too loud.

Annoyed, he listened as River began her campaign to add Beth to their group. She appealed to Teague—no doubt convinced if she could get him to agree, Finn would follow. Like some sort of puppy dog.

That was not how it worked. He was not Teague's pet.

River pulled out all the stops. Teague was falling for it. This only compounded Finn's irritation over the whole issue. He knew sticking around this town was a mistake. Now he had this Beth issue to contend with.

Tension rose in his body. Teague was pissing him off with his middle-of-the-road garbage. He fought back the urge to lash out. To yell at him... or worse. Growing angrier by the second, Finn needed to get away from everyone—to be alone. At least as much as possible with all these strangers everywhere. *Christ! Where did they all come from?*

"I'm walkin' around," he said, as he stood up and brushed himself off. It was not an invitation.

Weaving through the crowd, he made his way to the front of the makeshift stage. Men, women, teenagers and children. Every color, shape, age and size. He was searching for the right target. Someone who was both polite and preoccupied. It didn't take long.

A bearded man holding a toddler on his shoulders stood alongside the stage. Swaying with the music, the little boy giggled and kicked his feet. A string of drool glistened in the sun as it dripped down onto the man's head.

Disgusting.

Finn crept up behind the man and reached for his wallet.

"Dada Yook!" the toddler yelled, as he reached into the air. Making its way over the heads of the crowd, a red beach ball bounced toward them. Reaching up to hit the ball away, the dad stepped backward and bumped into Finn.

"Oh, geez!" the dad exclaimed. He smiled at Finn and uttered some inaudible statement—most likely an apology. These people were always apologizing.

The toddler babbled as he bounced up and down. Chubby hand holding tight to a partially dissolved cookie—or something. Finn couldn't tell what it was. Whatever it used to be, it was revolting... and the little boy was smearing it all over the head of his father. *Gross!*

The cookie-thing fell to the ground. The little boy reached down attempting to catch it, nearly falling in the process. With catlike reflexes, the dad quickly reached up to catch him.

During the commotion, Finn quickly swiped the man's wallet and melted back into the crowd, rolling his eyes as he walked away.

Oblivious, the father and son went right back to dancing to the music.

Finn stopped by a trash can and opened the billfold. Fifty dollars. *Nice.* Digging around a little more, he came upon a small photo of the whole, smiling, happy family. The dad, the toddler, a pretty mom and another baby.

Finn twitched his nose and flicked the picture into the trash bin. He pocketed the money, tossed the wallet in the can, and walked back toward his friends—taking the long way around the courthouse.

Circling around the building, his friends came into view. Beth and three other people were there. *Great! She's multiplying.* He thought.

He sat down on the back of a bench and watched. Beth and River were laughing, heads together. If he didn't know better, he would have guessed they were best friends. He couldn't deny there was a connection there. His anger grew. Why now? Why, with everything going on, did they have to run into her?

Making it even worse was the fact that everyone had turned on him. They dismissed his opinion as though it were meaningless. Nothing he could do or say would change their minds. They already decided. Like it or not, he had no say. Beth was coming along.

And Teague... What the hell? Why would he turn on him like that? Did he seriously believe that Finn would do whatever he wanted? Follow him like a mindless stray? River certainly did.

Why were they all being so stupid?

They had things they needed to do. Not only did they have to figure out how they were going to get the ashes, now they had to do it with a greenie under foot. She was going to get in the way. Someone was going to get hurt. Why don't people listen to him? This trip wasn't typical. It wasn't about them—it was about...

Cyrus and Craig. Sorrow diluted his anger. They were gone —forever.

He remembered a conversation he had with Cyrus long ago.

It was during one of their winter stops in Terlingua. Bored, they had ventured into town to one of the local bars. After getting a drink, Finn took a seat outside on the stone patio. A steady stream of tourists moved in and out of the restaurant. Each time the door swung open, country music would blast from inside only to go quiet again when the door slammed shut.

A girl—maybe nineteen—approached him.

"Hi," she said. "I'm Ava." She held out her hand and smiled.

Finn sneered. "And I'm supposed to care?" he snapped.

Ava looked as though he had slapped her. Her face turned red, her smile disappeared. Her shoulders bowed as she turned around and walked away.

Cyrus had been watching the whole exchange. "Hey, Finn, don't take this the wrong way, but, you're an asshole," he said. He leaned back in his chair and chuckled. "Man, you have got one hell of a wall around you."

"I don't like pushy people," replied Finn.

"She didn't seem pushy to me, she seemed kinda nice. She's just a kid trying to meet people. You shot her down pretty hard."

"I said four words to her. If that's enough to shatter her world, then... she should go back home to mama."

Cyrus shook his head. "Damn. That's pretty coldhearted. Now, imagine where you would be right now if Teague had the same aversion to newcomers."

Finn did not respond.

"We all do better when we let people in," said Cyrus. "You can't go through life pushing people away. I know, cause I used to be just like that. I hated everyone. That ain't no way to be. Sometimes it's good to make new friends—look at us. We've been friends now for at least a couple years. Your life is so much better with me in it. Admit it."

Finn snickered.

"Seriously though, man," said Cyrus. "Don't hide behind that wall of yours. You need to learn to trust the people you care about. Sometimes they're right. You might learn something new."

Trust the people you care about. Those words echoed in his head.

Across the grass, his friends were having a good time. He sighed, hopped off the bench and made his way back over to the group, sitting down beside Teague.

Beth smiled at him. "What have you been up to?"

"Nothin'," he replied. "Just a whole lot of nothin'." He pulled out the money and handed it to Teague, who added the new bills to the stack he had stashed in his pocket.

"Wow!" exclaimed Eli as he stared wide-eyed at the money. "That's a lot of cash!"

Finn jeered. "You always this nosey?"

Eli stepped back, looking as though Finn had slapped him.

Barely able to hold back a smirk, Finn stared back at Eli with cold eyes. He had to be tolerant of Beth—he did not have to be nice to anyone else.

Eli looked away. "I'm bored. Let's head home." He said aloud.

No spine. Thought Finn.

Liz stood up and brushed herself off. "Yeah, let's go to my house."

"You coming, Beth?" asked Kara.

For a brief moment, Finn had a glimmer of hope that Beth would leave with her friends and he would never see her again.

Beth tilted her head up and responded. "Nah, I'll stay here."

And just like that, all hope was dashed. She was not going away.

The trio said goodbye to everyone. Finn took great pleasure watching as Eli made every effort to avoid eye contact with him. With a wave, they turned and walked away. He was almost sad to see them leave. Messing with Eli was fun. Given a little more time, he bet he could get the kid to cry.

"You sure you don't want to go with your friends?" asked River.

"Nah, they're just gonna be bored at Liz's house," replied Beth. "Why walk all that way when I can sit here and be bored without all that effort."

The band stopped playing. The crowd dispersed. A little girl ran past, giggling as her dad ran up behind her, scooped her up in his arms and carried her off.

Beth became serious. "How did y'all know?" she asked. "I mean, how did y'all know you wanted to leave, to live the way you do?"

Zac shrugged. "The chance came along, and I went with it."

"All I knew was I didn't want to be home anymore," said Cash. "I left because I figured anyplace had to be better. When the opportunity came up to hop, I took it."

"I didn't really have a home anymore," said Teague. "So, leavin' it wasn't any big deal. Hoppin' trains wasn't anything I ever thought about—it just happened."

"None of us struck out intending to be doin' what we do," he continued, "Each of us left whatever our situations were at the time and let fate do its thing."

"There's really no plan. Do we know where we're gonna be in five years? Ten?" He chuckled. "To be honest, we don't know much about what the future holds for us, and I think that's exactly how we like it."

"What's going on in that head of yours, Beth?" asked River.

Beth sighed. "Don't laugh, okay," she said. "I hate it here. I hate my life—it's all so boring. I want to do something else. I want excitement. I want to live an interesting life. My life isn't awful. My family isn't awful. Nothing bad has ever happened to me. If I stay here, the worst thing that's gonna happen is I'll graduate from high school and go to college." She looked around at the others. A tear streamed down her cheek. "I don't know why, but sometimes I just wanna scream. I don't even know why I'm crying right now." She wiped her face and sniffled.

River put her arm around Beth.

No one said a word.

Finn locked eyes with River and sighed. "It's not crazy," he said. "Wanting to be free is normal—wanting to be caged, is abnormal. You're comin' around to the right state of mind."

River mouthed the words *thank you.* He rolled his eyes. *Yeah, yeah, you win.* Beth was staring at him with a pathetic, questioning look.

Finn sat up straight. His voice grew bolder. "There's a million different ways to live this life—the trick is figuring out which one works best for you."

He continued, "As for us, we like being in control of our own lives. We like being free to think, feel, and act however we want. Some of us are just born to wander. It's in our DNA."

Beth stared, unmoving.

He leaned closer and said in a conspiratorial tone, "You know, there was a time when people didn't live for things like views, followers, shares, up-votes, and likes. They actually lived their lives with close friends and family."

He sat back and said quietly, "They were happier for it too."

No one spoke—he had everyone's attention. Finn knew what they were all waiting for him to say. He couldn't believe he was about to do this.

He took a deep breath. "If you could do anything right now— anything at all, what would that be? Would you walk away and leave behind everything you know? Everything that makes you feel safe and comfortable?"

Beth nodded.

Finn stopped talking and stared at her. *Of course, you would.* He thought. Beside him, Teague was beaming. No doubt proud of himself for getting his pet to behave properly. Anger roiled inside. *We all do better when we let people in.* He sighed and brushed it aside. *Might as well get on with it. They're all waiting.* "So, I guess I should ask you then," he said. "What do you want to do? Do you wanna stay here and live a normal, predictable life? Safe from all the scary things out there. Or do you wanna come with us, be free and live forever?"

He could barely hold back a chuckle over that last bit. In the corner of his eye, Teague struggled to keep a straight face.

Beth blinked as she tried to process what he just said. "Um… wait, what?" she asked.

Laughter erupted.

"Don't be a dick, Finn," River said, as she hit him on the arm.

Finn smiled. "Nah, I'm just bullshittin'. We're not the Lost Boys— we ain't taking you to Neverland."

"Seriously though, no one lives forever. You gotta know there're no guarantees. You could get hurt—or maimed—or even die. It's a risk we all take. If you come with us, you'll see a part of the world most people never see. No more safety net. No more rules. You'll meet some wild, amazing people. It'll be a rush. It'll be downright terrifying. But you'll be more alive and freer than you've ever been."

He paused, then asked, "So, what do you say, Beth? Wanna come along?" He already knew what her answer would be. It was written all over her face.

Eyes wide, Beth slowly nodded her head. "Yeah, I do."

Finn glanced at Teague, then jumped to his feet. "Okay, Beth, let's go."

"Go where?" she asked.

He reached his hand out to her. "Show you the ropes. You can't come along unless you know what you're in for."

Chapter Twenty-Three

WALKING AWAY FROM THE SQUARE, BETH WAS LIGHT AS AIR. SHE could hardly believe what was happening. As if on cue, a train whistle rang out.

At the sound, Teague shouted to the others, "Let's go!"

They ran across the road, ducked into the bushes and emerged near the tracks.

Finn pulled Beth between himself and Teague. "Okay, so most of the time, we'll be catching on the fly," he said.

"That means you're jumping on board while the train's still movin'," explained Teague.

Beth nodded. As weird as it was being in between the two of them, she was happy that Finn was being nice. Whatever made him change his mind, she would not question it.

Finn continued, "We let several cars pass. You don't wanna hop on too close to the engine because odds are that close, an engineer could spot you. You don't wanna get caught. Especially if they have to stop the train because you jumped on."

The train rounded the corner.

Finn raised his arm, gesturing toward the cars. "That's the lead engine. Most times, the train will have two or more engines pulling the cars. The more engines, the better for us because that means it's a heavy, long train."

Teague interjected, "A long train is gonna move slower, which means it'll be easier to get on and off. It's also less likely anyone will ever know we were there."

Finn spoke rapidly, and Teague filled in the blanks. Beth held back a giggle. For the first time since meeting him, she was looking to Teague for clarification. Funny accent and all, he was easier to follow than Finn.

The first engine passed by, then the second and third. Still pointing at the cars, Finn explained, "Now, every type of car has its pros and cons; some are easier to ride than others."

"We prefer boxcars, or grainers," said Teague. "Boxcars for obvious reasons. Grainers because they have what we call a porch at the front and back of each car that you can sit on and enjoy the ride. Gondolas are good too—if they're empty."

"They're filthy though," said Finn. "Fine soot and dust flies out of the cars and blows all over the place. That's why you need a buff or a bandana and some goggles."

"They also have a small, open-frame porch. They're tricky to ride on," added Teague. "Ridin' on these cars exposed in the open is risky."

Beth listened and watched as the cars rolled past. They pointed out each area to grab hold of and explained how to get settled quickly, making room for the others. So much information. She wondered how she would remember everything.

"The easiest place to catch on is at a rail yard. We prefer side-outs," said Teague. "That's a spot where two trains will pass one another. One train will pull off to the side to allow the other to pass. We also like catching on in places where there's a bend in the tracks or at the edge of town. The trains don't stop, but they have to slow down. That gives you time to hop on. It's better to catch on where there are fewer folks who can see you doing it."

"Catching on is the easy part," said Finn, smirking. "Getting off is a little trickier."

"How's that?" asked Beth. She hadn't even considered hopping off.

"Well, for one, if you ain't getting off at a rail yard—the train won't stop to let you off, so you have to jump while it's moving," he replied.

He leaned closer. "It's not as bad as it sounds. You toss your pack off the train and wait for a clear spot and jump. Be sure to bend your knees and roll with it. You'll be fine."

Teague placed his hand on her shoulder. "We can practice the jumping off part easily enough. Don't stress about it."

Watching the rear engines pass, Beth's mind was whirling with all the information they just dumped on her.

"Any questions?" asked Teague.

"No, uh, yeah, uh, lots actually. I can't think of any," she replied.

He smiled. "Well, speak up when they come to mind." He stood up, hit Finn on the shoulder with the back of his hand, and said, "Come on."

Back on the street, River walked up alongside her and asked, "So, you're seriously gonna come with us?"

"Yes," answered Beth. "That is, if y'all are serious about wanting me to come along."

River giggled and said playfully, "Aw, she's adorable. I wanna keep her." She stopped walking, causing everyone else to pause in their tracks. "All those in favor of Beth coming along with us, say aye," she said.

"Aye" was the response from nearly everyone. It was official—Beth was now one of them. River gave her a hug. Beth's heart soared.

"So, when are you, I mean, *we* leaving?" she asked.

"Good question," replied River. "Hey Finn, Teague, when are we leaving?"

Teague spun around and, walking backward, said, "Tomorrow?" as he shrugged and glanced at Finn, who nodded in response.

Finn pulled his phone from his pocket. "I gotta find out when the next train heading to Austin is passing through. I'll do that now." He tapped away on his phone.

"What's he doing?" asked Beth.

"He's posting a message," replied River. "See, there's a schedule of

166 • N.L. MCLAUGHLIN

all the trains, what they're hauling, where they're going, and when. Let's just say this info isn't public knowledge. For obvious reasons." She grinned. "In some places, riders will pass this info along face to face. We have a friend, Porter, who fills us in."

Beth stopped walking and stared at River. "Porter?" she asked.

"Um, yeah," replied River. "No one knows much about him or how he knows the things he does. A while back, we asked him what we should call him, and he told us to call him Porter. I don't think that's his real name. Whoever he is, wherever he is, he has access to all the train times, destinations and what they're carrying. He also gives us a heads-up when a stakeout is happening—so we know to avoid the area and not get busted."

"So, he helps you out? she asked River. "Think he used to be a rider?"

"Maybe." replied River. "He does have a lot of knowledge about camps and squats."

"Camps?" asked Beth.

"It's a spot where lots of riders will gather," said River. "They're always moving—never in the same place, to avoid being raided."

"Wow. I had no idea," said Beth. "It's like there's a whole other world that exists just outside of the one I've been living in."

"Oh, Beth, there is so much more for you to learn," said River. "Just wait. You're gonna have the adventure of a lifetime."

As the sun set, it was time to head back to Beth's house to collect their gear and find a place to sleep for the night.

By the time they arrived at the cozy brick house, it was dark. Beth's mom had parked her red sedan in the driveway, and the lights were on in the kitchen. Through the windows, she could see her mom moving around. Dancing to music that Beth could not hear.

Beth's mom was a kind woman. Rarely did she lose her temper. She always told Beth that she preferred to put her energy into being positive. Making others happy. This was something Alicia was very good at.

Crouched outside, Beth watched her mom move about the kitchen. A swell of childhood memories flooded her mind. The nights they danced together, singing and laughing to some old music from her mom's youth. Learning to make cookies. Her mom patiently watching as Beth struggled to measure just enough flour for the dough. Alicia never scolded her when she got it wrong, she simply put the flour back and encouraged Beth to do it again.

Winter afternoons sitting at the table sharing a cup of cocoa. Her mom always made sure she had plenty of whipped cream and marshmallows on hand—Beth liked to fill her mug with both.

Holiday meals. Birthday cakes. Sadness bubbled up around the edges of her memories. She was scared that if she were to stand face to face with her mom, at that moment, she would cry—and possibly change her mind.

Beth didn't want that to happen; she wanted to stay with her friends. Quietly, she waited as the others snuck into the backyard, gathered their packs from behind the shed, then stealthily walked away from the house.

With each step, Beth's mood lightened. The urge to cry subsided. No more tug of guilt over leaving. No more childhood memories. Joking with one another and playing around, they walked through the neighborhood and across the tracks.

This neighborhood differed from Beth's. The houses were much smaller, older and not nearly as well maintained. With Beth as their guide, they walked until they came to a small home with tan siding, white trim and a little front porch. All the windows were boarded-up. Perfect.

On the back porch, Zac pried the board off one window and using his elbow, broke the glass. Reaching in, he unlocked the latch.

From outside, Beth watched as the beam of his flashlight slowly disappeared around a corner. There was a click at the back door, then it swung open.

"Welcome to our evening accommodations," said Zac, with a flourish.

While the others made themselves comfortable, he and Finn went back outside and replaced the board to block the window.

Cash and River pulled small, solar-powered lanterns from their packs and turned them on. The lamps filled the room with cool light. Cash rolled a joint and once again, the flask of moonshine made an appearance.

River handed Beth the flask. "Are you excited about leaving with us tomorrow?"

Beth nodded and looked at the bottle in her hand. *This stuff again.* She thought. "Honestly, I'm a little scared I'm gonna mess up getting on the train," she replied.

"Try not to overthink it," said River. "It's not as hard as they made it sound."

Beth took a swig and winced as she swallowed; the liquid burned the back of her throat. Outside, a train whistle blew.

"Come on," said Finn, as he jumped to his feet.

"What?" she asked.

"No better way to get over your fear, than a trial run."

Beth looked around at everyone and realized they too were standing up.

Next thing she knew, she was running out the back door, around the house, and down the street toward the tracks. The whistle called out. The train was getting closer. They picked up their pace, arriving at the edge of the tracks at the same moment the train roared past. The deafening rumble of the wheels made it impossible to hear anything that was being said. A metallic scent wafted on the breeze created by the cars as they rolled by.

"All right, Beth. See that grainer?" Finn pointed to a grain car.

Beth struggled to read his lips. She could hardly hear. The sound of blood pumping through her head was louder than the train. She nodded; her mouth was so dry she couldn't speak. Her heart raced inside her chest.

"That's the one," he said to her. "As soon as it comes by, we're gonna run alongside of it and hop on. Got it?"

Once again, she nodded. *Oh, god! Oh, God! Oh, God!* She thought.

The car came close. As it passed, they ran alongside. She was doing it! She was running and holding her own! Best of all, she was keeping pace with the others. The air was heavy with the smell of grease mixed with metal. It reminded her of the garage her uncle owned.

Zac and Cash reached out and hoisted themselves up on one car while River pulled herself up on the other. Teague hopped up next to River and leaned out, holding his hand to Beth. Heart pounding, she grabbed hold, and he pulled her off her feet.

With her free hand, she took hold of the cold, metal handle and pulled herself up. Teague's arm around her waist the whole time. Helping her. She lifted her legs and swung them around, landing on the metal floor. The train jerked and swayed. She looked over to see Finn appear beside her.

I did it! I did it! I did it! She thought.

Her heart raced—her whole body trembled.

"That's the adrenaline," said Finn, leaning close. "It'll calm down in a minute; just relax."

Beth breathed in deeply. She couldn't believe she actually just did that. It wasn't so hard. Sure, it was scary at first, but it wasn't difficult. Filled with pride, she stuck her arm out from between the cars and let it glide along the air current.

The train whistle blew one more time, and everyone stood up. Looking up at them, Beth asked, "What are you doing?"

Finn smirked and said, "This is our stop."

"What?" asked Beth, panic welled up inside her once again.

"This is where we hop off," he said deliberately. "I told ya, it's a practice run."

The blood pounded in her head again. Her stomach was in knots. She struggled to catch her breath. *This must be what it feels like to hyperventilate.*

The train lurched as it slowed to pass through the station. Rolling past the platform, Beth watched as the graffiti wall scrolled by.

Without warning, Cash hopped off, followed by Zac. Beth leaned over to see where they landed.

Finn's voice rang out beside her, "Just remember to bend your knees." He stood on the rail and launched himself to the ground. Beth watched as he rolled and came to a stop. It was her turn now. Teague nodded in encouragement.

She took a deep breath, stepped up on the rail, and glanced back at River and Teague. They stood still and nodded. She turned, faced outward, and leaped forward.

She was flying—untethered, like a bird. Her body was light as air. Her hair flowed in the breeze.

A sudden jolt knocked her back to reality as her feet hit the ground. The impact of the shock rang up through her body. Legs buckling beneath her, she reached out—arms flailing, finding no purchase.

Clawing at the air, unable to control herself, Beth tumbled on the gravel. She came to a stop on her bottom, legs splayed before her. Her ears were ringing. Her head was swimming. It took a moment for her to realize that the muffled sound all around her, was her friends— laughing. They were all standing around her.

River kneeled down. "Oh, Beth. That was the most ungraceful landing I have ever seen anyone make. Are you okay?" she asked, fighting back giggles.

Beth nodded, still a little stunned. The ringing subsided. She wondered whether she broke something—besides her pride.

They sat with her on the ground for a while as she regained her composure. Their teasing didn't offend Beth—she had been with them enough over the past couple of days to know that this was how they treated one another all the time. In fact, the teasing meant they already considered her one of them. This made it more tolerable.

"So, Beth," said Teague. "You made your first hop on and off. How'd it feel?"

Beth rubbed her head. "I think I need to work on my landings a little more."

This caused a round of laughter from everyone.

"Ready to head back?" he asked.

Beth nodded, stood up, and brushed herself off. Her legs trembled. She wondered if she could make it back.

Zac bent down in front of her. "Hop on," he said.

Thankful for the help, Beth climbed on his back, wrapping her legs around his waist and arms around his neck. He carried her all the way to the little, tan house.

They went over some tips for Beth to make hopping on and off a little less hazardous. For her, the fact that she didn't break anything this first time around made her feel much less nervous about it all.

It was near midnight when they turned their lanterns off and curled up to sleep for the night.

In the darkness, River whispered to Beth, "I'm glad you're coming with us."

"Me too."

River sighed sleepily. "I'm happy. I finally have a sister to travel with again." She rolled over on her side and closed her eyes to sleep.

Chapter Twenty-Four

RAYS OF LIGHT POKED THROUGH THE GAPS BETWEEN THE BOARDS AND windows, piercing the darkness like dozens of glowing blades. Beth rubbed her eyes, yawned, and sat up. Across the room, Finn sat against the dirty wall, using a splinter of sunlight to read a tattered paperback. He glanced up and nodded at her.

Beth stretched. Her neck and shoulders were stiff. Standing up, her legs cried out in pain—mostly her left knee. She flexed it back and forth until the ache subsided, then walked over to sit beside Finn. As soon as her bottom hit the floor, she realized how sore it was. The hop last night had taken its toll on her body. The others told her it would get easier—she hoped that would be sooner rather than later.

"So, is this how it's gonna be?" she asked. "You and me, the two early birds."

Finn glanced back at her. "We'll see if you're still up at the crack of dawn in a few weeks," he replied, then turned his focus back to his book leaving Beth to her own thoughts.

Curious about the title, she leaned forward and attempted a stealth peek. The faded cover was impossible to read. She leaned closer, squinting her eyes.

Finn cleared his throat.

Peering up, her eyes met his. His face wore a half smirk.

"I-I was just trying to see what…"

He closed the book and handed it to her.

"Oh! No need to stop. I'm sorry. I didn't want to interrupt."

He pushed the book at her. "Here, you can read it. You might like it. It's about hitting the road."

Teague's sleepy voice echoed out from the dusty darkness. "Go ahead, Beth, take it. He's read it enough times that he can probably recite it word for word by now."

"This is true," chuckled Finn.

Beth took the book and rolled it over in her hand. Ragged along the edges, it had seen better days. A tattered photo strip, like the ones you get from a carnival, was wedged between two pages. Four images of a much younger Finn and Teague played out before her. Smiling wide, they goofed around in front of the camera, making silly faces, kissing in the final one.

She handed the photo strip to Finn.

He shook his head. "That stays with the book. Just leave it there."

Beth nodded and placed it back between the pages like a book-mark. She fanned the pages—underlined passages littered the book. "Thanks! I can't wait to read it," she said.

Teague moved closer. "What's the story with the train?"

Finn pulled out his phone. "Looks like Porter responded. The next train out for us will be at 8 o'clock tonight."

This news came as a relief for Beth, she wasn't ready to go running off just yet. Her body was still very sore. She also had to figure out what to pack. It was good to know she had the entire day to take care of all that she needed to before they left. Thinking of packing, she wondered how much she could fit into her backpack.

From his corner across the room, Cash sat up, stretched, and yawned. "Anybody hungry?" he asked. "'Cause I'm starving."

He shoved Zac, waking him up. Zac responded by sitting up and pushing him back. Causing Cash to slam against the wall with a thud.

Beth giggled. She enjoyed watching the antics of those two. Cash always with the witty retorts and Zac right there ready to toss him

around like a toy. It didn't seem harmful in any way—all of it was
playful. She found them both endearing. This whole band of misfits
had stolen her heart.

River sat up, gazed around the room, then lay back down.

"Cool!" said Cash. "Now that sleeping beauty is up, can we go get
something to eat?"

River responded with a single finger thrust high in the air.

Not long after, they packed up and made the walk back to Beth's
house.

Upon entering, Beth was ill prepared for the tide of emotions that
washed over her. The house was empty—her parents had already left
for work. She was thankful for this, the last thing she needed was to
run into her mom or dad. All she wanted to do was to get her things
and leave.

Passing by the mantle with all the photos, she couldn't stop staring.
Every day of her life, she walked past these images—never giving
them a second thought. This time, however, her heart ached.

She entered her bedroom and sat down on the bed. Looking around,
she realized that she no longer had any connection to the items that
surrounded her—such an odd sensation considering that, two days ago,
this was her entire world. How quickly things change.

What, out of all this stuff surrounding her, did she need? She
sighed.

River entered the room and sat down beside her. "I figured I would
come to help you pack," she said.

Beth didn't say it, but she appreciated the help. She didn't think she
could dig through everything and not break down. River's presence
made it easier.

The two picked through Beth's belongings as she chose the things
she would need and a few precious keepsakes to bring along. She
picked up her laptop and went to place it in her backpack.

River stopped her. "Um, that's not gonna survive one jump from a train. It's best to leave it behind. Every town has a library, and every library has computers. No need to haul your own anymore."

Beth nodded, then shoved the laptop aside. Now came the part she dreaded the most. Saying goodbye.

She sat down at her desk and wrote a short note to her parents.

Dear Mom and Dad,

I'm sitting here trying to find the right words to tell you what I need to say. I suppose just being honest would be best.

I'm leaving today. Please don't look for me, don't call the police and report me. Understand this is what I want, and if you do drag me back, I will only leave again. I'm not leaving because of anything you or anyone has done. So please, just let me go.

One day I'll come back and visit, and I'll tell you all about my adventures.

I love you both and hope you find happiness. I'm on a journey to find mine.

Goodbye,
Beth

She got to her feet and tucked the chair under her desk one last time. Such an odd sensation. This would be the last time she tucked that chair in—the last time she sat at this desk.

From the pin board, River pulled down the photo of Kara, Liz and Eli. She handed it to Beth. "You're gonna want to keep this."

Beth attempted a smile as she placed the picture in a pocket of her backpack. It just occurred to her that she had completely forgotten about Eli. He would be so angry with her—she didn't even take the time to say goodbye face to face.

It was time to get rid of that last connection to her old world—her phone. River had informed her that she could not keep her phone as that would be an easy way for her family or police to locate and track her. They would purchase a new one before they headed out.

Turning it on, Beth wiped it clean of contacts, history and apps. She pulled out the memory card and placed it in her pocket, then set the phone down on top of the letter.

Before closing the door, Beth stopped and gave her bedroom one last look. Her comfy bed where she lay, snuggled up at night reading, imagining the life she would one day lead. The countless nights texting with Eli. The closet—so stuffed with items, the door could no longer close. Her army of stuffed animals that stood sentinel high on the shelf circling her room. She reached up to pick out a bear. A deep sorrow overwhelmed her. Lips trembling, tears welling up in her eyes, she pulled her hand back and instead clicked off the light.

She was saying goodbye to her old life and beginning something new. Excited and melancholy, she turned around and walked down the hall to where the others waited.

Zac came close, looked her in the eyes and asked, "You sure you wanna do this?"

"Yes," she replied. "Absolutely." But she wasn't sure at that moment.

He smiled, turned, and headed toward the front door.

As she moved to follow, Finn grabbed hold of her arm, stopping her in her tracks. He picked up the family photo from the mantle. Taking the picture out of the frame, he handed it to her.

"Last chance. You can stay here, go to college, and live a predictable, boring and safe life," he said. His face lacked his usual look of disdain—his voice had no sarcasm. It was almost as though he was feeling her sadness.

She took the photo and smiled half-heartedly, then tucked it away in her backpack.

"Let's go," she said, as she walked to the front door and waited for the others.

Choking back tears, she scanned the living room. The fireplace where she and Tomas spent cold winter nights snuggled up in front of a warm fire. The corner of the room where the Christmas tree stood every year. Her dad's favorite chair—all the Sunday mornings sitting on his lap, watching his car shows. Her mom's knitting basket, filled to the brim with colorful yarns. A tear escaped and ran down her cheek. Using her palm, she wiped it away. She closed the front door and stepped off the front stoop.

Beth looked out at the neighborhood. So many memories. Her pink bike with the rainbow tassels—the one that made her feel like a princess every time she rode it. Roller blading with Tomas. Snow ball fights. The old swing in the front yard stood alone and still. She walked up to it and pushed it twice, then let it swing silent and empty as she turned and walked away.

Chapter Twenty-Five

A PANG OF REGRET CREPT OVER RIVER AS SHE STOOD IN FRONT OF THE cozy brick home, watching Beth say goodbye to her old life. For the first time since meeting her, River realized how different they were. Never having known her mother, River had no frame of reference to understand how Beth was feeling. She never had the kind of home Beth was leaving behind. *Is this a mistake?* She wondered.

Beside her stood Zac. Based on the expression on his face, he could relate well to Beth's current state of emotions. His face was soft, his eyes sympathetic. A pale, red hue emanated across his forehead, nose and cheeks. He stood there, jaw clenched, hood pulled up over his head, hands buried deep in his pockets.

A few feet away, on the sidewalk, Cash shuffled his feet. Eyes darting up and down the street, he was restless—he was ready to get moving. They locked eyes; he gave her a sharp nod that said, *come on.*

She nodded.

Down the street, already four houses away, Finn and Teague strolled along. In their own little world. They weren't waiting—they never did. She watched as Finn laughed and did something that caused Teague to reach out and shove his head. Sometimes it was hard not to be a little envious of their relationship.

Beth pushed the swing one final time, then walked away.

Their train was not coming through until later that evening, so they had several hours to waste. After ditching their gear by the tracks, they split up into two groups. Cash, River and Beth went to the pawnshop. It was time to get Beth a new phone.

The shop smelled of old things. A thin layer of dust rested on top of the items on the shelves. Looking through the glass countertop, it was striking how many phones there were. So many options—some were still in their original sealed packaging. She couldn't help but wonder why someone would pawn a new phone. Emergency? Drugs?

Strolling down the aisle, the sheer volume of guitars hanging along the wall struck her as overkill. Stacked three rows high, they ran the entire length of the shop. Every model, every style, every color. *How many people play guitar around here?*

TVs, laptops, and gaming consoles cluttered the aisles. How many hours had people spent staring at these? How much time wasted?

Cash was busy haggling with the man behind the counter. River watched as he poured on the charm. She had seen this play out many times before. He was one of the rare people who could mask his thoughts and emotions quite well. He knew which words, facial expressions and body movements to use so people would let down their guard. If he ever wanted to stop riding, he could take Hollywood by storm.

The man caved and agreed to a lower price—no real surprise there. They quickly paid and left the shop, taking up a shady resting spot on the courthouse lawn.

Holding the phone in her hand, Beth asked, "So what do I do for service?"

"Same as us. You use the local, free Wi-Fi," replied Cash.

He took the phone from her and explained, "Everywhere you go, cities and towns have free Wi-Fi available to everyone. If they don't have it in public like this, you can go to any library, coffee shop or public building, and they'll have it there. It's everywhere, and it's free." He slid his finger down the screen, the little Wi-Fi icon became visible. With one tap, the symbol lit up. "All you got to worry about is keeping it charged, which is something we haven't mastered yet." He winked and handed the phone back to her. "Go ahead."

"What do you do if you end up somewhere that doesn't have any Wi-Fi?" she asked.

This time River replied, "We keep at least two of our phones set up with prepaid service. When that's used up, we buy more when we can. We only use that when it's necessary. You know, for maps and communication. It's not something we need to do often. Over time, you're gonna see that you don't need that thing for much other than maps and finding out specific info."

Beth nodded and turned her attention back to her new gadget.

It was seven o'clock when they met the others at the tracks to wait for their train.

The setting sun cast an orange glow. The smell of damp earth permeated the air. On the road, cars rolled by in a seemingly never-ending stream.

"How do you know if your friend is right or not?" asked Beth.

"Right or not about what?" asked River.

"About the trains and the schedule. Has he ever been wrong?"

"Nah, he's never wrong," she responded.

Beth was fidgety. She fiddled with the drawstring of her hoodie. The first hop was always the most nerve-racking. River decided that perhaps it would a good time to go over the routine with Beth once more. As she talked, Beth's fidgeting subsided.

The train whistle blasted, signaling its arrival into town.

This was it.

As the engines came into view, they crouched low waiting for them to roll past. River counted the cars, waiting for the right moment. Earlier, Finn had informed everyone that this train had several empty boxcars. At least Beth's first ride would be a comfortable one. The whistle blew once more—it was time. A boxcar came into view. The giant door stood ajar, which meant it was empty inside.

Cash and Finn glanced at each other and grinned.

"You thinkin' what I'm thinkin'?" asked Finn.

"Right there with ya brother," replied Cash.

They dashed for the boxcar.

The door was open just enough to get a firm hold and provide leverage. Finn grabbed the lip of the door with both hands and pressed his legs against the door frame. Opposite him, Cash did the same.

Using their bodies and all their strength, they applied every bit of pressure they could muster. Pushing and straining their legs, the door slowly gave way, sliding open to reveal a spacious empty room. After tossing their packs inside, they reached out to help the others.

First River, then Zac—not a single issue so far.

It was time for Beth. River leaned out the door and stood ready to help. Still holding onto the ladder, Cash reached out and grabbed hold of Beth's hand. Like a rag doll, he swung her around through the opening.

She landed safely in River's waiting arms.

A moment later, Teague was on board.

They were on their way.

Chapter Twenty-Six

BETH'S HEART RACED. BREATHING HEAVILY, SHE FEARED SHE WOULD pass out. Adrenaline raged through her body. She did it! She hopped a train and was on her way to points unknown. Beneath her feet, the wood floor creaked and moaned as the car buckled and swayed. A trace odor of oil and dirt permeated the air. Exhilaration gave way to nausea as her body struggled to adjust to all the stress of the past few minutes. Hand clasped over her mouth, she ran to the door and leaned out. A strong arm wrapped around her waist, holding her securely in place. She glanced up—it was Zac. She looked at him apologetically, then poked her head out of the car and threw up. Thank goodness he was on the other side of her.

Weak and trembling, she wiped her mouth with the back of her hand. Zac held her upright. She leaned against him, thankful for the support.

River was right there with a damp cloth that smelled of clean laundry soap. Like home. Trembling, she wiped her face, hands and the back of her neck. She was feeling much better.

Around the car, everyone was staring at her—Finn smirking while the others wore various looks of concern. She mouthed the words *thank you* to Zac and sat down on the floor.

Even though she wasn't feeling great, she was still very excited—she didn't want to miss anything. She scooted closer to the open door. The cool, evening wind blew through her hair. Her heart beat at a normal pace. She breathed in.

River sat next to her. "Looks like you're on your way."

Beth nodded.

The trees rolled by at a rapid pace; it was impossible to make out any particular one, instead they all blended together—the tops resembled a bundle of paint brushes standing upright in a jar.

A rush of warmth flooded up from deep inside her belly. As if a dam had burst open, emotions came rushing forth—holding back tears, she forced herself to think of something pleasant. Bad idea. The first memory her mind grabbed hold of was one of her mom, smiling at her across the table on a cold winter's day. *No, no, no! Not that one!* She blinked to clear her eyes. *Okay, Beth, think of something else. Think of something that will not make you cry.* She thought.

River wrapped her arm around her shoulder and squeezed. Beth leaned against her and sighed.

"All right, enough of this," Finn said, as he stood up and brushed his hands off on his thighs.

Beth watched, wondering what he was up to.

He reached out the door and climbed onto the ladder. Turning around, he peered down at her, grinning; he slipped out of sight.

Beth leaned forward and glanced out to the side. He wasn't there. Looking up, she glimpsed his boots disappear over the edge of the roof. Apprehension bubbled up inside her.

Teague got to his feet. He brushed himself off and climbed out of the car onto the ladder. Next followed Zac, then Cash. Beth wasn't sure what to make of this or even what to do. She peeked out—they were nowhere in sight. *I hope they don't think I'm gonna climb out there.*

River stepped out on the ladder and leaned back inside, extending her hand.

The thought of climbing out onto that ladder while the train was moving terrified Beth. *Nope! Ain't gonna happen.* She shook her head.

River smiled. "Come on," she mouthed.

Nope, nope nope. Beth didn't move—she couldn't.

River sighed and stretched her hand closer.

Beth hesitated. River signaled once again for her to take her hand —this time a little more insistent. Shaking with fear, Beth reached out. River's hand clasped tightly around her wrist.

Oh god! What am I doing?

Next thing she knew, Beth was standing on the ladder. Petrified, she pressed her body against the metal rungs as the landscape whizzed by at a dizzying pace.

I'm gonna die!

Refusing to look out, clinging tightly to the cold metal, Beth struggled to slow her racing heart. River pressed up against her; pinning her in place. This small gesture made her feel more secure.

"You're okay," said River.

Beth nodded, unable to catch her breath. But she wasn't okay. Who could be okay hanging on the outside of a moving train? She felt like a bug stuck against the windshield of the car as it drove along the highway. Thinking about this made her giggle nervously.

River stared down at her. The questioning look on her face only made Beth chuckle more.

"You gonna be all right?" she asked.

Beth collected herself and nodded. "I'm good." *Yep, perfectly fine clinging to the outside of a moving train. It's all perfectly normal.*

"Just hold on and don't worry," said River. "You're not gonna fall. I won't let that happen. Stay calm and climb." She pointed up. On the roof, looking down at them, was Teague—smiling.

River nodded. "Go ahead, just take it one rung at a time."

Terrified, Beth held her breath and took the first step. As promised, River was right there—holding her in place. She exhaled, then took a deep breath, swallowed hard, and continued to climb.

At the top of the car, Teague reached his arm down and they locked arms.

His grip was firm and reassuring. With little effort, he pulled her up over the lip and onto the roof. Wrapping his arm around her, he steadied her and helped her sit down. Her whole body trembled. Beth didn't know how much more of this she could take.

A moment later, River came over the lip and onto the roof.

The back-and-forth swaying of the car had a calming effect. Beth relaxed and let her body rock from side to side. Overhead, the stars shone bright against the black of the night sky. They dazzled like gemstones. She reached into the air as though she could touch one. So beautiful.

Flashing an impish grin, Finn stood up. The others did the same. Once again, Teague held his hand out for her. She stared at it as though it was a foreign thing. *Nope.* She was not standing up.

River's voice rang out over the noise, "Come on, Beth. Stand up."

Beth sighed, she took hold of Teague's hand, and allowed him to pull her to her feet. The train rocked back and forth. Her long hair whipped and twisted all around her face as if she were standing in a wind tunnel. Terrified, her heart pounded. She feared she might pass out. Beth stood stiffly—holding on to Teague with a death grip, too frightened to let go.

River gently took hold of her left hand. She leaned closer to Beth. "It's okay, we got ya." She winked. "Relax, bend your knees a little, and roll with it. Like a skateboard or surfing."

Beth took a deep breath and tried to relax. This was not at all like skateboarding. The pitch and sway of the train made her feel as though she could fall overboard at any moment. Allowing her body to sway with the movement, she relaxed—her confidence grew. Standing in place, she slowly released her grip on their hands.

There she stood, on the top of the train. Leaning into the wind, she was nervous, but exhilarated. She could not believe she was doing this.

In front of her, the others faced forward into the wind. They raised their arms high, allowing the air to rush past them. Beth slowly raised her arms. The cool night air blowing past her body was unlike anything she had ever experienced in her life before. She was free—completely, utterly free.

"Woooooo!" came a loud cry from Finn, followed by various calls from all the others. Beth took a deep breath and, with her hands extended into the air, cried out.

"How's it feel?" asked River.

"It's amazing!" shouted Beth.

The train jerked. Beth lost both her balance and her confidence— she scrambled to sit down. Unable to find anything to grab hold of, she crossed her legs and held tight to her knees. Around her, the others had no issues. She watched as they stood, faces toward the sky, arms out, like birds of prey soaring on the wind. She pulled out her phone and snapped a picture. Switching over to record mode, she zoomed in on Finn, panning out to catch as much of the dark sky ahead of him as she could. Her friends were gonna be so impressed when they saw this image. None of them had ever posted anything as cool as this. She bet they would be so jealous.

After several minutes, River and the others sat beside her. Finn walked past to the end of the car.

She studied him, trying to figure out what he was doing. It took her a moment to realize that he was relieving himself. She blushed and glanced away.

In the corner of her eye, she glimpsed River laughing. "At least he's doing it downwind," she said.

Beth chuckled and shook her head.

They lay down on the roof in a circle with heads touching. Once again, Beth pulled out her phone and turned on the video. Flashing a peace sign, she recorded a selfie of the group.

"You know," chided Finn, "if you put that thing away, you might actually see more."

Beth shrugged. "I wanna make sure I catalog everything. I don't want to miss any of it."

Finn scoffed. "You're so busy trying to make sure you aren't missing anything that you're gonna miss a lot. Put the phone away."

Beth rolled her eyes as she turned off the camera and stuffed the phone inside her pocket.

She lay there, staring up at the sky. The metal from the boxcar

188 • N.L. MCLAUGHLIN

pressed hard and cold against her back. The deep rumble of the wheels reverberated throughout her body.

"Beth, do you know your constellations?" asked Cash.

"Some, but not many," she replied. "I know that's the big dipper, right?"

"Yep," he replied.

Feeling more confident, she continued, "So, this is Ursa Major, the large bear."

"Yes," responded everyone.

"And that, is Orion's belt, so that," Beth made a sweeping motion with her arm, "should be Orion, right?" she said smiling.

Another "yes," from everyone.

"Hmm," Beth said, as she scanned the sky. "Like I said, I only know a few. I think those are all the ones I can see."

Pointing up, Zac said, "That right there is Scorpius." Beth moved her gaze over to see what he was pointing at. "You can spot it easiest by locating Antares. That's the brightest star right there. You see it?"

She nodded and said, "Yes."

"Antares is the heart of Scorpius. To the right of that are the five stars that make up the head." He waved his hand, showing their location. Waving his hand in the opposite direction, he said, "Down below here is the tail. See that?"

People who could spy the constellations always impressed Beth. It was not something she could do herself.

River chimed in, "See Ursa Minor, Beth?"

"I do," she replied.

"Here's one for ya," said Finn, pointing at the sky. "Right there to the left of Scorpius's tail, the weird little cluster that kinda looks like a triangle. See it?" He paused for the others to make out where he was pointing.

"I see it!" shouted Beth.

"That's Sagittarius. He's pointing his bow at Scorpius."

Finn continued, "His name is Chiron—the centaur. The story goes that one day, he was struck by one of Hercules' arrows that was dipped in the poison of Hydra. Hydra's poison killed mortals. For an immortal, though, it would just make a wound that could never heal. One that would hurt like hell, forever. Having no real future, he offered himself as a substitute for Prometheus."

"You know the story of Prometheus, right?" he asked Beth.

"Wasn't he the one Zeus punished for giving fire to man?"

"Yep," replied Finn. "They tied him to a rock where every day Zeus' eagle would come and eat out his liver. Every night it would grow back, only to be eaten again the following day. When Zeus sentenced him, he agreed—at the request of Hercules, to grant one option for a pardon. If a suitable substitute for Prometheus, meaning an immortal, were ever to offer to take his place, then and only then would he be able to go free. Keep in mind, doing this meant that the immortal was giving up his or her immortality, and they would die."

Beth lay there listening. She hadn't realized how distinctly masculine Finn's voice was before—so deep and gravely. It sounded as though it belonged to a much older, larger man. His cadence passed seamlessly between a Texas drawl and no dialect at all. It was rather pleasant to listen to.

Finn continued, "Anyway, back to Chiron. Knowing he was looking at an eternity of horrible pain, he offered himself up as a substitute for Prometheus. That way he could die and end his suffering, and Prometheus would be free. He went to Tartarus and took his place on the rock where he eventually died."

"To recognize his act of selflessness, Zeus placed Chiron in the stars as Sagittarius."

Beth stared up at the constellation. It was hard not to feel awe over such an amazing story of compassion and bravery. She would have to make it a point to read some of the old Greek tales one of these days.

"Let me just say," said Cash, "I love all of you, but I would never, ever volunteer to have my liver eaten out for any of you. I'm sorry."

"Yeah, I'd have to think about that one too," chuckled Zac.

"Y'all are weak." River said, as she laughed.

"I'd do it," whispered Finn. "That is, if it was Teague, who was tied to the rock. The rest of y'all could stay tied up. I'd come by and visit, maybe bring water, but I'd leave ya there to suffer the consequences of your idiotic actions."

"Wow," teased River. "You just said one of the most romantic things I've ever heard you say, then a second later," she snapped her fingers. "You became a dick again."

"That's my Finn," laughed Teague.

Beth giggled. She realized that being there, in that moment, there was nowhere else she wanted to be. Nothing else she would rather be doing. No other people she would rather be with. She lay there and breathed it all in.

When it was time to climb back inside, one by one, they crawled over the lip down the ladder, and inside. It wasn't so bad the second time.

Teague opened the map on his phone to see their location. He announced that they were about halfway to Austin.

Excitement rose inside Beth. She could not wait to see the city.

Beside Teague sat Finn, biting his nails. He looked anxious. He didn't seem that way earlier. In fact, Beth realized that his anxiety seemed to peak when Teague mentioned how close they were to Austin. She wondered what could be so worrying to someone like him.

Teague whispered something to him. Finn responded with a nod, then they lay down to rest.

In the corner, Zac put on his headphones, pulled his hood over his head and closed his eyes, while Cash lay prone on the floor, resting his head against his pack.

At the other end of the car, Beth and River stayed up and chatted in the corner. Beth was far too excited to do any sleeping, so she was happy to have company to pass the time.

Chapter Twenty-Seven

BLEEP, BLEEP, BLEEP. THE ALARM ECHOED AROUND THE BOXCAR, bouncing on the metal walls—such an annoying sound. Teague opened the map to see where they were. Right on time, they were outside of Austin. Beside him, Finn lay already awake. Teague wondered whether he even slept. He worried about Finn. The lack of sleep was showing—dark circles formed under his eyes and he wouldn't stop biting his nails.

He expected Finn to struggle with being back in Austin, but he had hoped that enough time had passed that it wouldn't be so difficult. Apparently, this was not the case.

Beth and River were sitting by the open door, staring outside. Wanting to see the city lights again, he convinced Finn to come with him and sit with the girls.

Tall buildings, aglow with bright lights, lit up the night sky. So bright—so alive with activity. The Colorado River loomed large up ahead, with its banks of soft sand.

A quick jolt jerked them about as the train crossed over the bridge that spanned the river. Gazing out across the water, the familiar sight of the Lamar Street Bridge came into view with its small concrete arches one after another.

Teague's heart raced. This was where it all began—so many years ago. The memory of that meeting came surging back to him. They were so young, Finn was so broken. Remembering that night, all Teague wanted to do was find a secluded place to sleep. To hide from the world. He was lonely and empty. Being on his own for so long, with no one to distract him from his darkest thoughts, had taken its toll. That night, when he lay his head against his pack, he closed his eyes and imagined the various ways he could best put an end to all the loneliness. Then, as if on cue, this skinny, frightened kid crawled up into his hiding place. Being the person he was, Teague's mind immediately switched over to caring for this wretch before him. He hadn't stopped worrying about Finn since.

Trying to glimpse the exact arch where they met, he leaned forward. The cool breeze carried the scent of the river below. He glanced over at Finn. Staring out over the water, biting his nails, his mind was elsewhere. Teague gently took hold of his hand. Finn relaxed. They sat in silence, fingers entwined as the train rode past the little arch where they met on that fateful day.

A few minutes later, they were already at the south end of the city. Behind them, the lights receded as they passed back into the countryside.

"Okay, looks like this is our stop—time to get ready," Teague said, as he stood up and stretched.

Beneath his feet, the train jerked as it slowed. He peered out the door. Pulling his head back inside, he said, "Time to jump."

They gathered in the doorway.

He took hold of Beth's arm. "Let some of the others go first."

She stepped aside.

Cash tossed his pack. He took a step back, then sprinted and jumped.

Next came Zac. Playfully, he tipped his imaginary hat at the others, then launched himself out of the car.

"I'll go next," said River. She touched Beth on her shoulder. "You'll go after that. It's Okay. We'll be out there waiting for you." She backed up two steps, gave a mock, exaggerated curtsy, then sprinted and launched into the air. She landed with the precision of a gymnast. After coming to a stop, she held her arms in the air triumphantly.

"Okay, Beth," Teague said, as he held her hand and gently moved her forward. He could feel her pulse racing. She was trembling. "Jump far as you can away from the train. Try not to hit anything on your way out. Got it?"

Beth nodded half-heartedly.

"When you touch the ground, relax, bend your knees, and roll with it."

She didn't move.

Teague handed her pack to Finn; he tossed it outside.

"Go for it," he said smiling. The look of fear on her face made him wonder if she would jump. She had to know this was the only way off this train. She stepped back, took a deep breath, exhaled and leaped.

As soon as she hit the ground, she bent her knees and let her body roll forward until finally; she came to a stop—on her bottom. Not nearly as graceful as River, but a vast improvement from the previous night.

Right after Beth landed, Finn tossed his pack and jumped, landing a few feet away from her followed by Teague.

As their eyes adjusted to the darkness, they dusted themselves off. The thundering noise of the train moved further and further away, leaving behind the loud yet different sound of the country at night. They collected their things, then strode away from the tracks, stopping at the edge of a dark road.

Not a single light to illuminate their way. No buildings, no street signs and no sign of people. Crickets, toads and frogs echoed in the darkness. Overhead, the pitch-black sky sparkled brilliantly with millions of stars.

Teague wanted to lighten Finn's mood. He didn't like it when Finn became sullen like this. More than that, he disliked his own feelings about Finn when he became this way. Somehow, he needed to remind Finn that not everything about this area of the state was bad.

"Anyone up for a quick visit to the spring before we head to the cave?" he asked.

"The spring?" asked Beth. "What's that?"

"It's a water hole," replied Teague. "Crystal clear and deep. It's fed by an underground spring. We haven't been here in a long time, it'll be fun to see it again."

"Sounds fine to me," she replied, shrugging.

Finn didn't respond, he was standing several feet away from the group, staring up at the sky. The others agreed enthusiastically.

It was a couple-mile trek over rolling hills covered in tall grass and mesquite trees. Zac took up the lead.

At the rear of the group, Teague lagged with Finn. He was being eerily quiet. Teague struggled to find the right words—any words to say that would pull Finn out of his funk. He settled on walking in silence. Sometimes the best thing to do was just be there; physically in case he wanted to reach out or talk.

The tall grass was nearly as high as Teague's waistline. He lifted his hands, holding them flat so he could brush along the tops of the blades as they walked. The grass was dry—the ground hard beneath his feet. He was okay with that. Strolling through a Texas field saturated with water was an awful ordeal. When wet, Texas dirt was pure clay, making it impossible to walk across without losing one's shoes.

They passed over a small rise and halted at the top. Below, a verdant line of trees stretched out as far as the eye could see, following the river's path. Millions of fireflies blanketed the meadow, undulating like waves of water.

Beth's voice called out in amazement, "It's so beautiful! I've never seen so many in one place before!"

The tiny bugs flashed and glimmered. Millions of flickering lights danced in the darkness. As Zac plowed his way through, the shimmering creatures parted, creating a path of darkness. On either side, glimmering lights sparkled and heaved. Behind Teague, the tiny lights floated back, closing the path as though it never existed.

Leaving the glowing creatures behind, they entered the tree line. Up ahead, the telltale sound of gurgling water. To their right, somewhere in the darkness, a twig snapped, followed by the unmistakable sound of fallen leaves crunching under running feet. Probably a deer. They found the stream and strolled along its shallow bank.

"Does the water get deeper?" Beth asked aloud.

To Teague's surprise, Finn responded, "It does. Give it a chance."

This was a hopeful sign, Finn's voice didn't sound detached or sullen, rather it was almost content. This was exactly what Teague had hoped for. Being in the woods, away from civilization, always made Finn feel better. It was his natural habitat.

They came to a series of large boulders set deep in the ground spanning from one side of the stream bed to the other. Years of erosion had worn away at the rocks in the center, creating a mini canyon. On either side, what remained of the boulders stood solid and firm. Single file, they climbed up the uneven rocks, halting at the top.

A steady stream of water cascaded down into an almost perfectly round pool. River clicked on her flashlight and shined the beam straight down to the center of the water. Along the edges stood a shallow lip of moss-colored limestone. In the center was a pool of crystal-clear water.

"Woah!" Breathed Beth. "It's beautiful!" She stood atop the rocks, staring in awe at the bottomless body of water beneath her.

They set up lanterns to light the area. Casting a cool glow, they illuminated the trees. Water glistened off the rocks.

Already stripped down to their boxers, Zac and Cash leaped off the ledge, crashing into the water. "Come on in, the water's fine!" called out Zac.

Beth looked around at the others, "Are we seriously gonna jump? There's not another way down?"

Beside her, River had already stripped down to her tank top and underwear. "It's the best way to get into the water. All at once."

A look of apprehension swept across Beth's face. "Y'all have a thing for jumping, don't you?" she quipped.

"The first step is always the worst," said Teague.

She took off her clothes, leaving only her T-shirt and underwear, then stood at the edge of the rock. "How's the water?" she asked.

Teague snickered. He shrugged. "C'est ce que c'est."

Finn leaned over his shoulder and said to Beth, "That means *it is what it is*." He laughed and gave both Beth and River a gentle shove. They jumped off the ledge.

Beth's voice cried out from the pool, "Oh my god! It's so cold!"

"I forgot to say the water's cold, cold," shouted Teague.

Finn and Teague waited until the girls were sitting along the ledge —it was now their turn. Shooting a glance at one another, they launched into the air.

Plunging into the water sent a shock of ice-cold through Teague's body from the bottom of his feet to the top of his head. The clear, chilly liquid enveloped him. Swimming up, he breached the surface. Beth and River were lounging on the slick ledge while Zac and Cash were busy making their way back to the top of the rock for another jump. Treading water, he and Finn splashed around for a minute before swimming to the ledge.

It was good to see Finn smile. Teague's little detour had completely transformed his mood. No longer sullen and distant, he was happy and alive—present with his friends. There was hope, after all.

Chapter Twenty-Eight

THE NIGHTTIME SWIM IN THE COOL WATER WAS A PLEASANT DIVERSION.
For Finn, it was a welcome reminder of two things he enjoyed most—
unbridled freedom and nature. His uneasiness slipped aside, replaced,
for a moment at least, with a sense of contentment. When it was time
to head out, he led the group to their next destination.

Walking along to the music of the night, Finn breathed in. The
country air was fresh, not stale like the city. He didn't know how
people could live like that. The air alone was enough to make you want
to run far away. Never mind having all those other people all around
you—all the time.

Beth broke ahead of the group and jogged up alongside him.
"Where are we heading?" she inquired.

"You'll see," he responded.

"I get the feeling it's someplace special for y'all. Am I right?"

"You could say that."

"Okay, man of limited words—care to elaborate? At all?"

Finn halted and faced her. "This whole area is full of limestone
caves and underground springs like the one back there. They spider
web all throughout the region. Some of them are open to the public
while others are on private property."

"Cool," said Beth. "So, are we going to one of these caves?"

"We are."

As they resumed walking, Beth adjusted her pack. Wincing, she slid her hands between the strap and her shoulder, pulling it away. That she said nothing while doing so impressed Finn. He would expect that someone like her would whine and cry at the first sign of pain. Perhaps she wasn't all that bad.

"You okay?" he asked.

"Yeah, yeah. I'm fine," she replied. "I guess I need to get used to wearing a heavy pack for long hikes."

Finn nodded. A part of him still enjoyed seeing her struggle. Another part of him respected that she didn't seize the opportunity to ask for help. "You will—don't worry," he said. "And this ain't nothin'. We've walked a lot longer than this before. You will too."

She flashed a worried smile. Still no whining or complaining —impressive.

As they passed a cornfield, he pulled an ear of corn off of its stalk and inspected the inside. Ready for picking and no worms. Excellent. After stuffing the ear into his pack, he told Beth, "Grab a couple. They'll come in handy for tomorrow." He took the time to show her how to inspect them. What to look for.

Beth did as she was told. No complaint—no argument.

At the end of the field, they came to a small bridge with a narrow creek flowing below. Tall grass grew between the rows of corn and the guardrail. It was dark green and as tall as Finn. He pushed aside a broad swath, exposing a worn footpath. He beamed at Beth, "This is where we turn off."

Beth leaned forward and peered into the darkness. "Um, we're going down there?"

"Yes."

"It seems buggy. Will it open up or is it all gonna be nothing but pushing through these tall weeds?"

Cash peered over her shoulder. "Just stay close. He'll clear the path and I'll make sure it's good before you go through."

Beth nodded and let him pass.

Deep in the thicket, a deafening squeal erupted, followed by grunts and more squeals.

Beth jumped and squeaked. "What was that?"

Holding back laughter, Finn replied, "Sounds like a feral hog or two are out here doing their thing tonight." He shrugged.

"Um, we're not going near them, are we?"

Finn smirked. "It all depends."

"On what?"

"On whether we create a ton of commotion and they come on over to check it out."

"If it's all the same," said Beth, "I'm gonna stay close to you." She stepped up.

"Suit yourself," replied Finn. "Stay close and don't get in the way."

More squealing followed by the sound of something substantial crashing through the brush—something that was not the hogs. It was closer. Finn glanced over his shoulder just in time to catch the subtle sway of the grass as the creature moved. He wondered what that could be. It appeared to be going toward the water. Whatever it was, it was doing its best to be stealthy.

The boars squealed again, startling Beth. She cried out and jumped, grabbing hold of his arm.

This time he laughed out loud. "I said stay close, not on top of me." He pulled his arm free of her grasp. "Try not to make too much noise. They don't want to mess with us any more than we want to mess with them. We probably won't even come close enough to see them."

Finn raised his knife and went back to work, hacking his way through the reeds. The tall grass gave way easily. His knife slashed and cut through the blades, creating a nice wide path.

The dense grass gave way to a cluster of short, twisted Devil Trees, with sharp thorns that covered their branches. A painful obstacle to cut through. Putting on a leather glove to protect his hand, Finn passed a message along through Beth to warn the others about the thorns. Around him, the crickets seemed to be much louder, if that was even possible.

After much effort, he cleared the brush and came out at the edge of a small stream. Across the water, a startled deer ran away into the woods. He waited for the others to clear the brush, then turned and followed along the bank for about a mile. The damp sand shifted under each step.

He halted in front of a dirt opening in the side of a bank. Weedy vines crawled up along the bank, stretching their thorny tendrils into the dark abyss of the cave. It had been years since he and Teague last visited this place. Based on all the overgrowth, it appeared no one had come along in all that time. He grabbed a handful of vines and pulled, clearing away enough of the hole to allow passage.

The entrance itself stood about five feet tall. It didn't look like anything significant. In fact, to the untrained eye, it would be a little disappointing. Something easily missed. A tall, mud hole being swallowed up by intrusive plant life.

As the others caught up to him, he smiled. "Here we are, home sweet home…"

Beth flashed a questioning look at Finn and examined the entrance. "Don't take this the wrong way, but I kinda thought it would be more like, I don't know… a cave."

Finn chuckled, he figured she would think that at first. "Well, little girl, this is a cave. Just wait."

"All right, I'll take your word for it," she replied, as she wagged her head in disbelief.

He turned on his small flashlight and led them in.

The entrance tunnel was a little tight as they made their way into the darkness. Clay earth lined the walls, floor and ceiling. A damp chill permeated the air with a distinct scent of dirt all around. They were heading down below ground level.

A few yards in, the clay gave way to a soft, dirt floor and solid, rock walls. The surrounding air grew drier, yet remained cold. Their footsteps echoed around their heads. Somewhere up ahead, water dripped—one tiny drop at a time—drip, drip, drip.

At last, a vast expanse of blackness opened before him, swallowing the beam of his flashlight. He stepped down and passed into a large room. This was the great room. He and Teague had called it that years ago, when they first found this cave. Solid limestone made up the soaring walls and cavernous ceiling. At their base, along the floor, stood many stalagmites. He shined the light up at the ceiling, casting an eerie glow over the stalactites that hung there like an upside-down, petrified forest.

Upon entering the room, Beth let out an audible gasp. "Oh!" Was all she said. She sauntered up to a stalagmite and touched it with her finger. "It's slick. How weird."

The others entered the room and spread out, placing their gear down. River pulled out her tiny LED lantern and turned it on. It cast a bright glow around the cave, creating shadows along the walls.

Beth strode past the others as she made her way across the great room, taking time to study all the oddly shaped stalagmites and fissures she came across. She scanned the ceiling. "That is amazing!" She spun around, facing Finn. "Okay, I take it back. This is so much cooler than I imagined it would be."

Finn smiled at her. He knew the cave would impress her—how could it not?

"This is huge!" shouted Beth. "It's incredible!"

"I take it the lady approves," said Teague, as he laid out their sleeping bags.

Beth pointed to another tunnel leading away from the large chamber. "What's down there?"

"That leads to another smaller room about a quarter mile down," replied Finn, "It gets kinda narrow along the way though." He pointed to another opening to the left. "That one over there just seems to go on forever. We never figured out where it ends."

"These are all over the place around here?" she asked in amazement.

"Yep," he replied, "They go on for miles."

"How come I never heard about these?"

"If you're not from this area of Texas, you don't know about them. During Prohibition, they used tunnels like these as speakeasies or hiding places for bootleg moonshine." he said. "Folks from all over the area would come out and party in these underground caves. Local cops either looked the other way or took part in the fun."

"Oh, my God! How cool is that?" exclaimed Beth. "Do you think this was one of them?"

Finn shrugged. "When we first discovered this one, we found some old whiskey bottles and decaying clothes. Not sure how long they were down here, but they were pretty deteriorated."

"How long ago was that?" asked Beth.

"A few years ago," he replied. "We spent a winter down here. It gets freezing cold outside, but down here, the temps stay the same as it is now all year round."

"It's nice and cozy," Teague said, smiling.

"So, wait, during the winter, what did you do for food?" she asked.

"We did what we always do for food," Finn replied, shrugging. "The rest of the time, we were in here, burnin' time."

He walked to the center of the room and kneeled down in front of an old fire ring made of small round rocks. Dust and sand had covered most of the charred remains. The winter they spent in this cave was one of his most precious memories. The evening hours talking—the days spent hunting and foraging outside. He and Teague were the only two people on earth. It was perfect.

He sighed. "Since we've been hopping trains, we haven't spent a winter down here—or any time, really. For the past couple years, we've ended up in the southwestern desert during those months, moving between Terlingua and southern Arizona."

"I can't believe how cool this is," Beth said, still looking around.

"I'm beat," interrupted Teague. "I could pass out right now... and you," he pointed at Finn, "need to get some sleep." He sat down on top of his sleeping bag.

Teague was right, Finn needed to get some sleep. He tried to remember the last time he slept. It was days ago. Not since the night before the tornado. Exhaustion settled over his body like a lead blanket.

River draped a bandana over the lantern, casting a warm glow around the room.

As the others went to sleep, Finn lay there, staring up at the shadows on the ceiling. He did not want to close his eyes, for fear he would fall asleep and dream. Instead, he occupied his mind by listening to the steady drip of water.

Drip, drip, drip...

Chapter Twenty-Nine

THE HOURS SLOWLY CREPT BY. LYING IN THE DIMLY LIT CAVE, THE turmoil in Finn's mind would not stop. Old memories, many of which he thought he had locked safely away, danced through like a circus of the macabre. Anxiety and anger overwhelmed him.

Agitated and exhausted, he pulled on his boots, grabbed his flashlight and snuck down the narrow shaft away from the others.

Several yards down the passage, the stone walls grew narrow. He remembered the first time he and Teague ventured down this tunnel. How nervous Teague was—especially along the stretch where the walls were so close, they had to slip sideways to fit through the opening. Teague hated that part. That was when Finn learned that Teague had a deep fear of tight, closed spaces.

Finn passed through the narrow section with ease. Another chamber, much smaller than the great room, lay just on the other side.

The walls rose out of the earth, arching inward, creating a rounded ceiling. This cave was dry, no water dripped or seeped through the walls. The ground was fine powdery sand that billowed with the slightest rush of air.

Holding the flashlight, he scanned the room. Old footprints remained in the soft earth. He knew to whom they belonged. A smile crept across his face. In a corner, his light fell upon a dark item laying forlornly near the wall.

He walked over and held it up for inspection. An old T-shirt—Teague's. He shook off the dust and held it high. There's no way this would fit him any longer. Holding the fabric against his face, he inhaled. No trace of Teague, just the earthy scent of the cave.

They were so young back then. He remembered his first impression of Teague. His scruffy hair, his calm manner and the air of control he radiated. There was just something about him that led people to trust him.

Shortly after they met under the bridge, they left Austin and headed south. Finn didn't want to spend another day in that city—he never wanted to see those streets again. They ended up in San Antonio. Together they managed to eke out a comfortable existence; as comfortable as one could be, living in abandoned houses. He remembered scoping out neighborhoods—watching the occupants, to see when they left and for how long. At least once a week, they would sneak back to those houses, wait till the occupants left, then break in. While inside, they showered and spent the better part of the day eating, watching TV, and doing their laundry. Teague always made sure they cleaned up after themselves—Finn never really understood that part. It was in one of those homes where he stumbled across a dog-eared copy of Jack Kerouac's On the Road. He read that book from cover to cover—then read it again. It made him want to travel, see other places. The freedom of the road beckoned him.

Teague could have stayed in San Antonio forever. Finn had a deep-seated need to move. San Antonio was too close to Austin.

It took several months and one horrible incident involving a group of locals before Finn convinced Teague it was time to leave.

Striking out on their own, there was no destination in mind, they only knew they wanted to be as far away from other people as possible. So, they did what was natural for them—they headed for the woods.

Finn preferred being in the wild to being in the city. Surrounded by tons of people was suffocating. People lied. They were cruel. At least in the wilderness, there were no manipulations, no lies. Just plain survival of the fittest. Truth be told, the wilderness wasn't much different from the city; it was just honest about it.

The words of Daniel McCann echoed in his head, "Predator or prey —pick one." That horrible deep voice made raspy from years of smoking was still vivid in his memory. The mere memory of it sent a shiver down his spine.

He twitched his nose and looked down at the ground. The darkness was creeping back in.

His parent's faces flashed into his mind. Daniel, with his thick beard, dark hair and cruel eyes. Tricia, with her doe-like expressions. The mask she wore that hid her true personality. In many ways, she was worse than her husband. At least with him, you saw it coming from a mile away. With her—it was a wicked surprise.

Daniel had a nasty reputation for violence, always determined to get the final word. The only thing he cared about was prepping. He believed the country was heading toward civil war. So, he prepared. Everything else was in the way. His wife—his son. Dead weight.

He beat them both regularly. Everyone knew. No one did anything.

Finn's most vivid, early, childhood memory was of Daniel barreling down the hall like a raging bull. Heading straight for him. He remembered flying through the air, crashing against the wall and slumping to the floor in a heap only to have Daniel storm over, lift him up and toss him across the room again. This happened at least four times.

All for the crime of misplacing a book he borrowed from the kindergarten library. The book was due back at school that morning. Shortly after the blow-up, while Finn lay curled up in the fetal position on the floor, Tricia found it tucked under a stack of magazines. Turns out, she had put it there by accident while she was cleaning up. She forgot that part.

"Quit crying," she hissed, as they sat in the family van, outside the school during drop-off. "I swear, if you say anything, I will set him on you again. And if you thought what happened this morning was bad, just wait."

Finn wiped his eyes and forced himself to stop crying—stop trembling.

The teacher opened the door. "Good morning, Mrs. McCann. Hey, Finn." Her bright, smiling face a welcome sight for the five-year-old.

Tricia grabbed his arm—nails digging into his flesh. "Give your mama a kiss, baby boy," she said with a sweet, loving tone. It was all a performance.

Finn gave her a peck on the cheek.

"Remember what I said, you be good and mind yourself," she warned.

He nodded and climbed out of the car. Just another day in the McCann household.

Over time, Finn learned to steel himself for what was coming when he heard the bastard heading his way. Sometimes he ran and hid; other times he stood his ground. The worst times were when Daniel would come at him during the night while he was asleep. Being awakened by a raging madman was a terrifying ordeal. There was no way to prepare for it.

Finn hated him. He hated her.

As he grew older, he did whatever he could to make their lives as miserable as they made his. For an entire month, he drained the radiator fluid from Daniel's truck. The miserable jerk lost his mind trying to find the leak. It was great. When Daniel figured out what was happening, he beat Finn. He couldn't open his left eye for a week. To this day, he still considered it well worth the price.

Finn smiled as he recalled how the mysterious leak unnerved Daniel. Even after the beating, Finn still took great pleasure in knowing he had bested the bastard—at least one time. He ran his fingers through his hair, feeling the scar that ran along the side of his skull. Another gift from Daniel. In a weird way, it truly was a gift—it brought about the end of the charade that was their family.

He remembered every vivid detail of how it went down.

Finn was thirteen. Sitting at his desk in his room, doing homework while listening to music through his headphones. In the living room, Tricia and Daniel were fighting again—a typical night. Home sweet home.

Something heavy slammed against the floor; he could feel the vibration through his feet. He pulled off his headphones and listened. That was when he heard the screaming.

Whatever was happening out there was not good.

His gut told him to stay put. He didn't. On his way out of the room, he picked up a baseball bat. Just in case.

Following the sound, he crept down the hall and into the living room where he found Daniel sitting on top of Tricia, hands wrapped around her neck. His face strained red with the force he applied, pressing against her throat while she clawed wildly at his hands.

Without hesitation and full of rage, Finn rushed in and brought the bat crashing down on the back of his father's head. Like a lifeless rag doll, Daniel slumped to the floor. Unconscious.

Could it have been that easy all along? He wondered.

He helped his mother to her feet. Together, they tied Daniel up, then Finn called the police. Tricia begged him not to. She was hysterical. He wasn't sure if she was acting or not.

When the police arrived, Daniel was alert and pissed. They hauled him away to jail. Finn would never forget the look of pure malice on Daniel's face as he stared at him through the car window.

Finn knew when his father got out, he would beat him worse than ever before. He didn't care. One thing Daniel had taught him over the years was that bruises fade—broken bones heal.

Before the police left, they informed Tricia that unless she posted bail, Daniel would stay locked up. They suggested she let him remain in lockup until the trial. She nodded and agreed.

She lied.

First thing Monday morning Tricia pulled all the money together and posted bail. By midafternoon Daniel was a free man.

What came next was the thing of nightmares. Finn spent weeks in the hospital afterward, playing it repeatedly in his mind. Like a bad horror movie—only it was all real.

At his desk, music playing through headphones, he never heard it coming until it was too late.

The door to his bedroom exploded in splinters off of its hinges.

Daniel charged in, grabbing Finn in a headlock. He dragged him out of his chair and flung him across the room. With all the rage to match his malevolent glare, Daniel lifted Finn up by his throat and slammed him against the wall.

Stars exploded around the corners of Finn's eyes. He couldn't breathe. His feet scraped against the wall as his lungs cried out for air. Daniel's hand pressed hard against his windpipe. He couldn't breathe. Finn wanted to gag, but the giant hand around his throat prevented that. He knew that if he didn't do something, he would be dead soon. Groping around desperately, he searched for anything he could use to defend himself.

He clawed at Daniel's face, trying to get him to let go. It didn't work. With the last ounce of strength in his body, Finn lifted his leg and kicked Daniel in the crotch. He held nothing back. It was him or Daniel.

Just like that, his father let go, and dropped to the floor, holding his groin. Blood on his face from the scratches.

Predator or prey—pick one.

Fighting back the urge to vomit, Finn picked up a baseball bat and swung. The vibration rang all the way up his arm. Daniel was down. He swung hard one more time, then tossed the bat and ran toward the front door.

Finn only got halfway down the hall before Daniel came up behind him and threw him into the wall—head first. His head broke through the drywall. A dull sound echoed inside his skull. It felt as though a rubber band had snapped somewhere deep inside his head.

Blood rushed into his right eye. Everything went red. Nausea swept over him. The room was spinning. Next thing he knew, he was on the floor. Daniel on top of him—punching with the full force of a drunken man in a barroom brawl.

Blow after blow. The metallic taste of blood. The feeling of shattered bones in his face. His jaw snapping, followed by the grittiness of tiny bone fragments grinding against each other.

There was a loud crash. "Police! Freeze!" boomed a male voice.

The beating stopped. Finn crawled on his stomach attempting to get away. Looking up through swollen eyes, he saw Tricia standing in front of him—staring.

His jaw broken, he could not utter a word. He lifted a trembling hand to her and pleaded.

Mom, please.

Tricia didn't move. She stared—cold, hate-filled and silent. She did nothing.

Then blackness.

Red haze—body numb. The only sound was a low buzzing deep in his brain. His head was resting on something soft and warm. It took him a moment to realize his head was resting on someone's lap.

A calm voice whispered above him, "Come on buddy, stay with me." It was a man's voice, and he was begging Finn to hang on.

A radio squawked. Fading in and out of consciousness, Finn heard a few words like trauma and something about a seizure.

Tiny flecks of light burst around the corners of his eyes. His body tensed and trembled. The world went black once again.

Finn awoke six weeks later in the hospital. Fearing further damage to his brain because of the seizures, the doctors placed him in a state of medical sedation until most of his head injuries could heal. By the time he came to, Daniel had pleaded out. He was in prison.

When they told him the news, Finn sobbed uncontrollably. It was over. He never had to see that monster again.

He spent another six weeks in the hospital recovering. Surgery, pain meds, and physical therapy—it was all so grueling. He would have to be mindful of his head. Due to his injuries, he was now prone to seizures under certain conditions.

Finn got to know the staff well. Chase, the RN, would come in after his shift and play games with him. Sonja, the head nurse, would sneak extra snacks in for him. Even one of his surgeons, Dr. Preston, a big, boisterous Texan, would come in and watch football games with him. They were all so nice. It was such a stark change from what he was used to.

His favorite visitor of all was Trevor. The police officer who begged him to hang on that night. Trevor spent hours at the hospital reading, watching movies and playing games with Finn.

The day he left the hospital, Finn held back tears as he said goodbye to his friends. Tricia was there—cold and emotionless as usual. The ride home was silent and long.

Walking through the front door of that house was the most surreal experience of Finn's life. He walked down the hall, stopping at the spot where he begged his mother for help. Running his hand along the drywall—there was no sign a hole had ever been there. The entire house was different. It smelled like fresh paint.

He entered his bedroom and looked around. Everything was foreign. He didn't feel like he belonged there anymore. He turned around to find Tricia standing in the middle of the hall. She said nothing—he didn't either. Staring at her, he closed his bedroom door.

A few months later, just after his fourteenth birthday, Tricia brought the phone to his room. She handed it to him and walked out without saying a word.

Not sure who it could be, Finn raised the phone to his ear, "Hello?"

"Happy birthday shithead." That gravelly voice—Finn trembled.

"Just wanted to let you know, I'm still thinkin' of you. I've been working real hard. I'm a model prisoner, if you can believe that." He chuckled.

Finn's guts churned.

"What's the matter? Surprised to hear from your dad?" Daniel laughed. "Don't fret. I'll be home soon enough. And when I get there —I'm gonna gut you like a fish, then tear you apart with my bare hands and bury your pieces in the backyard."

Finn tossed the phone across the room. His heart raced.

No more.

He gathered up all his camping gear, walked out the door and never returned.

Things didn't go smoothly. His first friend on the streets turned out to be one of his worst mistakes. As if his life hadn't been hard enough, the city of Austin seemed hell bent on making things worse. In Finn's eyes, the only good thing to come out of that city was Teague.

Ah, Teague. Finn wondered if he was awake. He wiped his eyes, brushed himself off and made his way back through the passage to the main chamber.

Chapter Thirty

B<small>ETH WAS RUMMAGING THROUGH HER PACK WHEN</small> F<small>INN, RED FACED</small> and disheveled, entered the cavern.

"I was wondering where you were," said Teague.

Finn smiled—If that's what you wanted to call it. What appeared on his face was more like a pathetic, half-hearted attempt of a smile.

A concerned look swept across Teague's face. He leaned closer to Finn, "Tout va bien?"

Beth strained to listen. She didn't know what those words meant, so she studied Finn, hoping to glean some sort of translation from his reaction.

"Yeah, it's okay," replied Finn.

At least now she understood what Teague asked. She needed to learn some Cajun.

She looked around to see if any of the others had noticed. Zac and Cash were not paying attention, instead they were in the middle of one of their card competitions. This one was silent, which made it impossible for Beth to figure out what was going on. She turned back to River. Her face wore the same concerned look as Teague.

Beth didn't understand what could be the issue. So, Finn woke early and went for a walk in the tunnel. He wandered off all the time. Why make such a big deal out of it? Her stomach growled.

"I'm starving," she said. "What are we gonna do now?"

"We," replied River, "are gonna eat."

Those were the exact words Beth wanted to hear. "Is the town far? Is there a diner or something there?" she asked.

River chuckled. Beth didn't understand what was so funny, it seemed like a reasonable question to her.

"We don't need to go into town," replied River. "We have all we need right here." She pulled out her cooking pot and grabbed her ears of corn. "Just grab the corn you picked last night and follow us."

Beth wasn't sure what they were all up to, but nevertheless, she did what River said and followed the others down the passage. As they emerged from the cave, she found herself blinded by the bright morning sun. Being down in the cavern was like being in another world; it made it easy to forget this one existed.

At the edge of the stream, Zac and Cash crouched down and splashed water on their faces. Some sort of scuffle ensued that resulted in Zac putting Cash in a headlock. The two stood there, deadlocked, ankle deep in the water.

Beth couldn't help but giggle.

"You two done?" River asked in mock disapproval.

"Not even close," replied Zac through his teeth. Cash mumbled an incoherent agreement as the two struggled a little more. Cash wrapped his arms around Zac's thighs and gripped as he shifted his footing.

"Oh, shit," was all Zac could say before Cash lifted him off his feet. With a loud splash, they both crashed backward into the water. Soaking both Beth and River in the process.

"Seriously!" shouted River. "Cut it out!"

They stopped tussling and stared up at River like apologetic children.

A loud whistle echoed in the small gully. Up ahead, shoes off— pants rolled up, Finn and Teague strolled along in the ankle-deep water. They beckoned to the others, then disappeared around a bend.

Continuing to shove one another, Zac and Cash stood up, removed their shirts and wrung them out. Still dripping wet, Cash jogged up alongside River and shook his head, spraying water all over her. She shoved him backward and gave him a playful, disapproving glare, causing him to feign an innocent shrug.

The thin stream widened. Soft sand gave way to stones that gave way to mud. Still ankle deep, the water ran clear. Rounding a tall bank, they came to a halt at an open area overgrown with patches of grass and mud. Finn and Teague were already there—waiting.

"So, what's the plan?" asked Beth, as she placed her items on the ground.

"Well," replied Teague, "there's crawfish all over this area, so we're gonna catch some."

"Oh! Cool!" said Beth. "I like crawfish. I've caught some before. Are we using a net? The stream doesn't seem deep enough for that."

Laughter and smirks.

She looked around, confused. "Did I say something wrong?"

"Nah," answered Teague. "You're fine. You're right, the stream's too shallow for anything like that. The crawfish we're going after are all right under our feet." He bounced up and down in place to illustrate his point.

"Oh, right!" she said. "I remember that. They can live under the ground in little holes. That's why they're called mudbugs."

She couldn't believe she forgot that bit of info. *Use your brain, Beth.* She thought. The others would never stop teasing her, if she didn't start thinking before she spoke.

"So, how are we doing this?" she asked, "I once had a friend tell me how he would get a little piece of bacon, tie it to a string, and drop it down into the hole. He'd wait for the little bugger to grab hold, then pull him out of the ground. Is that what we're doing?"

"Wow," said Finn, shaking his head. "That's a terrible waste of some perfectly good bacon." He took off his shirt and kneeled down on the ground in front of a crawfish mound.

"Yeah, no shit," chimed Zac.

Good job, Beth, another thing for them to laugh at.

Finn continued, "If I had a piece of bacon, I wouldn't be givin' it to my lunch for a snack. Fuck that. I'd use it to wrap the bastard up and eat both him and the bacon." He lifted the top of the muddy mound and moved it to the side, then peered down the hole. "There ya are, come on out."

"Wait!" shouted Beth, causing everyone to stop in their tracks and look at her. She fumbled around in her pockets and pulled out her phone. "I wanna record this," she said, as she focused in on Finn.

Finn shook his head. "Beth, I cannot wait till the day your battery dies and we're in a place where you can't recharge it."

He looked back down in the hole in front of him. After pulling back a little of the dirt, he reached his hand in. The ground made a wet, sucking sound as he forced his arm all the way down into the muddy soil. Shaking his head in disgust, Cash said, "Dude, you violate so many gut level instincts when you do that. There's something wrong with you."

Beth had to admit, watching Finn force his arm deeper into the hole made her feel squeamish.

"I can't believe you're sticking your hand in that mud like that," Zac teased, "Hey, Teague, your boyfriend's at it again."

"This ain't nothin'," replied Teague, with a grin. "He's put his hands in worse things than that." He winked at Finn. "I've seen him."

Zac shook his head. "This is why folks call you feral, man," he said to Finn.

This caused a round of laughter from the rest of the group.

Beth agreed wholeheartedly.

"Ha, ha, ha," replied Finn, sarcastically. With his arm buried up to his shoulder, he groped around for the small creature. "Y'all are just jealous because you're a bunch of pussies."

He pressed further, causing the ground to squish and make that sucking sound again—then he stopped. "Got ya!" He yelled out.

He pulled his arm out of the muddy hole. "One down!" he said, as he held out his catch for the others to see. Pinched between two fingers, a crawfish struggled. Claws opening and closing as it reached out—tail wiggling up and down, the little creature did its best to get

free. Its efforts were futile. Teague opened a container, and Finn
dropped it in with a thud.

Beth put her phone away in her pocket. All around her, the others
were getting ready to dig up their own crawfish. "Uh, I'm not gonna
stick my arm down in a hole like that," she said nervously, "I can't."

"Don't worry," said Teague. "No one expects you to be crazy like
him." He pointed to Finn, who removed another mud mound. "We all
got our own ways of doin' it. Aside from wasting bacon, just do it
however you can," he said, as he smiled.

"And if you do have any bacon," added Cash, "please speak up.
'Cause I would love some."

Teague kneeled on the ground and removed a mound, then peered
down the hole. "There ya are," he said, as he dug out the hole with his
bare hands. "Beth, open the container," he said, holding up the crawfish. She opened the lid and waited as he dropped it into the bin.

After that, they worked quickly, catching one after another. Beth
had all she could do to keep up as she ran from one to the other,
holding out the container so they could deposit their little captives. In
no time at all, they had caught so many, she could barely close the lid.

"Looks like we have enough," said Zac, looking at their haul as the
others wiped off some of the mud.

"Wait! I wanna catch one!" said Beth.

"Well, go ahead then," Finn said, as they all stopped and watched
her.

River winked at her, "Go on."

Beth got down on her knees in front of a mound. She removed the
muddy top and peered into the hole, then pulled up the dirt with her
hands, opening the hole wider. This wasn't so bad. Giggling, she
reached down and lifted the crawfish into the air.

"I got one!" she shouted, brimming with pride.

River quickly came up with the container. "Drop it in," she said, as
she held the lid open.

A sudden stab of pain shot up through her hand. "Ouch! Shit!"
shouted Beth, as the crawfish grabbed hold of her finger with its

pincer. Her eyes watered. Instinct made her let go, but the creature held on. It hung there, dangling in the air—pinching even harder.

"Hold on," River said, as she handed the bin to Cash and helped remove the crawfish. She placed it into the container with the rest, then carefully inspected Beth's hand. "It looks okay," she said smiling.

Beth nodded her head as she shook her hand to get rid of the stinging feeling. "Those little buggers are strong." She wondered how long it would take for the pain to go away. She was so wrapped up in the pain in her hand, she didn't notice the others were working on something else.

Cash and Zac were over by the water's edge, cleaning the corn. Finn and Teague were over by a mud bank. She walked over to see what they were doing.

"What is this?" she asked.

"This," Finn replied, "is what's called a snake hole fire. It's a stealth fire."

"Stealth fire?"

"Yeah, we don't wanna attract any attention; we're not exactly invited guests." He grinned. "So, we stay out of sight as much as possible and clean up after ourselves."

"This right here is the chimney," he said, pointing to the hole in the top. "This is where we feed the fuel for the fire." Finn pointed to the hole in the side. "The fire will get hot, and since it's focused, it'll help cook up our food quickly."

"Ah, okay," she said. "Can't wait to see it in action." Beth pulled out her phone and once again hit record. Finn shook his head in disapproval.

Holding a small bundle of dried grass, he lit it on fire. The flames caught instantly, licking around the dry blades. He moved the bundle around to help the flames spread, then gently shoved them into the hole. Black smoke billowed from the top of the chimney. Finn worked quickly to feed more grass to the fledgling flames, followed by some twigs. From the chimney, black smoke gave way to white smoke. Red and orange flames flickered out of the opening.

Beth wandered off to help the others prepare. As each pot was

Chapter Thirty-One

"RIVER, YOU'RE GONNA STAY IN TOWN WITH BETH," SAID TEAGUE, AS he dug through his pack. After spending the morning outdoors in the bright sun, he was having a difficult time adjusting his eyes to the dim light of the cave.

"Why's that?" asked River.

"Because Beth is new and not ready to help out the way we would need her to," he responded. "There could be cops, and we may have to run. She won't be able to keep up."

"You know, I'm standing right here," Beth said with a huff. "What is it that y'all are doing, anyway?"

"We're going to collect the remains of our friends," replied Teague.

Beth scoffed. "That doesn't sound very complicated."

"That's because he's oversimplifying," said River.

"So... explain."

Teague stopped and stared at Beth. He could understand how she might feel left out, but the way she was acting... she was being childish.

"Several days ago, we got a text from our friend. Another rider, like us." he said. "I guess you could call him our extended family."

"Two friends of ours, Cyrus and Craig, were squatting in an old, abandoned farmhouse outside of Austin. During the night, a fire broke out, and they weren't able to get out. They both died."

"That's awful!" said Beth. "Do they know how it happened?"

Teague shook his head. "You know what we know."

"The house was dilapidated. The siding was old wood. Most of the walls inside were crumbling—framing, exposed. The roof was caving in at some places. It was a big old mess of kindling waiting for a match."

Saying the words out loud, hearing them come from his own mouth made it all too real. That building was a mess—everyone knew it. Why, of all places, did Cyrus and Craig have to stay there for the night?

Why didn't you just camp by the tracks? He thought.

Beth stood silent, waiting for more information.

He sighed. "To answer your question, no. No one knows exactly what happened. It's all mostly speculation. All we know for sure is that the fire broke out, and the roof collapsed. We hope they went quick."

God! I hope they went quick.

Beth nodded solemnly.

"We," Teague continued, waving his arm in the general direction of the others, "are gonna collect their remains, so we can bring them down to Terlingua and give them a proper send-off."

"Um, how are you gonna carry two bodies that far?"

Everyone laughed.

Teague shook his head. "Nah, Beth, we're getting their ashes to bring with us."

"Oh," she replied. Her face changed color to a pale, pink hue.

"It took a while for the fire department to respond. I mean, after all —it was an abandoned house."

She nodded again.

"By the time the fire department got out there, the flames had engulfed the entire building. The only thing they could do at that point was control the burn and make sure it didn't become a wildfire."

"They let it burn?" she asked.

He nodded his head. "They had no way of knowing people were in there. Also, the fire was so out of control anyone inside was already dead."

Beth did not move.

"By morning, the fire burned itself out. They picked through the ashes and cinders, and that was when they found what was left of our friends—along with all the other poor souls that were trapped in the house."

"Ah, so you're going to claim the ashes. I get it now," she said. "So, why is it again that this is something I can't help with?"

Was she being difficult on purpose? He couldn't tell. "Because, Beth," he drawled, "we're not kin. We're not legally able to walk in there in broad daylight and ask for them. We have to break into the mortuary at night and take 'em."

He waited for her to process this information. At first, she stared with a cross look on her face, then slowly that gave way to realization.

"Oh!" she exclaimed.

"That's why you're staying in town with River, out of the way, safe in case anything goes wrong." he said, as he turned to get back to work organizing his things. The others were ready to go—all this chatter was holding him up.

"So, how are we gonna know if everything went okay or not?" she asked, looking around.

"They'll text us and stay in contact," replied River. "It'll be okay. They're big boys. They can handle themselves just fine." She smiled, then said, "If they get into anything they can't handle, we'll be able to come and save their asses."

"We'll meet up as soon as we can," said Teague. "We'll wait till it's dark, get in, get the ashes and get out. We should be back by midnight."

Teague did his best to mask his apprehension. Their plans never seemed to work out exactly how they intended. There was always some issue that cropped up somewhere along the way. He couldn't imagine what could go wrong, but he knew—deep inside, that something would go topsy-turvy tonight.

Beth tapped her chin with her finger. "So, if they were out in the middle of nowhere and no one knew who they were or even that they were there, how did y'all find out about them dying?"

"That's the awful part," explained Teague. "It took two weeks for the news to get around. Porter got wind of the fire and the bodies found inside. Knowing it was a Rider squat, he posted a message on our server about it. Our friend Gunner remembered that he saw a message from Cyrus saying that he and Craig were squatting out at the old farm-house for the night before heading to Tampa."

"Gunner sent them multiple texts and even tried to call. Nothing. No answer. He was too far away, so he posted a request to Porter for any more info. Porter did some research and found out the general age and race of the bodies. One was a white male in his early twenties, and the other was a black male, also in his early twenties. Cyrus and Craig."

"Not to be a jerk or anything," said Beth, "But—that description is vague. Millions of people could fit that. How do you know for sure that these ashes you're going to get are the remains of your friends and not the remains of two homeless guys who just fit the general description?"

She had a point. Teague had thought the same thing when he first heard the news. Then the other evidence weighed in.

He shook his head. "Unless you take into consideration that our community is small. There ain't millions of us out there riding the rails. In fact, there are probably a couple hundred—tops. Then take into consideration how many would even know about the Austin squat. Then the fact that we know—without a doubt that they were there during that exact time."

"I see that now. It's all so sad." Beth paused, then shifted her body. "Can I ask you something else?"

Teague nodded.

"How come you guys are the ones who are getting them? You said there are others who we're meeting up with. Where are they?"

"We were the closest," he replied.

"We were in Tulsa, heading east when the message with the info came through. When we got word, we switched direction and headed south."

"They were family. They don't deserve to be tossed in the ground in some pauper's field somewhere."

"So, you're getting the ashes," she said, "and then we're heading to Terlingua to meet up with others? How many?"

"Not sure on the exact head count," he replied. "It all depends on who can make it down in time. There could be nineteen or so folks—including us."

"Wow," she said with an incredulous sigh. "One more question."

"Yeah?" He wanted this conversation to be over. He had to get ready.

Beth tapped her chin with her finger. Talking with her, Teague realized this was something she did when she was deep in thought. He found it charming.

"So, what happens if, after all of this, you guys get the ashes, and everyone travels from all over to meet up… what happens if they show up one day—alive and well like it was all just a misunderstanding? What if they actually got to Tampa and have been hanging out on the beach this whole time—alive?"

Across the cave, Zac laughed. "Then, I am personally gonna kick their asses," he said.

"And when he's done, it'll be my turn," said Teague.

He became serious again. "It's not likely though. We all may fall off the grid from time to time, but we stay in touch. Someone would have seen or heard from them by now."

Beth nodded solemnly.

"What were they like? Cyrus and Craig?" she asked.

Teague stood in front of her. "Well, Cyrus was a big, old, southern boy from Alabama. He was smart—really smart. Craig was a city boy from Boston. That boy loved his Bruins. They were both great guys to have on your side. Funny as hell."

Their faces flashed in his mind. Cyrus with his big, happy smile. How he talked to everyone—homeless, business person, women, men, church people. It didn't matter, he would talk to them all.

Craig with his sly grin and his legendary sarcasm.

Teague's heart sank. He would never see them again.

Beth cleared her throat. "Did they have any family who would miss them?"

Teague shook his head. "Cyrus grew up in foster homes. He had no kin. Craig's dad was never in the picture—his mom died of cancer a while back."

"They sound like great people. I'm sad I'll never get to meet them."

Teague sighed and walked away from her. *Me too.* He thought.

It was mid-afternoon when they left the cave. There was plenty of time to get to the mortuary and do what they needed to do.

Chapter Thirty-Two

CRUNCH, CRUNCH, CRUNCH, THE SOUND OF THEIR BOOTS ON THE asphalt was a focal point for Finn's mind. Overhead, birds chirped and sang in the trees. Behind him, the occasional burst of laughter would disrupt his focus—at least someone was having a good time.

Staring down at his feet, he counted how many times the toe of his left boot came into view. *Thirty-six, thirty-seven, thirty-eight.* He had to keep his mind occupied. He couldn't allow his thoughts to wander. Random thoughts brought the darkness. Even as he counted, he could feel their inky tendrils reaching around the corners of his mind, poking and prodding, searching for a way in. *Keep them out. Forty-five, forty-six, forty-seven...*

The sound of squeaking brakes interrupted his counting as an old truck pulled up along the side of the road. The driver, a middle-aged man with weathered skin, plenty of tattoos and a thick beard leaned across the passenger seat.

"Y'all want a ride?" he asked, toothpick sticking out the corner of his mouth.

Zac trotted up, leaving the others to hang back. They moved closer for a better look. The odor of stale cigarettes emanated from the cabin of the vehicle. A sun-bleached, Christmas tree air freshener dangled from the rearview mirror.

The driver smiled and said again, "Y'all want a ride?"

Finn looked back, gauging the interest of the others. They were on board if he was. He glanced over at Zac who had been staring at the man, studying his behavior and the truck overall. Zac nodded approval.

"We'll take a ride," replied Finn.

The driver grinned. His teeth, amazingly white and straight for such a scruffy-looking man. "Then hop in the back," he said.

They piled in. Everyone settled, Finn tapped the side of the bed, signaling they were ready to roll. The warm wind rushed past, blowing his hair everywhere. He wished he would have let River cut it for him a few days ago. As if his own hair wasn't annoying enough, Beth's long locks were a wild mess flying all around her head. Hitting him in the face.

"Oops, sorry," she said, then twisted it up into a high bun.

Finn kept himself occupied by counting all the wooden utility poles as they flew past. *Fifty, fifty-one, fifty-two, fifty-three...*

The truck slowed and pulled into a small gas station. This was their stop—it was also where they were to split off from River and Beth. After hopping out, they took the time to thank the driver. He smiled, waved goodbye, then drove away.

The gas station stood alone at an intersection. Eighties music played over the loudspeakers. Except for the clerks working the counter, there was no one else around.

Finn looked up the map on his phone. "The mortuary is on the edge of town, about seven miles from here. We got at least a couple hours' walk ahead of us." He turned to River. "You two gonna be okay?"

River grinned. "Of course."

"Where the hell are we?" asked Beth, as she balanced herself on a concrete, parking barrier.

River grabbed her by the shoulders, spun her around facing west, and pointed. "The city's that way," she said.

Beth giggled.

Finn stared out along the horizon. The tall buildings of Austin were plainly visible. He shuddered. "We'll go do our shit and meet you two back here later tonight," he said to River. "We'll text when we're headin' this way."

"Sounds good," she replied.

They said their goodbyes and parted ways.

The road was empty of most traffic. Occasionally a giant truck would roll by, causing a gust of wind to whip around them. Fields of corn rose from the otherwise flat landscape, followed by open pastures. They crossed over small creeks and gullies filled with overgrown brush and trees. Once again, Finn struggled to keep his mind busy by counting steps.

After walking for hours, they arrived at their destination. Scoping out a shady spot under a group of mesquite trees, they sat down and took in the area.

Across the road cows milled around in an open pasture, munching on grass. They bellowed, snorted, and grunted to one another. A small calf nibbled at the grass along the edge of the barbwire fence. She paused and studied the newcomers. Seeing the humans nearby, the mama brushed along the fence, forcing the calf farther into the field away from the interlopers.

The wrought iron arch that spanned the entrance to the cemetery looked as though it had seen better days. A simple, worn out post and wire fence was all that surrounded the grounds. A narrow gravel road weaved its way around the gravestones—about ten rows deep. At first glance, they appeared weatherworn and old, but the surrounding grass was well maintained. Little vases with plastic flowers or flags decorated many of the graves.

Finn always wondered who left those flowers. Were there that many people who would come out to a place in the middle of nowhere just to leave flowers for a pile of rotting bones? What was the point?

Behind the small cemetery sat the mortuary. Nestled between giant oak trees, the old, farmhouse-style building was a serene sight. A beautiful, expansive front porch spanned the front of the building. At the center, a set of double doors, inset with ornate stained glass. To their right, stood two, white, wicker chairs with a small, glass-topped table between them. On the other end of the porch, a wooden swing swayed in the afternoon breeze.

From his vantage point, Finn could see the two, giant doors to the garage behind the house were open. Inside, the groundskeeper was working on the large riding mower. He noted that parked near the front, was a black hearse and a four-door sedan.

"Why's it gotta be next to a cemetery?" whined Cash.

"Cause it's a mortuary, moron. They kinda go hand in hand," replied Zac.

"Yeah, I get that smartass," he responded. "I'm just not loving the location."

"Actually, this is great for us," said Finn. "I mean, look around. No one's here but cows. Once the groundskeeper leaves, we're home free. We can do what we need to, and no one's gonna see us or call the cops."

Cash sighed. "Yeah, well, cemeteries creep me out," he said, looking around.

"Why?" asked Finn. "No one here's gonna bother you. They're all dead."

"You're kidding, right? Seriously, man. Did you not watch any horror movies when you were a kid?" asked Cash. "Zombie movies— ever seen any of those?"

"Never watched horror movies," replied Finn. "Never needed to." He shrugged. "If I wanted to have the shit scared out of me, all I needed to do was spill some milk or not put something back where it belonged. Hell, sometimes all I had to do was breathe." Finn shook his head. *No need to watch monsters on the screen when you had dinner with them every night.*

The afternoon sun scraped across the sky. Zac and Cash passed the time by getting into yet another epic card game. Teague tried to help Zac, but being as stubborn as he was, he didn't accept the assistance.

So, Teague and Finn found themselves watching as Cash won, hand after hand. It was almost sad.

The groundskeeper went about his tasks, then cleaned up and left for the night.

It was finally dark. The full moon cast its silvery glow around the cemetery. They crept out from the brush and walked between the graves, working their way to the house. After making sure there were no surveillance cameras, they snuck onto the porch.

"So, what's the plan for getting inside?" whispered Cash.

"Depends," replied Finn.

"On what?" asked Cash, still whispering, as they stopped in front of the giant front doors.

Finn jiggled the handle—it was locked. He smirked. "On whether or not they locked the front door."

Creeping along the porch, Finn ran his fingers across the base of the windows. Small bits of old paint chipped and fell to the floor. At each window, he poked and prodded in search of an opening—something large enough to use for leverage. Having found none, he hopped off the side rail and worked his way around to the back of the building, examining all potential points of entry along the way.

"So, anyone got an idea?" asked Zac, as he and Teague came around from the other side of the house.

They had exhausted every possible entry from the ground.

Finn stepped away from the building and scanned the upstairs level. *People don't lock second-floor windows.* He thought. Where he stood, he could see that two of them were easily accessible from the porch roof.

"I'll bet one of those is open," he said, pointing at the windows.

He climbed up on the railing, then hoisted himself onto the rooftop. The gritty asphalt shingles crunched under his feet as he walked toward the first window.

The screen came off easily. He flung it—frisbee style, across the yard.

Cash's voice called out from below, "7.0."

Finn scoffed. "No way asshole, that was clearly a 9."

"Mais non, there was a lot of wobble in that toss," said Teague.

"Wobble, my ass," argued Finn.

Zac interrupted their banter. "Are we here to rate screen tosses or get inside the building?"

Finn shook his head and placed his hands flat against the window glass. He pushed upward. The window slid open. A sheer white curtain billowed in the evening breeze. The only barrier between him and the room. He yanked them down, rod and all, then tossed them aside on the floor.

Leaning in, he inspected the room to get an idea of what was inside. It was dark. He pulled out his small flashlight and climbed inside.

The room was a simple office with a large, wooden desk, leather chair, filing cabinet, and a bookcase. At one time, this could have been a bedroom. A photo sat atop the desk—another smiling family. Finn scoffed and placed the photo face down. He crept out of the room and into the hall.

Narrow and long, the hallway was typical for an old farmhouse. Wooden wainscoting lined the lower half of the walls, while ornate wallpaper decorated the top. Wall sconces, made to look like gas lamps, hung dark every several feet. A worn and dusty oriental rug covered the floor. The place smelled old, musty.

Finn opened the first door to his right. It led to a split staircase. One flight of stairs went down and the other, up. No doubt, the one going down led to the kitchen.

Before heading down, he decided it best to inspect the rest of the second floor.

Two more offices and a bathroom. Random oil paintings adorned the walls between the sconces. At the end of the hall stood a giant sweeping staircase. The sheer openness of the entry was impressive. He turned and walked back to the stair closet.

This passage was narrow with a low ceiling. He had to duck down in order to avoid hitting his head as he descended the creaking steps. Just as he imagined, they led him down to the kitchen. It was clean and empty-feeling. Like a cafeteria.

On his way to the back door, he passed a pegboard with various keys on hooks. Each one had its own hand scrawled paper label. Shed, freezer, limo, and hearse. He swept his finger across—they swayed on their tiny pegs.

Finn opened the door and let his friends in.

All business, Zac scrutinized the room, then strode through the kitchen, flashlight in hand, followed by Cash.

Finn stopped by the refrigerator and peered inside. A half-empty coke bottle, a jar of mayo, a bottle of yellow mustard, and some habanero sauce. Two takeout food containers sat in the center of one shelf.

Over his shoulder, Teague pulled out the flat box and inspected the contents—half a ham and cheese sandwich and some chips. After removing the sandwich, he placed the container back on the shelf. He paused and offered a bite to Finn, who declined.

Finn pulled out the round soup container. He popped the lid, allowing it to fall and roll across the floor. Chicken noodle soup. It was still fresh. He doused the contents with the habanero sauce, then tossed the little bottle across the room. Sipping the broth, he followed the others out of the kitchen.

The first floor of the house was decorated with fake potted plants and more random oil paintings. Same dusty, old rug. There was a parlor off to the left. Spacious, with chairs set out in rows, all facing a podium and stand.

Across the grand foyer was another room, guarded by two, giant, mahogany pocket doors. Inside, several open caskets sat idle—all set up on display. Finn ran his hand over the silky, cool satin fabric. Such an extravagant expense for rotting flesh.

Beside him, Cash scolded, "No! Do not finger things."

Finn opened his mouth to reply. Before he could say anything, Cash shook his head and raised his hand. "Don't. Don't do it," he said.

Finn breathed in as if he were getting ready to speak.

"Stop now," said Cash, as he turned to follow Zac out of the room.

Finn shot Teague a glance and snickered.

Back down the hall, they came to another staircase. This one appeared to go down to the basement level.

"This must be where they keep the stiffs," said Finn. His voice echoed around the passageway as they crept down the stairs.

"Hey, I wonder if we're gonna see one on the slab," replied Teague. Finn laughed.

Up ahead, Zac chuckled over his shoulder. "We cannot take you two anywhere."

"Shhh!" whispered Cash. "Stop fucking around."

Finn leaned close behind Cash, "Why are you whispering?"

"He's afraid the dead are listenin'," teased Teague.

"You guys are total assholes," hissed Cash.

Teague chuckled. "He's got the frissons."

"Is that true?" asked Finn. "Got goosebumps? A little creeped out?" Leaning close, he whispered, "Scared there might be one down here that's movin' around?" He reached out and stroked the back of Cash's neck with his finger.

Cash spun around and shoved him backward into Teague. Shaking his head, he hissed, "Stop it."

The stairs emptied into an open room. At the base of the stairs, Zac clicked on the light switch. The fluorescent lights flickered and buzzed as they came to life, casting a sterile glow around the room. The walls were ceramic tile; the floor, polished concrete. This had to be the embalming room.

A strong smell of bleach hung heavy in the air. In the center of the room stood a single stainless-steel table—a massive light hung low above it.

They fanned out across the room.

A series of stainless-steel cadaver cabinets covered the wall opposite the stairs. Finn ran his hand along the smooth, cold surface. "Hey Cash, how many bodies you think are in here?"

Cash didn't respond.

Finn tapped on a hatch. "Anybody in there?"

Behind him, Teague chuckled. Nothing from Cash—he would have to try harder.

He leaned his ear against the door. "What's that? Do I hear knocking?"

A gentle tap—like a finger tapping on hollow metal—echoed across the room.

Cash jumped. "Stop it Finn!"

"I ain't doing anything," he replied, holding back laughter.

The tap rung out one more time. Cash spun around and glared at Teague, who was standing there—grinning from ear to ear. "I fucking hate you two right now."

Teague blew him a kiss.

Across the room, Zac was inspecting a tall, stainless-steel cabinet. "This has got to be where they are."

While waiting for Zac to figure out what he needed, Finn took a sip of broth from the soup container. He swirled the contents around then, using his fingers, fished out some noodles and dropped them into his mouth.

Cash watched in disgust. "Seriously?"

"Seriously, what?"

"Are you eating that with your bare hands?"

Finn smirked and walked over to the cabinet. After inspecting the contents of the drawers, he pulled out a stainless-steel pair of tongs. Staring at Cash—smirking, he dug them into the container, scooped up some noodles and fed them into his mouth.

Cash shook his head. "You're gross," he said. "You realize that's probably been inside some dead person's body, right?"

"I'm sure it has," responded Finn, as he licked the tongs clean. All while not taking his eyes away from Cash.

"I can't believe you're putting that in your mouth, man," said Cash.

Teague leaned over Finn's shoulder. "He's put worse than that in his mouth before." He smiled. "I've seen him."

"I need some new friends," Cash sighed under his breath.

"If y'all are done messin' around," Zac called out from the corner, "I could use some help over here." Finn placed the container and tongs down on the metal table and wiped his hands off as he walked over to Zac. The cabinet was sturdy. He tried to wiggle it from side to side—it didn't move. He grasped the handle and jiggled—locked. Zac scoffed, letting him know he had already tried both.

"Yo, Cash," Finn called over his shoulder. "You wanna do the honors and pick this lock open?"

Cash pulled out his lock pick and got to work. It only took him a second to open the latch.

Inside they found two, cardboard file boxes. Just as they hoped, the remains were there. The mood lightened—then quickly changed.

"Well, this sucks," said Zac. There were eight bags of ashes; not two. A random set of numbers was the only identifying information on each packet. He held one up, "I wonder which two of these are Cyrus and Craig."

"Fuck," Finn breathed.

"Maudit!" said Teague, as he lifted a bag to inspect it. "There's no identifying info anywhere?"

Zac shook his head. "It's not like they're anything but a couple John Does."

"Mais la!" said Teague, peering into the cabinet at all the pouches. "Makes you wonder how many homeless people die around here." He pointed to the number on one bag. "I bet there's a book or file some- where that has these numbers along with their identifying info."

They spread out and searched.

Over by the cadaver cabinets, Finn inspected a file cabinet. As he poked around, he noticed in the far corner—hidden by the stairs, a small, red light flashed. He moved closer to get a better look. That was when he realized what it was.

"Oh, shit!" he exclaimed. "Guys, we got a problem." He pointed to the flashing red light.

"Is that what I think it is?" asked Teague.

"It sure the hell is," he replied. "Looks like we triggered the silent alarm at some point."

"How long you think it's been goin' off?" asked Teague.

Finn shrugged.

"Time to go!" blurted Teague.

Over by the cabinet, Zac looked at Cash. "Take 'em all?"

"Do we have a choice?"

Zac pulled off his pack and stuffed all the bags of remains inside. They ran up the stairs, down the hallway, through the kitchen, and outside to the back porch. Standing there, they could hear sirens way off in the distance.

"How far ya think?" Zac asked Finn.

"Why the fuck you askin' me?" he replied—followed by, "Probably three minutes away."

"So, what? Do we take off into the woods?" asked Zac.

Finn remembered the garage and the group of keys in the kitchen. He ran back inside, grabbed the keys labeled *sedan* and *barn,* then ran out the door. After fumbling at first, he got the lock open. They slid the double doors open wide.

"Please tell me you did not take the keys to the hearse," whined Cash.

Finn opened the door to the sedan. "I ain't gonna lie, the thought did cross my mind. It's too obvious, though, so we're takin' this." He climbed into the driver's seat and fired up the engine. The others jumped inside and closed the doors.

Flooring the gas pedal, tires ripping up the gravel, they tore down the driveway past the tombstones and out onto the road. Lights off, they sped away in the opposite direction of the sirens. When they were half a mile away, they could see the glowing blue and red lights in their rearview mirror as two police cars pulled into the cemetery.

"Holy shit, that was close!" Zac shouted from the back seat.

He was right—that was close. Alarm thing aside—this was one of the easiest heists they had pulled off. Finn allowed himself to revel in their victory. Now to get back, pick up the girls and get as far away as possible from this area of the state.

All at once, their phones went off.

Chapter Thirty-Three

As River watched, the guys walk away, something felt wrong in the pit of her belly. She couldn't recall another time she stayed behind while they took care of business. This would not be a regular thing. She preferred being in the thick of things—keeping them out of trouble.

As their silhouettes disappeared along the horizon, Beth turned to River and asked, "So, what are we gonna do while we wait?"

River smiled. "We're going into the city."

Beth beamed. "Can we?" she asked. "Is it okay if we go watch the bats fly? I've only ever heard about them. It'd be cool to see them in person... can we?"

River nodded and looked around for someone to bum a ride with. Noticing a short, middle-aged man by the gas pump, she approached him with her most pleasant voice, and asked. Within minutes, they were sitting in the back of his truck, wind rushing through their hair, as they headed straight into downtown Austin.

The streets teemed with people. Shops—large and small lined the avenue.

She didn't hate cities the way Finn did, though she didn't care much for the big ones. Something about weaving your way through a seething mass of humans was unsettling. She preferred mid-size cities. Just enough people to be interesting. Austin was somewhere between both. It was a big city, by city standards, but it had a mid-city feel.

They poked around little, nicknack shops and purchased coffee from one of the local venders. Strolling along sixth street, they paused occasionally to listen to the music that poured out onto the street from the bars. Each corner a new sound. Glasses clinked. People laughed. Across the street from an old, stone hotel, they settled on a bench and finished their coffee.

Beth pulled out her phone. River watched as she slid her fingers across the tiny screen. She handled the phone as though it was a part of her body—a natural extension of her hand. River couldn't help but be impressed.

An image of Finn popped up on the screen.

"What's that?" asked River.

Beth smiled. "I'm posting about our adventures."

"Yeah, I get that—why the picture of Finn?" River fought to contain the protective anger that was rising inside of her.

"Because he was there... doing what he does. He's photogenic," replied Beth, with a shrug.

River knew there was no harm in Beth posting some images of the others. However, something deep inside her made her feel uneasy. "Just keep in mind what I told you. Be mindful of the things you post." She admonished.

Beth nodded.

As Beth played with her phone, River pulled hers out. She pressed the home button, and the screen came to life in her hand. It was eight o'clock. Glancing over, Beth was busy swiping and touching. River peered down at her screen. Aside from the server their group shared, she had no apps—no social media. Her friends were always with her, she didn't need to reach out and connect with random people online. She popped open the server app and scrolled—just a bunch of posts asking for and receiving train info.

She sighed and closed her phone. "Come on, let's head over to the bats," she said to Beth.

By the time they arrived at the riverbank, people were already gathering to see the infamous Austin bats. Touristy things like this made River giggle. The crowds were always the same. Women in floppy hats and oversized sunglasses. Men in cargo shorts. Children squealing and running around. It didn't matter what language they spoke, one way or another the same cast of characters always appeared.

They found a quiet spot under a majestic willow tree and sat down on the soft grass. The water gurgled and splashed as it swept along the bank.

"How much longer do you think they'll be?" asked Beth.

"The guys or the bats?"

Beth giggled. "The guys."

River looked up at the sky. "They won't get started until it's full dark. It'll be a few more hours."

"Think it'll be okay?"

"Yeah, they're big boys," she replied. "They can handle themselves fine."

A collective sound of awe emanated from the crowd to their left. Hundreds of bats erupted from beneath the bridge. Their tiny, black bodies fluttered and flipped against the darkening sky. Chirps and clicks echoed through the air as they called out to one another.

The bats flitted about for a minute as if performing for the tourists, then suddenly they were gone. The sky was silent and dark. The crowd of onlookers milled their way back to the parking lot or onto the street. Having nowhere else to go and plenty of time to waste, River and Beth stayed behind and lounged in the grass.

"Can I ask you something?" asked Beth, her voice had a tentative sound to it.

"Sure."

"Finn." Beth breathed in, then exhaled. "Why does he hate Austin? Is it because of his parents? Or is it something else?"

River sorted her thoughts. The subject of Finn and what happened to him was not something she was comfortable discussing—not even with him. Just thinking about the pain and fear he suffered broke her heart. According to Teague, the Finn he first laid eyes on under the bridge was a shattered, fragile mess. It was an absolute miracle of fate that they met up that night. By the time River came along, he was whole again—mostly. He had his moments when something triggered his demons. Things could get pretty scary when that happened. Luckily, those incidents were rare.

"It's not really my place to tell you his story," she replied. "I'm sure when he's ready, he'll tell you all about it." She hoped that would be the end of that line of questioning.

Beth nodded and smiled.

Behind them, something stirred in the bushes. River glanced at Beth and then turned around. Hidden among the shrubs, a young boy sat curled up—head resting on top of his knees, arms wrapped tightly around his legs. He whimpered and sniffled.

Was he one of the tourist children? Was he accidentally left behind? River tried to get a better look without startling him. He had short, light, brown hair; it was messy and greasy-looking. Not only were his clothes filthy, they were torn and his shirt was inside out. She knew right away—he was a runaway.

She leaned toward him and said, "You okay?"

Startled, the boy looked up. Scooting back against the shrub, his eyes darted from Beth to River and then past them toward the parking lot. Panic spread across his face.

"It's okay," blurted River. "We're not gonna hurt you."

The boy sat still, staring at her. He wiped his face with a grubby hand and continued to stare, not saying a word.

"I'm River, and this is Beth."

She waited for a response—nothing. The boy sat silent and unblinking.

"Um, okay," she continued, "You look like you could use some help. We want to help you, but we can't do that if you don't talk to us. You got a name?"

The boy did not answer.

River shifted her body to face him.

"Don't!" he hissed. He looked out beyond them once again and back at River. "Please. Don't turn around. Don't make it look like someone's behind you. Please."

At least he said something. She thought.

River faced Beth. To a passerby, it would appear as though the girls were talking to one another. The thought that they may have stumbled into something dangerous did not sit well with her. She took a moment to scan the surrounding area—no other people were visible.

"Okay, this better?" she asked.

The boy murmured, "Yes."

"Just so we're all on the same page here, who are we trying to avoid?"

The boy rubbed his head, then responded, "There're two guys in a red car."

River casually scanned the area; no red car in sight and no sign of the two, mysterious men. This was good.

"I think you're safe," she said. "I don't see anyone. Wanna come out?"

"No. I'll stay here," he replied.

"Why are you hiding from them?" asked Beth.

River touched Beth's arm and shook her head. She had an idea what was going on—what he might be running from. She also knew without a doubt that the boy needed their help. Reaching into her pocket, she pulled out a candy bar.

"Here," she said, as she passed it back to him. He devoured the chocolate as the two girls kept an eye out for the mysterious, strange men. His body relaxed. She was winning him over.

"What's your name?"

"Noah," replied the boy. He ran his fingers through his hair.

"How old are you, Noah?" she asked, as she looked him over. He had blue eyes and was rather skinny. There were a couple of angry bruises on his left arm and one above his right eye. This poor kid. She thought.

"Thirteen."

"These guys you're hiding from—do you think they're still looking for you?"

Noah hung his head low as he nodded.

River scanned the area again. Nothing. "Where you from?"

"San Angelo," he replied.

"You're a long way from home," said Beth.

Noah nodded.

A red, four-door sedan with dark, tinted windows slinked into the parking lot. It cruised along slowly, allowing the occupants to scour the area. As they passed, the two men glanced momentarily over at the two girls, then looked away—they were looking for someone else. The red car circled around the parking lot and drove slowly back toward the street.

Facing Beth, River said aloud, "Okay buddy, we gotta leave this area. You understand?"

Noah nodded.

River continued, "Looks like they're gonna head south on Congress. I think if we run for it when the car turns out, we'll be able to get clear and head north across the bridge without them seeing us."

"We're gonna have to run fast. Can you do that?" she asked him.

"Yes," he whispered.

She turned to Beth. "You?"

Beth nodded. Eyes wide, her bottom lip trembled as if she were holding back tears.

River didn't have time to worry about this. They were in danger and it was up to her to make sure they all got out of this unharmed.

The car turned onto Congress.

She signaled to Beth and Noah. "Come on, let's go now."

Ducking low, they ran to the edge of the bridge and peered down the road. The tail lights of the car were visible as it drove away in the opposite direction.

River grabbed Noah's hand. "We gotta run across the bridge to that alley over there." She pointed.

"You okay?" she asked Beth.

Beth nodded. But she was trembling. She was anything but okay.

"Let's go!" Holding tight to Noah's hand, River ran across the bridge.

Focused on the street ahead, she ran, pulling Noah along, while prodding Beth to go faster. They needed to get off the main road before the men in the car saw them. The distinct sound of screeching tires dashed her hopes. The engine revved as the car sped up the street— heading right toward them.

"Don't look back!" shouted River, as she gripped Noah's hand tighter and shoved Beth.

Running as fast as they could, they turned down the darkened street and ducked into an alley. She could hear the men shouting in Spanish behind them. River needed to stop and think about their next move. With terrified Beth and weak, little Noah, she had no hope of outrunning two grown men. *Shit, shit, shit.*

Crouching behind a dumpster, she whispered to Noah, "You okay?"

He nodded, bending over, holding his knees and struggling to catch his breath. His narrow chest heaved with every inhale and exhale.

She turned to Beth, "How about you?"

Beth swallowed and gasped. "I think they saw us." Her voice shrill. "What are we gonna do?"

River placed her hands on Beth's shoulders and looked her in the eyes. She needed her to calm down. "It's gonna be okay. I'm not gonna let anything happen to you or Noah. Just stay calm and do exactly what I tell you to do. Got it?"

Beth nodded.

The footsteps of the men came closer. Their shouts echoed out along the dark streets. Then silence.

River peeked around the dumpster toward the alley entrance. Two shadows moved stealthily—signaling one another.

One man barked an order in Spanish; the other man turned and disappeared.

Holding her finger to her lips, she signaled to Noah and Beth. "Shh."

She crept to the back end of the alley and spied around the corner. Nothing yet, but she knew they were trying to surround them.

The man at the entrance crept closer. River searched for something to use for defense. The only thing she could find was a metal pipe near

Noah's foot. Quietly, she picked it up and pushed Beth and Noah behind her.

Raising the pipe high, she stood and waited. Ready to swing.

The man edged close to the dumpster.

She tightened her grip and steadied her feet. Blood pounded in her ears. Thump, thump, thump.

His shadow appeared on the ground.

She inhaled and held her breath.

The shadow grew longer—he was inches from her, on the other side of the dumpster.

River lunged out and swung with every ounce of force she could muster. The pipe struck the side of his head with a hollow thud. A shock wave reverberated all the way through her body. The man let out a muffled holler, then fell to his knees. She swung a second time. This time he fell to the ground in a heap.

She grabbed Noah's hand and shouted, "Come on!"

Still holding on to the pipe, River led them back down the alley and onto the street. Behind her, she heard the shouts of the other man. He must have discovered his unconscious friend.

Running as fast as they could, they didn't slow down until they crossed over into a small neighborhood. Cozy little houses set close to one another—children's toys lay scattered about the front lawns.

River coaxed Noah and Beth to keep moving. She knew they were being pushed to their limit, but they had no other choice. She needed to find a safe place to hide. They continued to run until they came to a small boarded-up house. In its heyday, it must have been adorable with its pitched roof, white siding and gray trim. She pulled Noah with her and signaled for Beth to follow as they snuck around back.

Using the pipe, she pried the plywood from a window. She then broke the glass near the latch and reached inside to unlock it. After signaling for Noah and Beth to stay put, she climbed inside, turned on her flashlight and explored.

. . .

The linoleum flooring was torn and curling up on itself. Kitchen cabinets hung open, displaying their raw emptiness. A rat scurried out of a corner and into a hole in the floorboards. She rounded the corner and followed the hall past two bedrooms and the remains of what she could only guess was a bathroom. The house was gross, but it was secure. She went back to the window and collected the others.

Safe inside, they sat down in a tight circle on the filthy surface of the small, living room floor. Noah scooted closer to her, and once again he pulled his legs up to his chest, wrapping his arms around. River put her arm around him. He was trembling.

"What do we do now?" asked Beth. Tears streamed down her face.

River pulled her phone from her pocket and typed a group message. "I'm gonna tell the guys."

She typed. "Need help, call me now!"

She sent the message, then placed her phone on the floor in front of them and waited.

The house was dark and smelled of mold and mildew. Small rodents and various insects scurried around the corners of the rooms. The wood floor was littered with dirt and old bits of carpet and padding.

They sat there huddled together—waiting.

River's phone lit up; Cash was calling her. She held it to her ear and answered.

"The fuck is going on River?" He was on speakerphone. In the background, River could hear a car engine roaring as whoever was driving, pushed it to its limits.

"We found this kid, Noah. He's running from some guys, big guys. I knocked one out."

"Where you at?" asked Teague.

"We're hiding in a house a few blocks from downtown. Not sure on the exact address. I'll send you my location on the map." She opened the map app on her phone, and after zooming in on their location, she took a screenshot and sent it in a message.

"We're on our way. Don't move," said Cash, his voice anxious.

"Come around the back of the house," she said, "There's an open window you can crawl through."

"Got it," he replied. "Stay put. We're coming."

River hung up and put her phone back in her pocket. She pulled Noah close—and waited.

Chapter Thirty-Four

FINN PUSHED THE PEDAL TO THE FLOOR. BESIDE HIM, TEAGUE navigated, pointing out various turns and points of reference. All hope of avoiding the city was dashed. He was driving full bore straight into the heart of hell. Inside his head, anger and fear were at war with one another.

Why did they have to go into the city? He thought. *Christ! What were they thinking?*

"Turn left up ahead," Teague called out.

Finn hit the brakes and spun the steering wheel. Tires squealed. Revving the engine, he sped up and barreled down the road. Up ahead, the lights of the city came closer with each mile.

His heart raced. The strain of holding so tight to the steering wheel made his knuckles ache. His stomach was in knots. He didn't know if he wanted to scream or throw up—or both.

"Pull down any of these streets and park," said Teague. "We'll walk from here."

Slowing down, Finn turned down the first street. It was vacant. No cars, no people. He slipped into a parking spot and cut the engine. Doors opened and banged shut around him as the others climbed out of the car. Finn remained—clutching the steering wheel. Head pounding.

The driver's door creaked open. Teague leaned close. "Are you getting down?" he asked.

Finn climbed out of the car. Overhead, a street light flickered and buzzed. A cool breeze drifted through the air.

"You gonna be okay?" Teague asked, as he studied Finn.

Finn nodded, but he wasn't positive. He didn't want to be here. He wanted to climb back inside the car and drive out to the country. His head screamed at him to run.

Walking through the dark city streets, they came upon two men. One rested on a metal bench, holding the side of his head. Crimson blood oozed through his fingers, staining his hand dark red. The other stood close, speaking on his phone. Both men were large, athletic, and cleanly dressed with tattoos visible on their necks and hands.

Finn had seen their ilk before. They existed in every major city. Different sizes, shapes and colors, but they all had one thing in common. They were predators. The sort of people who made a living off of the innocent, the hapless and the hopeless. He knew these were the men River and Beth were hiding from.

His head pounded. Anger and stark, raw fear stirred up inside of him.

Leaving the strangers behind, their pace quickened. Like a harbinger of doom, traffic signals flashed red as far as the eye could see. At each crosswalk, sensors beeped informing non-existent pedestrians it was safe to cross. Not a single human being in sight.

They followed their map to the house where River and Beth were hiding.

Cash crawled through the open window first, followed by Zac, then Teague and finally Finn. The house was dark. It took him a moment to adjust his eyes. Cash crept toward the living room. The floorboards creaked under his feet. With a roar, River jumped out holding the metal pipe over her head ready to strike.

"Woah!" shouted Cash, holding his hands in the air.

"Shit!" She dropped the pipe on the floor and wrapped her arms around his neck.

Beth peered out from around the corner. Her face pale with grimy streaks of dirt on her cheeks. Behind her, huddled in the center of the room, a small, dark shadow rocked back and forth.

"Wanna tell us what's goin' on?" asked Teague.

River pulled away from Cash. "We were sitting by the Congress Avenue bridge when we found Noah here hiding in the bushes." She nodded at the pathetic figure on the floor.

Finn and Teague walked over to Noah and kneeled down in front of him. He was young and small. Not small as in size, though that was true. No, Noah was small as in diminished. Broken. His eyes were empty. His features blank.

"Hi Noah, I'm Teague, and this is Finn."

The young boy nodded and locked eyes with Finn.

"How old are you?" asked Teague. His voice reassuring.

Finn knew that tone well. It was the tone one used when approaching a tortured animal. Teague had a knack for that. An uncanny ability to evoke trust from even the most terrified and broken of souls.

Finn stared back, unblinking, at Noah; they had already formed an unspoken bond.

"Thirteen," replied Noah. His voice cracked.

"Can you tell us any more info about the guys who're chasing you?"

Noah sighed, tilted his head down at his feet, and shook his head.

"Are they armed?" asked Teague.

"I don't know."

Teague placed his hand on Noah's shoulder. "Hang in there. It'll be okay."

Noah nodded and stared back at Finn, begging for confirmation. Finn wanted to respond, he wanted to tell this miserable creature in front of him that it would all be okay. But he couldn't. He didn't know how things would play out. They could all be dead within the hour for all he knew.

Teague climbed to his feet and slapped Finn on the shoulder, jolting him back into the here and now.

River explained all the events of the night. As hard as Finn tried to listen, he couldn't take in anything she said. He caught occasional words. Bats. Bridge. Pipe. The sound in his head drowned out everything else.

Teague tapped him on the arm. "Ça va?"

Finn nodded, but he wasn't sure. The world was spiraling out of control.

"Is it just the two guys?" asked Zac.

"As far as we know, yes," said River.

Finn rubbed his head. They needed to get out of this city. He glanced over at Noah just in time to notice his body tense. Eyes wide, the boy stared at the kitchen; terrified.

That was when Finn heard a shuffling sound accompanied by soft footsteps from the rear porch near the open window. He raised his finger to his lips, "Shhhh." Silence swept over the room.

River pulled Noah to his feet. Shoving Beth ahead of her, she steered them down the hallway. They disappeared in one of the empty bedrooms and closed the door. Cash and Teague stood close against the wall on one side of the living room archway while Finn and Zac stood against the opposite side.

They waited.

Shoes hit the floor. Glass crunched under heavy footsteps. Time froze, held captive by the tension in the air.

A tiny creak at the threshold of the living room. Finn's hair stood on end. The ringing in his brain stopped. In its place, silence.

Finn jumped out from around the wall and shoved the man back into the kitchen. A fist landed square in his face. Blood burst from his nose. He felt no pain. The ringing was back, louder than before. The man had Zac pinned against the counter, punching his face.

Finn wrapped his arms around the man's neck and pulled him backward. The man bucked and kicked. They stumbled into the living room, slamming Finn against the wall.

Grabbing the man by the back of his skull, Finn slammed him into the wall three times. Dazed, the stranger fell to the floor. Finn lifted him up to his knees by his hair, blood trickled down the man's face; he was barely conscious.

Across the room, the man's partner was being restrained by Cash and Teague. He called out, "You don't know who you're messing with, little man! Our people will find you, and they will kill you!"

Finn stared at the yelling man and sneered. He was mistaken, Finn knew exactly who he was messing with. He knew the group, these men belonged to. With one mighty twist, he snapped the neck of the man in front of him. The lifeless body slumped at his feet.

The other man panicked. His eyes darted from Teague to Cash as Finn stalked toward him.

With a malevolent glare and eerie calm, Finn turned the man's head to the side, exposing a small, skull tattoo on the side of his neck.

"Te vas a morir, niñito," the man jeered.

The corner of Finn's mouth twitched. "Esto es verdad," he responded. He tilted his head left, then right, popping his neck, then pulled out his pocketknife. "But you won't be here to see it," he stated. Then, with a quick jab, he stabbed the small blade once in the center of the skull tattoo.

Teague and Cash released their grip. Gasping, the man collapsed to the floor, clawing at his throat while blood shot out from the wound.

Finn crouched down and watched, unmoved. Red liquid oozed out onto the floor. The man stopped moving. He was dead. It was all over so quickly. Finn studied the ribbon of crimson on the floor. Fresh blood had a distinct scent to it—almost metallic. The ringing in his skull gave way to a steady buzz.

Around him the room bustled with activity. Teague barked orders, the others complied. Somewhere in the shuffle, River left the house with Beth and Noah in tow.

"Snap out of it." Teague shoved him. "We got work to do now."

Finn stood up and rubbed his hands on his thighs. Without a word, he helped Zac drag the bodies into the kitchen.

Teague and Cash inspected the building to make certain they left nothing behind while Zac and Finn dug through the pockets of the dead men.

A disposable lighter, car keys, cell phones, pocket knives and some change.

Finn flipped open the wallet of the man with the bandana—Francisco was the name on the I.D. Tucked away in a side slot was a photo of a pretty young girl. He pulled out all the cash and tossed the rest on the floor beside the lifeless body. He removed the bandana and crammed it in his pocket.

Zac pulled the stove away from the wall, dislodging an empty glass bottle. It rolled across the floor.

Finn bent down and picked it up.

They waited.

Entering the kitchen, Teague signaled all was good, then he and Cash climbed out onto the back porch.

Zac kicked the gas line connected to the back of the stove. The smell of natural gas seeped into the room.

Finn stared down at the bodies. He felt no anger, no sorrow and no remorse. Nothing. He cast one more glance around the room, then followed the others.

Once outside, they went around to the front of the house. Finn— with the aid of Teague, wrested the plywood away from a window and smashed the glass. Standing in the middle of the front yard, he filled the bottle with moonshine from Zac's flask and stuffed the bandana into the top. He pulled out his lighter and lit the cloth on fire.

Blue flames licked at the fabric. He allowed the flame to take hold. Then he launched the bottle into the open window. A glimmer of light flickered in the room. They raced to the corner where River, Beth and Noah were waiting. Standing there in the dark, they watched. The neighborhood, quiet around them.

A deafening blast rang out. Glass shattered and flames burst forth from the windows. The street shook, setting off car alarms. Angry, red flames burst from the rooftop. The wood crackled and popped as the blaze destroyed the building.

People rushed out of the neighboring homes. Collecting on the sidewalk and in the street, they stood helpless as they watched the fire consume the tiny house. None of them seemed to notice the pack of strangers under the old tree.

Sirens wailed. Three fire trucks rushed past, accompanied by an ambulance. Nothing left to see. Casually, Finn and his friends turned and sauntered away.

No one said a word as they strolled back along the same dark streets they traveled earlier. Past the same traffic lights flashing red.

Pausing at an intersection, they peered down the road—this was where they left the car from the mortuary. Two police vehicles were parked alongside the sedan, blue lights flashing. The officers were too busy inspecting the stolen vehicle to notice the group of young people standing on the corner—watching. They crossed the street and made their way to the tracks.

As if on cue, a freight train lumbered near. With little effort, they hopped on. As they passed the Lamar Bridge one more time, Teague reached out to hold his hand—Finn pulled away.

They hopped off along the same dark road as the night before. The walk back to the cavern was long and silent. Finn lagged, wishing to be left alone. Teague hovered near the entire time as though he knew that Finn was considering making a run for the woods. A part of him was irritated—a part of him was glad Teague was there.

Back in the safety of the cave, River helped Noah clean up. She snuggled him in the down sleeping bag and pulled him close. Laying in the darkness, she hummed; gently caressing his hair.

Across the cavern, Finn lay staring up at the ceiling. The buzzing was gone. He reached over and took Teague's hand. Fingers entwined, he closed his eyes and listened to River's melody, as he drifted off to sleep.

Chapter Thirty-Five

WORN OUT AND ACHING ALL OVER, RIVER STRETCHED AND YAWNED. She reached out to touch Noah. He was not there. Bolting upright, she searched the cavern, taking note that both Finn and Teague were nowhere in sight. Assuming they were together, she put on her boots, and strode to the entrance of the cave to see if they were outside.

Bright, morning sunlight assaulted her eyes. Using her arm as a shield, she scanned the area. A soft breeze blew through the trees. The stream made a trickling sound as it coursed along. At the edge of the water sat Teague, bare feet buried in the sand.

Upstream, Noah and Finn sat on a boulder at the water's edge. Feet soaking in the cool water, deep in discussion, they didn't seem to notice her. She focused her eyes on Noah, seeking to glean how well he was doing. A much larger, black shirt had replaced his torn shirt. She recognized it as one of Finn's. She smiled, and sauntered up to Teague, then sat down.

"Good morning, mama bear," he said.

"Pshh." She scoffed.

She didn't want to admit it, but she had this deep need to keep Noah safe. When she woke up and found he was not there, she worried. That young kid had stolen her heart.

Nodding toward Finn and Noah, Teague said, "He's okay. He's in good hands. Finn's probably the only other person he can relate to right now."

As much as that bothered her, she had to agree. She studied the two figures, upstream. Finn splashed water at Noah, he jumped back and laughed. It was a joyful, natural laugh—raspy with a high-pitched crack. It was exactly the sort of laugh one would imagine a thirteen-year-old boy would have. River decided that she loved that sound.

The splashing continued, followed by more laughter. Noah's effortless smile made her heart sing. Then it sank. She knew all about Finn's past. All about the horrible things done to him. Her heart broke for Noah—for Finn. *Why are people so horrible?* She wondered.

Thinking about all of that made her want to cry. She settled back on the soft sand and let the sun warm her body.

"How long y'all been out here?" she asked Teague.

"Not long. You know Finn doesn't sleep in. Apparently, neither does Noah." He smiled warily.

Something about his demeanor made River uneasy. She gazed up at him. He stared down at his feet. For the first time, she noticed the deep furrow in his brow—the dark circles under his eyes.

She raised herself up on her elbows and watched Finn, who was busy playing with Noah. Nothing odd there.

Turning back to Teague, she asked, "How's he doin'? Finn, I mean." She studied his reaction.

Teague shrugged. "Good. I suppose." He paused, then shook his head. "I don't know. He hasn't said anything, but I imagine it's gotta be kinda weird for him to be here. Ya know?" he said, looking at River. His gaze more pleading than she had ever seen before.

Something had him concerned. River put her arm around his shoulder. Seeing Teague unhappy was not a typical occurrence. She worried about him. Looking at Finn one more time, she scrutinized his actions, hoping to see a sign of whatever had Teague so bothered. She saw nothing.

"Do you think it would help if I talked to him?" she asked.

Teague shook his head. "Nah, he'll talk when he's ready, not a moment sooner."

River nodded. He was right. You had to wait until Finn was ready to speak.

He sighed. "May be with us leavin', he'll have time to calm down and be more like himself again."

She hoped Teague was right—that whatever was going on between them would be over when they left. "Let's hope so," she said. "I can't imagine what he's feeling, especially after last night. For what it's worth, he looks like he's doing fine."

"Let's hope," he replied.

"And because of him, Noah looks happy." She watched as Noah played with Finn. Such a beautiful smile. She could almost forget he was the same boy from last night. "I mean, look at that smile," she said.

Teague smiled in agreement. "It is a great thing to see, isn't it?"

"I think everything's gonna be okay," she said.

"Think so, huh?"

She flashed a smile. "I do."

"I'm gonna hold you to that."

"I wouldn't have it any other way," she replied. "I'm here. And so are the others. Don't be afraid to speak up and ask us for some help if you need it. Or if you just need someone to talk to. I promise, I will drop what I'm doing and listen."

"You really are quite the mama bear," he quipped. "Seriously though, I'm fine. Besides, you've got your hands full enough already with Noah and Beth."

As if he heard his name, Noah shouted, "Hey, River!" He waved at her.

He really was an adorable kid. It was fate that brought her and Beth to the bridge.

Oh god! Beth. She thought. For the first time all morning, she wondered how Beth was doing.

She hugged Teague. "I just realized I haven't seen Beth since last night. I'm gonna go back inside and check on her." She got to her feet, brushed the sand away and went back into the cave.

Upon entering, she found Beth seated alone on her sleeping bag. A sullen look on her face.

River plunked herself down beside her. "Good morning!" she said, trying to sound upbeat.

"Morning," replied Beth, her voice distant. Without another word, she got up and packed her things.

River sighed. She had had her fill of worrying for the morning. In her heart, she was sure all they needed to do was pack up and leave. They would drop Noah off at home along the way. Safe and sound with his family. Finn could shed the darkness that Austin cast on him, and Teague would stop worrying. Whatever Beth was going through would subside as well—she was sure of this.

They just needed to get on the road.

Chapter Thirty-Six

BETH AWOKE HOPING IT HAD ALL BEEN A BAD DREAM. IT WASN'T. THE
events of the night before played out in her mind like a cheap, horror
film.

The two strange men. Running through the dark, empty streets, her
heart pounding in her chest. Her breath burning like fire in her lungs.
Noah. Cowering in the back room. Listening to the commotion taking
place just a few yards away, unsure who would be left standing when it
was all over.

The two dead men, one lying in a puddle of blood—Finn crouching
nearby. His face contorted in a malevolent sneer. Something about him
at that moment terrified her beyond description. The scream trapped in
her throat. The forceful grip of Teague's hand pressed against her
mouth as he leaned eerily close and whispered in her ear. "Shhh."

None of the others seemed affected by any of it. *Have they done
this before?* For the first time, she wondered who these people really
were. It was all very surreal, like being trapped in a dream. A terrifying
nightmare she couldn't walk away from. She missed her home, her
friends, her family. She wanted to go back. This wasn't fun anymore.

When River came up to her, she was in no mood. She packed her things and waited in silence until it was time to leave. As they headed toward the train tracks, she made it a point to lag.

Zac slowed his pace to walk alongside her. "You okay?" he asked.

"Yeah, I'm fine," she responded.

"You don't look okay. You wanna talk about it?"

Afraid of what might come out of her mouth, Beth shook her head.

Undaunted Zac continued, "You know what happened last night..." He shook his head. "Those guys were not good people. They were traffickers... gang members who treat people like merchandise. You've got to know, given a chance, they would have killed both you and River or maybe done something worse."

Beth looked up at him. "What could be worse than being dead?"

"Lots of things," he said. "Death ain't a big deal if you're the one who died. Depending on which theory is true, you'll either end up in paradise with all your long-lost loved ones or there's nothing, it's just over. Either way, you're not gonna care much anymore about anything." He shrugged. "Death only hurts the living—the folks left behind."

"You didn't answer my question," she said. "What would be worse than being dead?"

"Use your imagination," he replied, "or ask Noah. I bet he knows a few things that are worse than being dead." He paused. His tone softened. "Better yet, one of these days, maybe Finn will clue you in. He's got plenty of personal experience on what could be worse than being dead." There was no trace of sarcasm in his voice.

Zac was right. She knew, given a chance, those men would have killed them all. Beth didn't know what really happened to Noah, but she felt as though she had a good idea, and it broke her heart to think about that. She and her friends used to make fun of their parents whenever they tried to warn them about predators. In their world, this sort of thing was a myth. Something your parents told you to prevent you from doing anything fun. It was probably a myth for Noah, too—until it turned out to be real.

"Can I ask you something?" she asked.

"Sure."

"Has something like this ever happened before?"

Zac sighed and nodded. His jaw clenched as he formed the words in his mouth. "Yeah," he said. "We've run into our fair share of monsters along the way. I ain't gonna lie—we've had to make some brutal decisions. We've seen people do some horrible shit."

He stared at Beth. "The world ain't full of peace and love. There're some vile folks out there. The kind of people who'd slit your throat in an instant if they thought it would benefit them somehow."

He looked down at the ground. "It's also full of kind people. People who would give you the last bite of food they had if it meant you weren't hungry. Luckily, there're a lot more good ones than bad."

"Look, Beth," he said, as he stopped walking. "Life ain't supposed to be easy. Sometimes up is down, and down is up. You take it as it comes, and you have to learn to trust your gut; your instinct. Your heart'll trick you—it wants what it wants. That ain't always good. Others can easily manipulate your mind—making you believe things that ain't true or even realistic. Your gut... will always be right."

He took a step away, then paused. "Looks like you've got to decide what you want; if you wanna go back home or stick around. No one's gonna force you to stay, it's all on you. For what it's worth, I hope you stay." He smiled at her, then jogged ahead to join the others.

Beth didn't bother to keep up with the group. She wanted to be alone—to think about everything. *What does your gut say, Beth?*

It was noon when they came upon the little diner in Georgetown. The thought of a warm meal made Beth's stomach rumble.

The teenage waitress reminded Beth of Liz. As soon as she left the table, Beth pulled out her phone and opened her app. The red notification bubble appeared at the top with the number—two hundred thirty. Two hundred thirty-one. Two hundred thirty-two. The numbers were climbing right before her eyes.

Opening her profile, she saw that her latest post—the video of Finn digging out the crawfish, had over five thousand views already. It was going viral. People she didn't even know were commenting. Her follower count exploded. She scrolled to the earlier posts. Those too had gained likes and comments.

Her heart skipped a beat. She had all she could do to contain her smile. People were posting comments in real time as she watched. This had never happened before. She knew nothing like this had never happened to Liz or Kara. Smirking, she tried to imagine the looks on their faces when they saw how popular she had become.

"Something's got you grinning—care to share?" asked River.

Beth startled. "It's nothing. Just something one of my friends posted."

"Well, you better put that thing away," said River, "Food's getting cold and these guys will eat everything in sight. If you don't get yours now, there might not be another chance."

She closed her phone and shoved it back into her pocket. Her mind swirling with new ideas. She couldn't wait to record the next great thing.

She watched Noah across the table, River by his side. It was interesting to see how protective she was of this little boy. She hadn't let him out of her sight since they stumbled upon him. He was such a small kid. It was a good thing they ran into him. Who knew where he would be if they hadn't. "So, Noah," she said, "What made you run away from home in the first place?"

Noah hung his head low and responded, "I got in trouble at school."

"Yeah? For what?" she asked.

"I cheated on a test."

"Seriously?"

Noah nodded—his face red.

"So, how did that turn into all of this?"

"My teacher sent me to the office and told me they were calling my parents," Noah explained, "I was sitting outside the door when the principal called my dad. I knew he was gonna be mad. I would be grounded for sure, so I ran out of the school and walked. I walked so far, I got tired."

Noah sighed. "I didn't really know which way to go to get home. A pretty, blonde woman in a black car pulled up and offered me a ride…"

River put her arm around his shoulder. He leaned against her side. "Well, it was fate that we met you and we're gonna get you back home to your mom and dad," she said, as she hugged him.

After lunch, they hopped a ride on a train heading west. This one didn't have any boxcars, so they settled on a grainer near the end. Noah's face beamed with delight as he put his face in the wind. He reminded Beth of a puppy sticking its head out of a car window. She recalled how happy she was that first hop. How exciting it all was.

The ride to San Angelo was short and pleasant. A sense of purpose infused Beth with positive energy. Noah was almost home. A happy ending to what otherwise would have been a horrible tragedy.

They jumped off just outside of the train yard, stashed their gear and headed into town.

Noah's home was in a comfortable neighborhood with manicured lawns, big brick houses, and three-car garages. They turned a corner and entered a cul de sac. At the very end stood a large, red, brick home with white trim. A basketball hoop stood silent in the driveway.

River gave Noah a nudge, "This is it, buddy. Home sweet home."

Noah took two steps forward, then quickly spun around and flung his arms around her, hugging tightly. The initial look of surprise on River's face gave way to bliss.

Beth's heart melted. Saving this little boy made it all worth it. Everything.

He said his goodbyes to everyone with handshakes and hugs. Then he took a deep breath and walked up the driveway.

After pressing the doorbell, he glanced back at the group. They were standing across the street, watching. A pang of sadness bubbled up inside Beth—saying goodbye always made her feel that way.

The door opened. A pretty woman with long, brown hair, exactly like Noah's, stood in the opening. "Noah!" she cried, grabbing him and pulling him close. She kissed his face all over. A younger boy waddled up behind his mom and hopped around, shouting, "Noah! Noah!" They stepped back inside and closed the door.

Noah was home.

The walk back to the rail yard hardly felt like a walk at all. Everyone was in good spirits. Even Finn joined in the playful banter. This was the way it was supposed to be. Beth let go of her apprehension. She was where she belonged.

Sitting by the tracks, waiting for the train, Finn kneeled down beside her. "So, Beth," he said, "you still wanna come with us? Or do you wanna go home?"

His boldness surprised her. She looked at him and quickly responded, "I want to stay."

"Good, you've kinda grown on me." He smirked. "Besides, I'd hate to have to kill you." He winked and walked back over to sit with Teague.

Beth glanced around, stunned. A few days ago, she would have laughed if he had said something like that. Now... After the events of the past couple days, she didn't know if he was joking or not.

River leaned against her. "He's joking."

Beth chuckled nervously. Of course, he was.

Chapter Thirty-Seven

THE MOON CAST ITS PALE LIGHT OVER THE DESOLATE LANDSCAPE. After hopping off in Midland, they passed under a small overpass, and stopped to rest at a dilapidated gas station. Abandoned and seedy, graffiti covered every surface, accessible without a ladder. An assortment of old tires lay in a giant heap where the pumps once stood. The smell of oil and dirt permeated the air.

A sea of rusted oil rigs, tanks, and various other equipment stood silent, as far as the eye could see. Decomposing reminders of a not so remote history.

Teague was tired. Unable to sleep, he spent most of last night staring up at the rock ceiling of the cave, listening to the constant drip, drip, drip... of the water. Finn, however, slept like a baby. At least one of them had rest.

His muscles ached and a low-key buzz ran through his body, telling him that he was reaching his physical limit. It was a good thing that they were almost at the meetup point.

Before leaving San Angelo, Gunner messaged, letting them know that he and Nate were in the area and were camping at the old, stone house. They agreed to meet up there. Teague was looking forward to being around others—especially Gunner.

Things had been much more lighthearted since they dropped off Noah. He was thankful for that. Even Finn was in a much better mood —at least he seemed to be. Finn had a habit of holding things inside until they exploded with all the fury of an angry volcano. Sometimes Teague could break through and calm things before the eruption. Other times, all he could do was stand back and wait until Finn exhausted himself.

Few people could handle Finn when he snapped. Gunner was one of them. All the more reason it was good they were meeting up. Teague needed a break.

After a brief rest, he called out to the others. "All right, let's head out."

Random wreckage littered the ground. Old tires, rotting wood, and rusted metal shards were buried deep in the overgrown grass. Finn volunteered to lead the way, carefully picking out a narrow path the others could follow. They had to be careful. One wrong step could cause a nasty injury.

Walking behind Finn, Cash whined, "Are we there yet?"

"Shut up," retorted Finn.

"Why you gotta be so mean?" asked Cash, playfully.

Finn ignored him.

"This is taking forever," griped Cash.

Teague picked up a rock and hurled it past the others. It crashed into Cash's backpack with a thump.

"Hey, now." Cash whirled around and wagged an admonishing finger at Teague.

"Shut the hell up, couillion," said Teague.

Cash flipped him off and turned back around.

Silence descended upon them.

"What does that word mean?" asked Beth.

"Which one?" asked Teague.

"Couillion."

He snickered. "It means fool, idiot, or dumbass. Whichever you prefer."

"I see why you use it a lot." She chuckled. "Was it hard to learn French?"

"I didn't know I was learnin' it," replied Teague. "So, I suppose you could say it wasn't hard." He smirked. "The hard part was figuring out how to communicate with folks who didn't speak that way."

"I hadn't thought of that," said Beth. "It was the same way for me. I didn't know I was learning Spanish, it was just how my family spoke to one another. It was natural."

"Did Finn pick it up easily? she asked.

Teague smiled. "As soon as he figured out that it's mostly cuss words, he was all over it."

Beth giggled. "Somehow, that does not surprise me."

A moth fluttered and landed in her hair, causing her to shriek and flail about. When she calmed, she scanned the ground. "How many creepy crawlies do you suppose are living out here?"

Teague shrugged. "Way more than we wanna imagine. You're not freaked out by a little moth, are ya?"

"No," she replied. "Well, maybe a little. I don't mind them so much if they keep to themselves. Especially the ones with all the legs."

He chuckled. Beth had a tendency to open her mouth and have her mind flow out—one incoherent thought after the other. Like a child processing the world for the first time. When he first met her, he wasn't too sure about her. She was proving to be a pleasant surprise. He was glad they brought her along—and that she decided to stay.

"You know, Cash ain't a fan of spiders either," he said. "In fact, he freaks out when one is near him."

An evil grin spread across Beth's face. "Hey, Cash," she called out.

He glanced back at her.

"Imagine how many spiders are hiding all around us in this stuff," she said.

Teague laughed, up ahead, he heard Finn giggle.

Cash called, over his shoulder. "Hey, Beth, fuck you."

"Actually," Teague said to her, "spiders are cool."

"Cool? How?"

"Well, for one, they eat all those other creepy-crawly things, keeping their populations down."

"Birds and bats do that too," she said, laughing.

She had a point.

"Yeah, but they're nowhere near as badass about it as spiders are," he responded.

"You say badass. I say creepy."

He pulled out his flashlight. "You ever hunt for spiders in the dark?"

"No, I'm usually happy not knowing where they are when I can't see them."

"You're telling me that you, Beth Sepulveda, have never seen spider eyes in the dark?"

"Spider eyes?" She shook her head. "Do I even want to know?"

Teague smiled. "It's actually pretty cool."

She scanned the ground, then sighed. "Okay, what is it?"

"First, you start with one of these," he said, holding up his flashlight. "Next, you hold it up against your head at eye level like this." He demonstrated.

"Now, you slowly move it around pointing the beam to the grass, shrubs, and trees."

"You'll see these little things glistening in the dark. They look like little tiny reflectors—little bits of glitter all beaming back at you. That's the light reflecting off of the spider's eyes."

He handed the flashlight to her. "Here, you do it."

Beth took the flashlight and held it up against the side of her head. She skimmed the field.

"Holy shit!" she shouted. "They're all over the place! I had no idea!" Without skipping a beat, she shouted, "Hey, Cash, you wanna see how many spiders are out here in the grass? They're everywhere."

"Fuck you," was Cash's reply.

Teague couldn't help but laugh. Teasing Cash was one of the group's favorite pastimes. Beth took to it like a fish to water. She would fit in just fine.

"Aw, come on, don't be like that. It's cool," pleaded Beth. "You should check it out. The little buggers are everywhere."

"Oh, I can see you're gonna be a real pain in the ass," Cash replied. "Another smartass in the group. Awesome."

The flickering, red glow of a campfire came into view. At last, they were at the old stone house—or what remained of it.

Overgrown shrubs and grass encircled the remains of what used to be a tiny house. On top of the concrete slab stood two walls with a stone fireplace set in the corner. A warm fire blazed in its belly, illuminating the two figures who sat near. The steady crackle of wood burning echoed around the clearing.

As they stepped closer, a small dog barked and sprinted toward them.

"Gypsy! Stop!" came a gruff voice—it was Gunner. Gypsy stopped barking, but continued her approach, ears down, wagging her tail.

"Oh, my goodness! Gypsy! You little sweetie," said River, in a baby-like voice, as the little dog ran up to her excitedly. She lifted her off the ground, and Gypsy licked her face while wriggling around wildly.

"Hey, woman, stop spoiling the dog," said Gunner. "She's gonna expect that shit from everyone now."

He stepped off the slab. Gunner was an impressive sight. Tall, broad shouldered and muscular with short, dirty, blond hair and scruffy, facial hair. He had the look of a warrior.

"You guys finally made it," he said, as he hugged River.

"Gunner," she said. "You dirty bastard. When was the last time Gypsy had a bath? She's supposed to be white and she stinks."

"You act like she's my dog or something," he replied.

"She is," stated River. "You two travel together. She's your dog."

"We may travel together, but she doesn't belong to me," replied Gunner. "She can go off whenever she wants. She just sticks around for now."

Gunner turned to face Finn.

"Finnegan," he said, as he pulled Finn close. "You grew since last time." He stepped back and looked him over. An odd look washed over his face—almost like concern.

He turned his attention to Teague, wrapping his giant arms around him.

Now, it was Teague's turn to be scrutinized. Gunner's piercing, blue eyes made him feel as though he was going through an x-ray machine. Teague found this unnerving.

"So, who is this lovely lady?" he asked, as he smiled and stood in front of Beth.

"This is Beth," replied Teague. "She's traveling with us now."

"Ah, first time?" he asked.

She nodded in reply.

"Welcome. Any friend of theirs is a friend of mine," he said, as he wrapped his arms around her.

Chapter Thirty-Eight

GUNNER MADE BETH FEEL SMALL. STRENGTH EMANATED FROM THIS man—it oozed out of every pore. He smelled like fire and the outdoors.

"Hey!" Another male approached. "Long time no see." He appeared to be close to Beth's age, with blue eyes and wavy, blond hair. His demeanor was that of an older person trapped inside a younger man's body.

"Nate," said Finn as he greeted him. "You're still traveling with this creep and his dirty, little dog, I see."

Nate smiled, "Someone's gotta keep him out of trouble." He turned to Beth, extending his hand as he introduced himself.

His hand was soft. After Gunner, she imagined everyone would feel soft in comparison. "Beth." She responded. He had a pleasant smile.

"Put your things down and come on over to the fire," said Gunner. "We have a couple rabbits on the spit—figured you might be hungry."

Beth glanced up at the night sky—clear, black and full of millions of stars. She wondered what it would be like to sleep outside the tent, under the stars for one night.

Over by the fireplace, Zac and Finn divided up the meat. The savory aroma made Beth's mouth water. There was something about food cooked outside, over a wood fire that defied description. It was without a doubt some of the best food she had ever tasted. She gobbled down her portion.

A bottle of whiskey made the rounds. Gypsy waddled up to Beth, stood on her hind legs and pawed. She picked up the little dog, letting her sit on her lap.

"Looks like she likes you," said Gunner.

Beth laughed, as she continued to pet the little dog.

"Where you from, Beth?"

"Denton."

"I've been through there a few times," he replied. "Seems like a nice place."

Beth nodded. Gunner's voice was deep. He had one of the most authentic smiles she had ever seen. She tried to imagine him angry—it was probably a terrifying thing to behold.

"So, what do you think of train hopping so far?"

"I like it," she replied. "I need to get better at the whole, hopping-off part, but other than that, it's cool."

The bottle made its way to her. She took a small sip.

Gunner lit a cigarette. "Well, the good thing is, you're starting out with some of the best people I know to show you the ropes," he said. He pointed to Finn and winked. "Now, that one's a little feral, but the others keep him in check."

"There's that word again," Finn mumbled, shaking his head.

Beth giggled.

"Nah," said Gunner. "He can't help who he is. He's a little rough around the edges, but we like him that way."

Noticing a set of dog tags poking out of his shirt, Beth asked, "Were you in the military?"

He nodded, then tucked them away. "Yeah, I was."

"Which branch?"

"Marines," he said. There was a strange tone to his voice—it was faint, just enough to tell Beth he didn't want to discuss that topic anymore. She moved on.

"So," asked Beth. "Where are you from?"

"Up north," he replied. "A city in central Massachusetts called Worcester."

"I never heard of it before."

"Yeah," he replied. "Most people in this part of the country have never heard of it."

"What's it like there?"

Gunner looked at her and smiled, "Think Fort Worth, with a lot more colleges and a different accent. Oh, and no cowboys."

Beth grinned. She looked across the fire at Nate. He was staring at the flames—the orange light flickered on one side of his face. From her angle, she couldn't help but notice how long his eyelashes were. How perfectly refined his features were with his angular jaw and narrow nose. His face had a forlorn expression. "How about you?" she asked.

"Kansas City, Missouri," he replied.

Beth nodded. He was timid—the exact opposite of Gunner. "How long have you been riding?"

He shrugged, "A little over a year now."

His shoulders relaxed. Perhaps he was just shy around newcomers.

"What made you want to leave?" Beth prodded.

He glanced down at his feet. Beth noticed he had a hard time maintaining eye contact with her.

"Life wasn't going so great up there, so I left."

"What about you?" he asked. "Why did you leave?"

"I guess it was just the right time," she said. "I met these guys, and well, it just felt right to leave with them. Does that make sense?"

The bottle made its way to Nate. He took a generous swig, wiped his face and passed it along.

Gunner turned his attention to Finn. "We would have guessed you guys would be at least a day or two ahead of us. What slowed you down?"

Finn breathed in. "We ran into some trouble in Austin."

"Go on," said Gunner.

"There's not much to go on about," replied Finn. His voice dismissive. "We ran into some scumbags. Took care of them and saved a kid."

Gunner cocked an eyebrow. "A kid?"

Finn nodded. "Noah."

"Thanks for the watered-down version," Gunner said, "I look forward to hearing the full details tomorrow."

Finn's body stiffened. He clenched his jaw, then quickly released the tension.

Beth couldn't figure out if Finn feared Gunner or respected him so deeply he would do anything he told him to do. It was a whole new strange side of him—intriguing.

Somewhere close by in the darkness, a band of coyotes howled and yipped. Beth sat up and looked out in the general direction of all the noise. Gypsy cowered close on her lap. *Smart little dog.* She thought, as she wrapped her arms protectively around her.

The howls called out more rapidly. The pack was closer. At the edge of the clearing, a scuffle erupted in the brush. The poor creature they were hunting—whatever it was—gave out one, final, pathetic cry. A cacophony of noise erupted as the coyotes celebrated their kill.

From the safety of Beth's lap, Gypsy turned, facing the opposite direction, and growled as two figures emerged from the darkness.

"What's up, jackasses," said a man, as he stepped forward.

River jumped to her feet and ran over to one of them. They hugged for an extended period. Taking hold of his hand, she brought him over to the fire. "Beth, this is Tripp. He's a flirt, so watch out for him."

Beth smiled and said hello. He was tall and good-looking in a male model sort of way. With short, brown hair and big, brown eyes.

River pulled the second man forward. "This skinny guy right here is Sam."

Beth nodded hello. Sam had several piercings and a head full of overgrown, messy, blond hair. Tattoos were visible around his neck. On his temple, a tiny anchor tattoo. A series of red dots and lines spanned from cheek to cheek, crossing over the bridge of his nose. He smiled pleasantly and reached out a tattooed hand. Beth wondered how much ink this man had on his body. His handshake was firm, but gentle—not at all what she would expect from someone who looked the way he did. She realized that, had she met Sam a week ago, she would not have spoken to him—out of fear. Now, however, she didn't find him intimidating at all.

Tripp sat alongside River. The two immediately turned to one another, ignoring the rest of the group. The bottle of whiskey made its way to Sam. He took a large swig, then pulled out his guitar and strummed.

Chapter Thirty-Nine

COZY INSIDE HIS SLEEPING BAG, TEAGUE LAY, EYES CLOSED, LISTENING to the sound of the wind whistling across the deserted prairie. Somewhere nearby, metal things scraped against each other creating a rusty, metallic noise. The perfect soundtrack for a wasteland.

Beside him, Finn lay on his belly, head resting on his forearm. Deep in a dream, his fingers twitched as though he were tapping out a secret message in Morse code. Teague touched the tip of his fingers. The tapping continued momentarily, then paused. The corner of Finn's mouth curved up in a smile. His eyes remained closed.

Outside, footsteps crunched on the gravel. Gunner's voice sounded out. "Sun's up, buttercup. Time to take the dog for a walk."

A sleepy Finn responded, "I don't own a dog."

"Neither do I," responded Gunner. "But she still needs to go for a walk."

"So, take her," replied Finn, eyes still closed.

Gunner's feet shifted. "I want you to come with me."

"Nah, I'm good."

Silence.

Gunner sighed. "You seem to be mistaken. That was not a request."

The tent unzipped.

282 · N.L. MCLAUGHLIN

A brown eye snapped open and peered at Teague—questioning. Two, large hands reached in, grabbed hold of Finn by the ankles, and dragged him out, sleeping bag and all.

Gunner's face leaned into the opening. "You too, blondie, get your ass out here. We're going for a walk."

The sun was peeping over the horizon. The rest of the camp was still asleep as the trio wandered out among the scrap.

"What's the deal with this Noah kid?" asked Gunner.

"Not much to say. He was a kid who got tangled up with monsters," replied Finn.

They walked so far, the campsite was no longer visible. Gunner climbed up on an old tank and called them over. Sitting on top, legs dangling, they looked over the vast, sprawling prairie. Tall grass, sprinkled with rusted machines and decomposing wood. Teague remembered the first time he had seen this area. How overwhelmed he was with the sheer expanse of it—the sheer waste and deterioration.

On the ground below, Gypsy prowled, sniffing and digging through the wreckage.

"Humor me," said Gunner. "What went on with Noah?"

Finn shrugged. "We did what we had to do. The kid needed help. You know what they were doing. You've seen it before." He stared at Gunner. "We've all seen it before."

Gunner nodded. He looked back at Finn with an intense gaze. "So, where's Noah now?"

"Back home," answered Finn. "With his family where he belongs."

"I'm gonna assume the men behind all that are no longer breathing. Did you cover your tracks?"

"Come on." Finn scoffed. "Who are you talkin' to? Of course, we did. There wasn't much left of those two goons after the fire got through burnin'. We made sure of that."

"Think this Noah will talk?"

"Nah," replied Finn, shaking his head. "He's got other things to worry about." Finn twitched his nose. "I told him not to tell anyone about the fire. He was okay with that. He told me he was glad to see them dead."

"So, what about Beth? She okay with all of that?" asked Gunner.

"She had a hard time with it at first," responded Teague. "She's okay now."

Gunner's eyes followed Gypsy as she poked around, investigating an old oil rig. He took a while before he spoke again. "Sounds like you handled it just fine then," he said. "I got one more question about it."

Silence.

"Were these guys a part of the crew you ran into years ago?" he asked, staring at Finn.

Finn's jaw clenched. His nostrils flared. "They were—they had the same ink." He tapped his finger to the side of his neck.

Gunner sighed. "Then I suppose they got exactly what they deserved."

Once again, they looked out across the field. Teague was trying to assess what Gunner was thinking—it was impossible.

"I know going back to that city was rough on you, for multiple reasons," Gunner said to Finn. "I imagine just being there brought back a bunch of memories you'd soon forget. I'm pretty certain the whole Noah thing didn't help. So, I'm wondering—how are you doing?"

Unblinking with glassy eyes, Finn stared out at Gypsy. Not really focused on her, his jaw flexed. Teague didn't know if Finn was about to say something or drop down and walk away. Based on the visible tension in his body, Finn was grappling with the decision himself.

Finn shot a side eye at Teague. "I'm fine," he stated, as he turned his head toward Gunner.

Fine? Thought Teague. Fine would not be the word he would use to describe the past few days. The lack of sleep—the moodiness. The distance. The nightmares. Teague knew about the nightmares. How could he not? All the years sleeping on the streets, fine-tuned his senses to wake up at the slightest movement out of the ordinary. Each time Finn startled awake, Teague was aware. He mentioned nothing about it because he didn't want to deal with it. He wanted it to pass—for Finn to get over it and for things to be normal again.

Truth be told, sometimes he wanted to not be the one who cared about everything. Admitting this to himself made him feel guilty. What kind of person lets someone they care about suffer because they just don't want to deal with their problems at that moment?

Gunner's deep voice broke through his self-loathing. "You know, some people are pure evil. I suspect you know that better than most," he paused and studied Finn.

Tension hung heavy in the air.

"Those sort of people, deserve to be punished," declared Gunner, his tone dead serious. "Sometimes though, it's not a good idea for us to do the punishing. Taking a life is not something that gets harder, the more you do it."

He stared hard at Finn.

"We start out thinking we're the good guys—the next thing you know, we're not," said Gunner. "Somewhere along the way, we fall down a rabbit hole. We become exactly what we hate."

Finn's face twitched. His eyes narrowed. A vicious smirk swept across his face. "Okay, I'll call you when Teague finally snaps and goes all evil."

Teague got the sense Finn was trying for sarcasm. What came across just then was anything but. His tone was strange—almost menacing.

Finn flashed a wicked grin. He gripped the rim of the tank and thrust himself off, landing softly on the ground below. He nodded once, then strode over to the brush where Gypsy was poking around.

"Always the smartass," Gunner said, as he shook his head.

Teague nodded. His mind could not put together the words to describe the turmoil that were his thoughts at that moment.

"How about you?" Gunner asked him, "Everything okay?"

"I'm hangin' in there."

Gunner studied Teague.

Below them Finn had found a rusty rod of rebar and was using it to move around various bits of junk.

"Don't poke around down there too much," Gunner warned Finn.

"There's bound to be snakes. Get bit by one and I'm gonna have to kick your ass."

"Ah, but you'll save my ass first," Finn replied, not glancing up—still poking around.

Teague snickered.

Gunner turned his gaze to Teague. "Back to what I said earlier. I meant what I said," his tone somber, "It's hard to look at yourself in the mirror and realize you're the monster now. It causes regret and self-loathing. Regret is the real killer."

"He's not gonna go too far." Teague bristled. "I won't let him."

"Oh yeah? How are you gonna stop him?"

"The same way I always have," snapped Teague. "He listens to me."

"And when he doesn't anymore? What are you gonna do then?"

Teague did not respond.

"He's not going to know when he's crossed that line—he won't even see it," Gunner warned, "But you will. That's why you need to keep an eye open and don't be afraid to get some help when it's needed."

Teague nodded soberly. He didn't want to admit it, but every word Gunner just said had already crossed his mind.

On the ground, Gypsy barked. Her body taught, tail straight.

"What's she barking at?" asked Gunner.

"It ain't a snake," replied Finn.

"Then what the hell is it?"

Finn looked up. "A spotted skunk." He jabbed a shrub with the rod. "It's hiding in this bush."

Gypsy growled.

"Don't be an idiot! barked Gunner, "Don't fuck with skunks!"

"I thought you said don't fuck with snakes?" taunted Finn, as he continued to poke the shrub. Gypsy scratched at the dirt, all the while growling—hackles up.

"I mean it, smartass," ordered Gunner, "Don't mess with skunks and don't encourage that dog to mess with them either."

Finn peered up and flashed a mischievous smirk. With a grand flourish, reminiscent of a fencer parrying an opponent, Finn swirled the metal rod above his head, then thrust forward, stabbing deep inside the bush. The skunk shot out the other side and dashed over to a pile of debris a few yards away. Gypsy followed, running full speed. Her little body disappeared beneath the rubble.

"Shit! Gypsy! No!" Gunner yelled, as he dropped to the ground.

Too late.

The two animals burst from the mound like a geyser. Both running at top speed. Gypsy pounced—the skunk raised its tail and sprayed.

The little dog gave out an agonized whimper, then rolled around on the ground.

The skunk sauntered off, no longer in a hurry.

Finn and Teague exploded in laughter.

In the wreckage's midst, Gypsy thrashing around at his feet, Gunner spewed out a string of profanities that would have made the most notorious of pirates blush.

Chapter Forty

RIVER LAY AWAKE LISTENING TO THE COMMOTION GOING ON IN THE tent a few yards away.

"Sounds like they went for a walk," said a sleepy Tripp.

"Doesn't sound like they went voluntarily," she chuckled.

"If Gunner wants you to do something, you do it." Tripp leaned up on his elbows. "One time, we all met up in Northern Cali. The camp was packed with drifters. It was like an impromptu festival. Drugs, music, booze, sex..."

"Sounds like your ideal habitat," she teased.

"You know me well." He grinned. "Anyway, it didn't take long for things to get out of hand. It was the second night. I ain't gonna lie, I was a little high."

"A little, huh?"

He laughed. "Gunner came up deadass serious-like and told me we were leaving. He didn't ask and didn't explain. Just said it was time to go and started packing."

"Now, I was having a good time. I told him I wasn't leaving. He pressed—I argued. Things got heated. I punched him. Dude didn't even flinch. It was like hitting a solid brick wall. Instant regret. I knew I was about to die."

River giggled. "What did he do?"

"He raised his giant fist and slammed it right in the center of my face. I flew back so hard, I couldn't figure out whether my ass or my face hurt more. I literally saw stars."

"What happened next?"

"What do you think happened?" He smirked. "As soon as the stars went away, I got up, packed my shit, and we left."

"Where was Sam during all this?"

"Oh, he was right there—watching. Nate too. Unlike me, they started packing when Gunner told them to the first time."

"Did you ever find out why he wanted to leave?" River raised herself up on her elbows.

Tripp nodded. "Some guys got into a fight and one of them pulled out a knife and gutted the other one. We found out through the grapevine a month later that someone died that day. A big brawl happened, and the cops showed up and arrested a dozen people. We got out at the right time."

River sighed. "Those gatherings can get crazy real fast. So many people used to living without rules, coming together in a place where there're no prying eyes..."

"Yeah," replied Tripp. "I guess that's the downside to people like us. We don't play well with others."

He slid closer and kissed her cheek. "Enough about that. You should come ride with us." He said, as he kissed her neck.

River tensed.

He pulled back and looked her in the eyes. "It doesn't have to be permanent. Consider it a vacation. Just for a week or two."

She ran her fingers through his hair. As much as she enjoyed their time together whenever they would meet up, she did not have deep feelings for him. Not the kind that would warrant her leaving her family.

"I can't," she replied. "Beth..."

He sat up and pulled on his jeans. Reaching for his shirt he turned to face her. "No worries. I get it. No strings." He kissed her on the forehead, then crawled out of the tent.

River lay back down and exhaled. When she first hooked up with Tripp, it was all about having fun. He wasn't looking for a girlfriend and she didn't want a boyfriend. No strings.

"One of these days, you're gonna want to be with someone." Cyrus' voice echoed in her mind. *"You can't be alone forever."*

"I'm not alone," replied River. "I have my family."

Resting on a bolder they were lounging in the sun at the edge of a lake in the Rockies.

Cyrus shook his head. "That ain't what I'm talking about and you know it." He tossed a rock across the water. It skipped three times, then disappeared.

River laughed. "You know, there is such a thing as people who never get married or end up in a full-time relationship."

"Yeah, but that ain't you." He scoffed.

"So, what about you then?" she said. "You're not exactly searching for Mrs. Right."

"On the contrary. I am always on the lookout for the future Mrs. Reed."

River chuckled. "How's that coming along?"

"It ain't. Obviously."

"What happens if you never meet her?"

Cyrus rubbed his chin. "I suppose I'll cross that bridge when I get to it."

Across the lake, the others were swinging from a rope, jumping off into the water. They watched the antics unfold.

"Tell you what," said Cyrus. "How about we make a promise right now. If neither of us is married or in a serious relationship when we're forty, we'll get married."

"What like to one another?"

"Yeah," he replied. "Why not? It ain't gonna be like either of us would have anything else going on."

She laughed. "Cyrus, you are so romantic. For the life of me, I cannot imagine why you are having such a hard time finding your future wife."

"But seriously. Let's make the promise," he said.

"Seriously?"

"Yeah."

"You're weird. But okay." She shrugged.

"Pinky swear. You gotta pinky swear." He held up his hand and smiled.

They hooked pinkies.

"All right. It's locked in," he said with a smile. "And just so you know, the only way out of a pinky swear is death."

River wiped her eyes. *Cyrus, you idiot.* She thought.

Outside, she could hear muffled laughter. She sighed, pulled on her clothes and joined the others by the fireplace.

Sitting beside Tripp, she had just finished prepping her tea when Gypsy burst out of the brush. Tail wagging, she went straight for River.

"Aw, good morning Gypsy!" she shouted. This made the little dog even more excited as she reared up on her hind legs. "High five, Gypsy. High five!" The pup tagged her hands, then jumped up on her lap and tried to lick her face.

A pungent odor accosted River's senses—her eyes stung. "Oh, dear God! You smell! It's burnin' the inside of my nose!" she shouted, as she quickly put Gypsy down on the ground.

Oblivious to her own stench, the little dog turned and ran to Zac, tail wagging. He leaned forward, careful not to get too close, and sniffed. "Holy shit! Smells like someone got into a tangle with a skunk," he said, holding his arm against his face.

"Sorry," Gunner said, as he trudged up to them. "She ran ahead of me and got here before I could warn you."

"Dude, that is disgusting," exclaimed Cash. "It's burning my eyes."

"Tell that to dumbass here," scoffed Gunner, as he pointed to Finn, who came up behind him with Teague.

Finn feigned an innocent shrug. The impish smirk on his face told River everything she needed to know.

Gypsy tried to move closer to Zac who shoved her away, trying not to touch her with his hands. The whole area reeked of skunk.

"Finn, man, what the hell did you do?" Zac asked, as he used his boot to shove the pup toward River. She responded by using her foot to push Gypsy back toward him. They ended in a standoff with the little dog pressed between their feet.

"Dumbass found a spotted skunk a few yards back," Gunner explained, as he scowled at Finn. "He messed with it and got Gypsy involved."

"Well, there's your problem right there," replied Zac. "He ain't much more civilized than the dog."

Gunner agreed. He pulled a ball from his pack and whistled. Gypsy scampered over, waiting for the toss. As soon as it was airborne, she yapped and ran off into the brush, taking the pungent odor with her like a noxious cloud.

The smell dissipated. As long as Gunner kept Gypsy distracted, they were safe.

It was evening when they gathered their things. Rather than ride with a smelly pup, Tripp and Sam headed out on their own. After saying their goodbyes, they disappeared.

Holding out a bright-pink harness, Gunner called Gypsy over. River stopped what she was doing and watched. She tapped Cash on the arm to get his attention. Oblivious, Gunner put the harness on the little dog and secured the clasps.

"Not my dog, huh?" teased River.

"That sure is a pretty, little, pink harness with matching leash she has there," Cash quipped, laughing. "How many shops did you have to visit before you found the right one?"

"It's got little pockets!" Beth shouted, as she stepped closer. Catching a whiff of the skunk smell, she raised her arm to her face and backed off.

"She got a matching, pink sweater?" River giggled.

Behind Gunner, Nate nodded, letting them know that there was indeed a pink sweater.

Laughter broke out.

Gunner sighed and shook his head. "Haha, yeah, go ahead laugh, dumbasses," he continued. "The leash keeps her from running onto the tracks. The harness allows me to pick her up easily and get her on the train. It also makes her feel safe because it wraps around her."

Chuckling.

"... and don't even give me shit about the sweater. She needs that —it can get cold out here at night."

"Aw, how adorable!" River said, over all the laughter.

"Not adorable!" Gunner defended, "Functional." A small toy fell out of his pack. Still trying to hold on to some vestige of his masculinity, he hastily stuffed it back into a pocket. Barely fitting, it gave out a slow, tortured squeak as he forced it inside.

The laughter was deafening.

Gunner rolled his eyes and groaned. "You guys are assholes, sometimes," he said with a voice that sounded so unlike Gunner, it made the others laugh even more.

Chapter Forty-One

THE GENTLE NUDGE OF TEAGUE—NO WORDS, JUST A SHOVE AND A quick nod awakened Finn.

His mind reluctant to wake, he couldn't recall falling asleep. Gradually, he realized, the soothing sway that tempted him back to slumber, was the gentle movement of the boxcar cruising along the tracks. All around him, the others were in various states of readiness. He stood up and stretched. Outside, the dawn sky was a tranquil, steel blue. Up ahead, the radiance of distant city lights drew near.

The train slowed. Time to go. He tossed his pack, then jumped.

His feet struck the ground, jolting his body as he rolled with his momentum along the sharp gravel. Coming to a halt, he gained his footing and brushed himself off. Without skipping a beat, he gathered his gear and took off away from the tracks as speedily as possible. Being in the desert, there was no brush to deal with. That also meant there was no cover.

He stopped at the edge of a nearby road and waited.

It was a desolate stretch of asphalt. No street lights, no buildings, no cars of any kind—just hills, sand, the occasional desert plant and power lines. The faint smell of petrichor lingered in the air. It must have rained recently.

Behind him, the noise of shuffling feet on gravel drew near, as the rest of the group caught up.

"Everyone off ok?" he asked Teague, who was the first person to arrive.

Teague nodded. "Looks like it."

Finn waited until everyone was accounted for. Giving out a sharp whistle, he took up the lead as they headed toward town.

A few miles down the road, they reached an abandoned gas station. The old sign stood broken and dark high atop a rusty pole—$2.35 was the last price listed. Metal bars barricaded the windows. On the front doors, a heavy, steel chain and a rusty padlock held secure.

Finn took hold of the lock and tugged—it did not give. No surprise.

"Wonder when this closed down," Gunner said, stepping closer. "It was still open when we came through last time."

"Yeah?" asked Finn. "When was that?"

"About a year ago."

Finn walked around the building to the bay doors and cupped his hands to peer through one of the small windows. It was dark—too dark to see if anything of significance was inside. Deserted gas stations like these were great places to scavenge useful things. Especially if they had recently closed. He needed to get inside and poke around.

Gunner was by the rear door rummaging through his pockets. Finn joined him and tried the knob. It was locked. He reared back and kicked the door. It crashed open with the loud splintering noise of wood that echoed all around. To their left, something darted out of the shadows, away from the commotion. Finn flashed a triumphant grin at Gunner, who responded with a grunt of disapproval as he shook his head and put his lock pick kit away.

He glanced back at the others, shrugged, then ventured into the dingy garage.

It took a moment to adapt to the darkness. Broken fragments of metal and various bits of debris littered the stained floor. The smell of old tires, dirty oil and sweat permeated the air. Tiny pieces of dust danced about in the beams of his flashlight. In the corner of a window, a black widow worked undisturbed, building her web.

He examined the empty bay, venturing to the far side, searching in all the corners for anything that might be of use. Gunner disappeared into the darkness that was once an office. From where he stood, Finn could hear the shuffling sound of drawers being pulled open. A tiny whimper came from the threshold of the entry. It was Gypsy. When Gunner entered, he ordered her to stay. She remained still, her little body quivering as she waited excitedly for his next command.

Finn squatted beside an old workbench. The floor was thick with a sticky substance mixed with gritty sand. The scent wafting up from the floor was familiar—almost like waffles. That explained the sticky substance; it was antifreeze. The sand was kitty litter.

Standing up, his hand brushed across the top of the bench. Something small hit the floor with a metallic clang, then bounced. He dragged the bench away from the wall to get a better look. Scattered about in the dirt and grime, were half-a-dozen, small, perfectly round, half-inch ball bearings. Smirking, he gathered them up and looked them over in his palm. The little, metal orbs glimmered in the light. They were perfect. Exactly the sort of thing he hoped to find.

Gunner joined him in the bay. After one more cursory glance around, they joined their friends outside.

The morning sun was climbing, casting its warm glow on the sandy landscape. The golden light warmed Finn's skin, giving him a sense of renewed energy.

Along the road, cars rushed by, the occupants wrapped up in their own worlds, going about their daily tasks. It never ceased to astonish him that the only smiles he ever saw on the faces of people in cars belonged to the children. The adult facial expressions varied from detached to outright sneers. It was as though modern life sucked the joy right out of them. He wondered why it hadn't occurred to them that it didn't have to be that way.

They walked the main highway past small, rural homes. Sometimes a donkey or two would be in the front yard, nibbling on weeds. Passing by a house with goats, two kids hopped toward the fence, poking their heads through the wire. Beth giggled like a child as she scratched their fluffy, little heads.

An old horse—ribs showing, ambled up to the fence and neighed. They spent an extra several minutes rubbing his head. Nate even dug an apple out of his pack. The horse gobbled it up.

By mid-afternoon, they found themselves a pleasant, shady spot under a metal awning in one of the neighborhood parks in town. Leaving the others to rest, Finn and Cash wandered off to explore. It would be much easier to convince someone to give them a ride if they didn't approach with a large group.

The sun was out in full force. Except for the odd, stray dog, they were the only people walking around in the high heat of the day. They had turned down so many streets, Finn was losing his sense of location. Everything looked the same. It was all so dusty, flat and tan. When Cash suggested they stop at a little diner, he agreed enthusiastically.

Upon entering the building, the cool air struck him, causing a slight chill all over his body. It was a stark contrast to the temperature outside. They sidled up to the counter and perched themselves at the far corner where they could have a clear view of all the customers coming and going.

The server was a middle-aged woman, heavyset with dark, home-dyed hair and several, missing teeth. Her skin was a dark shade of bronze. Not the kind you would get from a tanning salon—this was the sort of deep tan you get living a hard life in a hot, sunny environment. Her name was Leta. She was friendly, but she over shared. Before they could even place their order, they knew she was a single mom with three, adult kids living at home. That she had suffered a heart attack four days before, but because she was the only source of income for her family, she couldn't stay home and rest. She smiled a huge, prideful smile when she informed them that her kids were so concerned about her health; they cooked her a huge breakfast before she left for her shift that day. After all of that, she pulled out her pen and pad and asked them what they would like to order.

Finn was still processing all the personal information Leta had just dumped on him when Cash gave him a shove. "Well? What are you getting?" he asked.

Snapping out of it, Finn realized they were both staring at him—

waiting. He quickly ordered a strawberry shake and some French fries. The server finished her notes, then wandered off. Finn was thankful she was gone. Turning to Cash, he let out a sigh, shook his head and spun around on his seat.

Country music played from the jukebox in the corner. The smell of onion rings and burgers on the grill permeated the air.

An elderly couple sat side by side in a booth by the window. Holding hands, they spoke in happy whispers and smiles as though they were the only two people on earth. There was something special about two people who had shared a lifetime together.

Next booth over sat a young couple facing one another. He couldn't see the man, but the girl was pretty with long, dark hair and brown eyes. Her makeup was perfect and heavy. Done up in that way that someone who spends too much time watching beauty videos would do. She stared down at her phone, tapping at the screen with her long, painted nails. Her male friend was busy doing the same. Neither of them spoke with one another.

At the counter, two seats away from Cash, sat a leathery, gray-haired man. His sweat-stained, cowboy hat sat on the stool beside him. Oblivious to the others in the cafe, he was reading a newspaper, pausing every so often to dip one of his fries into a puddle of ketchup on his plate.

Realizing his hands were filthy, Finn went to the men's room to wash off. When he returned, his food was waiting. Cash had struck up a conversation with the gray-haired cowboy. The old man's name was Travis. Finn nodded in greeting, then scooped up several French fries, dipped them in his shake and shoved them into his mouth.

From that moment until his plate was empty, Finn didn't pay much attention to anything Cash was saying to Travis.

At some point, Cash had found out that Travis lived in Lajitas—a halfway point between where they were and where they wanted to be. He also got the old man to offer them all a ride.

When it was time to leave, Travis paid for his meal and theirs. They climbed into his old truck and rode to the park to gather up their friends.

"Hey! Guys, this is Travis," Cash said, as they approached. "He says he'll take us as far as Lajitas."

Travis spit some chew on the ground, then smiled and said hello to everyone.

"You're welcome to ride along in the back. It'd shorten some of the walkin' you have ahead of you at least," he said, smiling.

"Sounds good to us," replied Gunner, with the others nodding in agreement. Gypsy barked and wagged her tail as she wriggled up toward Travis to check him out.

Seeing the little dog come near, he leaned down to pet her. "Ain't you the cutest little mess," he said, as she waddled over. When she came within arm's reach, Travis got a good whiff of the skunk smell. He quickly stood up covered his nose and said, "Dear Lord. Don't take this the wrong way, but your dog stinks to high heaven."

"I'm sorry. She ran into a skunk a-ways back. I guess I don't smell it anymore," Gunner said, as he pulled Gypsy back.

"Well, you probably fried your senses. Shit makes your eyes water," Travis said, as he shook his head and chuckled. "I once had a dog who did the same damn thing. Son of a bitch took over a week before I could even get close to him." He laughed.

"Well, all right then, let's get goin'," said Travis. "I don't have all day; I'd like to get home."

They piled into the truck bed and settled in.

Desert plants dotted the landscape as they rode through the rolling hills. In the distance, the mountains grew larger with each passing mile. To the right, the Rio Grande meandered with its lush, green vegetation—to the left, hills and the vast expanse of the Southwestern Texas desert. The sky was a vivid blue. Not a cloud in sight.

As promised, Travis brought them to the center of Lajitas.

They were roughly a half day's hike from their destination. Rather than continue walking, Gunner suggested they find a spot to camp for the night and head out fresh and early the next day. Tired from the long hike in the exhaustive heat, the entire group agreed. They found a remote spot along the river and set up camp.

"Is it okay for us to camp here?" asked Beth.

River responded, "Sure, why not?"

"I don't know." Beth shrugged. "I just imagine the local police wouldn't like it too much."

Finn scoffed, "First off, there ain't no local police force in this town. There's like seventy or so people who live here. The only law enforcement that would come through here would be border patrol. They got bigger issues to deal with—a few campers by the roadside are nothing by comparison."

Beth nodded.

Finn continued, "Most people who live this far away from the rest of civilization live by a simple code. Live how you want, love who you want, just don't be a dick."

"Mais oui! My kind of people," Teague said, grinning.

Gunner carried Gypsy to the river bank and removed his boots and socks. Holding the little dog with one hand, he stepped into the water and held her, limbs dangling as he soaked her down.

"Hey, you know that water is not even close to clean," Nate called out. "Seriously, man, it's really nasty. It probably stinks…" He paused, then let his words trail off and die.

Back in the water, Gypsy was not happy, but she remained still and allowed Gunner to lather her up then rinse her off. Standing there, soaking wet, she looked more like a drowned rat than the fluffy, little dog they all knew. He let her shake off, then wrapped her in a blanket and carried her over to sit with the others. She lay on his lap, snuggled up, little, black eyes and nose peeking out of her cocoon.

It wasn't long before the bright, blue sky gave way to the brilliant red and orange colors of sunset. Minutes passed, and the colors became more vivid, more electric. The sky was on fire. It cooled to an icy blue. Small bats flew overhead. The only sounds were the coursing river, the wind and the occasional chirp of the bats. They sat in silence, watching the little creatures perform their aerial acrobatics.

To Finn, this was paradise.

Slowly, the sky turned black, bringing with it the fantastic spectacle of billions of stars shining bright.

Laying atop his sleeping bag, Finn stared up in silent awe. The magic of lying there in the open, witnessing the beauty of the universe was awe-inspiring. Experiences like this made traveling worthwhile— this was what he lived for.

"There are just so many of them," Beth sighed. "The sky is absolutely crowded! There're billions." She pointed to her left. "Is that the milky way?"

"Yep, it sure is," replied Zac.

"I've only ever seen it in pictures. It's gorgeous!" she said. "So many different points of light, so many different colors! I had no idea stars were so colorful! I feel so small."

"It's like laying under a glittery, rainbow blanket." She reached into the air. "I've never seen so many at one time."

"C'est beau," Teague breathed.

Far away, a group of javelinas got into a loud scuffle. As quickly as the noise erupted it stopped, leaving them in silence once again.

In the dark wilderness across the river, a band of coyotes yipped and howled. From her blanket cocoon, Gypsy growled as Gunner snored.

Chapter Forty-Two

TWELVE MILES TO THE CENTER OF TERLINGUA. IF THEY MANAGED A modest pace, they would arrive around noon.

The highway snaked its way through the valley. Up hills and back down again. The Chisos Mountain Range loomed in the distance. This was one of Teague's favorite places to be. Rugged, wild and untouched by contemporary civilization, the entire range had a tranquil beauty to it. He imagined this is what it would be like if no other people existed on earth.

As the morning hours passed, the sun cast its rays down on them with the full measure of a blast furnace. Up ahead, heatwaves blurred the asphalt like a mirage. The dryness of the landscape coupled with the absence of trees did not do much for limiting the effect of the sun —the temperature climbed. Sweat oozed out of every pore, drying rapidly in the arid breeze.

When Gunner suggested they take a rest before the last stretch, Teague was more than ready. Finding the most abundant shrub, he tossed his gear to the ground and sat down under the sparse branches, hoping to take advantage of the minimal shade it provided.

Finn's pack hit the ground beside him. Teague glanced up to see him staring across the open field. Several yards away, a rabbit nibbled on desert weeds.

Without breaking his gaze, Finn pulled out his slingshot. As he crept forward, he fished a ball bearing from his pocket.

A slight shuffling sound diverted Teague's attention; Beth, who had taken a seat beside River under a nearby tree, had pulled out her phone and was recording. She winked at him and smiled.

Teague looked back over to Finn, who was inching closer to the small creature. Watching Finn stalk prey was like watching a video of lions on the African Savannah. The way they snuck up on their unsuspecting quarry—the tension in their bodies as they ramped up to pounce.

Finn crept closer, making no noise. Nostrils flaring, eyes unblinking, he concentrated on the bunny. He placed the bearing into the pocket of the slingshot and pulled the band back. The muscles in his arm and shoulder strained as he took aim. His jaw tightened. His eyes narrowed. He released the ball bearing.

The rabbit collapsed with a soft thud.

"Yes! Got lunch!" Finn shouted, as he flashed a victorious grin at Teague.

Beth and River cheered while Cash and Zac silently clapped.

Their celebration was short lived. A loud screech came from the sky. A golden eagle soared against the crystal, blue backdrop. It was a sight to behold. Teague watched in admiration as it cruised along the currents of the air. Wings wide, tail tilting left and right. It circled and flew closer to the fresh kill.

"No, no, no, no, no! Finn shouted, as he scrambled—slingshot still in hand—slipping on the loose sand.

The giant bird dove. It wrapped its massive talons around the rabbit with one fluid motion, then flapped its enormous wings and raised itself into the air.

Finn slid across the gravel like he was sliding into home base, reaching out to catch the bird as it lifted itself off the ground and over his head. A plume of dust billowed around him.

He jumped to his feet. "Fuck!" he yelled, as he raised his slingshot.

He picked up a small rock from the ground and let loose—it missed. Reaching his hand out to Gunner, he said, "Gunner! Give me your gun!"

Lying under a mesquite tree, hat pulled over his face, Gunner replied. "No."

"Come on. I can get that thing from here. Just give me your gun."

"That's debatable, all the same… nope."

"Come on," pleaded Finn.

"No."

"Come on; it's got my kill."

"And it's gonna keep it, son. I'm not giving you my gun," replied Gunner, decisively.

Teague giggled, then stopped instantly when Finn glared at him.

Finn scoured the ground for another rock. Firing it off, it went wide and missed. He found another one, and once again, let it fly. It missed. Overhead, the giant predator stretched its wings as it circled, almost as though it were mocking him.

"Fuckin' aye!" cried Finn, as he took to throwing random rocks in the air. "Goddammit!"

With one final screech of triumph, the majestic bird turned and disappeared into the hills.

"Come on, this is just sad now. Let it go, Finn," Cash said, laughing.

"Screw y'all," replied Finn, turning to face at the others. "That damn bird stole my kill." He peered at the sky in the direction the bird flew and shouted one last time as he raised his finger in the air, "Fuck you!" Then he stomped back to the tree and plopped himself down on the ground.

Fighting the impulse to laugh, Teague handed him a bottle of water.

Between guffaws, Cash asked, "So, ah, what exactly was it that you were tryin' to do there, when you were hopping up and down reaching for the damn bird? Did you not see how big it was?"

Finn swallowed and wiped his mouth with the back of his hand. "Yeah, I was right next to it. I know how big it was. Stupid bird."

"Yeah, but if you actually grabbed hold," Cash continued, "what the hell would you have done? It's freaking wingspan, was at least six feet wide."

"I wasn't thinkin' about that. I just wanted my rabbit back."

That was it. Teague could hold back no longer. He joined the others in laughter. Finn stared at him, making him laugh even harder.

"Teague, your boy here is feral," Zac said, shaking his head.

"This is true," Teague replied, with an enormous grin. He turned to look at Finn. "Part of me wonders who would've won."

"Me. I would have won," replied Finn.

Teague knew that Finn would have fought to the death with that eagle over the rabbit. When it came to food, he did not mess around. He nudged Finn, and the others continued to needle him.

Gradually, Finn's anger diminished, and he laughed with the others, even though he made it clear he was still not happy.

Their rest ended when Gunner stood up and donned his pack. "Okay, everyone, we've lounged long enough. Time to get back on the road. We're almost there."

Chapter Forty-Three

"WELCOME TO TERLINGUA." BETH READ ALOUD. THE SIGN WAS weather worn and riddled with bullet holes. Behind it, stood a follow up. "You won't stay long, if you don't belong." *Well, this is gonna be interesting.* She thought.

Their long trek was almost over. She shifted her pack; the straps pulled on her shoulders, and one specific spot near her collarbone was rubbing raw.

This was rougher than she imagined. The scorching heat was draining. The extra burden of the pack made each additional step more arduous than it needed to be. She could not wait to shed the surplus weight and stretch her neck and shoulders. Though no one complained, the others had to be feeling the same. There was no other explanation for why their jovial banter had died down to nothing.

Up ahead, Finn and Teague were the only two people who didn't seem fatigued. They had paused a while back and saturated their shirts with water, then tied them around their heads. From that time on, they walked at the head of the group chatting away with animated gestures. No hint of exhaustion. They acted as though they were meandering down a shady, tree-lined street as opposed to the dry hell-scape they were plodding through.

Turning off the main highway, they paraded down a dusty, gravel road. Finn and Teague whistled. Gypsy took off running, disappearing around a bend.

Shielding her eyes, Beth squinted and searched ahead. The bleached sand reflected the sunlight, causing what she could only think of as the desert's adaptation of snow blindness—sand blindness. She giggled, then felt silly for laughing at the joke in her head.

At the far end of the road, a dark rectangle came into view. Stark against the backdrop of the tan hills, it blurred like a mirage. She squinted and focused her eyes. "Is that a freight container?" She asked, surprising herself—she didn't mean to say that out loud.

As they neared, more details came into view. It was a large, red, metal box with Chinese lettering along the side, broken up by three, wide windows. The windows themselves were new—modern additions to the otherwise used and abused hide of the container. There were distinct patches of different-colored paint speckled all over the side. Olive green, navy blue, dark red and black. Someone was trying to choose a color. At one end, a metal awning stretched over a generous glass door.

The door shot open, and a scruffy-looking man came outside. He was slim and tall with gray hair.

Gypsy reached him first. He leaned down and patted her on her head, then turned and greeted Gunner. Without skipping a beat, he spun around and hugged Nate like a long-lost son. One by one, the stranger worked his way through the group.

At last, he stopped in front of Beth. "Hello." He beamed. His face was like tan leather, his eyes were pale gray. There was an intensity and inner joy to him that was indisputable. His clothes were dusty and well-worn, though not dirty.

"This is Beth," said Cash. "She joined us a few days ago from Denton. Beth, this is Stoney. The old curmudgeon of the desert."

Beth reached her hand out.

Stoney laughed. "Nah, get over here."

He pulled her in and gave her a hug, then released her. "Welcome to Stoney's Retreat. You're welcome here just like everyone else."

Beth smiled. Stoney's happiness and openness were contagious. It was impossible not to feel accepted.

"Stoney here used to be a hobo, like us," said Cash. "He rode for ten years." He halted, turned to Stoney and asked, "Was it ten? I thought I heard you say that once."

"Too many," replied Stoney. "It was probably more like fifteen. I just got tired and too old. Catching on became a real drag. Nothing like a couple of near misses to make you realize you ain't no Dirty Kid no more—you're an old man and it's time to retire." He chuckled. "So, I came here and made this little oasis in the desert my home."

Stoney winked at Beth and spun around on his heels. "Well, don't stand around in the hot sun. Come on to the back and let's get you all settled. There are some other folks dying to see you."

Up close, the container appeared less of a metal box and more like a bright, modern, small home. As she sauntered past the entrance, Beth peered inside. The door opened to a bright, narrow room with a sofa on one side, a wood stove and bookshelf on the other. Just beyond that, a kitchen with a small table and in the back, a bedroom—partially shielded by an old, barn door.

Behind the house stood four more containers. Each one had a covered porch and large windows. One had a spiral staircase that led to the roof, another had two front doors. They reminded Beth of small cottages. Off to the side, another large container sat baking in the sun. This appeared to be a new project as it had no fancy door or windows. Tools were strewn about on the ground. She wasn't sure, but they appeared to be welding equipment.

In the center of the yard, located to be the focal point, stood an enormous, rock-lined fire pit. Mismatched lawn chairs were arranged all around.

At the rear of the home, a stone patio awaited, topped with a metal roof. In the corner, an old refrigerator hummed away. Beth ditched her pack and plunked herself down in a chair. Her legs tingled and throbbed. The temperature was twenty degrees cooler in the shade. She sighed.

Zac passed her a bottle of water. The icy-cold bottle made her feel cooler as she rolled it along her forehead and the back of her neck. She peered out across the backyard beyond the little units; each one had its own gorgeous view of the mountains off in the distance. Such a peaceful place.

The door to the unit with the spiral stairs flew open. A tall, thin man with messy, brown dreadlocks and a beard walked outside. He was wearing sandals, shorts and a tie-dye tank top. A slender woman followed. Her dark, brown hair was a cascade of long dreadlocks hanging down to the small of her back.

"Spinner, my man," shouted Cash.

Close up, Beth could see he was older—not as old as Stoney, but older than Gunner.

The woman wandered up. "There are my babies," she said with a serene, feminine voice as she wrapped her arms around Finn and gave him a long hug. She worked her way through all the members of their group.

The woman turned and beamed at River. "Get over here baby girl."

Noticing Beth, she stood in front of her. "Who is this beautiful new thing?"

Beth found it difficult not to stare. This woman had a powerful, earthy presence. She was elegant and athletic. Years of living under the sun made her skin a dark, golden bronze. Her bright, blue eyes were striking. Everything about her was natural—authentic.

"Oh, this is Beth," River responded. "She travels with us now."

"Beth, this is Bella," she said smiling.

Bella tilted her head and stared at Beth. The kind of stare a person does when they are reading into your soul. No judgement, just acknowledgement. "Where you from, Beth?"

"Denton."

"Denton," repeated Bella, nodding her head. "I've been there. Quaint little city." Her eyes drifted past Beth toward the hills. "Great local music scene." A sincere smile stretched across her face. "Welcome! You have to tell me all about yourself when you get a chance."

Beth nodded and smiled. She took a sip of water, savoring the sensation as the cool liquid flowed down her throat.

"Anyone else here yet?" asked Gunner, as he lit a smoke.

"Yeah," replied Stoney. "Tanner, Ben and Mara came in a few days ago with some guy from Australia. His name is Josh. He's been tagging along with them for a few months now. Seems like a decent guy."

"Tripp and Sam got in yesterday. They said they ran into you and that you weren't far behind."

Stoney continued, "Last I heard, Max, Bells and DB were in transit somewhere up north outside of Olympia. They were hoping to catch a ride south, but it seems something happened to the tracks up there. No trains can pass until they clear or repair whatever it was. It's a remote enough area that there aren't a lot of options for hitching a ride. They're not gonna make it. They're pissed."

Beth listened to the discussion. That was quite a few people she didn't know. For the first time since leaving home she felt like an outsider. Letting her mind go, she turned her face to the hills, closed her eyes, and breathed. A soft hand settled on her shoulder. It was River.

Stoney fed them a lunch of burgers, salad, fresh fruit and beer. After the long hike in the heat, Beth didn't realize she was even hungry until the aroma of grilling burgers wafted her way. When River finally placed a plate on her lap, she gulped it down like a person who hadn't eaten in days—like Finn. She didn't care, it was the best tasting food she ever had.

Feeling better, she turned to Stoney. "So, is this where you grew up?"

He shook his head. "No, I grew up in Georgia. Haven't been back in decades, though."

"How did you start riding?"

"I got out of the Marine Corps after Desert Storm. Didn't want to go back home." He shrugged. "I suppose I wasn't ready to settle down yet, so when I left Camp Lejeune, I just hopped a train then another and another. Traveled alone mostly, but I spent time with many other riders. Got to know most of the community."

"I bet you have tons of interesting stories."

"I do," replied Stoney, as he nodded. "Life is supposed to be an adventure, especially when you're young."

"What made you choose here?"

Stoney grinned. "I don't really like most people. Only a certain kind of person can come out here and live full time. When it was time to stop, this was the only place for me. I worked, saved up some money, and bought this plot of land. This container was already here. I built it out with my two bare hands." He patted the wall.

"Wow! That's so cool."

"Added a few other units," he nodded toward the cottages. "Been working on them over the past couple years. I rent those out to tourists when these guys aren't in town."

"Which reminds me," he said aloud, "I told the others to double up as much as possible. Those of you who are inclined to sleep in a tent can set up anywhere you'd like."

The discussion shifted to who would sleep where. Beth let her mind process all that Stoney had told her. What he had built here was remarkable.

"So, who's up for the hot springs?" asked Teague.

River chuckled. "I thought you were never gonna ask."

"I'm in," chimed Cash.

Finn stood up. "Can we borrow one of your trucks?"

"Ben took the blue truck. The red one's still there in the driveway. As for whether you can take that one—sure, as long as someone else drives. You..." He pointed his finger at Finn. "Ain't getting behind the wheel of my truck ever again."

Finn flashed a sheepish grin.

"I'll drive!" shouted Cash.

"That's just as bad as him driving. As I recall, you were very much a part of the last fiasco. No." Stoney said. "It took me a week to get her out of that ravine. You know there are no tow trucks out here."

"Looks like it's me," River said, as she rose.

"Finally, a grown-up." Stoney tossed his keys to her.

She took hold of Beth's hand. "Grab your bag and come with me."

They ran over to the container with two doors. This was the shower cabin. Beth went in one side—River the other.

Inside, warm, tan colored tile covered the entire room from floor to ceiling. A deep sink stood against one wall, toilet on the other. Along the back wall was a giant shower with what had to be the largest shower head Beth had ever seen.

She ran her fingers through her hair and cringed as they snagged on greasy knots. Dried sweat clumped together thick strands. Her neck and face had an oily feel. She gazed into the mirror, stunned by the young woman she did not recognize. The sun had burned her face. Grime settled deep into her pores. Remnants of eyeliner remained smudged around her eyes. She couldn't recall the last time she put on makeup. Trying to wipe it clean, she ran a finger under her bottom lid —this only made it worse. What a mess she was. Well, she was undeniably a Dirty Kid now. She wasn't sure if she should laugh or cry.

She wandered over to the shower. The fresh fragrance of soap made her aware of her own smell. Reaching in, she turned on the water and held her hand in the stream. Warm yet cooling. More than anything, she wanted to strip down and stand under the water.

River pounded on the door. "Come on! We're burnin' time."

Beth sighed, then turned off the shower and quickly changed into clothes for swimming.

By the time she and River got to the truck, the others were already piled into the back, waiting. She hopped into the passenger side and buckled up, as River adjusted her seat and mirrors.

Chapter Forty-Four

STONEY LOVED USING THINGS UNTIL THEY FELL APART. EVERYTHING HE owned was a dinosaur. His trucks were prime examples, with no A/C and hand-crank windows. River opened the window, letting in a blast of hot, desert air. Small flecks of dust glinted like tiny crystals settling on the dash.

She threw the truck into gear. "You are in for a treat, little sister," she said to Beth.

A moment later, she was driving down the dirt road, kicking up a dense cloud of dust in their wake.

The ride through the park was breathtaking. She held her arm outside the window and let the wind blow against her hand. The untouched landscape scrolled by like a postcard. Birds flew overhead, roadrunners ran across the road. Out here, in the middle of nowhere, it was easy to forget about the rest of the world.

In the parking area, she pulled up alongside Stoney's blue truck. Before she could even open her door, Finn and Teague hit the ground and took off running. They disappeared down the trail.

River laughed, she could relate to their enthusiasm. She scanned the area. There was one other vehicle—a red jeep. Hopefully, whoever they were, they would leave soon.

They crossed over the dry creek bed, into a clearing where the remnants of the old general store stood. Giant palm trees hovered overhead. Beneath their feet, the soft, powdery earth was more like beach sand than typical desert soil. Behind her, Zac was busy telling Beth all about the history of the place. How it used to be a resort for adventurous travelers.

Steep rock ridge to their left—lush plant life and flowing water on their right. They followed the path as it snaked along the banks of the Rio Grande.

The sound of laughter up ahead told River that they were not far. Rounding the corner, she pushed aside the tall grass.

The remains of the bathhouse rose from the muddy clay, creating a near perfect square filled with hot spring water. Outside, the cool river water rushed along the edge of the wall.

"Ahhhh!" shouted Mara, as she ran up and wrapped her arms around River. "You made it!"

Mara was one of a short list of females that River actually liked. She traveled with Tanner and Ben—the love of her life. She was one of the happiest people River had ever known. She had a flair for seeing the good in others. When Mara was around, the mood was almost always cheerful.

"This is new," River said, pointing at the septum ring dangling beneath Mara's nose. The tiny, emerald-green stone set in the middle brought out the color in her hazel eyes.

Giggling, Mara brushed her wavy, brown hair aside, exposing her neck. "I got this too." She tilted her head sideways, exposing a tiny, green, sea-turtle tattoo.

Mara's favorite color was green. Olive, emerald, grass—it didn't matter the shade. She loved them all. She even dyed the tips of her hair green. No small feat considering the nomadic way they all lived.

"Who's this?" she asked, studying Beth.

River had forgotten she was there. She pulled Mara forward. "This is Beth. She's new to our group."

"Beth, this wench is Mara," River said. "Yes, she's always this happy."

Mara chuckled and wrapped her arms around Beth, hugging her as though she had known her for years. "Welcome, Beth!"

River looked around to see who was there. Finn and Teague were lounging in the spring, chatting with Sam. Tanner sat on a rock nearby.

Tanner towered over the other members of their group, standing a foot taller than River. Tattoos covered every inch of his upper body. When plied with the right amount of alcohol, he would happily tell the story behind each one. However, he was most proud of the sleeve that covered his right arm. It was the story of his time spent in the Army. The focal point being an elaborate set of crossed swords with the word 'MOUNTAIN' centered above.

Mara squealed as Ben snuck up from behind and lifted her in the air. "Ben, this is Beth. She's new."

Ben reached his hand out. "Hello there Beth."

He put Mara down and hugged River, soaking her. The faint smell of wet clay emanated from him. When River protested his wetness, he laughed, ran his fingers through his short, brown hair then flicked the water at her. She scoffed and shoved him.

"Come on! The water's amazing!" shouted Mara, as she grabbed hold of River's hand.

Stepping into the spring was sheer bliss. River bent down on her knees and let the warm, earthy water envelop her body. She closed her eyes and breathed in.

The scent of weed wafted her way. She opened her eyes to see Ben hovering nearby, waving a joint inches from her nose. Pulling herself up on a ledge, she accepted the offering and took a hit.

"River, say hello to Josh." Ben said, in between hits.

She took in the newcomer. He was fit with well-defined arms and a golden, tan body. His hair was an unruly mop of wavy, brown hair. *Not bad.* She thought.

"Hello River," He said with his thick, Australian accent. He flashed her a gorgeous smile. His eyes were a striking shade of warm brown with very long eyelashes.

Blood rushed to her face. "Hello." She reached out to shake his hand, accidentally knocking the joint into the water. There was a moment of fumbling as they both tried to rescue it, followed by cries of dismay coming from everyone. Then came the teasing. River rolled her eyes and moved away from Josh. There would be plenty of time for her to get to know him later.

Laughter and voices erupted from the trail as Tripp and three young women cut through the grass and came into view. All three of the girls had the distinct look of young, college students. One of them, a redhead, was riding on his back, giggling. Coming to the edge of the spring, he let her slide off his back.

Locking eyes with River, he smirked, "I see you all finally made it." The young girl sidled up next to him in the water and pulled his arm around her shoulder.

River rolled her eyes. Typical Tripp. Seeing him with another girl didn't bother her. She wondered if he thought it did. *Whatever.*

The girls went on and on about classes, professors and parents. It all sounded the same. When Cash finally came to the rescue with a bottle of whiskey and a way out of the conversation, River was relieved. As she waded away, she blew a kiss at Tripp. He winked at her and went back to listening to the redhead.

River climbed out of the warm water and sat on the wall next to Mara, letting her feet hang over the edge into the cool river.

"So, Josh," she said loud enough the get his attention. "What brings you all the way out here in the middle of nowhere USA?"

"Backpacking," he replied. He climbed out of the water and took a seat beside her.

"I was supposed to get off the plane in LA then work my way north. For some odd reason, I got stuck there. I didn't leave."

"Sorry to hear that." She chuckled. "I can think of at least five other cities I'd rather get stuck in."

"True," he replied. "It's strange. When you're in the city, it's so chaotic and busy—it smells, and it's noisy. You always feel stressed out. You get all uptight and irritated like you don't want to be sur-rounded by all of those people, but you don't want to leave either."

River was enjoying the sound of his accent. She wanted him to keep talking.

He sighed. "In hindsight, I think I was lucky things went down the way they did and forced me to leave. I'd probably still be there."

River's curiosity was piqued. "What went down?" she asked.

A sly smile swept across his face. "Let's just say I'm not as sweet as I come across at first."

"Oh?" she replied with a smirk. "I am intrigued."

He laughed, then cleared his throat. "Anyway, I ran into Ben, Mara and Tanner on the beach one night. They told me what they did and how they traveled. I decided I had to give it a try."

"So how long have you been in the US?"

"A little over a year now, I think." He paused and thought about it. "Yeah, my visa expired a little over a month ago."

"When do you plan to go home?"

He shrugged. "We'll see what happens."

"Sounds like a solid plan," she replied. Mara gave her the bottle of whiskey. She took a sip and passed it along to Josh.

Chapter Forty-Five

BETH WAS HAVING A TOUGH TIME KEEPING UP. ALL THE UNFAMILIAR names and faces were overwhelming. Their closeness and ease with one another made her feel even more like an outsider. Like she just wandered into the midst of a family reunion. Terrified she would say something improper or offensive, she elected to keep her replies as simple as possible.

Mara was nice. Ben was a little more complicated. She didn't know how to react to his caustic wit. Was he joking or serious? She couldn't tell sometimes. When she met them, she noticed right away that they both had the compass tattoo. Mara's was on her left hip and Ben's was on his rib cage. She wondered if the others had it.

Glancing over at Sam—sure enough, it was there in plain sight on his upper arm.

Beth shifted her attention to Tanner. A set of dog tags hung down around his neck. Tattoos covered his entire body. At least every area she could see. She traced the lines with her eyes, trying to see if any of them lined up with the familiar circle. So many images—like a mural. She examined his abdomen, then moved up to his chest and finally his neck. There it was, on the left side, the compass. Celebrating her minor triumph, she smiled.

Her private celebration was short lived. He was staring at her—wearing a grin that spread across his entire face, all the way to his deep, blue eyes. *Oh god!* She thought as she glanced away. How long had he been watching her stare at him? Awkwardly, she tried to pretend she was part of the conversation between River, Tripp and the college girls.

Mara's cheery laughter drew her attention to the other side of the pool. Beth decided she genuinely liked her. Through their conversation, she found out that Mara grew up in Sandy, Utah. Raised in a faithful Mormon family, she had two older sisters and two younger brothers. This fascinated Beth. She always wondered if things would have been different if she had a sister or another brother or two.

The afternoon sun hovered low on the horizon. It was time to head back. The walk to the parking lot was full of banter and laughter. This was the lifestyle Beth had imagined.

Tripp and Sam decided to spend the night camping with the college girls. They left in the red Jeep. Everyone else piled into the two trucks and sped back to Stoney's.

Beth stuck her head out of the window, letting the wind rush through her hair.

Arriving at Stoney's, they were greeted by an ecstatic Gypsy, a warm fire blazing in the pit and an amazing dinner of brisket and salad. She snagged a plate, piled it high with food and took a seat beside Spinner and Bella.

"How did you like the hot spring?" asked Spinner.

"It was nice," she replied.

Spinner smiled. "One of my favorite places."

"You never got around to telling me where you're from, Spinner."

"Northern California," he replied.

"And you, Bella?"

"I grew up in central California." Her words came out as an almost wistful sigh.

There was something about Bella that intrigued Beth. She didn't require fancy clothes or makeup. Gorgeous, powerful and maternal; confidence and femininity emanated from her.

"So, what's your story?" she asked Spinner.

He grinned. "Well, back in the day, when I was in high school, I would head out backpacking around the west coast during summer break. As time moved on, I went to college, then stayed in college. I guess I stayed there a little too long. I kinda lost sight of how much I loved roaming."

"How many years were you in college?"

"I wanna say eight or nine." He smirked. "Some of it's kind of foggy—we did a bit of partying back then."

"Wow," said Beth. "Does that mean you have a master's degree?"

Spinner smiled.

Bella interjected, "He has a Ph.D."

"Really?" asked Beth. "In what?"

"Ancient history."

"Cool," said Beth. "So, were you a Professor?"

"I was," he responded. "For a few years. In fact, that's where I met Bella." He wrapped his arm around Bella's shoulder and pulled her close. "She was working on her master's."

"Why did you leave? I mean, lots of people would kill for a chance to teach at a university."

Spinner sighed. "I guess for some of us, being in one place, doing the same thing every day is just not what we're meant to do. Truth is, I found the life of an academic to be sterile, void of any honest interaction with the real world." He shrugged. "Living that way just never felt like a good fit for me. I tried, but I need freedom and a change of scenery from time to time. I'll take nomads any day over anyone else. They're far more interesting."

Beth mulled over those last words. Spinner was right, nomads were a lot more interesting than normal people. She thought about her friends back home. *What are they doing now?* Probably staring at her posts wishing they were the ones on the adventure. For the first time in her life, she was getting all the attention—all the likes, shares and comments. *I bet Liz and Kara are so jealous.* A sly smile swept across her face. Dying to see how many more responses were posted, she pulled out her phone.

"That might not work out here." It was Teague. He was sitting on the other side of the fire—Finn beside him, glaring.

The light from the fire cast an eerie glow on Finn's features, making it appear as though he was sneering. A chill ran up her spine.

"He's right," said Stoney. "Connectivity is spotty out here. It's part of the reason I love this place. No modern distractions."

Beth sighed and put her phone back in her pocket. She would check tomorrow on the drive. Surely there would be a signal somewhere. She couldn't wait to post her newest clips of the Spring. It was a sure bet that none of her friends had been there before.

Her mind drifted back to the compass. "Bella, Spinner, do you two have a compass tattoo?"

They nodded. Spinner pulled his sleeve up to show it was on his right, upper arm. Bella pulled up her pants to show hers on her left calf.

"Wow, so everyone has it," she said. "Did you get it done here? By who?"

Bella nodded toward Cash.

He sat up. "By me," he said.

"Cash is our resident scratcher," came a voice, the speaker just out of view, it sounded like Ben.

Beth looked over at Zac. "I thought you drew it?"

"I did," he replied. "I just created it. I'm more of a pencil-and-paper kind of guy. Cash is the tattoo artist."

"Why do you think mine's right here?" Cash said, holding out his arm. "It's an area I can reach."

"You should decide where you want yours," said River.

"Huh?" Beth asked. Her voice quaking.

Cash stood up. "Stoney, my gear in the house?"

"Right where you left it."

"Okay, Beth, figure out where you want it," Cash said, over his shoulder as he walked into the house.

Beth glanced around. "Did he mean that?"

"He sure did," Bella replied.

"Only if you want to," said River.

She peeked over at Finn—he was staring at the ground.

Teague chimed in, "You kinda earned it."

Was this really happening? Was she about to get her first tattoo? Beth's mind was reeling. To be a member of this tribe was all she wanted. "Yes!" she shouted. "Yes, I do."

Soon after that, Beth sat at the kitchen table, surrounded by the others.

Straddling a chair, Cash asked, "Where are we putting it?"

Adrenaline coursed through her body. "Um, I don't know," she replied. "How about my left shoulder, opposite River's?" She peered up at River.

"Sounds like an excellent spot to me," said River, smiling.

Beth's heart raced—she hugged the back of the chair to keep from trembling. Cash leaned closer, the machine in his hand buzzed.

"Is it gonna hurt?" she asked. Her voice sounding pathetic in her own ears.

"Nah, not at all," replied Cash. His tone wasn't very convincing. He touched her shoulder.

The tattoo machine vibrated as it hovered just above her skin.

Cash paused, snickered, then said with an impish tone, "Hey Beth, wanna talk about spider eyes again?"

She groaned.

The bite of the needle was sharp and instant. She could feel every poke as the needle dragged along her skin. Beth sat as still as possible, doing her best not to let on that she felt any discomfort. Gradually, the sharp pain gave way to a burning sensation. The buzz of the machine became more of a vibration she felt throughout her body.

From time to time, a person from outside would stray in and see how it was going. They would look at her shoulder, nod in approval, then wander back out.

Beth could not wait to see it—the anticipation was killing her.

Alas, a little over an hour after they began, it was done. Her skin burned like a bad sunburn. Beth went to the bathroom and turned around in the mirror to see her new tattoo. Ignoring the angry, red outline, it was the most beautiful tattoo she had ever seen. She ran her fingers across the top to see if she could rub it off—it was permanent.

She spun around and squealed with delight, then pulled out her phone to take a picture.

Chapter Forty-Six

PERCHED ON THE COUNTER IN THE LITTLE KITCHEN, FINN WATCHED Beth parade about with glee showing off her new ink. Right away, she pulled out her phone and preened before the mirror trying to take the perfect shot. No matter what was going on, there was Beth fondling her phone. The worst part of all was how she stared down at the screen with zombie eyes. Her shoulders stooped over as she folded her body around the one thing in the world she coveted most. He had seen that posture before—in the dark alleys of every major city he had been in— it was the posture of the addicted.

The commotion moved outside. Thankful for the moment of quiet, Finn sat alone listening to the hum of the electric lights. With a heavy sigh, he hopped off the counter and went outside.

"She's loving her new tattoo." Bella's soothing voice wafted out of the darkness.

Finn paused, allowing his eyes to adapt to the absence of bright light. "This where the old folks are hiding?" He sat down beside Gunner who passed him a baby food jar filled with moonshine.

"You've been holdin' out on me," Finn said, then he took a swig. The liquid burned as it cascaded down his throat and into his belly. He

326 • N.L. MCLAUGHLIN

gasped and wiped his mouth. "Tastes like turpentine with a slight hint of apple pie." A warm sensation spread throughout his body.

"180 proof," replied Gunner. He took a sip and handed the jar to Spinner.

"No, thanks, man. That shit'll cause you to go blind. I'll stick to the lower-proof whiskey."

Stoney scoffed. "Well, give it on over here." He drew a swig, then whistled. "That's good." He gasped. "I got something better. Hold up." He bolted into the house letting the door slam behind him.

Teague's arm slid over Finn's shoulder.

Finn handed him the jar.

He sniffed the contents and recoiled. "That's potent." He stated, then took a swig. Gasping, he handed the jar back to Finn.

The door swung open and Stoney bumbled out carrying a mason jar filled with clear liquid. "A buddy of mine in town makes his own moonshine. He's been experimenting with different flavors." He unscrewed the cap and handed the jar to Finn. "This one reminded me of you two. It's infused with habanero."

Finn took a whiff of the contents and cringed. He handed the jar over to Teague, who smirked and took a swallow.

Nostrils flaring, Teague exhaled. "Ça c'est bon! Clears the sinuses."

Finn took a drink. It was hard to say which burned more—the alcohol or the pepper. Eyes watering and nose running, he could feel sweat seeping from his pores. Teague was right.

Shouts and laughter erupted from the people around the fire. Someone had poured whiskey on the flames, causing them to shoot into the air like a rocket launcher.

Bella chuckled. "Looks like you boys are missing out on all the young people's fun."

Finn shrugged. He didn't feel like he was missing out on anything.

"So, how do you like having a new, little sister?" pressed Bella.

Finn could sense her eyes looking through him—searching for something that would reveal his true feelings. Truth was, he didn't know how he felt about it. One minute he would be fine, the next, Beth would do something that made him question whether she belonged.

"She's young," he responded.

"That she is," replied Bella. "Give her some time. She's just a young woman trying to figure out who she is and where she fits in this world."

Finn didn't want to talk about this. The moonshine was dulling his senses; he wanted to enjoy the numbness.

Ben staggered up onto the patio and into the house. A moment later he appeared carrying a bottle of Everclear.

Slapping Finn on his shoulder, he said, "Come on you two, time to play."

"I got 'em! Ben yelled, as they stepped into the light around the fire.

Finn dropped to the ground beside Zac. He took a hit from the jar of moonshine.

"You holdin' out on me?" asked Zac.

"Here, have some literal firewater," Finn said, as he handed the jar over.

Zac smirked, then took a huge swig. His face went red. His nostrils widened. "Holy shit, that's hot!" He declared through watery eyes. He coughed a few times and gasped for air—then took another pull.

Across the fire, Beth was busy interrogating Ben.

"I hitched a ride to Burlington and got dropped off at a bus terminal. It was late, so I had to wait till the morning. So, I made myself comfortable over by the seating area. That's when I met this dumbass," Ben said, pointing to Tanner.

"He was all curled up on the floor, talking in his sleep, kinda like how a dog will yip and whimper, you know?"

Beth giggled and nodded.

Ben went on, "He woke himself up while I was gawking at him. It was pretty uncomfortable. We got to talking, and he told me about riding around on trains. I was sold on it right away. We headed out together a few hours later, just before sunrise. Caught a train heading south, and well, that was that."

Beth turned to Tanner. "Were you riding long before that?"

He shook his head. "Not really—maybe about six months."

"What made you start?"

Based on her expression, Finn could see that Beth was interested in learning all she could about the people of the group. Watching her from this angle—minus her phone, he saw the young woman that Bella was talking about. He liked this Beth.

"I just didn't fit in with the folks at home," replied Tanner.

"Why so?" she pressed.

Tanner flashed a wry smirk. Without speaking, eyes locked with Beth's, he pulled his pant leg up, uncovering a prosthetic leg.

Finn studied her reaction. What Beth didn't know was that Tanner did this to everyone when they first met. He liked to make people uncomfortable.

"Oh," exclaimed Beth.

Ben came to her rescue. "Don't worry, Beth, he knows that freaks people out. That's why he does it."

"Blew my mind the first time he showed me," said Cash. "He waited till I was super high to do it."

"I'm sorry," Beth said awkwardly.

"Sorry for what?" asked Tanner. "Did you make the bomb that did this?" He held up his left hand, his ring finger and pinky were not there.

"I, I didn't. Um, I mean, I… Oh god! I don't know what to say," she sputtered.

Ben slapped Tanner. "Come on man, don't be a dick."

Tanner chuckled. "I'm just messing with you. No need to get all nervous."

A strained smile inched across Beth's face. The fire crackled. No one said a word.

Out of the silence, Ben's merry voice broke out. "Enough of this dark shit. Time to play a game." He held up the bottle of Everclear.

"What game are we gonna play?" asked Beth.

Ben grinned mischievously. "The best game to get to know one another: Never Have I Ever."

"Do you know how to play?" asked Mara.

Beth giggled and nodded. "Yeah, I've done it with my friends."

"Cool!" exclaimed Ben. "So, each time someone calls out something that they haven't done, but you have, you gotta take a swig of this here bottle. Got it?"

He glanced around the group. "No lying. I'll know if you are." He warned.

Everyone agreed.

"Great! Let's get started then, shall we?" He gave the bottle to Beth. "Okay, Beth, you're the greenie, so you get the first question."

Beth cleared her throat. "Never have I ever...." She looked around the fire, smirked, then said, "Shaved my face." She giggled.

The guys groaned. "All right, all right," said Ben sarcastically. "Good one. Kinda lame, but you got all of us the first time out of the box," he said, as he took a swig and passed the bottle.

The bottle made its way to Finn. Mason jar in one hand, Everclear in the other, he leaned close to Teague. "This might be a short night."

Teague snickered.

The bottle made its way back to Beth, who handed it over to Mara. "Your turn."

Mara grinned. "Never have I ever," she said, "peed while standing."

"I'm sensing a pattern here," Cash said, as the bottle made its way around the circle.

Teague had a mouthful of moonshine when the bottle landed in his hand.

"Maybe we should stop with the hooch for a while," said Finn, as he hunted around for the jar's lid. He must have left it on the patio. He lifted the jar to see how much of the liquid remained. Only about one more swig—he may as well just down it—no sense in wasting. He lifted the jar to his lips only to have it wrenched out of his hand.

Zac winked at him. "I'll take care of that for you." He took the final swallow and shuddered.

Mara retrieved the Everclear bottle and handed it over to River who flaunted an impish grin.

"You realize you're setting a precedent here," said Ben.

River winked. "Never have I ever," she said, "kissed a girl."

"I do believe we are being set up," said Zac, as the bottle came to him. He took a swig and handed it over to Finn.

Finn handed it to Teague, who took a swig, then passed it along. The bottle made its way back over to the girls. Mara took a swig and smiled.

"Well, looks like we did all the damage we could do this round, ladies," said River. "Brace yourselves, this could get messy."

"All right Tanner," said Cash, as he rubbed his palms together. "Don't let us down."

The guys started quietly chanting, "Tanner, Tanner, Tanner…"

"Never have I ever," said Tanner, "kissed a guy."

"Drink up ladies," chortled Ben.

"I thought you were supposed to get them," Finn said, as he took a swig and passed it over to Teague.

"Sorry man," replied Tanner, "You two are collateral damage."

"I think we're screwed," Finn whispered to Teague.

Teague nodded drunkenly.

Ben took the bottle. He smiled and said, "Oh, I got this," looking at the girls.

"Never have I ever," he paused, "slept with a guy."

"Y'all are comin' up with some lame shit," declared Finn.

"Shh," said Ben. "This is war. I think we already covered the fact that you two," he pointed to both Finn and Teague, "are casualties of said war. Now, be quiet, drink up, and pass that bottle along to the girls."

Finn took a swig, then handed it to Teague. "We're just gonna keep gettin' hit in the crossfire, ain't we?"

Teague chuckled and took his drink.

Grinning, Ben gave the bottle to Mara, who took a drink and passed it off to River. When she finished, she offered the bottle to Beth. She passed.

"Gimme the damn bottle! shouted Finn. "I'm callin' it before it's too late. It's my turn now." He flashed a smirk at Teague, who nodded in drunken approval.

Finn raised the bottle high. "Never have I ever..." He paused and glanced over at Teague. "Shit! My mind's blank." He rubbed his head. His thoughts were hazy bubbles floating in his head. "Help me out here."

Peering at Finn with unfocused eyes, Teague ran his fingers though his hair. He shook his head and lay back on the ground. "Sorry, you're on your own. That last pull did me in. I'm out."

"Come on, Finn," called out Ben. "Either shit or get off the pot."

"Hold up, don't disrupt my concentration."

"Ah, they're already drunk," said Ben. "Lightweights."

Teague lifted his hand in the air and flipped a middle finger toward Ben. "Beck moi tchew." He slurred.

"I'm sorry, I don't speak drunk Cajun." Ben cupped a hand around his ear. "Care to clarify?"

"I got this," said Zac. "I believe he just told you to bite his ass."

Teague shot a glance at Finn, and they burst into laughter. At that moment, Finn realized he was done. He held the bottle into the air, smiled and took a swig.

Zac grabbed the bottle. "Y'all are just lame as hell," he said. "Now, watch how it's done."

"Never have I ever shaved my legs." He turned to Finn. "There, I saved you two that time. You owe me."

The whiskey made its rounds. First Beth, then Mara and on to River. After taking her swig, River handed the bottle over to Cash. "Come on," she said, smirking. "Drink up."

Cash sighed and took a hit.

Ben leaned toward Cash. "Seriously?"

"Wait," said Zac. "How the hell did I never hear about this? And how does River know?"

"Okay, okay," said Cash. "I told her." He pretended to glare at her. "In the strictest of confidence."

River giggled. "Sorry, baby, this is war, don't ya know?"

Finn's ability to follow along with the conversation faded in and out. He laid back on the ground surprised at how soft the gravel felt beneath his body. Staring up at the sky, the stars were out in full force. The booze had taken its toll. Closing his eyes, the world spun out around him as he released control and fell into the darkness.

Chapter Forty-Seven

TINY FLECKS OF SAND FLEW IN AND OUT OF HIS NOSTRILS WITH EACH breath. He had the distinct taste of dirt in his mouth. Teague opened his eyes. A small lizard stood inches away, staring at him with disapproving, unblinking eyes.

He sneezed, racking his body against the rocky ground. His head exploded in pain. Moaning, he sat up and held his head, waiting for the pain to subside.

Aside from Finn, who was sleeping on the ground beside him, no one else was around. Teague shoved him. Finn groaned and batted pathetically at the air. He was fine—gonna have one hell of a hangover, but fine.

The door to the main house opened and banged closed. Stoney was up and stirring about.

Teague ran his fingers through his hair. Fine sand settled to the ground. Tiny bits of gravel remained embedded in his cheek—he brushed them away. Still groggy, he pulled himself to his feet and wandered up to the patio. Stoney handed him a bottle of cold water, which he guzzled before sitting down. Leaning his head against the post, he closed his eyes.

. . .

334 · N.L. MCLAUGHLIN

Voices. He opened his eyes, a group had gathered on the patio. He must have fallen asleep. Yawning, he raised his arms over his head and arched his back feeling several vertebrae pop into place.

"How's your head?" Stoney asked.

"I'll let you know when my hair stops aching."

Someone handed him another bottle of water, which he promptly drained.

"Looks like your other half survived," Tanner said, "Well, at least he's moving around."

The sound of stumbling feet drew near followed by a pitiful whimper as Finn collapsed beside him and leaned his head against Teague's back.

This was not a good day for a hangover—if there ever was such a thing. Pulling his phone from his pocket, Teague remembered how spotty the connectivity was. "Stoney, you have to do something about the service out here."

"I know, I know," Stoney replied. "Some folks in town are saying it might get better soon." He shrugged. "It just doesn't feel like a priority."

Teague stared down at his screen and frowned. "Anyone got any service?"

"I got one bar," replied Ben.

Tanner chimed in, "Fading in and out between one and two."

"I have one also," said Nate.

"What are these bars of which you speak?" asked Cash.

"I suppose, we're gonna have to wait 'till we get to Marathon to find out which train we're gonna ride tonight," said Teague.

"Actually, I think I can help." Josh held up his phone. "Never travel internationally without a satellite phone," he said, as he wiggled it in his hand.

"It's not perfect, but I can access some basic things." He glanced at the gadget. "Do you have the number of the person you are trying to contact?"

Teague shook his head. "We only connect with him over our private server."

Josh smiled. "Well then, I can set this up to be a hot spot, and you can use it to access your forum to send him a message."

After connecting to the hot spot, Teague posted his inquiry for Porter; task completed, he disconnected and put his phone away.

"Now, we wait," he said. "We should have a response when we get into Marathon. Thanks Josh, that saved us a few hours of waiting."

Finn hadn't moved in a while so Teague nudged him. He sat up— eyes red, hair a dusty mess.

"So, who's doing the eulogies?" asked Ben.

Cash chuckled. "This is where it gets kinda weird. Eight of us."

Ben cocked an eyebrow. "Come again?"

"We, had a little issue while getting the ashes," said Teague.

"Go on..."

Teague explained the events that unfolded at the mortuary, the close call they had getting out just in time, and how they didn't have enough time to figure out which ashes belonged to their friends.

Ben could not contain his laughter. "So, wait, are you telling me that you dumbasses brought the remains of eight people, six of whom you don't even know, all this way?"

"Yeah," replied Teague.

"So, we don't know which ones belong to Cyrus and Craig?"

Teague shook his head.

"Sweet Jesus." Ben laughed. "So, are there families out there without their grandma's ashes?"

"These were all homeless people in the county," replied Teague. "None of 'em had names."

"Well, shit," declared Ben, "Only you idiots would end up breaking into the one mortuary with a bunch of homeless dead people.

Mara, Beth and River joined the group. The soft smell of soap wafted through the air, making Teague aware of his own sweaty stench. Suddenly all he could think about was taking a hot shower and washing away the grit from his body.

Tanner's melancholy voice cut through his thoughts. "Man, it's hard to believe they're gone."

Teague nodded. "Oui. It doesn't feel real."

He reflected back to the last time, everyone had gathered in one place. That was almost a year and a half ago. It was fall—in Boston. The scent of dead leaves mixed with crisp air and car exhaust would forever be lodged in his memory. The city was a hive of energy. It was much too busy for him. Ordinarily, Teague would avoid large cities, but this was a special occasion.

Craig's mom Tammy, was diagnosed with terminal lung cancer. After months of chemo with no improvement, she finally broke down and told her son the bad news. He promptly returned home to be by her side.

Both Cyrus and Craig spent the next month with her. They made it their personal mission to fill her last days with as much love and laughter as possible.

She passed quietly one evening, her son and bonus son, by her side, looking through old photo albums of their life together.

Cyrus posted a message letting the others know. The response was unanimous; they would all make their way to Southie so they could be there for the funeral.

The tiny, two-bedroom apartment on the third floor of the old, three-story building, was cramped. No one minded. They were there for Craig.

By the look of it, Tammy loved two things—lighthouses and her son. Pictures of young Craig adorned every wall. His entire history was on display. Certificates, awards and even his high school diploma were hung with pride.

Scattered everywhere else were tiny replicas of lighthouses. Lamp bases, salt and pepper shakers, pillows and coffee mugs. You name it, if it had a lighthouse on it, Tammy owned it.

Her favorite lighthouse was in Marblehead. Tammy always said she loved it because it was not as pretty as the others. An ugly duckling. Craig decided that would be where he would release her ashes.

One evening, around midnight, they drove north out of the city. Teague recalled his surprise standing there peering up at the curious structure. The tower was a single, metal column soaring into the air with the lantern room sitting precariously on top. Metal rigging surrounded the entire structure. It was nothing like anything he'd imagine when visualizing a lighthouse.

They ascended to the top and gathered for the farewell.

Tears streaming down his face, Craig opened the container and let her ashes fly. "I love you, Ma." Were the only words he could say.

The fine dust swirled as it mingled with the salty ocean air. *Like smoke.* Thought Teague. The wind blew, scattering the ashes into billions of tiny particles until all of it disappeared. All that remained of Tammy Doherty was her memory.

That's how it ends for all of us.

The tantalizing aroma of bacon cooking on the grill made his mouth water. When Stoney handed him a plate full of eggs, bacon and biscuits drowning in gravy, he dug in.

Chapter Forty-Eight

THE MOOD WAS GLOOMY WHEN THEY LEFT STONEY'S. EVERYONE silent, lost in their own thoughts, barely any conversation. Beth didn't know how to act. It was such a stark contrast to the previous night.

Having never dealt with death before, she didn't know the proper etiquette. All of her grandparents were still alive and healthy. She had never even lost a pet—her mom wouldn't allow one in the house. Cyrus and Craig were strangers. She couldn't feel sad because she didn't know them. All she could do was wait for it to be over.

After traveling for hours, they finally reached Lake Amistad. As they drove across the bridge, Beth peered down at the river below. The water was a brilliant blue, flowing deep within a vast canyon.

River tapped her shoulder and pointed to the nearby trestle bridge. "We'll be riding across that tonight," she stated.

Beth studied the bridge. She tried to visualize what was to happen, but for the life of her she couldn't recall the discussion earlier. She couldn't wait for this day to be over so they could get on with the business of having fun again.

They rode into town and parked in a strip mall parking lot. While a few of the others ran into the grocery store for supplies, Beth took advantage of the Wi-Fi to check her online stats. More followers. Her follower count was growing by the day. Her comments were exploding. People were sharing her videos and images while praising her and her friends. For the first time in her life, strangers from all over the world wanted to be her.

Even Kara had posted. "Wow! This is so cool," she wrote under the video of the train ride on the first night. Beth smirked. *You bet it's cool. Too bad you won't ever do anything like it.* She thought. She liked Kara's post, then, barely able to contain her glee, she uploaded another video.

A phone chimed. It wasn't hers. She glanced around. No one else seemed to hear the alert.

"Is that someone's phone?" she asked, feeling annoyed. *Who hears their phone go off and doesn't want to see who it is?*

There was a moment of confusion as the others looked around.

"Shit! I think that's mine," said Gunner, as he fumbled around in his pockets. "It's Max. He wants to know where we are."

He read aloud as he typed. "Del Rio. We'll be heading to Box Canyon to set up camp in a few minutes. Where are you?"

The phone chimed in response. Once again, Gunner read loudly. "Portland. It sucks."

Bella sighed. "Too bad they couldn't make it."

"I'd be pretty pissed myself," said Gunner.

Beth had an epiphany. She knew how to make it so they could at least be part of the farewell. "Video chat!" she shouted.

Everyone stared.

"They could be here virtually," she said. "We would need to use Josh's hotspot, just to be sure we don't lose the connection." She turned to Josh. "Can we?"

"Um, sure," he replied.

"With his connection, and my phone, they can be a part of everything." She waited for their response.

Spinner nodded. "That's a great idea." He turned to Gunner. "Find out if they're at a coffee shop or if they can get to one."

Beth smirked at Finn and stuck out her tongue.

"Yeah, that's real mature, Beth," he replied, waving his hand dismissively.

After Gunner relayed the plan to the trio in Portland, he turned to Beth and said, "You're a lifesaver."

Beth reveled in the praise. Watching Finn cringe with each compliment made her enjoy it all the more.

The chime rang out one more time. The distant trio was in place.

Beth connected her phone. A few moments later the screen lit up with three smiling faces.

"Hello, hello, hello. What's up my people?" said the blue-eyed, young man on the screen. His dark, brown hair was short with a twisted mass of dreadlocks on top. He had many piercings on his face, most notable were the two on his bottom lip and his septum.

Beth stared at the screen. She couldn't think of any clever words to say.

"What's up?" said Gunner. His tone was lighthearted—more so than he had been all day. It was a nice change.

The man on the screen leaned forward and squinted. "Who's the new face?"

"I'm Beth," she replied.

He nodded and smiled. "I hear we have you to thank for this idea. So, thanks."

She blushed.

The man on the screen continued, "I'm Max." He gestured to the woman to his left. "This here is Bells and this jackass," he gestured to his right, "is D.B."

The blonde woman nodded. She was pretty in a masculine sort of way, with piercing, brown eyes and sharp features. Her hair was short, and choppy, longer in the front, so it fell over her face. She wore one ring near the left corner of her bottom lip.

D.B. nodded. "Hey there," he said with a shy voice. Even though he was sitting, it was clear he was very tall. He had the darkest, brown eyes Beth had ever seen—they were almost black. On the side of his face was a small tattoo. She could not make out what it was.

Gunner took over the discussion as he laid out the plan. Before hanging up, they thanked Beth one more time.

Shortly after, they crowded into the bed of the red truck and, leaving the blue one behind, they traveled back across the bridge to a campsite in Box Canyon.

Chapter Forty-Nine

CROUCHING DOWN AMONG THE THICKETS, BETH MARVELED AT THE beauty of the black sky as it shimmered with the lights of a billion stars. She wondered if she would ever become bored with seeing such a sight.

Beside her, Zac handed out the plastic bags. "Okay, when it's your turn, just say something and let them go."

There were a few snickers followed by low murmurs over the number of bags.

Gunner placed Gypsy inside a small pack that he fastened around his chest. Her little face peered out of the opening, happily looking around at everybody.

The train whistle blasted a lone cry into the night. A gust of air blew past as the engines roared by. The whistle blew once more—the sound was deafening. In the shadows, she waited as the others counted the cars.

"Let's go!" shouted Gunner.

Beth's heart raced, her palms were sweaty, sprinting out of the brush, she gripped the ladder and clambered onto the car. Once aboard, she quickly made room for Josh.

River climbed to the rooftop—Beth waited for her turn. Adrenaline coursed through her body. On the roof, she perched herself between River and Josh, then connected to his phone. The signal was strong. In seconds, the little screen lit up with the smiling faces of their three friends in Portland.

Shoving his face close to the camera, Max said, "Hey there, fellow travelers. Sounds pretty noisy out there."

"Little bit," replied Beth.

D.B. shoved him back. "Man, get your face out of the way. I wanna see."

Beth giggled as they scuffled with one another.

When they settled, Max grinned and leaned into the screen again. "Hold us up. I wanna see everybody."

Beth held the phone high over her head, facing it out toward the rest of the group.

"What's up, my people?" said Max. As he spoke, the train blasted its whistle. "Ah dammit, that's loud! he shouted.

The bridge loomed on the horizon. The car jolted as it rolled onto the iron structure. A moment later, they were above the river.

At the front of the car, Finn and Teague stood up. Finn remained silent as Teague spoke.

"Adieu my brothers, rest in peace," he said, as Finn tore open the bag. Holding it high above his head, he released the ashes into the air.

A soft cloud of powder floated into the night. At first dense, then quickly dissipating as the particles spread out and went their separate ways. Into the cosmos—the person they once were—gone forever.

When the bag was empty, Finn signaled for Gunner.

Gunner, with Gypsy safely secured in the pack, stood up and tore open his bag. "Ride the steel rail in heaven, my friends." Once again, a cloud of dust erupted and disappeared into the night sky.

It was Spinner's turn.

Standing up while Bella remained seated, he held out his bag. As he released the ashes, Spinner said "Peace be with you, my brothers. We'll meet again someday." He sat back down and wrapped an arm around Bella who buried her face against his chest.

While Tripp spoke, Sam held the remains. "Not sure what to say other than—this sucks. I'm sorry, man. I wish we had one more chance to hang together."

Sam wiped his face. "I don't want to say goodbye, but I have to for now. Till we see each other again—goodbye." He let the ashes fly.

Cash and Zac were standing by.

Zac held the ashes while Cash spoke. "Goodbye, my brothers. It sucks that you'll never be able to pay me back the twenty bucks you owe me, Craig. Dying is a hell of a way to get out of paying for losing a bet." He smirked and glanced at Zac, who shook his head admonishingly. "Nah, I'm just kidding," he said. "Peace." He held up two fingers.

Zac stood silent. His lip trembled as a tear dripped from his cheek. His mouth moved, uttering not a word. At last he spoke, "Take care of each other." He released the ashes.

Next was Stoney and Nate.

"Be free, little brothers," Stoney said, as Nate released the ashes into the wind. He nodded toward Ben, Tanner, and Mara.

"Love you, babies," said Mara sadly.

"May we catch on together in the afterlife," Ben said. Mara rested her head against his shoulder.

"Fly home," said Tanner, he set the ashes free.

The cloud wafted past Beth and disappeared into the night like a fading memory.

Still holding the phone high, Beth stood with the help of Josh. As she swayed with the movement of the train, he wrapped his arm around her waist to keep her steady.

River tore open the final bag and slowly began releasing its contents into the air. "Fly to heaven, babies. We'll see you again one day. Until then, peace and love." The bag emptied. She placed her fingers to her lips and blew a small kiss.

From all the way in Portland, the trio on the tiny screen said their farewells.

"Farewell," said D.B.

Bells kissed her fingertips and placed them on the screen. "Fly with the angels, babies," she said.

Max wiped a tear from his eye, "Ride on," he said.

Cash stepped into the center of the car and, with his arms above his head, shouted, "And to those other poor bastards who had the misfortune of being cremated and tossed in a box with our friends, may you all have a glorious afterlife!"

There was an abrupt jolt as the train crossed onto the other side of the river. Beth lowered her hands and said goodbye to the trio on the phone. Max winked and flashed a sorrowful smile as he held up a peace sign.

Beth put her phone away. Melancholy settled deep inside her soul. When the evening began, she didn't understand what was happening. After witnessing their sorrow, seeing their tears and hearing their beautiful farewells, she finally understood. It all made sense now. Zac was right, death hurts the living—it cuts deep and leaves a messy scar.

She wiped a tear from her cheek and silently hoped she caught it all in her recording. Her followers will enjoy seeing the love these nomads have for one another. How tight their bond. She smiled. The video was bound to go viral. She could hardly wait to see how many followers she would gain.

Chapter Fifty

GYPSY YAPPED AND RUSHED OVER TO RIVER. TAIL WAGGING, SHE licked her face until River was forced out of the warm comfort of her sleeping bag.

"Okay, okay, okay, I'm up. Stop," she said, as she tried ineffectively to fend off the happy, little dog. Gypsy crawled up on River's lap and lay down, tummy in the air. "You are such a baby," she said, as she rubbed Gypsy's belly.

Her friends lay asleep all around her. Gunner being the only exception.

"You're spoiling her," he said gruffly.

"Yeah, and it's not like you don't already spoil her, huh? Mister cute little pink harness and matching leash?" She teased. "Or should I point out the seemingly limitless supply of squeaky toys? Hmm?"

Gunner scoffed and shook his head.

A few feet away, Nate sighed and stretched. He sat up and ran his hands down his face, rubbing the stubble on his chin.

"You coming back to Stoney's?" asked Gunner.

Nate nodded.

"You know, you can head out with the younger folks," said Gunner.

"It might be more fun for you to hang with them instead of us old people."

"I like old folks. Besides, you'd be lost without me," responded Nate.

Gunner nodded and let it be.

River knew the story behind Nate, how he grew up with his drug-addicted mom and never knew his father. Gunner was the big brother—the father figure Nate never had. She suspected that Gunner needed Nate just as much. It gave him someone to take care of.

Gradually in almost zombie-like fashion, the rest of the group crawled out of their sleeping bags and joined the conversation. It had been a whirlwind time for all. A roller coaster of emotions. A small part of River wanted to remain with the group for a longer time— another part was keen to hit the road again.

"So, who's all going where?" asked Stoney.

"Looks like Nate, Gypsy, and I are heading back to Terlingua for a few days," replied Gunner.

"We'll come along too," said Tripp. "At least for a day or two. Then we're heading west."

Sam agreed.

Bella chimed in, "We're gonna head back as well for a little while. We might head on south from there. I think Belize is calling our names." She put her hand on Spinner's shoulder, as he nodded his head in accord.

Ben turned to River. "Where are you guys headed?"

She looked around for Beth, finding her sitting alone on her sleeping bag, staring at her phone. "Hey Beth, where are we goin'?" River asked.

Beth glanced up. She put her hand on her chest. "Why you askin' me? I don't know." She shrugged back, looking puzzled.

"Well, it's up to you now," River responded. "We're gonna go wherever you want. So, come on, if you could go anywhere in the US, where would it be?"

River smiled at Beth, nodding her head in encouragement. At this moment, she kind of envied Beth—the entire world just opened up for her.

"I guess I've always wanted to go to Florida," replied Beth. "I've seen pictures of people on white, sand beaches. I would love to dip my toes in the ocean. Would that be okay?"

River glanced at Teague, who nodded. She looked over at Finn, who was staring down at his feet.

"Florida, it is!" shouted River. "We know of some cool beaches along the panhandle and near Tampa. Great fishing off the bridge too." She turned to Ben and asked, "Where are you going?"

"Mara says she wants to head northeast. She'd like to get up to the Cape and maybe eventually Maine," he replied. "Hey, Josh, you in?" he called over his shoulder. "If not, it looks like you have several options to choose from."

Josh grinned. "The Cape sounds great, as does Maine. I think I've had enough of the west coast for now."

"Where you guys heading first?" asked Ben.

"I think we're good on Texas for a while," replied Teague, as he shot a sideways glance at Finn. "I suppose it's off to New Orleans for a couple days. After that—Florida."

"Oh! Can we tag along?" asked Mara, excitedly. "At least until New Orleans."

Ben smiled. "Sounds like a plan to me."

"New Orleans sounds cool," said Josh. "I always wondered what it would be like."

"Looks like we'll be traveling with you for a few days," Ben said to River.

"You're gonna love New Orleans," River said to Josh.

"Will I?" he asked.

"Yeah, it's a great place with amazing food and music. And the company is top notch." She flashed a coy smile.

He grinned. "Then I look forward to you showing me around."

River chuckled and shoved him playfully.

"Well, now I know I'm the luckiest one in the group. I've got the prettiest tour guide," Josh said, as he winked.

. . .

They spent the next couple hours enjoying each other's company. No one knew when they would see one another again, so every moment shared was precious. The passing of their friends, made this point even more apparent.

When she finished packing, River spent a few moments alone with Tripp. Their relationship—open as it was—had drawn to a close. He didn't seem to mind, and neither did she.

After sharing a long embrace, River kissed him one more time on the cheek, then joined the others as they loaded their gear into the trucks.

They rode across the bridge to a side-out at the edge of town. In the distance, they heard a train whistle.

River took the time to say farewell to everyone they were leaving behind. She disliked the leaving part. Goodbyes were always sad.

The train roared into view—she hunkered down. A blast of metal-scented air tossed sand in the air as the engines passed, followed by double stacks, several boxcars then finally a few grainers. Waiting until the third grainer came into range, they sprinted out and hopped on board. Taking a seat alongside Beth and Mara, River settled in for the scenic ride ahead.

As the whistle rang out one more time, the train moved away from civilization, into the open expanse. River sat quietly gazing out as the landscape scrolled by—this was her favorite part.

THE END

Daniel

THE HEAT OUTSIDE MADE BEING IN THE EXERCISE YARD UNBEARABLE, so he headed back inside to the rec room. The instant blast of cool air chilled the sweat on his body, causing goosebumps to raise up on his arms. In the corner, the television played some random talk show. No one paid it any mind.

He paused and watched for a minute, reading the captions—the sound was never on. Uninterested, he scoffed and wandered over to the game table.

Two men were playing a round of poker. He watched as the younger man made a bad play that cost him the game. With a sound of exasperation, the young man tossed his cards down on the table. Nothing more to see.

Along the wall, a group had gathered around a computer. Unable to see what they were watching, he turned to walk away when a voice called out to him.

"Hey, McCann! Come on over here, man," said the man, as he made room for him. "Check this out. Remember those survival things you're always talking about?"

Daniel nodded, walking closer.

"This kid here in these videos does all that shit, even some things you haven't mentioned. It's a riot man, you need to watch this."

Daniel twitched his nose and stepped closer to the computer.

The man sitting in front of the computer looked up at him. "This kid is a trip, man. He's got some skills."

Leaning closer, Daniel stared down at the screen. There in the video was a young man, tall and muscular with a head full of wavy, dark hair.

Rage surged through his body. His heart raced—the blood pounded in his skull. Everything around him disappeared as he glared at the monitor.

Well, hello there, shithead.

He sneered.

Every time Finn smiled or laughed, red-hot rage exploded in his gut. He fought back the urge to demolish the damned device into a million pieces.

Daniel let the hatred pour over him. Motionless, seething inside, he imagined the ways he would take that smile off of Finn's face and make him wish he was never born.

The buzzer sounded. It was time to go back to their cells.

Daniel took his place in line. A malevolent smile swept across his face. He only had three more months to go before he was up for parole —plenty of time to hammer out a plan.

Luckily for him, someone was kind enough to leave a trail of bread crumbs behind. Thanks to them—whoever they were—tracking Finn was gonna be a whole lot easier. He made a mental note to follow that account the next time he had computer access. Wouldn't want to lose track of his dear son. It was just about time for a good old family reunion.

Acknowledgments

When I first set about committing word to page, I did not know the incredible journey I was about to embark upon. Life is busy. It's messy and uneven and filled with distractions. There were times when it didn't look as though I would ever finish—there were times when I questioned whether I even wanted to.

I had a great deal of encouragement from my amazing friends and family. I feel they deserve some special recognition. First, there's Meagan. She read the first snippet I had written; it was more of a short story. Her enthusiasm for the characters encouraged me to write more.

Samantha McLaughlin read the first written manuscript. Let's just say it had serious issues. She dutifully read through it all, pointing out holes and problems. Her feedback was priceless. After hearing her input, I went back to work, revising and rewriting.

Samantha Dayton, Vic Willette, Jackie Lowry, Carol Kielty, Bill Bishop, Rory, and Shannon, all of these beautiful people, read various revisions along the way. Their feedback and critique helped the book take its ultimate form.

And through it all, Robert McLaughlin was there the whole time, listening to me rattle on about ideas and plot holes. He is my road trip partner—my sounding board—my anchor.

I am lucky to be surrounded by so many loving, compassionate and intelligent people. This book—this series was begging to be brought to life. Thanks to the help and encouragement of some very awesome people. I was able to pull it all together.

A Word From Nancy

Thank you for reading American Nomads. If you enjoyed the ride so far, please take a moment and leave a review, it would be greatly appreciated.

For more Nomad stories, including special shorts and origin stories of the characters, visit my website and sign up for my newsletter. You will also receive news about upcoming releases and special deals and, of course, this free content.

https://www.nancylmclaughlin.com/

I am currently finishing up work on book two of this series; Valley of The Sun. It should be ready to publish by Fall of this year (2021) After that, there will be two more books in this series. I hope you will stick around to see how it all ends. I promise it's gonna be a wild ride.

Printed in the USA
CPSIA information can be obtained
at www.ICGtesting.com
LVHW042323151123
764097LV00009B/45